The Terror & The Sword

The Hueik Trilogy: Book 1

Trevor Warren

Dedicated to Justin Green

Acknowledgements

I am very grateful to Justin Green, who, out of everyone I sent a draft to, was the only one who made the time to read all of it. For that reason, this book is dedicated to him. And special thanks to Elden Liu, who was kind enough to listen to me talk about this book and discuss it and my ideas for the broader series with me. Those conversations were a catalyst of inspiration. And special thanks to my sister Melanie and my cousins Colby and Lindsay, who refrained from telling my parents about this book so I could surprise them with it.

Chapter One

MY SOLE LIGHT SOURCE came from a window barred by thick iron bars. Centered high enough to be out of my reach, it gave me no hope of escape. Adjacent to the uneven stairs, a hazardous pass leading out of the subterranean prison was another barred window. The light that came through the windows beamed two rectangles onto the wall across from my cell, though each was broken up by the window bars.

Since my cell faced west, I knew it was past noon when those two luminary planes appeared on the bottom of the wall, softly stretching out across it. As the day went on, I watched them levitate to the top of the wall, condensing as they crawled up it, and the shadow of the bars became more defined.

Both signaled that the day was waning and the sun would soon set when the two rectangles reached the top of the wall. They were replicas of the windows, striped by the shadows of the bars.

The king descended the crooked stairs. He wore no crown and carried no scepter. There was no reason for him to have either. I knew who he was. Instead of royal regalia, the king wore a shirt and pants without embellishments. I thought the clothes made him look like a commoner.

With a reluctant pace, the monarch walked towards my cell, the look on his face betraying that he was rethinking whether to speak to me. The debate was not because the king was the self-doubting type. The firmness of his stride confirmed that he was confident.

He needed something from me. While walking towards my cell, he tried to think of a way of getting what he wanted without dealing with me. There was another reason he could have come down to the dungeon, but he was alone, so it couldn't have been that.

After ten slow, meditative steps, he stopped before the cell. Not saying a word, he stared at me as I lay on the stone floor that was my bed. I didn't acknowledge him.

The king didn't speak. He knew I would address him when I was ready. If he spoke first, then I wouldn't talk. If I were the type of person who revered kings, then I wouldn't have been in that cell in the first place.

As I lay there, the stone pressing against my back, I wondered why he was there. I had expected him to visit me, accompanied by at least two guards who would escort me to the gallows. But there weren't any guards, which made me wonder why he was there. What could he want from me other than my execution?

When curiosity got the better of me, I got up and turned to my visitor.

"I will not repent," I said.

"I didn't expect you to," the king replied.

"Then why are you here, brother?" I asked.

"You killed someone," he responded.

"That's why I'm in here," I reminded him.

"Recently," he clarified.

"How recent?" I asked.

"Not more than a few days before your capture," he detailed.

"I need more information, brother. It's either that or you tell me who I killed since you know who it was," I said.

"Does the name Lord Gaenic mean anything to you?" he asked.

"Is this about that noble's death a couple of weeks ago, the one I stabbed to death in the market at Tureni? Brother, the man didn't have one ounce of good sense, let alone the mental capacity to run whatever lands he would inherit. I was doing you and the whole kingdom a favor getting rid of that simpleton. On top of it, he had horrible business instincts, thinking it was a good idea to try to betray me," I explained.

"No, he was not the one I was referring to, but thank you for confessing to yet another murder. As if I needed more reasons to hang you," he said, and I could hear the exhaustion in his voice.

"Then I need more information," I stated.

"He was the most recent person to try to kill you," my brother said, at last, providing me with useful information.

I smiled. "He's dead too."

"What did he look like?" my brother interrogated.

"I don't remember. Why does it matter?" I asked. Being bored of the interrogation, I turned around, desperate to find some source of amusement in my barren cell.

"How did you kill him?" my brother inquired.

"Stabbed him through the heart," I told him.

"Where's the body?" he asked.

"I don't know. If I kept track of every corpse I made, I wouldn't have time to do anything else," I lied. I knew where the body was, and by the look on my brother's face, he knew it. How he knew and why he bothered to come down to get me would remain a mystery to me for some time.

Then I heard a series of noises that puzzled me so much that for a moment, I thought I was hallucinating: the rattle of keys, the scrapping of a key entering a keyhole, the quiet but brisk click of a disengaging lock, and the rustic squeak of my cell door opening. My brother, the king who was forever relentless in his pursuit of justice, would never unlock my cell.

But when I turned around, I was shocked to realize I was not hearing things. The cell door was open. I could feel the blood drain from my face, and I stood paralyzed with shock.

"Let's go, brother," he said, not even acknowledging the state of incapacity I was in.

I followed as he ascended the stone stairs. Every time my bare feet landed on the frigid stone stairs, it felt like they were giving me frostbite. When I climbed the first flight of stairs, my toes had turned a light purple, and my brother had finished his ascent. A few minutes later, I arrived at the top of the third and final flight and was out of breath. My brother was there, leaning against the doorway.

"Out of shape?" he asked, then threw me a pair of shoes.

We were outside the door to the dungeon in a small room tucked away on the right side of the palace. The barren stone that made up the room created the feeling that it was an extension of the dungeon. The entire palace was constructed of lusterless, grey stone.

Our father built the palace so it wouldn't feel like a palace. Most kings want their palaces to be grand and splendorous to invoke regality. Father was not like other men, let alone like other kings. He believed a person's surroundings play a large part in shaping them and did not want us to be soft. He hoped the hard surroundings of what we called home would ensure this.

Then, there was the effect a stone palace had on foreign diplomats. Within moments of walking into the throne room, Father could assess the quality of their characters: whether they were accustomed to hardship, which few were, whether they were reliant on luxuries, which was most, and their intelligence. Intelligence was whether they had enough sense to know that objects of wealth don't always equate to a king's power.

Usually, the diplomats understood this and realized that the spartan nature of the palace was the greatest indicator of Father's power. The ones who did not understand this, most of whom were haughty and found themselves easily manipulated.

All Father had to do was have them believe they came out on top of every deal. Seeing him do this taught me and my brother the dangers of arrogance from an early age. My brother would charge me with arrogance, amongst other things. Most would be crimes and rightfully leveled.

But my brother never learned the difference between being arrogant and projecting arrogance. The latter can be used to manipulate someone in negotiations and is a valuable skill. My father was a master of this skill, yet my brother didn't bother to learn it because of his distaste for arrogance.

Though made of stone, the palace's layout was typical. It included a grand hall, a throne room, numerous bedrooms, two kitchens, an armory, three libraries, servant quarters, two dining halls, a small ballroom, and a dungeon.

Growing up, the palace had few decorations and signs of wealth. Our father did not want his sons to become soft men, a gift for which I am grateful. My brother must have appreciated this, too, since as we walked through the palace, there was a scarcity of lavish décor and expensive furnishings.

I was speechless for the second time that day when I stepped out of the palace and saw horses. Rono was holding the reigns of one and a palace guard, wearing a conical helmet with a nasal guard, a breastplate with the Eshtaran deer, the national animal, painted on the front and back, bracers, and greaves, was holding the reigns to another. Each piece of armor was the pristine white of the Eshtaran royal guard.

"My king, I must advise against this," I heard the guard say as I approached.

"You have Gontrill. Several times," Rono said.

"And as someone who has sworn to protect you and your family, I do so again. My king, it is unwise to travel alone with your brother. Please, at least bring one guard with you," Gontrill pleaded.

"Gontrill, you have been a part of my guard since my reign began, so I hope you know what I am about to say is coming from a place of sincerity and candor, not of insult and offense. We both know I'll be as safe traveling alone with him as if twenty guards traveled with me. I have no guard, yourself included, who can survive against Bowv in combat. Nor can any guard stop my brother's subtle stratagems; he is too cunning by far. If my brother moves to kill me, only the gods can protect me." Rono said.

"I understand, my king," Gontrill said bowing as he did.

"I don't think you've ever given me such a fine compliment," I said as I approached the two.

Rono ignored my remark. "Take me to the body," he commanded as he mounted his horse. Gontrill remained close to his king, hand wrapped around the hilt of his sword.

"After hearing that compliment, you leave me no choice," I said as I mounted my horse. While I was doing so, Rono dismissed Gontrill.

"Where is it anyway?" Rono asked.

"About five miles north of Bihendum," I told him.

"Bihendum?" he asked as I mounted my horse.

"Yes," I confirmed as we began our journey.

"What were you doing there?" he asked.

"Murdering a lord, apparently," I answered.

"Be serious, Bowv. That's not the reason you were there. What were you doing in Bihendum?" he asked again, now annoyed.

"Besides checking to see how my criminal enterprise within the city was running, I got word a lord, Eshtaran but ethnically Udenian, was closing in on one of my illicit operations..."

"Must have been Lord Hundono; he's the only Udenian who's a part of the Eshtaran nobility. He served as a mercenary under Father and was rewarded with a noble title for his service. And what illicit operation?" he asked

"That doesn't matter, brother. The point is that while protecting my profit margin, I heard rumors another lord, a Diefetian, said to be much wealthier, was out in the woods close to the city without any bodyguards," I explained to my brother.

"You decided to rob him," he guessed.

"No, I decided to kidnap him," I said.

"Then he put up a fight, and you killed him," Rono deduced.

"Yes," I affirmed. "To my surprise, he was a good fighter."

My brother fell silent. He just sat there on top of his horse. A few moments later, he told me we were stopping at Bihendum before I took him to the body because he needed to talk to some of the town guards. I told him that was fine, figuring he would probe the guards with questions to verify my story to ensure I hadn't lied to him.

I was honest, though I doubted the city guards would be well informed of my illegal operations in the city. The people my underlings killed for their indiscretion would ensure that.

Night fell, yet we rode on with the full moon illuminating our path. We could hear the nocturnal animals of the forest, the totting of our horses' hooves, and nothing else. Within hours, we arrived at Bihendum. At the gates, five city watchmen were waiting for us. Their uniforms were adorned with emblems given to guards for fifteen years of service.

"Sire," one of them spoke. "We are here as you requested."

"Thank you for coming, captain," my brother said.

"What do you need?" the guard asked.

"I need you to make sure no one leaves the town until we come back, which should be before first light," my brother explained, and I wondered why he said this when we weren't concerned about anyone leaving the city.

"Will do, my lord. Is there anyone we should look out for?" asked the captain.

"No, Jenkins, just make sure no one leaves the city," Rono answered. Rono knew about my illegal operations in the city, but it wasn't why he wanted me to take him there. And why were the guards outside before we had arrived in Bihendum? Royal messengers are quick, but I didn't see my brother send one out after he released me.

He could have sent a rider when he exited the dungeon before me, and I was still climbing up the stairs. But I would have heard him speak to the messenger and saw the messenger when we got to Bihendum or on the road to the city. And if my brother did send a messenger right before he released me, there wasn't enough time for the guards to assemble outside the gate before we got to the city. Rono must have sent a messenger before he retrieved me, which meant he knew where we would be going.

How did Rono know where we were going? Why did he release me if he knew the body was in Bihendum? Why did Rono have the city watch bar anyone from exiting the gates? What did my brother know that I didn't?

Jenkins nodded, and my attention returned to the matter at hand. He called for the gate to be raised and, when it was lowered, walked out of sight along with the rest of the watchmen.

"How far is the body?" Rono asked.

"About a two-hour ride. The body should be a little way into the woods from the road," I said.

"I'll follow you then. Let's get going," he ordered, and we rode off.

We rode in silence for most of the journey until we reached the point where we needed to proceed on foot.

"Why is this dead noble so important to you? I've killed dozens of them before. What makes this one special?" I asked.

"Hopefully, it isn't," the king replied.

I was confused as I led him into the dense grove of trees. The moonlight slipped through the trees enough to illuminate areas the size of a fist. Our walk through the woods would have been more difficult if Rono hadn't brought a torch. Within ten minutes, we arrived at a circular clearing within the woods with a torn tent in its middle. A man's body lay on its back ten paces from the tent

"We're here," I announced, and we walked over to the body.

Rono leaned down, brought his torch close to the body, and examined the corpse. Despite being weeks old, the skin wasn't rotting, there was no smell of death, and animals hadn't scavenged the body. There was a lack of blood, something I had noticed when I killed Gaenic but had forgotten to inform Rono about.

My brother moved the torch towards its chest, then picked up a nearby stick and inserted it into the wound that was on the chest where the heart was. Within moments, the stick prodded what remained of the heart after my blade pierced through it. Satisfied, my brother pulled it out and placed his impromptu investigative tool back on the ground. Rono then instructed me to hold the torch and handed it to me. Rono picked up the same stick and used it to pull back the corpse's lower lip, then began examining the mouth.

"Come closer; I need more light," he commanded.

I brought the torch closer and leaned in to see what my brother was so fascinated by. Then I saw them, two teeth that tapered to a point as lethal as any spear tip. They were more akin to animal fangs than human teeth. My brother saw them, and his face became flush, but ever persistent, he used the stick one final time to push back the upper lip. He found two more fangs.

"The legends are true," uttered Rono. "I had hoped they weren't."

"Legends are just legends," I told him.

"Do you know what you have done?" he asked, standing.

"I've lost the chance to make some money by killing this noble," I answered.

"You killed a vampire," Rono said, his eyes locked with mine and his face more serious than I had ever seen it before.

I laughed. "Vampires. Brother, don't be absurd; they are stories told to frighten children. Similar stories are told about me. You can't seriously believe this dead nobleman was a vampire."

"The Sacred Texts speaks of them. It is not as if I am believing the word of a drunken bard," Rono countered.

"You can go on about the Sacred Texts all you want, brother. When will you learn that the gods you vehemently worship do not exist? If your gods were real, then they would have struck me down a long time ago, and the corpses I have made would still be animated flesh, let alone permit vampires to run amuck," I explained.

"You saw the fangs," Rono pushed back.

"So, what a man has four pointy teeth? That hardly counts as evidence," I said.

"When you fought him, what weapon did he have?" my brother asked.

"A sword," I answered.

"And did the blade have a grey color to it, one that looked like the color of the moon?" he asked, though I felt he already knew the answer to his question.

"Yes," I answered.

"You know where it is, don't you?" he asked.

"Why does this sword matter to you?" I asked. "A blade is a blade."

"Do you know who Lord Gaenic was?" Rono answered my question with another.

"He was that dead body," I said, pointing to the corpse behind him.

"He was a keshgu," Rono began to explain.

"Brother, don't insult my intelligence by making up words; it reflects poorly on you," I pleaded.

"Keshgus were elite warriors amongst the vampires, having roles from assassins to generals and everything in between. Lord Gaenic was said to have possession of *Hueik*, a sword with the power to kill a vampire as if it were a normal man," explained Rono.

"Enough with your stories. Almost the entire Continent is at war, and instead of working to maintain your neutrality, you want me to take you to a sword you believe is magical. Have you lost your mind?" I asked.

"Where is the sword?" he pressed.

"An associate of mine should have it in town," I answered, and then it dawned on me why Rono ordered the town guards not to let anyone out. My brother knew I would have taken Gaenic's sword and stashed it somewhere close. Bihendum was the closest place, and Rono must have known I had connections in the town.

"Let's get going then," he said.

We walked to the horses and rode back into town. My brother looked determined. Taking the same route, the journey back felt shorter than the trip to find Gaenic's body. When we rode up to the town's gates, the sky was lit by the gentle touch of dawn. We dismounted and approached the city gate, where Captain Jenkins waited.

"Did you find what you were looking for?" he asked.

"We did, Captain, thank you," my brother answered. "Did anyone try to leave town?"

"No," Jenkins answered.

"Good," my brother said.

"Let's get going then. The sooner we meet my associate, the sooner we can resolve this nonsense," I urged.

"We are not going anywhere," Rono told me.

"That doesn't make sense. We can't meet my associate *within* the town if we stay *outside* it," I explained, thinking about what must have been the tenth time that day my brother had gone insane.

"I'm sure Captain Jenkins can find your associate and bring him outside the gates," Rono said. "Not to mention, if the townsmen recognize you, they will hang you."

I laughed. "If they knew who I was, then they would shake in their boots, not wrap a noose around my neck," I corrected my brother. If the captain brings my associate out to the gates, people will notice, and there'll be a scandal. And if anyone realizes the king is here, we will be surrounded by people and unable to go anywhere."

"Then what do you suppose we do?" questioned Rono.

"You and Captain Jenkins stay here while I talk to my associate," I proposed.

"No," he said, knowing I planned to grab the sword and disappear.

"Then let's all go into town. It's still early, and people will be busy opening their shops, so we should be able to move without drawing too much attention. If anyone sees us, they will assume we are leading him to some disturbance," I suggested.

"That's reasonable," Rono said, agreeing to my plan.

"Lead on, captain," I urged.

The captain yelled to his men to open the gates, and we heard the gate's heavy wood scape the ground. Twenty of his men pushed the huge doors open, revealing the city of Bihendum. The city began as a trading post, which grew into a town and then a city. The houses were wooden, one-storied buildings made from logs felled in the nearby forest and were built along a near-deteriorated cobblestone road. The only sign of the town's status as an important trade center was a store sign on every block.

At a pace that would not arouse suspicion, Captain Jenkins led us to the market in the town's center, allowing us to go anywhere.

"Where do we go from here?" Jenkins asked, not knowing who my associate was. I turned to the government district of the town and pointed.

"There?" Jenkins asked.

"Yes. Now, let's go before people start wondering who we are," I urged.

The street leading to the government district should have been better quality, but it was the worst road in the city. There were no crooked or extruding cobblestones like in other parts of the city. No, the road was dirt and riddled with potholes.

Why were there such poor roads in an important trade city? The people of Bihendum are some of the kingdom's riches and are the stringiest people on the Continent. They only spend money when necessary and believe in purchasing in bulk to get the best deal possible. For the citizens of Bihendum to spend money on their roads, every cobblestone must be eroded, and the dirt roads must be untraversable.

The last time that happened was well over twenty years ago. But their extraordinary cheapness has permitted fortunes to be amassed and concentrated, which I had the pleasure of draining one way or another. They were bigger fortunes than most because the citizens of Bihendum have simple tastes and don't want to spend money on luxurious items.

We continued down the road, Captain Jenkins walking slower. As we passed each house, Jenkins would give me a questioning look. Each time, I told him to keep moving.

"Bowv, just tell us which building we are going to. With the Captain slowing down at every house, people will start wondering who we are," Rono ordered.

"We are going to the Mayoral Mansion," I revealed.

"I assumed so," my brother said.

"Sure, you did," I said, not hiding my skeptical tone.

We arrived at the mayor's Mansion. It was like all the other buildings but longer and had two stories. We walked in through the set of double doors. With Captain Jenkins leading, no one questioned us. It was around eight in the morning, and when we entered the lobby, the mayor was walking in from the dining room, no doubt finishing his breakfast and going to his office to start the day's work. He saw Jenkins first.

"Captain, to what do I owe the pleasure? And who is with you?" he asked.

"Sardenel, have you forgotten me already?" I asked, walking towards the mayor.

When he saw me, flames of terror lit his eyes. He took a few steps back, shaking as he did. Then he froze, sweat pouring down his brow.

"Answer me!" I yelled.

Fear still in his eyes, Sardenel unparalyzed and mumbled that he remembered me.

"Where is my sword?" I asked.

"I... I don't have it," he stuttered.

"What do you mean you don't have it?" I asked, moving close, hands clenched in two fists.

"Enough brother! I will not have you intimidate a mayor while I am in the same room," Rono spoke.

"You're right, brother," I said, turning around from Sardenel and walking towards Rono. "Why am I the one talking? After all, you are the one who wants the sword. And if Sardenel here doesn't give you an answer that you like, you can have Captain Jenkins here arrest him, then have him hanged for treason."

When I said "hanged," the mayor froze with fear again. Or maybe it was when I said "arrested." Who knows? Sardenel was afraid of his own shadow. Either one was enough to chill him to the bone.

"If you don't have the sword, then who does?" my brother asked Sardenel.

"I sold it to a traveling merchant not too long ago," he answered.

"Did you get the merchant's name?" Rono asked.

"Hearik," answered the mayor.

"I know him," I said.

"Where was he heading?" pressed Rono.

"Traevelios," informed Sardenel.

"When did he leave?" asked Rono.

"Yesterday afternoon," he answered.

"It's a two-day ride from here. You may be able to catch him," informed the captain.

"Let's get a move on then," my brother decided, turning away from the mayor, and walking out the door.

I followed him. I turned around when I got to the door and said, "I won't forget this Sardenel. I will be back, and if you're lucky, your town will still be standing when I'm done with you." I saw terror fly into the mayor's eyes again before I turned around.

"Did you have to say that? We have more important concerns right now," Rono asked as we returned to the city's gates, where we had hitched our horses.

"Yes," I answered.

"You know if vampires have returned, you will have more to worry about than punishing Sardenel," Rono told me.

"If the foolish old tales are true," I rebutted.

"You saw Gaenic's corpse. It was undecayed when the forest should have consumed it. How do you explain that? Or the fangs in his mouth? Or the absence of blood? Everything is consistent with what you call 'foolish old tales,'" Rono hounded me.

"Brother, I have walked the entire Continent and traveled to the Desolate Lands that lay beyond it—pillaging, raiding, and killing as I saw fit. Many times, I have witnessed the impossible. It is a fact of life that the more you live, the more likely it is that you'll see something unexplainable," I explained.

Rono, clearly agitated, changed the subject. "How do you know this, Hearik?" he asked me.

"I robbed him," I answered.

"Of course you did," my brother said with a sigh.

We walked in silence after that until we got to the gates. Finding our horses, we unhitched them and mounted them. It was high noon. By this time, we rode off on the road that leads to Traevelios, and merchants were coming in and out of Bihendum. No doubt the market was teaming. We didn't stop to make camp until we had an hour of light left in the day.

We set up camp close to the road, wanting to get back on the road quickly when the time came. We both had a small tent, and we made a small fire. After we ate, we went to sleep. The next day, when we got back on the road, the sun had just peaked over the horizon, beginning to illuminate the forested landscape.

After riding for half the day, we encountered three armed men blocking the road. The lack of armor and an army banner made it obvious they were highwaymen. We slowed our horses to a stop, and Rono looked at me.

"They're not mine," I told Rono, knowing he would ask. "Mine are dead or in prison, and they would never be stupid enough to stand in the middle of the road where everyone can see them."

"I didn't think they were," he informed me. "What do we do? I only have a sword."

"Stay here and let me do the talking," I told him, and Rono nodded in agreement.

I rode up to the bandits. Each was armed with a spear, their ends resting on the ground and the tips pointed up to the sky. "Stop right there," the one in the middle ordered. "There's a toll on this road."

"You are right, there is," I said, my tone ringed with authority. "Now, hand over a gold piece."

The bandits turned to one another, looking puzzled, then laughed.

"What's so funny?" I asked.

"You want us to hand over a gold piece," he answered.

"I do," I reaffirmed. "I wouldn't want to keep me waiting."

"Strong words for a man who's outnumbered and unarmed," the highwayman replied.

"Neither matters," I said, smiling.

"Why?" the ruffian on my right asked.

"Do you know who I am?" I asked with my arms outstretched to both sides.

"Someone who's going to get robbed," the one on my right said.

"Who are you?" the leader asked.

"Bowv," I said.

The man on my left froze, his muscles tensing to such a degree that I thought they would explode from his skin. While the other two stood there, I looked at them like they had just come out from living under a rock. They should have reacted in some way after I told them my name. After a few moments of silence, the one on my left spoke.

"Bbb... boss," he stuttered. "We ought to let him and his friend go."

"Why, who is he?" the leader asked.

"The Terror of the Continent," he answered.

"He's not even armed," the man on my right argued.

"He doesn't need to be," the one on the left assured him. "You haven't heard the stories about him?"

"Stories are just stories," the man on the right said, and I smirked in amusement.

"No, there not," the one on my left insisted, raising his voice as he did. "I passed by Fadiru once after robbing some merchants on the road, and there were thick clouds of smoke coming from the city. I saw heads mounted on pikes along the walls when I got closer. The skin was cut so the flesh was peeling off and dangling past the jaw.

"Flames were jumping higher than the walls, and I could feel their heat from where I stood. The stench of death surrounded the town, worse than the plague, and it lingered around me for a week. If this man says he's Bowv, give him the gold and let him pass; it's not worth the risk."

Their leader turned to look at me, and I looked into his eyes. He must have known my reputation because I could see he was debating whether he should give me the gold or call what he suspected may be a bluff. While he was doing that, a wicked grin ran across my face, and the possibility of a fight breaking out where I could kill the three of them brightened my eyes.

"Fine," the leader said, obviously concerned with the look I was giving him. His hand flashed to his pouch, opened it, grabbed a gold sovereign, and threw it to me.

"You can't be serious, boss," the one on my right said.

"I am. Now shut up and move off the road," ordered the leader.

I signaled to Rono that everything was fine with a wave. Rono caught up to me, and we passed the bandits without any more problems. When we got out of sight, Rono asked me what had happened.

"The fools thought they could shake me down," I said.

"I understand that, but how did you convince them to let us pass without a fight?" he asked.

"Were you paying attention, brother?" I chastised. "They not only let us pass without a scratch, but I got them to give me a gold piece."

"How in the name of the gods did you do that?" he asked.

"Being the most feared man on the Continent has its perks," I replied.

"I suppose it does, though I don't believe the benefits of such a reputation outweigh the savagery it takes to gain it," commented my brother.

"Believe what you wish, but not because of my reputation and the savagery it's built on, blood was not spilled today," I remarked.

"It would be a valid point if your savagery was confined to bandits and highwaymen and wasn't reserved for the innocent," he rebuked.

"If that's the case, then perhaps you should double-check how much innocent blood I have spilled," I suggested.

Rono had brought his horse to a halt. "The Wretched King was not innocent, I will give you that, though you acted outside the law. But you have slaughtered a dozen towns. Defend your actions, but don't think I'm dumb enough to believe your lies. You are not hanging from a rope right now because something much greater is happening."

That ended our conversation. We remained silent for the rest of the day's ride, and the sun began to set before we were close to Traevelios, so we had to make camp for another night. Like the previous night, we set up camp a bit from the road, and Rono made another stew. After our meal, Rono broke his silence.

"What do you think of the war?" he asked.

"Which war?" I asked, knowing that the Diefetians were fighting wars against the Kytrenabins, the Gofrudins, the Nutharicans, the Renvolies, and the Huderians.

"All of them," he said.

"Why would you care about my opinion?" I asked.

"You always had a better grasp on warfare than me," my brother admitted.

"That's true, but a nonsensical answer. You're worried about your neutrality," I deduced.

"Always so direct, brother," he said.

"Only when people waste my time," I reminded him.

"Yes, I am worried about Eshtar's neutrality, so tell me which wars the Diefatians will lose," he ordered.

"Lose?" I asked.

"Yes, lose," he reiterated.

I laughed.

"Why are you laughing?" Rono asked.

"I'm laughing because the Diefetians will be victorious by year's end," I told him amused by his ignorance.

"Victorious against whom?" Rono asked.

"All of them," I said.

"Why?" he asked, leaning forward.

"King Salroon knows what he is doing," I gave the simple answer since it was obvious to anyone who followed the wars.

"What's that supposed to mean?" Rono asked.

"Do you want the short answer or the long one?" I asked the king.

"We have time," was his response.

"Salroon has already won, even though peace has yet to be declared," I put it simply because though he said we had time, Rono never took well to understanding war.

Politics my brother could understand quite well. He maintained the power and autonomy of the king during a time when the nobility hated our family because of the Wretched King and I. But there was a reason the Wretched King took me and not Rono on campaign with him: my brother barely knew the difference between infantry and cavalry, let alone how to use them in battle.

Rono's strong suits were diplomacy and politics, and they needed to be. When my brother took the throne after I abdicated, the Eshtaran nobility was at the point of revolt. The nobles didn't care that I had killed my father. They all wanted the Wretched King dead. I had gotten their hopes up by killing Father. They thought I would slay the monster they called king and turn the kingdom around. The nobles thought the wars would end once I was king, and the bogus trials and executions of political adversaries would cease.

The nobles were too scared to do anything themselves, even when dissenting nobles began to disappear without a trace. They knew if they rebelled against the Wretched King, they couldn't win, not even when he was fighting a handful of wars. I was their only hope if they wanted the kingdom to be turned around, or so they thought.

I shattered that hope when I abdicated. At that point, Rono was fifteen and had no experience governing a kingdom and no experience in war during a time when the kingdom was fighting three of them.

The nobles were ready to rebel and put someone else on the throne. I was never afraid for my brother, though. From the time he could speak, he was a diplomat, and he spent most of his education studying politics. Within a month, he had calmed all the nobles, and within three months, he had negotiated the end of all the wars. Never had I been so proud of him.

"How is that?" he asked.

"The Kyntrenbins are cut off from their supplies, every Nutharican army has been outmaneuvered, the Gofrundin capital was taken a week before I was captured; it's only a matter of time before their king surrenders, half of the Renvoly fleet has been wiped out, and the Huderian Empire was dying long before the war started. They cannot sustain a long war," I explained.

"Will Salroon stop?" my brother asked.

"He won't want to, but when he reaches Luferia, he will," I said.

"But the Luferite army is only five thousand men. Salroon can field far more than that," he pointed out.

"Yes, but the terrain won't allow him to. When it is not narrow mountain passes, it is densely packed forests ill-suited for moving around with large armies," I explained.

The king nodded his head.

"I am surprised, brother," I said.

"About what?" he asked.

"You are picking my brain instead of condemning me," I told him.

He shrugged.

"Don't give me a shrug. Tell me, what's with your sudden change of heart," I demanded.

Rono didn't answer. Instead, he stared into the fire with a grim look, anticipating a near future, a desperate one that drove him to do something he never thought he would do: free me from prison.

"Good night, Bowv," Rono said, looking up from the fire and walking to his tent.

Chapter Two

WHEN SUNLIGHT GENTLY RAN OVER THE MOUNTAINS to the east, we awoke and got back on the road. It was a pleasant morning for a ride, with a gentle southern breeze and a cloudless sky. For about half the day, we rode until the city of Traevelios came into view. The City of Arches lived up to its name before we entered it.

Arches reached up from the ground and peaked at the top of the city's walls. Within the boundaries of each arch was a mural depicting historic buildings or spots in the city that the locals took pride in, such as the city's garden, which boasted the oldest trees in a public space anywhere on the Continent. Each arch was painted with vibrant colors that the Sun's rays brought to life.

However, the mural that we could see was the exception. Instead of depicting a scene within the city, it depicted a religious one. The nine gods of the Protectorate were seated on their thrones, arrayed in a semicircle that conformed to the pattern of the arch. On the bottom left was AAeruno, god of smiths and craftsman, with a long scraggly beard, muscles bulging from his arms, and a blacksmith's hammer resting on his lap.

Further up the arch was Kalrekos, the master of the sea. A dolphin was leaping over the god's head. Next was Junyl, the goddess of mothers. The goddess sat on her throne with a toddler beside her, tugging gently at the hems of her dress to get her attention. Next to Junyl was Heques, the goddess of beauty. Her throne had flowers growing on it, and her skin was flawless and glowing.

At the pinnacle was Numveron, leader of the Protectorate and patron of justice, law, order, and righteousness. The king of the gods sat with a crown upon his head and held up the scales of justice with his right hand.

To the left of him was Pafix, the god of war, who had a spear resting against his throne on one side and a shield on the other.

The next god was Ferjera, the goddess of the arts. She sat with one hand resting on her throne, the other gripped a paintbrush. Then there was Wusneric, the god of wisdom and the one who is said to intervene the most in mortal affairs. A scroll lay across the god's lap as he sat on his throne. At the bottom right, there was Xaretgriu, the god who wards off disease, with a potion in each hand.

Standing in the middle of the semicircle was a man wearing a ragged shirt and torn trousers. Chains slung to the ground from the iron cuffs that gripped the man's wrists and anchored him to the floor. Tolunfie, the god who guides the dead, was standing to his right, indicating the man was dead, and the chains marked him as a criminal. Now he stood before the Protectorate to be judged.

Numveron would list all the man's deeds, whether benign or malicious, heroic or cowardly, just or criminal. Then the king of the gods would ask the members of the Protectorate whether he deserves a peaceful afterlife or one filled with torments. If the Protectorate thought the man lived a righteous life, they would vote to reward him in the afterlife; if they didn't, he would be punished for his sins.

I believed it when I was younger before Father became the Wretched King and before Mother died. I believed everything the priests told me, even the stories about vampires. But what gods permit a man as pious as my Father to descend into despotism?

The early wars he fought were in defense of his kingdom and his people. I remember many nights he was on his knees praying to Numveron. Father asked if the wars were unjustified in the god's eyes, then to send him a sign and he would seek peace. Prayers to Pafix followed to grant a swift end to the war.

"We're here," I said, bringing my thoughts back to the present.

"Where will Hearik be?" Rono asked me as we rode towards the gates.

"Trying to sell the sword if he hasn't already. Though that's assuming he doesn't know it's mine," I said.

"The market then," Rono said, unfamiliar with how Hearik operated. I shook my head and told my brother to follow me.

We rode to the city's gates. Two guards posted outside stopped us as we rode up.

"Why have you come to Traevelios?" one guard asked.

"We're here visiting a friend who's holding an item for us," I said.

"What's the item?" the guard asked.

"A sword," I answered truthfully.

"How long will you be staying?" he asked.

"No more than a day," I answered.

"Very well, be on your way," the guard dismissed us.

We rode through the gates and trotted along the dirt road. When we were out of earshot, Rono said he couldn't remember when guards controlled who entered the city, so thoroughly.

"You're their king, brother; it's bad business to hold up monarchs at the gates," I remarked.

He sighed.

"And Hearik's probably been smuggling illegal goods into the city," I told him.

"I thought you said he was a merchant," Rono said.

"I did," I said. "He's a legitimate merchant until you need something pawned or smuggled."

"What are the odds that he has the sword?" my brother asked.

"There's a good chance he has it if he knows it's mine," I said

"Good chance? What do you mean by good chance?" the king asked.

"Hearik is prone to making stupid decisions if the monetary reward is high enough. However, his good luck normally protects him from serious consequences when he makes a poor decision. But selling the sword when he knows it is mine would be a stupid decision even by his standards," I explained.

"Where is he exactly?" Rono asked.

"He'll be at the inn on the south side of town called the Golden Rest," I said.

"Are you sure?" he asked.

"Yes, I'm sure. He owns half of the business, and I'm sure we'll find him there trying to sell something," I explained to Rono.

In about half an hour we had walked to the inn, having been told by a city guard to hitch our horses by the city's gate if we weren't staying in the city overnight. Waves of people were coming in and out of the Golden Rest, always a good sign for an inn. We walked underneath the customary arch that curved over the short pathway connecting the inn and the street. As we walked up the stairs Rono turned to me and asked how to find Hearik.

"It's easy," I said as we entered the lobby. "He'll be the man telling tall tales and outright lies while trying to sell something. But don't let his sales pitch fool you. He's the best smuggler on the Continent and can get you anything you want."

It took only a moment to find Hearik because I could hear his voice before I stopped talking. Hearik was sitting at a table to the right of the entrance towards the far side of the inn attempting to sell a bracelet to a man who was not being fooled.

"The queen of the ancient kingdom of Arundia once wore this very same bracelet, and I am willing to give it to you for the fair price of three hundred gold pieces," Hearik told his potential buyer.

The man got up from the table and walked away.

"Two hundred," Hearik shouted, arms extended to the side, but the man kept walking.

"You're lucky you're an owner. Else, you would be kicked out for harassing the patrons," I said, approaching the table and taking a seat, Rono shadowed me but did not sit down, not wanting Hearik to have a good look at him. If Hearik saw the familial resemblance, then things could have gotten complicated. And it wouldn't have been hard for him to see it.

Rono and I had both inherited our father's strong king and our mother's eye shape, though Rono's eyes were a lighter shade of blue and mine were on the darker side of green. Rono kept his blonde hair shorter than the length of the time's prevailing style, while I wore my dark brown hair longer down to about eye level. But the eye shape and the jaw lines were typically enough for people to figure out we were brothers. Though if Hearik saw the resemblance he didn't say.

"Bowv, I thought you were in chains," he greeted me. His thin face, unobstructed by hair from his bald head, accentuated his look of shock.

The man was so pale-skinned that someone who didn't know him might have thought him a ghost shocked to be seen.

"And I thought you were a better negotiator," I said. "And a better liar."

"Well, some people don't know a good deal even when it appears right in front of their face," he said. "And I wasn't lying. This bracelet was found in the tomb of an Arundian queen right on her corpse."

"I didn't know you moved into grave robbing," I said.

"I haven't," Hearik said. "I took it as payment for smuggling certain items into Pujinto."

"Interesting," I said.

"Anyways, I suppose you're looking for the sword," he guessed. "Heard it was yours after I bought it off of Sardenel."

"I am," I confirmed. "Now explain why you bought something that was mine."

"I didn't know it was yours at the time. I got a message from Goreson yesterday saying you barraged into Sardenel's office looking for it," Hearik defended himself.

"I'll believe you for now," I said, knowing it was possible that Goreson, a business associate of Hearik's in Bihendum, could have sent a message via pigeon. "You know what I will do to you if I find out you're lying."

"Who's this?" Hearik asked, turning to Rono and changing the subject.

"The man who got me out of my cell," I told him.

"Huh, I was wondering how you got out," he said. "Follow me. The sword is upstairs."

We followed him up the stairs and walked down a hallway to its end, where there was a small square door on the ceiling, an entrance into an attic. Hearik opened the door, and a ladder fell then he climbed up. We could hear the creaking of wooden boards. No doubt any guests in the nearby rooms were unhappy with the noise. After a minute or two, the creaking stopped, and Hearik came down the ladder with the sword.

The sheathe was made from weathered leather that was smooth to the touch. The pommel was a dulled sphere that reflected a minuscule amount of light. Knicks and dents covered the cross guard, providing the weapon with an air of authenticity and acting as a testament to its reliability. The handle was wooden, with grains running from the pommel toward the blade.

The sword looked like it was passed down from father to son for three generations or more, a veteran of the last century. It was not until you drew the sword that you realized you were holding a curiosity and not a weapon kept throughout the generations.

Hearik didn't unsheathe the sword, and Rono stood with his arms crossed. Rono no doubt looked at this battered weapon and thought I had tricked him. Hearik noticing this as well, shot me a glance, looking for confirmation to draw the sword. I nodded.

Hearik then drew the sword, revealing the blade in all its splendor. I wouldn't have kept the sword if I hadn't seen the blade when I fought Gaenic. Like the moon, the blade was made of a unique metal with a pale gray color. Ancient runes were inscribed from the tip of the blade to the bottom. The symbols were of a language I didn't recognize but were simple. My brother stood there amazed, with wonder in his eyes.

"*Hueik*," he said awestruck, his voice barely audible.

Hearik sheathed the sword and handed it to me. Rono just stood there, shocked. Thoughts about the ancient tales surged through his head.

"Thank you for not selling it," I said to Hearik.

"No problem," he said. "But I was tempted. A man came in here the other day looking for the sword. I thought I recognized him from when I was in Bihendum," Hearik told me.

"Did he threaten you?" I asked.

"No, but he told me someone in the Diefetian court was looking for it and said there would be some money for me if I could get my hands on it," explained Hearik.

"What did he look like?" I asked.

"Can't remember. It was dark in the lobby when he approached me," Hearik said.

"Did you get a name?" I asked.

"He wouldn't say," Hearik told me.

"Did he know the sword's name?" Rono asked him.

"Before you told me, I didn't know the thing had one," informed Hearik.

"And I bet you already forgot it," I guessed.

"Yes, I did," Hearik said with an honest smile. The smuggler dealt with so many rare items he stopped remembering names he didn't need to know for current deals. He once told me if he remembered the name of every antique piece he ever dealt with, then he wouldn't be able to remember anything else.

"Anyways, we better not hang around if this Diefetian is looking for the sword. Thank you again for not selling it," I said.

"I may be stupid at times, but I keep a small list of people not to cross, and you are at the top of the list," Hearik said.

I shook hands with him, and then he handed Hueik to me. Shortly after, Rono and I walked back down the stairs into the lobby.

"I thought you said you robbed Hearik," Rono said, recalling our conversation in Bihendum as we exited the Golden Rest.

"I did rob him," I said.

"Then how are you on good terms with him?" he asked me.

"I needed a good smuggler, and he's the best," I explained.

"But you robbed him," he repeated like a child.

"And by utilizing his services, I have given him a hundred times the value of what I stole from him," I said. "Now I trust you can get yourself back to the palace."

"We're not done, brother," he reassured me.

"You have the sword; therefore, you don't need me anymore," I countered.

"We're not done yet, particularly because you have a loose definition of me having *Hueik*," he said, pointing to the sword now attached to my hip.

"Not done yet. Need I remind you that you let me out of my cell to help you find the sword?" I asked him.

"I let you out to lead me to Gaenic's body," Rono said.

"Then I exceeded your expectations," I concluded. "Besides, we didn't have a deal, brother; you just let me out of my cell and demanded I take you to that noble's corpse, so the sword is mine, and I don't have to help you anymore."

"Why did you do it?" Rono asked me.

"Do what?" I answered with another question.

"Take me to Gaenic's corpse," he specified.

"Because I thought you came down to the dungeon to tell me I was about to be executed, but instead, you opened the door to my cell, something I never thought you would do," I explained. "I was in shock."

"And saw an opportunity to escape," he pointed out.

"Of course I did," I said, admitting the obvious.

"Goodbye then, brother," the king dismissed me.

"You're letting me leave?" I asked.

"Yes," Rono answered

"You are letting me go knowing that I will travel back to Bihendum and kill Sardenel in the most painful way I can think of," I said.

"Yes," Rono affirmed, not concerned with the idea of me torturing someone to death.

"Why is that?" I asked.

"Because if I am right about what this all means, then you running amuck will be the least of my worries," he explained.

"What could be more worrisome than me?" I asked him.

"Vampires," he said with a straight face.

"Brother, just because I killed a noble with some pointy teeth doesn't mean vampires are real," I argued.

"Then why is someone from the Diefetian court looking for the sword?" he asked.

"It's probably their inheritance," I said beginning to walk away down the street to get rid of my brother, but misfortune struck, and he followed. "Why are you obsessed with the sword anyway?"

"It is *Hueik*, the Sword of the Gods," he said.

I stopped in the middle of the street. It was noon, and most people were at the market where they couldn't eavesdrop on our conversation. "Don't let those runes on the blade kid you, nor its color. The sword is a forgotten relic of a bygone age, nothing more."

"A sword said to be gifted to Frood the Half-god for the express purpose of killing vampires," he elaborated. "It's too much to be a coincidence, Bowv."

"Fine," I said.

"Fine, what?" Rono asked.

"We'll track down this Diefetian, he's in the city after all, and torture him for information," I proposed if only to prove Rono the sword was nothing special.

"Bowv, we're not doing that," Rono rejected my idea.

"You don't need to," a voice from behind said.

I turned around to see a well-dressed man with Diefet's insignia, a red scorpion, on the breast of his blue shirt. He appeared to be around the same age as Rono and I. A dagger rested on his hip, typical for noblemen since they believe swords are too cumbersome. His black hair was longer than the average and covered his ears and touched his neck, but was cropped just before it would fall into his eyes. He had the fairer complexion of the Continent's north and not the tanned, almost bronze tone of a native Diefetian.

But what caught my eye was the large coin purse running parallel to the dagger, secured to the opposite hip. I silenced the greed enflaming my heart and continued to examine the man. What struck my curiosity was that the man had no guards. And his boots, which were weathered so much that the black leather was becoming gray.

"Who are you," I asked.

"A representative of the Diefetian court," he said.

"That's a long way of saying courier," I remarked.

"I'm no courier," the man assured me with a smile.

"Really, because I don't know a noble on the Continent who travels without a guard or has boots as beat up as yours," I said.

"I am here to offer you a hundred gold pieces for the sword," the stranger said, ignoring my deductions.

"What's your name?" Rono asked.

"Leernu," the man said. "And my king wants the sword."

"King Salroon won't be getting it," I assured him. "The sword is not for sale. I've been without a weapon for the past few days, and I like this one."

"Two hundred gold pieces," Leernu offered.

"If Salroon wants the sword, he'll have to fork over his kingdom," I stated.

Leernu smiled. "Ah, Bowv, you're as stubborn as your father was," he remarked.

"My father?" I asked.

"Yes, the Wretched King was one of the most stubborn men I've ever known," Leernu told us.

"Why should we believe you knew him?" my brother asked.

"Because King Rono, I was a military advisor to your father. Bowv would remember me from the Derierian Campaign when he was around twenty," explained Leernu, turning to look at me.

I remembered a military advisor talking to Father, hunched over a table decorated with sprawling maps and reports. But I couldn't remember what the man looked like. He couldn't have been Diefetian because, at the time, Diefet had a policy of strict isolation. Other than necessary trade, there was little interaction with Diefet, let alone Diefetian interaction with the rest of the Continent. There would only be one way of knowing if the man was my father's advisor.

"Towards the end of the campaign, what did you advise our father to do?" I asked, knowing if he were the advisor, then he would know exactly what advice I was referring to.

"I advised a retreat, for which your father threw a nearby axe at my head," Leernu answered.

Rono shot me a glace, a silent request for confirmation. The information Leernu gave was accurate, but a king throwing an axe at an advisor's head was the type of story that trickles into taverns across the Continent.

"If you are who you claim you are," I said. "Then tell me why you advised a retreat and who gave my father the advice that won the day."

"I advised a retreat because we were outnumbered four to one, the enemy had carried out a successful raid, and our supplies were dwindling," Leernu began.

"I didn't see a way out of the situation, but you did, advising your father to fortify our position and launch a counterraid against the enemy's camp to steal back our supplies and burn the rest. Being without supplies, they would be forced to assault our position or retreat, knowing they would starve without supplies. It was the last thing the enemy expected."

While we spoke, Rono had not taken his eyes off me. I could feel the tension building within him as he waited for me to confirm or deny Leernu's credibility.

"Who led the raid?" I pressed.

"Most people think it was your father, but it was you, Bowv, and I dare say none of us could have pulled it off except for you," Leernu said.

"He is who he says he is," I told Rono without looking away from Leernu. "Though he should be walking around with a cane."

Leernu chuckled. "I should be," he said with a grin. "Now, will you give me the sword or not?"

"You already have my answer," I said.

He began to reach for his dagger, and I reached for my sword.

"Don't be a fool," I told him.

"You are a capable fighter Bowv, but that won't deter me. My king wants that sword at any cost," Leernu said as he drew the dagger.

"Even at the cost of war?" Rono asked.

"You think you stand a chance against Salroon in a war? If so, then you are a fool," Leernu replied.

"He's already at war with half the Continent. He can't afford another war," my brother pointed out.

A smug grin worked its way across Leernu's face as he looked directly into Rono's eyes, a small mistake. "Salroon will conquer the Continent. Our armies will destroy yours within a week, then after your soldiers are all impaled on spikes..."

Faster than the blink of an eye, I drew my sword and lunged forward for a thrust, my motions a blur. Most people wouldn't have seen me coming, but Leernu did. The Diefetian representative began to move his dagger with the speed and precision of a veteran warrior. His goal was a parry to knock back my sword, but there was too much distance to travel. I smiled as I felt my blade pierce through his flesh, then rush through his gut, tearing apart his delicate organs.

He looked down at the blade; the arrogance vanished from his face, replaced with disbelief. I twisted the sword, and disbelief fled as anguish rushed onto Leernu's face. He let out a cry as his eyes became alive with pain. I smiled.

I never liked fanatics, particularly those devoted to their political leaders. People used to say I was the monster because I raided, burned, extorted, and slaughtered villages. But that is what armies do during war.

I always thought I was more honest since I never wrapped my crimes in the cloak of flag and country. Money and infamy were always my motives, but I never used politics or claims on land to justify my crimes. The conquerors of old did and were called great because of it, but I was condemned as a criminal because I didn't do my pillaging with an army.

In one smooth motion, I pulled the blade from the Diefetian. Leernu fell to his knees in a state of disbelief, and his hands moved towards his wound. I went to wipe the blood off the blade and was puzzled as I looked at the sword: there was no blood on it. The blade's moonlike gray color began to glow. It was faint, but it was there. I was flabbergasted. The barely audible voice of Leernu carrying his final words brought me back to my senses.

"Who would have thought an atheist would wield the Sword of the Gods?" he asked, gave a last laugh, and then his corpse fell face first to the ground.

I stood there for a moment, looking at the body and processing what he said. It matched with what Rono had been telling me all along, what I had been dismissing as nothing more than nonsensical old tales.

"Two bodies without blood..." I mumbled.

"They were vampires, Bowv. Do you believe me now?" Rono asked.

"Whether I believe you is irrelevant. Right now, we need to get out of here before a city guard finds us standing in front of a dead body," I urged him.

"Let's go then," he agreed.

We walked out of the alley, back to the horses, and then rode to the main gate. No one was around to hear our exchange with Leernu. We were lucky. If someone had, city guards would have blocked the alley to take care of the corpse and begin an investigation. If that had been the case, we would have been detained, and a scandal would have ensued.

It was around two o'clock when we reached the main gates. Unlike coming into the city, there were no guards questioning people. It made sense, considering they were concerned with people smuggling illicit goods into the city, not with what was being moved out. We walked back towards the gate, unhitched our horses, got through the gate without a guard giving us a hassle, and rode off before anyone found Leernu's body.

We didn't say a word to one another after we passed through the gates. My brother knew his insistence on the existence of vampires would only irritate me. The silence was broken when we rode well out of earshot of the city guards.

"Bowv..." Rono began.

I cut him off, "I don't know what we saw, but insisting the fantastical stories of your senseless religion are real doesn't change the fact that Salroon wants the sword and is willing to go to war for it. So, I suggest, brother, whatever speech you were about to give me, save it for someone else and go back to your capital and begin preparing for war."

"I will take that suggestion," the king told me.

"Good," I said.

"Under one condition," he continued.

"Condition?" I asked, confused. "Rono, suggestions don't have conditions to them. They're friendly advice. Either you take the advice or don't."

"If Salroon declares war, I want you to help me fight it," he said.

I laughed. "Brother, I'm a criminal, not a soldier."

"You were a solider during Father's reign and a skilled general. Leernu was right. No one else would have thought to raid the enemy camp."

"Are you sure?" I asked. "Just over two weeks ago, you had me imprisoned awaiting execution."

"I am," he assured me.

"Why?" I asked.

"Because, as you pointed out, Salroon is winning the wars he is fighting, which means I don't have anyone else to turn to," he explained.

"You have generals," I told him as we rode on.

"The ones that served Father are all dead," my brother informed me.

"What's that supposed to mean?" I asked.

"It means I have no generals with any experience in war," clarified Rono. "And I've sent them all to oversee the defenses of key cities"

"There aren't any lower-ranking officers who served under Father who you could promote?" I asked.

"No," the king informed me.

"Why is that brother?" I asked, thinking it was impossible, with the number of wars Father fought, for any officer in the Eshtaran army not to have fought in a war.

"Because either you killed them when I sent the army after you following Father's death, or they died in the bout of plague we had a few years back," explained Rono.

"Then you can't blame me entirely for your lack of experienced generals," I told him. "Putting that aside, it sounds like you want to make me a general."

"Military advisor, not a general," he stressed.

"Which is another way of saying general," I pointed out.

"That's what you think," my brother said.

"Well, I guess it depends if you have enough sense to take my advice," I said.

"So, you're taking my offer?" Rono asked.

"It's better than hanging," I said. "And it means if Salroon wants the sword, he will have to fight an army to get it."

"Then, as King of Eshar, I declare you to be my military advisor," Rono said, making my status official.

The sun was beginning to set, so we stopped and made camp for the night. Rono must have anticipated traveling for a while when we left the capital because he still had plenty of food despite us traveling for most of the week. After the tents were pitched, we ate dinner and sat by the fire, then we went to bed, woke up, ate breakfast, and traveled some more. This was our routine until we got back to the capital, Kiholp.

When we rode up to the Stone Palace, servants came out to take our horses. Rono entered first, and I followed him from behind. Everyone in the palace approached him, asking if he was okay, and what struck me was that they were genuine. They weren't trying to gain my brother's favor.

Instead, they were concerned about his health, the difficulty of the journey, and whether I had made any attempts on his life. In my experience, those who surround kings are petty men shadowing the monarch to fight over, then devour, whatever scraps of power that fall from his hands.

But for those who approached my brother that day, there was no denying the look of concern on each of their faces. Within a few minutes of walking into the palace, Rono was surrounded by dozens of people inquiring about his health and safety. I could have snuck out right then, when all eyes were on Rono, and my presence was unnoticed; the thought certainly crossed my mind.

It would have been easy. We had just entered the palace, and people swarmed my brother. I was right by the door. I could have turned around, walked out the door, grabbed one of the horses, then taken off. I doubt anyone would have bothered to stop me since I was seen riding with the king, and the few people who knew who I was wouldn't have dared to stop me. With just a few steps, I could have been out the door and riding towards Bihendum to kill Sardenel in the most painful way possible.

But I didn't. Salroon had authorized Leernu to kill me for the sword, something I couldn't let stand. If Eshtar were going to war with Diefet, then the best chance I had of killing Salroon would be with the Eshtaran army.

After what must have been ten minutes of people expressing their concerns, a young aide came up to my brother. The aide beckoned Rono to the throne room, and they entered. I was out of earshot to hear what was going on. But once I saw both go into the room, I waited a few minutes before I went in, thinking it was nothing more than two court nobles who butted heads with one another while their liege was away. When I realized Rono would have told the nobles he would hear their squabbles later since he needed to prepare for war, I decided to go in and see what was happening.

As I walked in, I heard the voice of a man who thought he could make demands to a king. Before Rono introduced the stranger, I knew who he was. The stranger wore a dark blue robe. Embroiled on both the front and the back was a red scorpion, the symbol of Diefet. Its right claw held an olive branch, and in its left claw, a spear.

Unlike Leernu, the man had the tanned complexion of someone raised in the desert kingdom. His black hair was short and barely touched his forehead, and his eyes were green like a reptile's hide.

The robe was dramatic, in my opinion, since the words "Diefetian Ambassador" stitched onto it would have given the same message. I did make a mental note that the robe was expensive but would require a skilled fence to sell it to. Then, the ambassador's obnoxious voice broke my train of thought.

"As I already told you, King Salroon will overlook the death of Lord Leernu if you give him the sword," the ambassador explained, his voice possessing the sleaze of a man offering a promise he knew may not be kept.

"And as I have told you, I do not have it," Rono said, remarkably maintaining a respectful tone. I don't know how he did it, considering I wanted to cut the vocal cords out of his throat whenever the ambassador spoke.

"No, you are not, but you can order your brother to give it up," the Diefetian ambassador argued.

"If I obeyed, that would make me a poor outlaw," I said, walking into the center of the room. Rono was on the throne with his aide to the right while the ambassador and I stood side by side before the king.

"And let's not forget you are the eldest," my brother added.

"Who won't allow his younger brother to boss him around," I said in agreement.

The ambassador turned away from my brother and toward me. "Tell me, Bowv, what is your price?" he asked.

"I'm not selling," I stated.

"There must be a price," insisted the Diefetian.

"There isn't," I told him, my tone flat and uncompromising.

The ambassador turned back to face Rono. "King Rono, my liege will get the sword somehow. This may be your only chance to resolve this matter civilly."

Anger lit up in my brother's eyes for the briefest of moments, then faded away quicker than it came as he recomposed himself. "Is that a threat, Ambassador Zimkoo? Your king was uncivilized when he first tried to get his hands on the sword in an alley in Traevelios. Lord Leernu's death was the cost of such incivility."

"Yes, it is," Ambassador Zimkoo confirmed.

I grinned. Those words put me into a state of bliss. In one smooth motion, acting as quick as whitewater rapids, I drew *Hueik* and drove it through Zimkoo's chest. The ambassador gave a blood-curdling scream that echoed throughout the palace. The palace guards rushed into the room with weapons drawn, ready to defend their king. But that wasn't important. What was important was that Zimkoo's scream was much less obnoxious than his voice.

I took a moment to appreciate the fact I would never again hear his voice before I pulled the blade from the dying ambassador. Yet again, the blade didn't have blood on it. This time, I was not shocked but annoyed because it meant Rono was likely correct about vampires, and I would have to listen to speeches about the gods. Once the sword was removed, the fresh corpse fell to the ground.

"Was that necessary, brother? He was unarmed," Rono asked.

"Yes," I said with a wicked smile.

Rono sighed, then dismissed the guards. "There will be war now," the king said.

"War was certain when Leernu was willing to kill you to get the sword," I reminded him.

He turned towards the aide, who looked about twenty with dirty blonde hair cut short in an army style, light blue eyes, and a defined jawline, and told him to see that the army was mobilized.

"I didn't think aides could give orders to mobilize the army," I observed.

"He's not an aide," Rono said.

"Who is he then?" I asked.

"Your oldest nephew," my brother said.

"Nephew? Ah, that's right. You got married, what twenty years back? Who did you marry, anyhow?" I asked, not caring that I didn't see the resemblance earlier.

"Hydela," he said as if I knew the woman.

"Should I know the name?" I asked.

"She's the daughter of Father's old chancellor," my brother explained.

"The sane one," I presumed.

My brother sighed, "Yes, the sane one."

"How many kids do you two have?" I asked.

"Four: two sons and two daughters. Jorn is the oldest; he turned seventeen last month," he answered.

"Good for you, brother," I said.

"What?" he asked, probably thinking he misheard me.

"I said, 'Good for you, brother.' You always wanted a family," I said.

"Thank you. Now, getting back to the dead ambassador in my throne room," he said, steering the conversation back on track.

"I was doing you a favor. Ambassadors can't be allowed to threaten kings. It makes the king look weak," I explained.

"Though I suspect that is not your reasoning," he pushed back.

"Of course not," I admitted. "If I had to listen to his pompous voice another minute, I would've killed someone else."

"Sounds about right. With this unpleasantness finished, I have to plan how to fight this war," the king informed me.

"That's why I'm here," I reminded him.

"What do you advise?" he asked.

"Assess your forces," I gave my first piece of advice.

"What then?' Rono asked.

"Worry about a plan after seeing what state your army is in," I told him.

"Right," my brother agreed. "But as far as strategy goes, what do you suggest?"

"To worry about strategy after you know your army is capable of fighting," I said.

My brother sighed. He knew I was right, and we both knew that the army was in worse shape than when Father was around. As king, Rono had never gone to war, managing to bring the wars he inherited to an end with diplomacy. He insisted the people of Eshtar needed to heal after the Wretched King's wars, and he was right. During the last war Father fought, most of the country was devasted.

Refugees flooded the capital, and widows mourned in the streets of every town that was left standing. Food was barely obtainable since most of the farmland was torched, and the economy was in shambles. Within a few years, Rono had fixed what could be fixed, as I knew he could.

It makes my abdication more altruistic than it was. My father, for all his faults, was one of the rare kings who could run a kingdom as well as he could run an army. He was as brilliant of a political administrator as he was a great general. Rono took to the administrative side of kingship, while I preferred the martial side. Rono learned the art of governance, while I learned the art of war.

In reality, I abdicated because I wanted people to fear me, to have my name bring dread whenever anyone heard it. That is where true power lies. I knew after Father's reign; the nobles would revolt if I were as feared a king as my Father was. So, I left the throne to my younger brother. To be feared on the level I wanted to be, I had to become the most infamous bandit on the Continent. Or at least this is what I told myself.

"What happens if the army is not ready to fight?" the king asked me.

I looked at the body of the dead ambassador. "Slaughter," I said, looking up back at my brother.

He fell silent. A few moments passed before Jorn entered the room again and approached his father, informing Rono that the orders had been given. They began to talk, and while they did, I walked over to Ambassador Zimkoo's corpse. I leaned over the body and began to search for blood, thinking that maybe the elegant robes had wiped it off my blade when I pulled it from the Ambassador's body, but I didn't find any.

I should have known there wouldn't be any because blood hadn't gushed out of the wound and pooled around the body, but I didn't want to believe I killed another man who didn't bleed. I pulled back the lower lip and found two fangs, and I found the same when I pulled back the top lip. Rono saw what I was doing and came over. Jorn just stood there by the throne observing the both of us, though he had a hateful glare whenever he looked at me.

"Another one," Rono said.

"No blood and pointy teeth," I said.

"Just as the Sacred Texts describe vampires," my brother said.

"I still don't know about this vampire nonsense, but we've seen three bloodless bodies of three Diefetian nobles, each completed with a set of fangs," I said.

"You think it's something Salroon is doing to his men?" my brother questioned.

"It's more plausible than a connection between Salroon and vampires," I said. "How long until the army is mobilized?"

"Jorn has given the orders. It will be a couple of days at the most," the king informed me.

"That quickly," I said with skepticism.

"I already ordered about half of our forces mobilized before I released you," my brother told me. Then I remembered that he mentioned sending his generals to oversee the defenses of key cities.

"I understand the army will be a lot smaller than during Father's reign, but how small are we talking about?" I asked.

"Three thousand men," Rono answered.

"Three thousand," I repeated in shock. Soon, my shock was replaced with a boiling rage. "Rono, when you took the throne, you wanted peace, but an army of three thousand men isn't enough to defend a kingdom as large as Eshtar."

"That is why I wanted you to be my advisor," admitted Rono.

"I don't know what you expect from me," I said.

"I know the situation is desperate, Bowv, but whether it was while you were on campaign with Father or running a bandit clan, you have always found some way to beat the odds. That's what I need. For you to pull us from the jaws of misfortune," explained Rono.

"It takes more luck than you think," I admitted. "But fortunately for you, it also takes great skill."

Chapter Three

I BEGAN TO WALK OUT OF THE THRONE ROOM.

"Bowv," my brother called me. "Where are you going?"

"To see an old friend," I told him.

Walking out of the room, I heard Rono say something to Jorn and then heard someone behind me. I turned around, expecting my brother to be behind me, but instead, I found my nephew.

"I thought you were your father," I said, turning back around.

"He told me to come with you," informed my nephew, displeasure clear in his voice.

"Huh," I mumbled. "All right, but if you can't keep up, that's not my problem."

I began to walk at a brisk pace, not caring if Jorn could keep up. As I walked, I noticed some details I hadn't before. First, about every six steps I took, there was a silk banner on the wall. There were two types of banners, and they kept alternating. The first was a silken banner that hung vertically with a deer, the national symbol of Eshtar, on it.

The second was less consistent, yet a clear theme bound them together. Each banner was made from silk, but instead of having the Esharan Deer, they had a symbol of one of the nine gods who made up the Protectorate: Aeruno, Kalrekos, Junyl, Heques, Numveron, Pafix, Ferjera, Wusneric, Xaretgriu. It always amused me how piety was an expensive virtue.

In comparison, Father had two banners with the Eshtaran Deer, made from the cheapest material he could find, and considered them a formality. The man was practical to a fault. The palace was built out of stone partially because he wanted it to be fireproof so that in a siege, the enemy could not set the palace ablaze, something he was fond of doing while on campaign.

"Why are you helping?" Jorn asked. I had stopped to admire the banners.

"Helping who?" I asked in response.

"The kingdom," he clarified. "You are a cutthroat who doesn't care about the wellbeing of others."

"Don't confuse altruism with necessity," I said, then walked away.

He followed me. "Then why did you abdicate?"

"Necessity," I said.

"What necessity?" he asked as we were exiting the palace.

"The necessity needed to become feared beyond my father," I said.

"That doesn't make any sense," the prince told me.

"It makes sense to me, and that's all that matters," I told him.

"So, you are a self-centered sociopath," Jorn concluded.

"Believe what you want. I don't care what some boy thinks of me," I said, and Jorn fell silent.

We exited the palace and started to walk down the street. It was a long time before Jorn spoke again.

"Who are we going to see?" Jorn asked.

"An old friend," I answered and left it at that.

We turned right onto the first adjacent street. The city hadn't changed much since I was younger. Most houses were made from stone, and their roofs were made from ceramic shingles. Father paid for it, saying it was not just the palace that needed to be fire-resistant but also the surrounding homes. I guess he was paranoid about some other king burning down his capital instead of the other way around.

Most of the shops I grew up with were still there, now owned by the shop owners' children. The roads were far better maintained than when I was younger. The Wretched King would work on the roads only if needed since most of the royal treasury went to the army.

Back then, the brick roads had several holes in them, restricting travel, though never posing any considerable hindrance to trade. My brother, on the other hand, had prioritized trade when he took the throne, and naturally, he ensured his capital's roads were suited for the task.

I took a left and headed onto the next street, with Jorn walking beside me. We walked down the street until we reached a small blacksmith shop. I could hear the distinct echoing of metal being hammered against an anvil. I opened the door and walked in, my nephew following behind me.

Inside, we found a young man about Jorn's age, an apprentice behind a counter. Swords, daggers, polearms, axes, maces, and bows decorated each wall. The young man greeted us, asking if we were looking for anything in particular.

"Is Billen here?" I asked.

"He is. I'll go get him," the apprentice said, walking away from the counter and down the nearby hallway, which led outside to the forge.

"How is a blacksmith supposed to help us in a war?" my nephew asked.

"Besides from making weapons and armor?" I asked, not bothering to hide the sarcasm in my voice.

"I don't think you came here to work out a deal for weapons and armor," Jorn stated his suspicion.

"You would be right," I revealed. "But depending on Billen's mood, that may be all we leave here with. Oh, and let me do all the talking."

"Father said you would say that. He also told me to tell you not to make any threats," Jorn informed me.

"As if you could enforce that," I said.

"I bet I could," he snapped back.

"Watch your tongue, boy, or you'll lose it," I said and moved my hand to the pommel of my sword.

Before Jorn could reply, Billen walked down the hallway with his apprentice. He saw me, his eyes narrowed, and a scowl ran across his face. Then he turned to his apprentice, said something to him, and the young man walked back down the hallway towards the forge. Now alone, Billen walked towards where we were standing.

It had been several years since I'd seen the smith, but it seemed like little had changed other than the beard he had grown. His brown hair fell to about shoulder length. Why any blacksmith would wear his hair so long is beyond me, but when I looked at the ends of Billen's hair, I was surprised to see no damage from heat or flame. His eyes were light brown and still held the same intensity I remembered. Billen's muscles were always big, but his biceps had gotten bigger since he had taken up the smithing.

"What do you want?" my old friend asked, his voice laced with hostility. "I thought you were supposed to be in the palace dungeon."

"Believe it or not, I was released," I said. "I have an offer for you."

"No," Billen flatly said. "And I don't believe you were released. It's not possible. Now get out of my shop."

"Come on, old friend, you haven't even heard my offer yet. A man can't refuse an offer before he even knows what it is," I argued.

"If he knows the man who is giving it, he can," Billen rebutted.

"It's nothing illegal," I revealed.

He chuckled. "Nothing illegal," he said with wonderment. "By the Protectorate, are you feeling okay, Bowv?"

"Never better. In fact, I have put my criminal activities on hold for the moment," I informed him.

"I don't believe you," the smith said again. "But tell me your offer anyway. I may find it amusing."

"Eshtar is at war with Diefet, and my brother made me his military advisor because he lacks experienced generals. I accepted. My offer is for you to join me and be my personal blacksmith," I explained.

"I thought you said you were a military advisor. Why would you need a blacksmith? You'll be in a tent," he asked.

"I plan to be an active advisor," I told him.

"What you told me is true?" he asked with a skeptical look.

"Yes," I said.

"Why should I believe you?" he asked.

"Because I have never lied to you. Though I know that's not a good enough reason for you. So, you should believe me because Prince Jorn is standing beside me," I said, turning towards my nephew.

Billen looked over to Jorn and took a good look. After a minute of silence, he turned and looked at me in the same detail.

"Well, the resemblance is there," he admitted. "All right, Bowv, I believe you, and I accept because I can serve the kingdom, not because I want to help you. And I am not fighting. My fighting days are over."

We shook hands, and then Jorn and I left the shop.

On our way back to the palace, Jorn asked me how I knew Billen.

"He used to be a lieutenant in my bandit clan. There was not a weapon on the shop's walls that he couldn't use," I answered.

"How did he learn blacksmithing?" Jorn asked.

"His father was a blacksmith," I answered.

"Then why did he become a bandit?" he asked.

"I'm not the one you should be asking," I said.

"Then why did you become a bandit?" he asked. "And give me a real answer this time."

"Because the gods aren't real, so they won't be there to protect you. Because we live in a dog-eat-dog world where power over others is the only way to ensure you don't get eaten. And the Wretched King's reign taught me power is derived from fear," I told him.

"After your grandfather's reign, the nobles were at the point of revolt. If I wanted to rule with fear, then I would have to put down a rebellion, and the army would be on the side of the nobility. But I still wanted the power from being feared, so I became a bandit lord. When people began calling me the Terror of the Continent, I had more power than any king, including the Huderian emperor."

"You terrorized the entire Continent because you wanted power," my nephew said in disbelief and gave me a disgusted look. "You're a monster."

"What I am is a man who has accepted that savagery is the name of the game in this godless world. There will always be someone willing to commit horrors against you, whether they be a pillaging army on the march, a king brutalizing his people, or a thug mugging people in a back alley. All I have done is take the world's natural order to its limits."

He fell silent after that. We took the same path back to the palace. When we arrived, there were four palace guards at the entrance, two more than when Rono and I arrived early that day. As we entered, the sun was beginning to set. We walked to the throne room and found Rono sitting on his throne, talking to a man, most likely some courtier. Rono saw us enter and dismissed the man.

"So, who did you go see?" my brother asked.

"The blacksmith, Billen," I answered.

"Not surprising," he said and nodded his head as if it made perfect. I thought Rono was bluffing, but later, I would learn he knew that Billen was in my clan.

"I need him to join me on campaign," I informed the king.

"Why is that?" Rono asked.

"Because I will need someone to fix my gear, and I trust Billen," I answered.

"When I asked you to be a military advisor, I thought that would imply you *wouldn't* be fighting," my brother informed me.

"As your military advisor, I would advise you to let me fight for two reasons. The first is that I will fight no matter what you say. The second is that I am the best fighter you have at your disposal. It would be a waste of my talents to sit in a tent for the entirety of the war," I explained.

My brother knew I was right. "Fine," he said. "But you can't bring anyone else along."

"I don't need anyone else," I said. "Now, who were you speaking to?"

"A courtier of mine. He thinks that there are Diefetian spies in the palace," the king answered.

"Of course, they do. It's probably how Zimkoo knew I killed Leernu," I guessed.

"What are we going to do?" asked Jorn.

"I'll take care of it," I volunteered.

"No, I need you ready when the army has fully mobilized," the king said. "And I don't want any more murders in my palace."

"Even with half of the army mobilized, it will take time to mobilize the other half, leaving me time to solve your spy problem," I argued.

Rono took a few seconds to think it over. "Fine, but restrain yourself," Rono ordered.

"You may need to respect the rights of nobles, brother, but I do not," I told him.

"No killing Bowv. You already murdered an ambassador within ten minutes of being in the palace," Rono pointed out.

"I will try," I promised. "Now, where can I find your courtier?"

"He should just be outside the throne room; he's my most trusted courtier," the king informed me. "In the meantime, I will look into the possible connection between Salroon and vampires."

"Don't waste too much of your time," I said, turning around and leaving the throne room.

The courtier was there, as Rono said he would be. His name was Paderok, and he was in his mid-thirties. His clothes were of better quality than those of a commoner and were of a different style, but they were far less elegant than those of a noble. His eyes were light brown, and his hair was dark brown and medium length. When I approached, his posture suddenly became erect, and his eyes filled with terror. I smiled.

"I hear we have a spy problem on our hands," I said.

He nodded his head.

"I have volunteered myself to investigate the matter until the army is fully mobilized. So, tell me what you know," I ordered.

"That... that... ambassador you killed," he began, his words staggered with fear. "He knew that you killed Leernu, but he also knew what happened in the palace while the king was traveling with you."

"Such as what?" I questioned.

"Details like the chancellor writing to various mayors assessing the status of their defenses and how many men they could muster if the kingdom were attacked, and the chancellor assuring the mayors that the king will send generals to oversee the defense of their cities," he said.

"Who knew about the chancellor's letters?" I asked.

"The king, the chancellor, and until recently, I did," he answered.

"Where's the chancellor?" I asked.

"I don't know where Chancellor Marilok is," he told me.

"Well, if you see him, don't tell him anything about our conversation," I said, staring him down.

Fear brightened in his eyes, his jaw clenched, and sweat ran down his brow. He nodded in agreement. I walked back into the throne room, where I found my brother with Jorn and another man, one in navy-blue robes that marked him as a priest of Wonderun, the god of history. Though not a member of the Protectorate, Wonderun is venerated by commoners and scholars alike.

His priests are mostly sought after by nobles to record family histories or by mayors to record a city's history. But Wonderun's priests also specialize in the history of the gods and are the most well-versed in the Sacred Texts out of all the priests. Traditionally, one priest of Wonderun resides in the palace to serve as a court historian. When I entered the room, the conversation had just begun.

"That was fast," Rono said as I entered and walked towards the throne.

"I work quickly," I said, not wanting the priest to know about the spy problem. "Who's the priest?"

"This is Frel; he's going to tell us about vampires," the king informed me.

"A king at war should not be concerned with old myths," I told Rono.

"You killed three men who did not bleed," Rono reminded me.

"Point taken," I said.

"So, you'll listen?" Rono asked.

"I will," I affirmed, and Frel began his tale.

"Long ago, an empire of great wealth and technological advancement ruled over the Continent. For a thousand years, the empire was governed by emperors who knew they owed their success to gods rewarding the piety of the empire's people. These emperors saw to it that no god's feast was missed and every year put on festivals of thanksgiving.

"They were devoted in their worship, never forgetting a sacrifice, nor failing to pray. Because of this piety, the gods favored the empire and it conquered the Continent, ushering in three thousand years of peace and prosperity.

"Then a man who thought himself equal to the gods ascended to the throne. The emperor preached this to his people, and his arrogance captured the entire empire. He went to the temple his forefathers built and demanded the Protectorate make him a god.

"The next day, a plaque broke out throughout the empire, yet this did not humble the emperor or his people. Even when the bodies were piling up in every corner of the empire the emperor went to the temple, not to repent, but to demand divinity for a second time. Again, there was no response. He waited a week then returned to the temple to make his demand again. Still, there was no answer from the Protectorate, and the plaque continued.

"Knowing the plagues were a punishment from the gods, cities and towns lost faith in their emperor and seceded from the empire. These new kingdoms, principalities, and republics abandoned the emperor's teachings and chose to resume their devotion to the gods. The plague stopped in each state which repented. Undismayed, the emperor continued to demand divinity.

"One night the demon Allemar visited the emperor and made him an offer. The demon would grant the emperor and what was left of his people immortality. They would live forever, be almost invulnerable to wounds, and be immune to all diseases, even the plaque that was their punishment.

"The emperor, wanting to spite the Protectorate and reconquer his lands, took the demon's offer. He went to sleep. Allemar killed him and his remaining subjects while they slept, capturing their souls, twisting them, and infusing them with his essence before returning them to their bodies.

"Thus, the first vampires were created. They formed a kingdom of their own from the remnants of the empire, worshipping Allemar and feasting on the blood of the living to access demonic powers. Wars were waged against the vampiric empire but to no avail. Vampires could only be killed by fire, beheading, or piercing the heart.

"The vampires were posed to conquer the Continent until the Protectorate forged *Hueik* from a sliver of the moon and gifted it to Frood the Half-god. The sword could kill a vampire as if he were a mortal man. With this divine gift, the living began to drive back the demonic servants. The vampires were defeated, their empire toppled, and they were hunted for centuries until the last one was killed."

"What about Diefet?" I asked

"I do not know of any connections between Diefet and vampires," the priest informed me.

"Is there anyone who would know?" Rono asked.

"No one endorsed by the Temple of the Protectorate," Frel told his king.

"Heretics," I deduced.

"Precisely," said Frel.

"And they would have information on Diefet and vampires?" my brother asked.

"I believe they would," Frel said.

"Why would they have information about a connection between vampires and Diefet?" Rono asked the priest.

"A certain sect of the Heretical Temple believes the vampires weren't hunted to extinction. They claim the Protectorate Temple covered up their existence and they claim to have been hunting the demonic undead for the past six thousand years," explained Frel.

"That's nearly the whole history of the Temple," Rono said in disbelief.

"Where can we find them?" I asked.

"The sect you seek are the Veroliks and they find you," Frel told us.

"Thank you for the information; we won't take up any more of your time," Rono said dismissing the priest.

Once the priest left the throne room, Rono and I were left alone.

"What did you learn?" the king asked.

"If there are spies, it's either they're in a position to intercept your chancellor's messages, are people close to the chancellor and are passing on information, or Chancellor Marilok is the spy," I said.

"Which do you think it is?" Rono asked.

"I don't know yet, but I know how easy it is to intercept messages. It will take some time to determine if the messages are being intercepted or if there is a traitor," I admitted.

"Do you think Chancellor Marilok could be a traitor?" asked the king.

"I couldn't say. I've never met the man," I said.

"Then, I must watch the Chancellor closely," concluded my brother.

It was getting late, and Rono offered to let me stay in the palace. I declined, not wanting to deal with the nonsense that was court politics, which always seemed to intensify in times of war. If anything went missing, I would be the obvious culprit, and it would be a Herculean task for me not to kill the person who accused me. I told my brother I would be staying at a nearby inn; he knew which one.

The inn was a short walk from the palace and operated by an old friend of my father. It was a small inn with two dozen rooms for guests, plus a lobby and the innkeeper's room. The exterior of the building showed signs of wear and tear, but considering the inn had been in operation for forty years at that point, it was understandable.

The wooden door greeted me with a long creek as I entered. Before me, a bald old man was behind the counter, writing in a ledger. I walked towards the counter, and he looked up to greet me; a warm smile started to form on his lips, causing the wrinkles on his face to bend. That was until he got a good look at me, then the smile chilled and sunk into a look of great disappointment that a father would give to his son.

"I told you never to come back," the old man said, anger providing weight to his voice.

I remained silent and continued towards the counter.

"Get out!" he shouted as he pointed to the door. His face was now red with anger.

"How are you Glendeo?" I asked, choosing to ignore his poor welcome.

"Considering I have a murderer in my inn, not well," Glendeo said, his voice laced with bitterness.

"The Wretched King needed to die," I defended myself.

"There are rites for removing a king," the old man argued.

"Ah, yes, these rites which make regicide just in the eyes of your gods. What's the difference anyway? Killing is still killing even when you wrap it up in the guise of tradition and ritual," I countered.

He fell silent and conceded defeat in our little debate. I could tell he was still angry, but what was once a roaring forest fire settled into a crackling campfire. "Why are you here?" he asked.

"I'm working with my brother and need a room because I don't want to stay in the palace," I told him.

"I got one," Glendeo said.

As he led me to the room, I remembered the days when I would come to the inn every morning. Glendeo was my father's best warrior and best friend, serving with him during the conquest of Eshtar's immediate neighbors and in the War of Reconquest before that. When Glendeo retired from the army, Father granted him land by the palace for a home and a shop. Glendeo chose to start an inn thinking that foreign diplomats would want to stay at an inn close to the palace.

When I was seven, Father sent me to train with Glendeo. Every morning, at the crack of dawn, I got dressed and walked down to the inn. In the back, Glendeo would teach me how to fight. He taught me how to wield every weapon known to man and how to fight unarmed. By age ten, I was more deadly than any soldier.

I owed Glendeo a lot; his training saved my life more than once. When I told him I killed the Wretched King, and I was abdicating, he couldn't look at me anymore. I remember him yelling for me to get out, that he trained me to be something greater than a murderer. He didn't blame me for doing it, though; he knew what my father had become, and there was no denying that the Wretched King needed to die. But he still wanted me to leave, so I left.

Glendeo led the way through the short hallway of the inn. Stopping at a room on the right side of the hall he pulled out a key and opened the door. The room was small with a bed and a dresser across from the bed. It had one window and it gave a wonderful view of the courtyard in the back of the inn where Glendeo spent countless hours training me to be the best warrior on the Continent. I got a rush of nostalgia for a far simpler time.

"How much do I owe you?" I asked the innkeeper.

"I don't want dirty money," he said.

"I have legitimate businesses," I assured him

"A half-silver a night," he said, knowing I probably did.

"That's fair," I agree.

He nodded and began to walk away.

"You aren't going to ask why?" I asked.

"If your brother chose to release you from your cell instead of executing you, then we are living in desperate times," he concluded.

I explained everything that happened over the last couple of weeks to Glendeo. How I was awaiting execution in my cell, then Rono showed up asking about a nobleman I killed then told me to take him to the corpse. I detailed my travels with Rono, going to Bihendum to investigate the body of Lord Gaenic, how it was undecayed, and how we began looking for Gaenic's sword.

Then, I recalled how we traveled to Travelios to retrieve the sword after we learned that Sardenel had sold it, how we recovered it only to have Leernu try to take it from us, and how I killed him. Finally, I told him about how we returned to the palace and how I killed the arrogant ambassador.

I explained how Rono thought vampires were returning, the possible connection with Diefet, and that he thought the sword we recovered was *Hueik*. I couldn't tell whether Glendeo was surprised or didn't believe me because as I told him of all this insanity the old warrior's face was a portrait of stoicism.

After a minute or two of silence, Glendeo spoke. "I knew times must have been desperate for your brother to release you, but war with Diefet is suicidal," he said.

"We don't have a choice. Salroon would have come anyways," I said.

"But this talk of vampires is even more concerning," he said.

"I don't know what's going on with bloodless corpses," I admitted. "But it is far more likely it's Salroon's doing than vampires."

His eyes looked to the sword resting by my hip. "Do you think that is the Sword of the Gods?" he asked.

"I don't believe in gods," I reminded him.

"Well, now might be the time to start," the old man said as he walked out of the room.

With that, I shut the door and went to sleep. It felt good to have a comfortable surface to sleep on after being on the road for many days. I drifted off into a deep, rejuvenating sleep. In the morning, I woke up, checked on Glendeo, then walked back to the palace.

The palace guards didn't give me any trouble as I walked in. Rono must have given orders for them to let me in without his permission. I did get a few skeptical looks, though, which was expected. I thought I would get more, considering I was the most infamous man on the Continent. But they trusted their king, and the few dirty looks didn't turn into insults.

When I walked into the throne room, my brother had dark circles under his eyes, threatening to close every few moments, and his head was tilted slightly downward. It was the look of a man who couldn't sleep after realizing how desperate his situation was. Though I thought we had better odds of winning a war against Diefet than Rono. It was because Rono was concerned with winning by honorable means and I wasn't.

Honor is a lie told to soldiers so they can justify killing one another and allows generals to ignore the blood on their hands. They can all kill without shame or limit if they do so with honor, otherwise they will be branded as war criminals. After I killed the Wretched King, I accepted I was a killer. There was no need to shield myself from that reality with the trappings of an illusion.

Rono and Jorn were standing in front of the throne, talking. I couldn't make out what they were saying when I entered, but my brother had a look of desperation on his face, his eyes drained of anything resembling hope. Jorn had the same expression.

"What's wrong?" I asked as I approached them.

"A Diefetian army has been spotted in the Ventiller Forest," my brother informed me.

"Salroon probably planned to invade whether he got the sword or not," I guessed. "How many men?"

"We don't know," the king admitted.

"How much of the army has been mustered?" I asked.

"About two thousand men," Jorn informed me.

"How many are here in the city that you can spare?" I inquired.

"Only 200, since the others would be needed to defend the city," my brother told me.

"And how many are in the Ventiller Forest?" I asked.

"Besides municipal garrisons, none," Jorn mumbled. "Father has sent his generals to the major cities to sure up their defenses. One is at Gregoros."

"200 men will be enough," I said.

"Be enough to do what?" Rono asked.

"Slow the Diefetians down," I said.

"Two hundred men against an army. Are you crazy?" Jorn asked.

"Salroon's forces are spread too thin, and he knows that the Eshtaran army is small and lacks veteran troops. So, he probably sent a smaller army, possibly around five thousand, maybe less, to invade. Give me command of the 200 hundred men, and I can slow the Diefetian army down while you continue mobilizing the rest of the army," I explained.

"I want you here as an advisor," Rono objected.

"I know you do, but I'm the only one who can slow down the army and has the experience to pull it off. I have spent all my adult life raiding, pillaging, extorting, robbing, and killing.

"While I did that, I avoided armies searching for me and struck at them with a small group of men when they least expected it, then disappeared. This will be no different and is a reasonable strategy, and I'm the perfect man for the job, you know this," I said, defending my proposal.

Rono fell silent and thought about it for a moment. He knew I was right, but he also knew that he would be taking a chance allowing me to lead men, no matter how few they were. The king did not want to deal with an invasion and his criminal brother running around his kingdom simultaneously. And he knew the odds were near suicidal.

Then again, he knew if anyone else led those men, the odds would be suicidal. He thought he could keep a close eye on me by having me as an advisor. If I was in a forest, then he couldn't. After what felt like ten minutes of silence, he agreed to my plan.

"Father, you can't be serious about this. He's the one who started the war by murdering an ambassador. Imagine what he will do when he is out of your sight," Jorn said.

The kid had a point, but Rono was not persuaded. "I have already decided. I will give you the men Bowv since you are the perfect man for the job. There are two conditions though: no criminal activity, including war crimes, and you take Jorn with you," Rono said.

Jorn looked at his father as if he had grown a second head.

"Can you fight?" I asked turning to my nephew.

"No," he admitted.

"He's liable to die," I said, turning back to my brother.

"Keep him alive then. I want him to learn how to fight and to learn from the best," explained Rono.

"Slowing down an army is a lot easier when I am not teaching someone how to hold a spear," I complained hoping my brother would see reason.

"Work around it," the king ordered.

"Fine," I yielded. "Where will the men be assembled?"

"They'll be right outside the northern gate, hopefully by the time you finish any preparations you need to," my brother informed me. "I will send a messenger letting them know you are my military advisor and are their commander."

"Let's go then," I told my nephew.

"I don't have a weapon or armor," protested the prince.

"Don't worry about it. We have to get Billen anyway. I'm sure he can outfit you once we are there," I reassured him.

When Jorn and I left the palace, we took the same route to Billen's shop. However, I wanted to test Jorn's endurance, so this time, we ran. It looked like the boy kept in good shape, but I needed to be sure. My nephew kept up with my pace to the blacksmith's shop, though I will admit that it was only a couple minutes run, and when we stopped at the door, he was breathing heavily. When we walked into the shop Billen was behind the counter.

"I suppose the war has started," Billen said.

"A Diefetian army has been spotted in the Ventiller Forest," I told him.

"Thank the gods I'm all already packed," Billen said.

"Good, because the kid needs a weapon and some armor," I said.

"What weapon and how much armor?" Billen asked.

"A spear and minimum armor," I told him.

"No sword?" he asked.

"No, he needs the reach, and if the spear breaks, he's dead anyway," I explained.

"He hasn't been trained?" asked the bewildered smith.

"No, he hasn't," I confirmed.

"Light and mobile it is, then," he said. "Though I can't promise the armor will fit."

"I'm sure you could make adjustments on the road if need be," I said.

"Sure can," Billen assured me as he walked over to a spear hanging on the wall, taking it off, and handing it to Jorn.

I instructed Jorn, who looked uncomfortable with a weapon in his hand, to give the weapon a thrust, and he thrust the spear with caution. It was a four-foot-long spear, short for a spear but good for mobility. After a quick examination of the weapon, Jorn cautiously placed the end on the ground so the tip could be pointing safely to the ceiling. Billen then walked to the back of the shop and quickly returned with a metal breastplate complete with a backpiece and a small round shield big enough to offer protection to its wear's arm and a bit more. Both lacked any design.

The smith instructed Jorn how to hold the shield. While Jorn got accustomed to holding the shield Billen began to loosen the straps on the breastplate.

Billen asked Jorn to hand me the shield and the spear so he could put on the breastplate. Jorn did so, and Billen fitted the breastplate. Billen took no more than a minute to adjust its four straps. Then he had Jorn do some movements: twisting his torso, lifting his arms, and walking to the end of the shop and back. While Jorn performed these tasks, Billen looked for whether the breastplate was too loose or impaired Jorn's mobility and asked Jorn how he felt wearing it.

"Billen, there's a war going on," I reminded him, not bothering to hide the impatience in my tone.

"I would be a poor blacksmith if I sold him some gear without making sure it at least fit him," Billen defended himself.

"Yes, and I thought we agreed you could make need adjustments on the road," I reminded him.

"How am I supposed to make adjustments if I don't know if anything fits first?" the smith argued.

"You have a point, but we need to go. The men should be assembled by now or close to it," I said.

"Everything seems to be a good fit. I'll grab my bag, and we'll be off," Billen said as he walked down the hallway to the back of the shop where his traveling bag was. After he returned, I paid him for the weapon and armor. Then we headed out.

It took us half an hour to arrive at the city's north gate. The guards opened the gate and let us through without a problem. Standing right outside the walls were two hundred men who were now under my command. I hadn't led men as part of an army since Father was alive.

The only men I had led in combat in recent years were bandits. And my clan did everything: raids, skirmishes, ambushes, small battles, and, when I had the numbers, a few sieges. But commanding in an official capacity was different. The men did not choose me to lead them. Bandits flocked to me because they knew who I was and sought me out. They wanted me to lead them.

The two hundred men I first saw that day followed me because their king ordered them to. They didn't want me; they were given me, and I knew that could be a problem because I was a criminal, not a soldier. We approached the camp, and the lieutenant in charge came out to greet us.

The lieutenant was a bit taller than average, had coffee-brown hair cut short according to army regulation, and had hazel eyes. Despite standing tall and straight, he did not radiate the confidence of a commanding officer, a sign that he thought our mission was suicidal.

He saluted Jorn. "Prince Jorn, it's a pleasure to meet you. I'm Lieutenant Halerod," he said.

Jorn returned the salute. "The pleasure is mine, Lieutenant Halerod," Jorn said. "But my uncle here will be in command."

"Ah yes... I was hoping that was a mistake in the orders," the lieutenant said with a shaky voice.

"It was not, lieutenant. Now get the men ready to move out," I ordered.

Lieutenant Halerod nodded, turned around, and ordered the rest of the men to pack up.

"You're not going to say anything else?" Jorn asked.

"They should know the mission," I said.

"But do they know the odds?" Billen asked.

"We aren't quite sure of the odds ourselves," I reminded him. "The Diefetian army could be anything from three thousand to ten thousand men."

"How are we supposed to slow them down?" Jorn asked, his voice filled with doubt.

"I have seen your uncle pull off crazier things," Billen told my nephew. "It normally involves deception, fire, and fear."

"Yes, but fire is largely off the table since we'll be marching through a forest," I told him.

"It's not completely off the table?" Jorn asked and gave me a worried look.

"Fire is never off the table. But we won't be burning down the Ventiller Forest if that is what you are concerned about," I reassured my nephew.

After I finished talking, Lieutenant Halerod walked over to us and informed me that the men were ready to move out. I ordered them to start marching, and within an hour, we were on the road marching towards the Ventiller Forest. Towards the first war, Eshtar had fought since my father's reign. A war that would have consequences for the whole Continent.

Chapter Four

AS THE SUN SET, I gave the order to make camp and saw the looks the men were giving me while they were doing it. Some were disgusted, a few were stares of hatred, but most were looks of fear as if, at any moment, I would start killing them. I didn't mind since I got the same looks wherever I went and had long accepted them as the price of my notoriety.

The ones who looked afraid weren't concerning to me. I knew from experience that they were the ones who only heard stories about me. The ones giving me disgusted looks were braver than those who were afraid, but like their companions, they only heard stories about my crimes.

I was concerned about the few soldiers giving me hateful glares. It meant I had either harmed them or someone they knew. If any of the men were going to dare raise a weapon against me, they would be the ones. I knew I would have to address the men at some point, but at that time, I had to focus on the mission. So, during those first few days, I ignored all the looks as we marched.

When it was time to stop for the day, we pitched camp a way off the road but close enough to see it. I ordered a night watch so that we would have eyes on the road. Billen thought I was paranoid, claiming that the Diefetians could not have marched that fast to threaten the capital. Then I reminded him about the numerous times we had attacked a camping caravan or a force of soldiers who thought the same, and he fell silent.

Our tents offered us some shelter from the elements. More importantly, they could be set up in a minute and taken down in half the time since the design was a long wooden pole running horizontally, resting on two forked poles driven vertically into the ground.

Sopunic, a special waterproof material invented during my father's reign, served as the exterior. The tents were designed to be light and mobile so the army carrying them would be likewise. Lieutenant Halerod came to speak with me when the tents were all pitched.

"Are we really trying to slow down a Diefetian army?" he asked.

"Yes," I answered.

"Is that... even possible?" he asked, then tensed his body as if bracing for a punch.

"Do you know who I am?" I asked, turning to the lieutenant to look him in the eyes. His posture straightened, and his jaw clenched.

He nodded.

"Do you know what I have done?" I asked, walking closer to him.

He gave a nod, jaw still clenched.

"Of course you do. At one point, most of the Continent's armies were hunting me. They all thought I couldn't escape, but I did. Would you like to know how?" I asked.

"Yes," mumbled the lieutenant.

"I did the unexpected," I said.

"I see," the lieutenant said, his voice now softer. "Certainly, taking two hundred men to slow down an army is unexpected, but specifically, how do we slow down the Diefetian army?"

"That's not a concern right now," I told Halerod.

"Not... a concern?" he asked, the fear he once had now replaced with confusion.

"You can't slow down an army if you don't know where it is," I pointed out.

"Then how are we going to find the army?" he asked.

I pointed to the road. "That road goes all the way to Gregoros. If anyone is fleeing the Diefetians, they will be traveling on that road," I explained.

"And we'll run into them, and they will tell us where they last saw the army," Halerod reasoned.

"Exactly, now get some rest, lieutenant. We break camp at first light," I ordered.

When dawn emerged from the night, I ordered the men to eat and break camp. Within an hour or two, we were back on the road. When there was time, I would teach Jorn about fighting, teaching him the basics of striking and defense. He wasn't ready for practice fights, but I wasn't concerned. My brother had said to teach Jorn how to fight. He didn't say Jorn needed to do any fighting.

Once Jorn became comfortable with the basics, I began yelling when he should strike, increasing the speed at which I called the commands. The prince's spear began to shoot out faster, and once the strike was completed, it rapidly snapped back to guard. Jorn's brow began to shimmer with sweat, his movements began to slow down, and his strikes became less powerful.

I yelled for him to move faster, and he began to strike with the same speed he had minutes ago. The sweat had moved down past his eyebrows. Seeing Jorn's power waning again, I yelled for him to strike harder. With sweat running down his nose, my nephew managed to put more strength behind each spear thrust.

Jorn began to slow down getting back into guard, so I shouted at him to get back into guard quicker. He did as the sweat reached his chin and began to drop onto his chest. After ten minutes had passed, I ended the training.

My nephew, now thoroughly exhausted, gave me a hateful glare which was all too easy to see.

Realizing how he was looking at me, Jorn asked me if I had worked that hard when I was being trained.

"No, I worked harder and at a younger age," I told him.

"When did you start your training?" he asked.

"I was seven," I said.

"Seven!" he exclaimed.

"You grew up in a time of peace. I was born in a time of war. Your grandfather knew Eshtar needed a prince who could fight in battles and command them, so that's what I was brought up to do," I explained. "But we can talk about that another time. Get some rest. You look like you're going to collapse."

We continued to march, and I continued Jorn's training until two days later when we ran into a small merchant caravan. The leader informed me that the Diefetians were besieging the city of Gregoros and were only a couple of days into the siege. The caravan was going to the town to trade but turned around when they saw the Diefetian army. After we made camp for the night, I pulled aside Jorn, Billen, and Lieutenant Halerod to discuss the situation.

"It's great news," I said.

"How is Gregoros getting besieged with great news?" Jorn asked.

"It's great news because while the Diefetians are besieging Gregoros, it gives the rest of the army time to assemble. We don't have to trek across the Ventiller Forest searching for the enemy," I explained.

"We don't have the numbers to break a siege," Halerod said.

"We don't know that for certain," I said.

"How are two hundred men going to break a siege?" Jorn asked.

"We would be slaughtered!" Halerod exclaimed.

"If we were dumb enough to charge them, yes, we would be slaughtered. But I don't think that is what Bowv has in mind," Billen stated.

"Then how are we going to do it?" Jorn asked.

"There's always a weakness to exploit. All we have to do is find it and hope it's big enough to break the siege," I said.

"So, your plan is to hope for a weakness?" Halerod asked in disbelief.

"No, I plan to find a weakness or, if need be, make one," I answered.

"So, we're going to do nothing," Jorn said.

"You can't defeat an enemy with more men than you do if you don't figure out their weak points first," I explained.

"But how are we going to find their weak points?" asked Jorn.

"Scouting," I said as if the answer was obvious because it was. Then I dismissed everyone, telling them to get some sleep. As Jorn and Halerod walked away towards their tents, Billen came up to me.

"Even if we find a weakness, do you think these men stand a chance?"

"In a direct fight, no. But we're not going to do that," I told him.

"Fair enough," he said. "Though I thought with you helping to fight a war, it wouldn't involve the same tactics we used as bandits."

"Having the smaller army doesn't permit us such luxuries," I said.

With that, we both went to get some sleep. In the morning, we ate, broke camp, and continued our march. As we got closer to Gregoros, the more travelers we encountered. Each one informed us that the Diefetians were still besieging the city.

I continued Jorn's training each day, though these sessions were shorter than the first ones since we had a siege to break. He grasped the basics of fighting with the drills I had him perform, but he was far from ready to fight.

I don't know what my brother expected when he sent Jorn with me. I assumed to make him a competent fighter. However, my nephew was starting late in his training. When I was Jorn's age, I was already a veteran. My nephew was learning how to wield a spear properly.

By the time we were a day's march from the city, Jorn had a respectable number of hours of practice, but if he entered combat, he would most certainly be killed. After the day's training session, he asked where I learned how to fight.

"At the inn down the street from the palace," I answered.

"An inn?" he asked confused.

"Yes, an inn," I confirmed. "Its owner, Glendeo, was the greatest warrior in your grandfather's army and a close friend of his. When he left the army, your grandfather granted him land near the palace as a reward for his service."

"And he trained you?" my nephew asked.

"Every morning, no matter what," I informed him.

"Did Father train with him?" he asked.

"If he did, I wouldn't need to teach you how to hold a spear," I pointed out.

"Then why didn't Father train with him?" Jorn asked.

"Because I was being groomed to be a king who could fight wars," I answered. "Your father was too young at that point to be trained. And Rono was interested in politics and diplomacy, even at a young age, so your grandfather provided him with an education that matched his interests."

With that said, I told Jorn to get some rest, then found Lieutenant Halerod, and I asked if we had anyone with scouting experience. He said we didn't, which meant Billen and I were the only ones. Considering the size of the Eshtaran army, I wasn't surprised my brother had neglected to send us with scouts. I told Halerod he and Jorn would be in command for two or three days while I scouted a head with Billen.

"Is that a wise decision?" he asked.

"We have no other scouts," I said.

"What should Prince Jorn and I do in the meantime?" the lieutenant asked.

"Keep the rest of the men here," I ordered.

"What do we do if you're not back in three days?" he asked.

"Then run back to the capital because it means the Diefetian army is on its way there, and we're dead," I told him.

He fell silent but nodded his head in understanding. I left to get Billen and told him we were going on a scouting mission.

"You told me I was coming along to fix equipment, that's it," he protested.

"I promised you wouldn't be fighting. Look, you and I are the only ones here with any experience scouting, and I want a second set of eyes with me in case I miss anything," I told him.

"We seriously don't have any scouts?" Billen asked in disbelief.

"No, we don't," I said.

"Then what do we have?" he asked.

"Two hundred men who've never seen combat," I told him.

"Not much,'" my old friend said.

"It isn't, so if you want to increase their chances of survival, you need to do more than fix my equipment," I told him.

"Fine, I'll help," he said.

"Gather whatever you need. We leave in an hour," I said.

It didn't take an hour to be on the road, considering I had already packed my supplies, and Billen, used to having to move quickly from his time as a bandit, had gathered his supplies quickly. Within half an hour of me speaking with Billen, we were on the road, walking towards Gregoros. We were silent for the first hour until Billen suddenly spoke.

"Why are you doing this, Bowv?" he asked.

"Because my brother didn't have enough common sense to send us with scouts," I said.

"You know what I mean. Why did you agree to become your brother's military advisor? And don't say necessity," he clarified.

"I'm doing this because Salroon authorized one of his lackeys to kill me if I didn't give him what he wanted," I explained.

"So, it's as simple as vengeance? I can't say I'm surprised," the smith said.

"You shouldn't be. Now that I've answered your question, let's get moving. There's no telling how long Gregoros can hold out for," I urged him.

"That depends on how many Diefetians there are," countered Billen.

"It doesn't matter how many Diefetians there are if the city starves," I argued.

"They probably have more supplies than you give them credit for," Billen countered.

"We don't have any scouts," I reminded him.

"Good point," he said.

We both fell silent after that. Despite Gregoros being on a significant trade route connecting the frontier to the rest of the kingdom, no one was on the road. Night fell, and we made camp; then, once the first light of dawn crept up over the horizon, scattering the darkness of night, we ate and got back on the road. It must have been late morning when we first looked at the Diefetian army and the city.

The Diefetians had cleared some of the forests around the city to erect their camp. Billen and I diverted from the road and entered the forest to get a better look. With years of experience ambushing caravans and hiding from authorities, we moved through the forest with a hunter's grace, approaching the camp with perfect stealth.

Once we were close enough, we found spots that offered good concealment and began analyzing the camp. The tents were arranged into small square clusters of twenty, and forty of these clusters formed a bigger square, and there were six of these large squares. Judging by the size, the tents were for one man each. After a quick calculation, I estimated the army was about 4,500 men strong.

We stood almost completely still, observing our enemy for a few hours. All types of soldiers were rushing around the camp: archers, skirmishers, light and heavy infantry, and a few cavalrymen. The Diefetians had enough manpower to take the city.

To my relief, I saw no signs of siege towers, though they had enough wood from making their camp to construct at least two. Nor did I know of any scaling ladders. Whoever was in charge was hoping to take the city without a fight. But I couldn't figure out why they would bother taking Gregoros.

Taking Gregoros would provide the Diefetians with a place to retreat and regroup. Starving a city takes time, but the Diefetians had the advantage of arriving before my brother finished gathering his army. They caught my brother off guard and ill-prepared, so why were they bothering to capture Gregoros? I decided to talk it over with Billen and signaled him to return to the road.

Neither of us made a sound as we left our hiding spots and snuck back through the forest to a spot further down the road from where we entered the forest. When we arrived, we stayed silent and still for an hour, listening to every twig crack and rustle of leaves to ensure no one from the Diefetian camp did not follow us. When I nodded to Billen that we were all clear, the sun was beginning to set. We found a clearing in the forest and quickly made a camp, then sat down to talk about what we saw.

"Why are they bothering to take Gregoros?" he asked after we both agreed the Diefetians didn't need to.

"I was thinking they would need a place to retreat to, but they shouldn't be expecting too much resistance," I said.

"Maybe they're trying to lure the Eshtaran army out and defeat them, so it's an easy march to the capital," guessed Billen.

"That could be it, but Salroon wouldn't launch an invasion without knowing the strength of his enemy. He knows he has the numbers to take Eshtar and quickly. What if Salroon is using the invasion as a cover for something else?" I asked Billen.

"Cover for what," Billen asked.

"The sword," I said.

"The sword you have?" he asked.

"Rono thinks the gods make it," I explained.

"*Hueik*," BIllen said.

"Yes," I confirmed.

"You're telling me you have the Sword of the Gods strapped to your hip?" he asked me in disbelief.

"That's what Rono thinks," I said.

"And you didn't tell me this sooner," he said.

"I'm an atheist, so it wasn't at the top of my to-do list," I defended myself.

"What in the gods' names happened after the king released you?" he asked.

I gave him the short version of my travels with my brother. I began by explaining how we searched for Gaenic's body, found it undecayed, and how Rono insisted I take him to the sword. I skipped to how we were redirected to Traevelios and how I retrieved the sword from Hearik. Then I moved on to how Leernu found us in a back alley, how he tried to buy the sword, and how after I killed him, there was no blood on my sword.

I told him that once Rono and I got to the palace, Ambassador Zimkoo was waiting for us. I described how when I killed him, there was no blood. I talked about how my brother thought vampires were returning and stopped there.

"You killed three vampires," he said.

"I killed three Diefetians who didn't bleed and had pointy teeth," I corrected him.

"Which would make them vampires," Billen said.

"Believe what you wish, but it's getting dark, and I'm going to get some sleep," I said dismissively.

Not wanting to give up our location, we went without a fire that night. As seasoned travelers, we brought plenty of blankets to keep us warm. When morning broke, we didn't bother with breakfast; instead, we packed our belongings and took down the tents. Within an hour, we had returned to the road and headed back towards the camp.

It was an uneventful walk back to the camp. There were no travelers or soldiers on the road. Regardless, we were still on the lookout. There could have been a Diefetian scouting party returning to their camp, but if there was one, we didn't see them. We arrived at our camp late in the afternoon and were greeted by Jorn and Lieutenant Halerod.

"How did it go?" asked Jorn.

"They have under five thousand men, as I expected," I informed him. "And it looks like they are trying to starve the city out rather than assault the walls."

"Why would they bother to do that? They have the numbers to take the city," Halerod asked.

"I think they want to make the entire army come to them so they can have a pitched battle and have a clear path to the capital," explained BIllen.

"Make sense," said Jorn.

"Though Bowv thinks something else is going on," Billen added.

"I think the invasion, or at least the siege, is cover for something else, though I can't say what right now," I said.

"The enemy is in one place. We should send a message back to Kiholp to inform the king the city is under siege and ask him to march the rest of the army here?" the lieutenant asked.

"That could work," Jorn said.

"What happens if they take Gregoros and hold up in the city once they learn the rest of the army is coming?" I asked. "Then we will have to besiege them, and we don't have the numbers for that. Our odds aren't good even with the rest of the army. We need to do something else."

"What do you suppose?" Jorn asked.

"We go after their food supply. Billen and I didn't see any baggage trains with them, so they must be getting supplied by caravan," I said.

"Where would the suppliers be coming from?" Jorn asked.

"Would have to be coming from the west," Halerod said.

"It would mean they are bringing supplies from Gofrund," Billen deduced.

"Which means Salroon has at least control of the territory along the border; if not, then he has full control of the country," I said.

"If we cut off the supplies, there is a chance they may go back across the border and come back after being resupplied," Jorn guessed.

"Yes, but it will buy the rest of the army some time. They will wait a day or two after their supplies don't arrive before they send anyone out to check on the supply line. Then it will take them time to pack up and leave," I explained.

"It could work," Billen said. "Our smaller numbers would work to our advantage since we can move faster. But we'll have to worry about their calvary because they will be sent out to investigate."

"And we will need to know when they are going to be resupplied," Halerod pointed out.

"Good points," I told them. "Here's what we are going to do. Billen, you're going to keep an eye on the Diefetians, see if you can gauge how much food they have, if they are getting it from across the border, and if there is anything we can do about the calvary. In the meantime, I will prepare the rest of the men for an ambush." With that said, I told everyone to get something to eat. Jorn followed me and said he wanted to talk.

"What's the problem?" I asked.

"An ambush?" Jorn asked. "That's what we are going to do?"

"Yes," I said. "If you have a problem with it, then say so."

"Ambushes are for cowards with no honor," the young prince informed me.

"Who told you that? Your father?" I asked.

"He did," Jorn answered.

"What does your father know about war?" I asked the boy. "How many battles has he fought? How many armies has he commanded?"

"A king does not need experience in war to know what is honorable," my nephew assured me with an edge to his voice. I clenched my fists but then unraveled them before I could do anything. My brother had sent Jorn with me so the boy could learn how to fight. I decided the boy needed a lesson in something other than the spear and pulled out a pair of dice from my pockets, one of the sets I keep on my person.

"If the sum of the pair is seven or more, you win; if it is less than seven, I win," I told him.

"What? We're having a conversation," Jorn told me.

I rolled the dice. "A six and a four. You win," I said.

"This is ridiculous. We were talking about...," Jorn continued, but I ignored him. Instead, I leaned over, picked up the dice, and rolled again.

"A two and a one. I win," I said, and as Jorn brought a hand to his face and shook his head in frustration, I switched out the pair of dice for another.

"As I was saying," Jorn began again.

"Your turn to roll," I said as I threw him the new pair of dice, then stood with my arms crossed.

The prince then explained that honor was a moral concept, one that a king did not need to fight in war to possess. I couldn't tell you what he said word for word because I was only half-listening, waiting for my nephew to follow my simple instructions.

"Roll the dice," I interrupted.

"No," Jorn said, then went back to his lecture. He got three sentences in before I interrupted again and told him to roll the dice.

"You're going to keep interrupting me until I roll the dice, aren't you?" he asked.

I nodded, then with a sigh, Jorn rolled the dice, and both landed on twos.

"You win. Now," he began again.

"Roll three more times," I ordered, and knowing I wouldn't let this go, Jorn did so. The sum of the first roll was two, the second four, and the third five.

"Are you happy now?" Jorn asked after the final roll.

"That depends on what you have noticed," I responded.

"I've noticed we both won at first, but after you gave me the dice, you won all the time," the prince said.

"Good. Now, do what else?" I asked.

"You have good luck," Jorn answered.

"I thought your father paid for a first-class education," I said, shaking my head. "What do you notice about the dice?"

Jorn took a second to examine the dice, inspecting the combined twelve faces. "The dice only have the numbers one, two, and three on their faces," he observed.

"And these have all six numbers," I said, holding up the original pair of dice.

"So, you switched them out and rigged the game. I don't see the point," Jorn told me.

"If you already knew my point, then this wouldn't be much of a lesson," I said.

"A lesson in what? Cheating?" Jorn asked.

"No, if it was, then I would be showing you how to switch out two sets of dice without being noticed," I assured my nephew. "Consider this your first formal lesson in war."

"And why are you giving me this lesson now?" the young man asked.

"Because you complained about ambushes not being honorable," I answered.

"They aren't," the prince insisted.

"You aren't thinking like a general. You are thinking like a philosopher," I said.

"A general? Father told you to train me to become a warrior, not a general," Jorn countered.

"I figured, since I'm his military advisor, I might as well do both," I told him. "Now, shut up and listen. I don't care for your notions of honor and don't want to hear them unless I ask you about them. A general is not concerned with honor because he is not concerned with morality. He can't be because morality says killing is wrong and war is killing.

"A general is concerned with ensuring the odds are stacked in his favor. He must find a way to put himself in a position that is favorable to him and unfavorable to his enemy. A general can never fight fairly; he must rig the game if the odds aren't already in his favor.

"I know you don't like hearing this, but it's true. When at war, kingdoms, empires, and republics rely on the general to win the war; otherwise, whatever the war goal is will not be achieved. Right now, Eshtar is counting on its king, your father, for its survival, and your father is counting on me. The fate of an entire kingdom rests in my hands because I am its de facto general.

"Our enemy outnumbers us, and if I fail, then the Kingdom of Eshtar becomes another Diefetian providence. Fighting fair is not an option. We must ambush the supply caravan because we don't have the manpower to fight honorably. If we can't break the siege, then the Diefetians gain a foothold in Eshtar where they can gather strength, and we will have a much bigger army to deal with," I explained.

"I suppose you're right," Jorn mumbled.

"You don't have to like the truth, kid, but you have to accept it," I told him. "If your father didn't shrink the army to its current size, then maybe we wouldn't need an ambush. But he did, and it would be suicidal for us to charge at the Diefetians when they have the larger army and more experienced troops," I said.

"I understand," the young prince said.

"Good, now get a good night's sleep. You don't want to be falling asleep while we're waiting for the supply caravan," I told him.

"Do you think I'm ready to fight?" he asked.

"No man is ever ready to fight in war," I told him. "But since I need you to stay alive, I'll have you stick with Billen."

"Why not you?" he asked.

"Because I'll be too busy trying to keep everyone else alive," I said.

Billen set out towards the enemy camp the following day without any argument about being a blacksmith and not a scout. I began getting the rest of the men ready for an ambush. I told Halerod and Jorn to assemble them after breakfast. They assembled as I had instructed: forty men in a row and five men in a column.

Each of them had the unsteady aura of nervousness around them, and like a vile stench, there was no denying it was there. This was the first time I had assembled them all, so they knew it was necessary. What didn't help was that they were terrified of me. I didn't mind because if they were terrified of me, they didn't have time to fear the Diefetians.

"You all know who I am, yes?" I asked, standing in front of them. Two hundred men slowly nodded their heads. I addressed them:

"You all wonder why I'm leading you, not Lieutenant Halerod. The kingdom is in desperate times, and my brother, your king, needs all the help he can get. You all think I am a cutthroat, and you're right.

"Let me assure you, most of the stories you have heard about me are true. I've been in the situation we find ourselves in, a small force up against a much larger one hundreds of times. None of you like me, that's fine, but follow my orders, and you might make it back to Kiholp alive."

After my speech was finished, I taught them how to hide in the forest for the rest of the morning. When afternoon came, I broke them up into ten groups of twenty men. One group would hide in the forest near the camp, and another group was tasked with finding them while standing in the camp. Then, the groups would switch.

To save time, I took three groups and gave three to Jorn and three to Halerod. The group that wasn't playing hide-and-seek was tasked with watching the road. Once a group finished with both roles, they would be rotated in. Each day, we repeated the process.

Everyone was easily spotted on the first day, which was not a shock considering limbs were sticking out from bushes and poking out from behind tree trunks. The second day was a bit different. Everyone was still easily spotted, but not as quickly as before.

They all appeared to have more awareness of their limbs, but not by much, though they all were reasonably quiet. They improved more on the third day, and most weren't found. I cut the drill short on the fourth day because Billen returned about two hours before noon.

"I overheard an officer talking to one of the camp's sentries. We were right; they are moving supplies from Gofrund, and the next shipment will be there in four days," Billen informed me.

"Let's get going then," I said.

Chapter Five

I GAVE ORDERS FOR THE MEN TO PACK UP CAMP, and two days later, we were hidden in the forest, not too far from the road. I was with Jorn and a hundred men on one side of the road, while BIllen and Halerod were on the other with the same amount. The men had not gotten great at hiding, but with the cover of the night, I was confident they wouldn't be seen.

Earlier, I sent Billen ahead to confirm that the supply caravan was coming. Not much later, he returned and told me there were ten slow-moving supply wagons and about fifty guards. The plan was simple: once we saw the first supply wagon, we would spring the ambush, take the first wagon, and then work our way down the road to the other wagons, overwhelming the guards as we went while cutting off their route to Gregoros.

We heard the first wagon's creeping wheels before we saw it. The loaded wagon crawled across the road, burdened with crates of food on its back and guards on either side, each carrying a shield on their arm and a spear in the opposite hand. When the wagon got towards the end of our line where I was, I gave a loud and high-pitched whistle, then rushed out with the men beside me. Soon, all the men on my side were running toward the enemy, spears, and shields in hand. Billen's men were doing the same on the other side.

The Diefetians didn't see us coming. Not because my men had gotten any better at hiding over the last few days but because the Diefetians weren't looking very hard for threats. Why would they be? We were only about half a day's ride from Gregoros, the last stretch of their journey; safety was near. Even the most experienced soldiers begin to drop their guard when they almost reach a place of safety, be it a town, city, or camp. I exploited this sense of security countless times as a bandit.

That day, the surprise was greater than usual. The Diefetians knew their rear was secure, and they were marching towards a besieged town on the edge of the enemy country. If there were an enemy army, it would be marching to break the siege. The Diefetians were shocked when they saw my men and me rushing out from the woods.

Once I got close enough, I drew *Hueik* and engaged one of the guards. I had a sword, while he had a spear and a shield. He should have been able to put up a good fight; however, shocked by the ambush, he had little opportunity to defend himself. I was on him before he could lift his shield, and with a well-aimed thrust, *Hueik* ran into his gut, just above his waist, where his chainmail shirt failed to protect him. I retracted my sword in one fluid motion, and the guard fell dead.

Another guard came rushing over, thrusting at me with his spear. I hit its shaft with my sword, knocking the weapon aside. He quickly recovered, raising his shield to his chest, then stepped forward, brought his spear above his head, and drove the weapon downwards, intending to drive it through my torso. While he brought the spear down, I stepped to the side, which gave me a clear path to strike, and I thrust my sword between his ribs and hips. There was no chainmail to protect him.

Unlike the previous guard, this one wore a helmet and relied on his shield to protect his body, not able to afford the expensive chainmail his comrade had, or maybe his chainmail was being repaired. The guard cried out in pain and dropped to the ground as I pulled *Hueik* back.

I smiled. It had been too long since I had fought a battle. The clinging of metal against metal, the cries of men struggling against one another, the sounds of the dying, they all sound horrible to the average person but not to me. Violence is what defined my life; war and killing are what I was trained to do and what I excelled at. Killing Zimkoo and Leernu was satisfying, but it wasn't a proper fight. Adrenaline course through my veins. It wasn't from nerves or fear. It was from excitement.

With a grin, I worked my way to the next wagon and found that my men had already engaged the guards. But the outnumbered guards were not intimidated. To their credit, my men were competent in their attacks, but they had never seen combat before, and the threat of death provided each of their strikes with quickness and strength. However, most of the time, the adrenaline flowing through their veins caused them to be too quick, and impatient spear thrusts were blocked by enemy shields.

One Eshtaran soldier got his spear stuck in a Diefetian shield. The Eshtaran should have let go of the spear, but instead, he held on and tugged several times, trying to get the spear out. I didn't feel bad for the fool when the Diefetian's spear, which he had forgotten about, pierced through his stomach and exited out his back.

As the guard began to remove the spear from the body, which he could do because the weapon wasn't stuck in any bones, I had already managed to get close to him. I swung *Hueik* high. My blade cut through his neck, and a moment later, his head fell from his shoulders.

One of the dead Diefetian's companions let out a scream and charged me. His shield was raised and pushed forward, hoping to use it as a battering ram, and his spear was held back. As he rushed forward, any Eshtaran soldiers near me moved away. I didn't move.

If his shield didn't hit me, his spear would act as insurance and shoot out to impale me. As he barreled in with his shield, I sidestepped and dropped *Hueik* to a low guard, its tip pointing down to the ground. Within an instant, his spear shot out, its tip quickly moving towards my chest. I let it get within inches of me before my hand shot out and grasped the shaft from just below the spear's sharp head with my left hand so that my palm was on the bottom and the knuckles of my grasping fingers faced upwards.

Shock came across the Diefetian's face as I guided his spear forward instead of attempting to force it away from me. As I pulled the spear towards me, I turned my body so that my left shoulder pointed back, its opposite pointed towards the caravan guard, and my torso and stomach became parallel with the spear.

The Diefetian was now turned to the side, his torso, and stomach facing the same direction as mine. His shield was on the other side of his body, the side whose shoulder was facing away from me, and it was useless to him as I brought *Hueik* up and stabbed him at an upward angle, my blade entering his body through his right side, blowing the ribcage and sliced apart his delicate inners. I pulled my sword out from his body, and the guard fell dead to the ground.

The rest of his comrades were engaged with my men. Our numbers ensured that my inexperienced soldiers were pressing the Deiefetians to the point where the caravan guards were fighting defensively. I saw two Diefetians nearby fall to the ground and decided my men close to me didn't need my help.

I looked around to see what else was happening. I was surprised when I saw Halerod and another Esharan soldier fighting a Diefetian. The guard, like his comrades, was no novice. His spear struck out with precision, speed, and strength, and when not held firmly in a guard, his shield was quick to intercept any spears aimed at him. Above all, the Diefetian was calm despite facing two foes at once.

Both the lieutenant and the soldier fighting beside him were stiff in their movements, especially compared to the fluidity of their opponents. But Halerod and his comrade's strikes were powerful and quick, and both quickly raised their shields. They were obviously trained as soldiers, but this was their first real battle.

Despite this being the first time the pair fought together for their lives, they worked as one. Halerod would thrust with his spear; then his partner would immediately after. There were more complicated techniques when two spearmen were fighting together against one, but if the pair knew them, they didn't show any signs that they did.

The pair were triumphant, with Halerod ramming his spear through the Diefetian's stomach. The caravan guard fell to the ground, bleeding profusely, and was soon dead.

I looked around for Billen and Jorn, who, if all was going well, would be staying out of combat. About a third of the men surrounding me were part of Billen and Jorn's group, but there was no sign of either.

I didn't waste time thinking about how my brother would have reacted if I had to tell him his son was killed. I knew Billen could keep the boy alive, something I had less chance of doing because I was in charge. I knew as soon as the Diefetians realized I was the one giving out the orders, they would target me, hoping that killing the commander would plummet morale and send the other ambushers running. So, I put Jorn with Billen, figuring the enemy would pay Billen less attention.

When I began barking orders for men who had taken an enemy out of action to join other groups still fighting, the Diefetians noticed me. Three Diefetians who were already engaged turned their heads toward me and noted my status, but they couldn't get to me.

By this point, the guards from the other wagons had realized they had walked into an ambush and were coming to aid their comrades. I ran into a few of them as I walked to the third wagon, but they were all running ahead of one another, not moving in as a group. As each guard approached me, we engaged man to man, which was fortunate for me, considering it would have been hard to fight off a group of spearmen with a sword. They paid for their stupidity with their lives.

Over the clash of weapons, I heard a Diefetian yell, "The commander has the sword." Six Diefetians made their way towards me. Two moved directly towards me while their comrades split up into pairs, with one pair moving around my right side and the other around my left, no doubt trying to surround me. That didn't concern me because while they were moving, their spears weren't pointed towards me, which made them vulnerable.

So, when the spears of the two guards in front of me were shooting out towards me, I didn't step back. Instead, I leaped to my left, avoiding the spear coming at my right side, while bringing up my sword to quickly parry the spear on my left, sending it safely over my shoulder to stab open air.

I landed next to one of the Diefetians, trying to encircle me. We were perpendicular to each other, with me facing his left side and him facing straight. His shield, strapped to his left arm, was no problem for me because his spear was in his right hand, which meant he couldn't thrust at me without turning his whole body. He knew it, too, and raised his shield higher to protect his upper body.

It was the wrong move. With the speed that only hundreds upon hundreds of hours of practice can produce, I brought *Hueik* down low and sliced his calf. The soldier let out a scream as he fell to the ground.

His companion quickly turned toward me, raised his shield, and pointed his spear's tip at me. No doubt, his other four friends were behind me, rushing forward, hoping for the opportunity to stab me in the back. All he had to do was keep me in one spot until they reached me, and the fight would be over. But I wasn't going to let that happen.

I charged forward.

The Diefetian's spear came rushing towards my head. He put his full weight behind the strike, turning his body to the side as he did. Still keeping my forward momentum, I dodged the attack with a duck and then stabbed my sword through his lower body. As I pulled *Hueik* from the dying man, I moved behind him with swiftness and fluidity, putting him between me and his four comrades, who were approaching from behind.

I stood there with my bloody blade held out in front of me. The four Diefetians stopped their advance, realizing I had taken out a third of them within two minutes. They stood there, not daring to step in my direction. One looked confused as if no swordsman could have pulled off what I had just done, no matter his skill. Another had wide eyes, sweat accumulating on his face, and tightly grasped his spear. The other two, the older ones of the four, looked at each other, and over the clash of the battle still raging around us, I heard one of them say "the Terror," and the other gave a grim nod.

They then began to debate whether to fight or run. I pointed behind them. My men, who at this point had either killed or driven off the Diefetians in the immediate area, were coming towards them. The Diefetians ran down the road away from Gregoros.

I led my men down the line of wagons, but few caravan guards were left to deal with. No doubt, the four guards who ran away were yelling at every Diefetian that the Terror of the Continent was behind the attack and they needed to run. It would be far from the first time something like that had happened.

But there were some Diefetian stragglers, and I took it upon myself to deal with them. Each deadly contest was decided in seconds with quick strikes and blocks. One by one, I descended upon them, and each fell, unable to withstand the rapid movements of my flashing blade.

I don't know how many guards I killed, but it took a while before the remaining ones had the common sense to try and surround me. They did not get close, though, because my men, finally done with taking out the guards of the second wagon, appeared behind me. Realizing they were outnumbered, the Diefetians turned and ran. They must have had sacred off the remaining guards because as we walked down to the rest of the wagons, there were no other guards to be seen.

I gave the orders to take what supplies we could carry and to burn the rest. I was shocked to find there were only a few casualties on our side, around a dozen killed and three wounded. However, I knew it would have been a different story if the remaining guards hadn't fled.

Jorn and the lieutenant came up to me and asked what was next.

"We disappear," I said. "The Diefetians will send out cavalry to find out what happened when the supplies don't arrive. I don't want to be around when the cavalry shows up because we stand no chance against them."

"Do you think they will break the siege?" asked Halerod.

"If their commander has any sense, he will," I told him. "They could try taking the city, but if they had wanted to take the city by storming the walls, they would have built siege equipment and done so already.

"If they decide to take the city to gain food, then they will have to wait and build siege engines, which takes days, and if they fail, they will need to go to Gofrund and gather more supplies, all while their food dwindles. Besides, they were starving the city out, probably to conserve men. No, they'll go to Gofrund for more supplies, which will take at least five days to deliver."

"So, what do we do now?" Jorn asked.

"We get back to Kiholp and tell your father our mission was a success. By now, the rest of the army should have had enough time to assemble," I said.

"Then what?" asked Halerod.

"We plan our next move," I answered.

We gathered the men and began to travel back to the capital. Once we reached the main road without any signs of the Diefetians hunting for us, we made camp for the night.

It took us a week to get back to Kiholp, and each time we made camp, I taught Jorn about fighting. He had done well in the ambush since he managed to stay alive. Before the ambush, I instructed Jorn to stay behind after the initial charge, and he obeyed. Jorn's fighting was minimal but tired the young prince more than he expected.

During training, there was no doubt Jorn improved in the sessions after the ambush. Jorn's movements had begun to lose the rigidity of a novice and begun to gain the fluidity of familiarity. And the prince's stamina had improved, his strikes remaining strong for a much longer before they began to weaken. By the time we reached Kiholp, I had determined he was ready for some sparring practice.

When we arrived at the city, a royal courier approached me and informed me that the men would report to the barracks while Jorn and I would go to the palace. I told Halerod to take the men to the barracks and told BIllen he was free to return to his shop. As Jorn and I worked our way through the city, we noticed more soldiers, a good sign considering that the city's garrison couldn't hold out against the Diefetians for long.

We reached the palace and walked straight to the throne room. My brother was sitting on the throne talking to Paderok, the courtier I had talked to about the spy problem. Rono dismissed him once he saw us enter.

"I assume all went well, considering you're not rushing here to tell me that a Diefetian army is marching this way," my brother guessed.

"The Diefetians were besieging Gregoros, trying to starve the city into submission. There were about five thousand of them, and they were supplied from Gofrund," I explained.

"Sounds like your prediction was correct, brother: Salroon won the war," Rono said, recalling our earlier conversation. "Anyways, what did you do?"

"I planned an ambush, and we cut their supplies off," I reported.

"What about the army?" the king asked.

"Either they did the smart thing and marched back to Gofrund or foolishly continued the siege and sent a message to be resupplied, which will take too long to be delivered," I said.

"What if they attacked the city to get supplies?" the king asked.

"It still wouldn't help them. They didn't have siege equipment built to take the city, and considering they didn't get resupplied, they wouldn't have the time to wait around and construct any," I explained.

"Fair enough," said my brother. "So, what do we do know?"

"Is the army fully mobilized?" I asked.

"It is," he answered.

"Then we plan our next move," I told him. "What about the problem you had me look into?"

"It's still being investigated," my brother informed me, knowing I was referring to the spy problem.

"What about the Verolik heretics? Is there any news from them?" I asked.

"Nothing," my brother said. "But we can talk about this another time. You both have been through a lot. Go get some rest."

"I'll be at the inn," I said, walked out of the room, and headed for Glendeo's inn.

Chapter Six

I WALKED INTO THE INN and found Glendeo behind the counter. He asked how the war was going, and I told him about Gregoros. The old man nodded, understanding I couldn't tell him all the details.

"While you were gone, someone came in looking for you," Glendeo informed me.

"Who?" I asked.

"An Estaran. He said he had information he needed to share with you. I told him I didn't know when you would be back, but he could rent a room and wait," the innkeeper explained.

"Where is he?" I asked.

"In his room, the first one on the right in the east wing. I figured I didn't know who he was, so I put him on the other side of the inn," Glendeo told me.

"Thank you," I said and began to walk to the room.

I walked across the lobby and entered the hallway. Turning to the first door on my right, I knocked.

"Come in," a man said.

I opened the door and found an unassuming man in traveler's clothes studying a scroll behind a desk. His darker blonde hair fell and ran to the bottom of his neck.

"I hear you're looking for me," I said.

"Yes, Bowv, I am," the man said, turning towards me. I noticed his green eyes.

"Who are you?" I asked.

"I am Ilkon," the man answered.

"Why have you been looking for me?" I asked.

He pointed to *Hueik*.

"You're a Verolik," I guessed.

"I am," the heretic answered. "I heard you and the king were looking for my order. My superiors initially hesitated to send me, considering King Rono's devotion to the Protectorate Temple. Still, I was sent once my order learned you had killed three vampires and had *Hueik*."

"My brother will want to speak with you," I told him.

"I suppose the king would," Ilkon agreed. "But if I am overheard talking about the lies the Temple spreads about vampires in the center of the palace, it wouldn't turn out well for him. People would begin to believe their king was supporting heresy."

"What do you want to do then?" I asked.

"I want to set up a meeting," he said.

"That's reasonable. Stay here, and I will be back in about half an hour," I said and walked out of the room.

I returned to the palace and went straight to the throne room, where I found Rono sitting on the throne, talking to Jorn. Paderok must have left after I did. They were talking about the ambush and how Jorn's training was going. Once they heard me walk into the room, they both fell silent. A worried look worked its way across my brother's face. He did not expect to see me again so soon.

"It's not bad news," I assured him. "On the contrary, I have good news."

"What is it?" Rono asked.

"I have a surprise for you at the inn," I said.

"Bowv, this is not the time for surprises," he said.

"It's about the thing that priest said would find us," I said.

Rono thought about it for a minute, then recalled our conversation with the priest. "I had forgotten about that. Let's go, Jorn, stay here if anyone asks; I went for a walk. Oh, and check in with your mother. She was worried while you were gone," instructed the king.

We left and headed for the inn. I thought there would be some protests from the palace guards about how the king should not leave the palace without a bodyguard during the war. But there was none. I don't know if this were because they knew Rono wouldn't have gone with me if he thought I wanted to kill him, or they thought no one was dumb enough to attack the king while I was with him. Either way, they didn't stop us.

Within a few minutes, we arrived at the inn. Walking through the door, we found Glendeo sweeping the lobby, the old man's head tilted down, looking for any specks of dust he missed. Once he looked up and saw us, he put down the broom and came over.

"Ah, you're back," he greeted me. Then, the old man knelt and bowed his head once he noticed Rono. My brother knelt and told the innkeeper; while he appreciated the gesture, an old friend of our father's, someone we had both known since we were children, did not need to greet him in such a way, then helped the old man up from the ground.

"Is our guest still here?" I asked.

"He is," confirmed Glendeo.

I walked to Ilkon's room with Rono beside me. I stopped at the door and knocked. Ilkon said we could enter, and I opened the door and walked in.

We found Ilkon at his desk studying a scroll. Taking a closer look, I noticed it wasn't in a language I recognized. The writing was runic and didn't resemble any modern alphabet. The words started vertically from the bottom of the scroll, working their way up to the top. The language was ancient, but the scroll was modern. Ilkon took the time to finish what he was reading before he turned around and greeted us.

"You're quick Bowv. You took fifteen minutes at the most," he said, then turned to my brother and gave a bow. "King Rono, it is an honor."

"The pleasure is mine, but you have me at a disadvantage. I don't know your name," my brother pointed out.

"I am Ilkon," the other said, introducing himself.

"Now that the formalities are out of the way, what information do you have?" I asked.

"You're always so eager to get to business," Rono complained.

"There's a war going on, brother, be grateful I didn't skip the formalities altogether. I bought us time at Gregoros, time which cannot be wasted," I countered, then turned to Ilkon. "Now, what information do you have for us?"

"That depends on wheiher the sword you're carrying is *Hueik*," he said.

I drew the sword, and the moonlight color gave off a soft, faint illumination. However, I doubt Ilkon noticed it because his eyes were focused on the runes carved into the blade. Ilkon's eyes widened as he studied them, and disbelief swept across his face. He smiled as his eyes traced the runes from the blade's tip to its end.

"The Sword of the Gods," he said in awe of the blade.

"We know the history of the sword," Rono began. "But we were hoping you could tell us if there is a connection between vampires and the Diefetians."

"Specifically, Lord Gaenic, Leernu, and Ambassador Zimkoo," I added.

"Whom Bowv murdered in my palace," Rono informed the heretic.

"You're welcome, by the way," I said.

"Lord Gaenic and Leernu were keshgus," Ilkon said, steering the conversation back on track. "Specifically, Lord Gaenic was the vampire who wielded *Hueik* for the last two thousand years. I should have known that was how you came across the blade, Bowv."

"Rono knew Gaenic was a keshgu," I said.

"How?" asked Ilkon.

"I came across an old book when I was studying the Sacred Texts in my younger days," Rono revealed.

"Do you remember what text?" asked Ilkon.

"I do not, I'm afraid, though it was one my father had in his personal library," my brother admitted.

"But what does this have to do with Diefet?" I asked, not caring why Father would own a book about vampires.

"I don't know. My order has suspected that vampires had infiltrated the Diefetian court, but when we investigated, we couldn't find any hard evidence," Ilkon told us. "Based on recent events, we will have to investigate how many vampires are in Diefet and in what positions," Ilkon answered.

"They are in high places already," noted my brother.

"Assuming there are vampires," I said.

"You killed three men who did not bleed and doubt the existence of vampires?" Ilkon asked, surprised.

"My brother is a die-hard atheist. He thinks it's all silly," explained the king.

"I do," I agreed.

"Why?" Ilkon.

"Do you know who I am?" I asked in response.

"The Terror of the Continent," he answered.

"Now tell me, Ilkon, if the gods of the Protectorate are real, then why would they allow a man such as myself to live? I have lost track of how many cities and villages I've burned down and left behind the charred corpses. So, if the Protectorate were protectors, shouldn't they have stopped me at some point?" I asked.

"Perhaps they didn't stop you because they knew you would eventually wield their sword," he responded with a certain calm in his voice, which had the ring of authority.

"I doubt it," I said.

"How would you know?" asked the heretic. "How do you know the gods want to punish you in this life? Perhaps they want to punish you after death and give you their sword as a last chance to prove you can do something good in the world, so your punishment is not as harsh. If I'm right, then they are taking pity on the Terror of the Continent."

I fell silent, not knowing how to respond to the ludicrous argument.

"Well done, Ilkon, it's not every day my brother is at a loss for words," Rono complimented.

"We should stop talking nonsense and get you back to the palace before anyone comes looking for you," I said.

"Yes, I should, and we should let Ilkon pass the information we gave him to his order," my brother agreed.

"I will be here at the inn if you need me," said Ilkon.

After saying our goodbyes, we left Ilkon and the inn. While walking back to the palace Rono took the chance to talk to me about our other problem.

"How would I know if Chancellor Marilok is giving information to the Diefetians?" the king asked me.

"The Chancellor doesn't have to be a traitor for his information to be compromised," I explained.

"How would you go about doing it? You said intercepting official documents is easy," he asked, recalling our first conversation about spies.

"There's a bunch of ways to steal a letter. You can arrange for the messenger to be one of your men, then have him open the document, copy its contents, and place the copied message in a hiding place for someone else to pick up and deliver it to you. Or they can steal it and have someone deliver it to you," I explained. "But typically, messengers are turned by blackmail or coin. I've found my reputation or a threat is enough to persuade a courier to do what I want."

"So, one of my messengers may be working for the Diefetians," he said.

"Yes, or the Chancellor himself is working for them," I said. "Like I said, there are various possibilities, so you need to be thorough in your investigation."

"How do I catch whoever is giving information to the Diefetians?" he asked.

"Good question," I told him.

"You don't know?" he asked.

"I'm typically doing the intercepting or ordering it. This is my first time being on the other side," I explained.

"Then tell me how you usually get caught," the king ordered.

I laughed.

"You don't get caught, do you?" he asked.

"No, brother. I rarely do it knowing that targets change their messengers, ciphers, or plans once they realize their message has been intercepted," I explained.

"Then how am I supposed to catch the spy?" he asked.

"Lay a trap," I answered.

"How?" Rono asked.

"You give information to Chancellor Marilok concerning some made-up threat, then have someone follow him and anyone he gives the message to," I explained.

"That sounds like a solid plan," the king agreed. "Now we need a war plan."

"I don't have a plan yet, but we have an advantage," I informed him.

"What is that?" asked the king.

"We know Salroon is after the sword, so we know we have bait if we need to set a trap," I explained.

"Ilkon said Lord Gaenic had the sword for the past two millennia. For the first time in two thousand years, the most dangerous weapon to vampires is not wielded by a vampire. If Salroon is a vampire, he will want the sword," agreed Rono.

We had arrived at the palace and ended our conversation. We went right to the throne room. There, we found Jorn standing by the throne, reading a letter.

"What's the matter, son?" asked Rono.

"News from Gregoros, the Diefetians have retreated towards Gofrund, just as uncle anticipated," informed Jorn as he handed the letter to his father.

"They must have retreated quickly if a message has arrived," I said.

"Yes, the Diefetians have withdrawn," said Rono as he took the letter and read it. "Gregoros is requesting more supplies and men."

"Should I make the arrangements?" asked Jorn.

"What do you think, Bowv?" the king asked.

"Send supplies but not men. We are too thin on soldiers as it is." I advised.

Rono took a moment and thought about it. "What happens if the Diefetans come back with a larger force?"

"You're assuming they will attack Gregoros again," I told him. "For all we know, they besieged the city to draw you into a battle. I would say this is the likely case, considering the only strategic significance Gregoros has is its proximity to the Gofrundin border. If the Diefetians take the city, they can secure their supply lines from Gofrund.

"But I don't think they will be worried about their supplies. The Diefetians know we aren't a match for their cavalry, so they must add a cavalry escort to any supply caravan to secure their supply lines. They outnumber us and will want an open battle, so they can afford to ignore Gregoros while extending their supply lines and using their calvary to protect them. They can afford to pass the town. What harm could our little army do?"

My brother took a few moments to think about my advice. I knew he wanted to send men to Gregoros, believing a king should not abandon his people in their time of need. But he also knew I was right; if he took men from the main army to reinforce Gregoros, he would weaken our ability to fight the enemy.

"We'll send supplies. Bowv is right, but we can't spare any men," the king decided. "Now, what is our plan? The Diefetians will be back within the week at the earliest."

"I would worry about the problem we were discussing on the walk back to the palace," I said. "Besides, the Diefetians that besieged Gregoros will need time to resupply; it will be some time before we hear from them again."

"I suppose you have come up with a solution," guessed my brother.

"Yes, have the Chancellor write the message to Gregoros, then watch him, or better yet, I'll watch him. If he is in league with the Diefetians, it's likely the message won't be sent," I proposed.

"That's not what I would call a trap," Rono said, recalling our conversation.

"You need to make traps not look like traps. In this case, we have legitimate information that is not vital to the war effort to send. We can catch the perpetrator without needing false information that could tip them off," I explained.

"Wouldn't you look suspicious following people around?" asked Jorn.

"Considering I'm the military advisor to the king, no," I argued.

"He's right, Bowv; people will be suspicious of you," my brother told me.

"No one else knows how messages are intercepted better than me," I argued.

"True, but I want Jorn to go with you so you look less suspicious," he said.

"Brother, two people will increase the level of suspicion," I argued.

"Considering the level of suspicion people have when they see you alone, I think having Jorn with you would decrease it," explained Rono.

"Fine," I said. "Just send the message."

"Good. I'll summon Chancellor Marilok and instruct him to write out the message, then give the orders for the supplies to be delivered," Rono said.

After Jorn and I exited the throne room, he asked what we would do. I said we would wait until the chancellor entered and then see what he did with the letter. However, Jorn thought we would look suspicious hanging around outside the throne room. I reminded him he was a prince, and I was his father's military advisor, so if anyone asked what we were doing, we would say the king had ordered us to stand outside while he spoke with the chancellor in private.

My nephew was unaccustomed to waiting around. How he managed to sit still while we were waiting to ambush the Diefetian caravan is a mystery to me. Maybe he was nervous and thought we would tip the chancellor off if we weren't talking.

"Who taught you strategy? Was it Glendeo?" Jorn asked me.

"Your grandfather," I answered.

"Who taught him?" my nephew asked.

"His father," I said, and he registered the pattern.

"Why didn't Father learn strategy?" he asked.

"Same reason he wasn't taught how to fight," I explained.

"You took to the art of war, not just the martial arts," concluded Jorn.

"Yes, and I already told you that. Your father took to diplomacy and politics. It's why he needs my help fighting his war," I explained again.

"Father knows nothing about war?" my nephew asked, getting to the heart of the matter.

It wasn't that Jorn didn't believe me when I told him his father wasn't trained as a soldier; it was hard for him to accept it. Growing up, Jorn must have seen Rono handle all types of political and diplomatic situations with ease, so the concept that his father couldn't do the same with military problems must have been incomprehensible for the boy, considering his grandfather was a master of war.

"He knows a little, considering he had enough sense to have the army mustered before he released me," I stated.

"Did he ever go on campaign?" Jorn asked.

"Never," I answered.

"Were you taken on campaign?" asked Jorn.

"I was," I told him.

"And the world would have been better off if you had died in battle," a woman behind us said.

I turned around to see a woman a bit younger than Rono, maybe three years his junior, with long blonde hair, fair skin, and pale blue eyes, staring at me. Her stare was an uncompromising wall of hate and disgust. When people are aware of who I am, they respond with terror or hatred if they are brave enough. Who this woman was and why she reacted with the former was a mystery until Jorn spoke.

"Hello, Mother," he greeted the queen.

"Hydela, how are you?" I asked my sister-in-law.

"Considering you are in my home, not well," she said, spite dripping from her mouth like foam from a rabid dog's mouth.

"You two know each other?" asked a confused Jorn.

"We do. My father was your grandfather's second chancellor. I grew up with your father and uncle, though Rono tells me he had to remind you of my name, Bowv," said an offended queen.

"You have to forgive me, considering you spent much more time with Rono than you did with me," I said.

"Why are you here, Bowv? You don't care about the kingdom," she asked.

"You're right, I don't, and I couldn't convince you otherwise. I'm here helping my desperate brother because King Salroon wants me dead, and my best odds of survival is to be with an army," I explained.

"Why are you standing outside the throne room," clarified Hydela.

"On the orders of your husband," I said.

"Really?" a skeptical queen asked.

"He's not lying. We're doing something important for Father," interjected Jorn.

"Then I won't bother you any longer," Hydela said, and then she walked away.

"Should we leave?" asked Jorn.

"Yes, because your mother has made a scene," I said.

"I don't blame her," Jorn said.

I ignored his comment and began walking down the hallway. I didn't take ten steps before a man wearing an expensive shirt and pants walked towards the throne room. He had short chestnut hair and dark brown eyes. His skin was uncommonly pale but was healthy and unscarred, typical for a man who spends most of his time in palaces and doesn't fight. Not knowing who I was, the man walked right past me; however, when he saw Jorn, he stopped and struck up a conversation, confirming my suspicion.

"Jorn," the man greeted the prince with a smile. "It's good to see you made it back in one piece."

"Thank you, Chancellor," Jorn said.

"Chancellor Marilok, I do not believe we have met," I said and walked over.

"I don't think we have. Who are you?" he asked.

"I'm Bowv," I informed him.

After I introduced myself to the chancellor, I watched his reaction like a predator analyzing its intended prey. The chancellor's reaction wasn't one of a stoic spy; his pupils dilated, and his breathing dramatically increased, far more than what I've seen most people do when they realize who I am. Breathing was the only thing the chancellor did other than stand there and stare at me with terror in his eyes.

The chancellor's reaction was all I needed to know: he was not the spy. The man could be threatened, but he would be unnerved. It's not a trait you want in someone you're coercing into committing treason. He could have been bribed or blackmailed, but I kept tabs on which high-ranking officials I could bride or blackmail, and Marilok wasn't one of them. The Diefetians may have found something I didn't, but that would be unlikely even for a king as crafty and informed as Salroon.

"I believe my brother was waiting for you in the throne room," I told the chancellor.

"Yes... he was," Marilok said.

"We won't take up more of your time then," Jorn told him.

A wave of relief swept across Marilok's face. "I better get going."

After he walked out of earshot, Jorn asked me what I thought of the chancellor.

"I don't think he is a traitor," I said.

"I didn't think he was," admitted Jorn.

"Why?" I asked the prince.

"He's a good man and has always been loyal to father," answered Jorn.

"A good man does not always have good judgment," I told him.

"What do you mean?" asked my nephew.

"He may not be giving Salroon information, but that doesn't mean someone who works for him isn't," I explained.

"What do we do then?" Jorn asked.

"We go talk to your father and the chancellor to see if the chancellor has any ideas why Ambassador Zimkoo was so well informed," I said.

When we walked into the throne room, Rono gave Marilok the details of the supply run. When he saw Jorn and I enter, he turned away from the chancellor and shot us a puzzled look, wondering why we were there and not sticking to the plan.

"I trust this is important, Bowv," Rono said.

"Yes, I have some questions for the chancellor," I stated.

"Questions?" my confused brother asked, not knowing I changed the plan.

"Yes, questions," I confirmed. "For instance, Chancellor, do you know why Ambassador Zimkoo was so well informed about what happened in the palace when my brother was gone? Specifically, do you know how the Diefetian ambassador knew which mayors Rono was corresponding with?"

A grim look came upon the chancellor's face, mixed with a great deal of regret. But Marilok did not look have the despairing look of a traitor caught. Instead, he looked like a trusted servant who had unfortunate news to share with his liege. The chancellor's regret was not caused by the actions he had performed but was caused by a different burden: having to inform his king about the failings of another he held in high regard. Marilok was not a traitor about to confess; he was a messenger with unwelcome news.

"What is it, old friend?" asked the king.

"I have good reason to believe that Paderok is giving information to the Diefetans," answered the chancellor.

"The courtier?" I asked.

"Yes, he's the courtier you met," my brother answered.

"What makes you think Paderok is a traitor?" asked Jorn.

"These last couple of weeks, he has been going outside the palace early in the morning," Marilok answered.

"He could be going on an early morning run," Jorn proposed.

"He never comes back sweating," countered the chancellor.

"An early morning walk, then," Jorn pushed back.

"We need more, old friend if you want us to think your suspicions are credible," urged the king.

"He always has a bag with him, the one he uses to carry around official papers," the chancellor informed us.

"Which isn't suspicious for a trusted courtier," Jorn pointed out.

"It is when I go into my office and find papers missing that suspicion arises," the chancellor defended himself.

"And Paderok is one of the few people allowed in there," my brother said.

"Who else is allowed in?" I asked.

"The chancellor, Jorn, and myself," the king answered.

"Well, brother, I think the chancellor is telling the truth," I said.

"Me too," the king said. "But what do we do about Paderok?"

"We need more evidence before we can arrest him," Jorn said.

"Yes, we do," agreed Rono. "If it turns out he is the spy, I don't believe he is."

"If you don't think he's the spy, I could ask around and see if any of the less illustrious citizens know anything about his morning activities," I proposed.

"You mean criminals," said Marilok with disdain.

"Yes," I said.

"Why would criminals know whether one of my courtiers is a traitor?" asked Rono.

"Because if anyone is walking about the city early in the morning, they would know about it," I said.

The king took a moment to think about it. "Fine," he said. "But don't do anything illegal. I have enough to worry about with the war."

"My lord, you can't let him go about the city unaccompanied. For the gods' sakes, he'll burn it to the ground," protested the chancellor.

"He is my military advisor, chancellor. If I can't trust him to go around the city alone, then Eshtar will be conquered by Diefet," Rono told Marilok.

"He's the Terror of the Continent; he can't control himself. Whenever someone looks at him the wrong way, he kills them. For the gods' sakes, he killed an ambassador within ten minutes of being in the palace!" the chancellor reminded his king.

"I am a brutal man, chancellor, there is no doubt about that, but if I did not know restraint, then right now you would be thrashing around on the ground bleeding from the throat for having insulted me," I informed him, my hand on *Hueik's* pommel.

"Enough, brother," Rono commanded, then fell silent.

Rono knew the chancellor was right, and a month ago, he would never have dreamed of letting me walk around freely in the streets of his capital, let alone release me from a cell he put me in. But desperate times change people, and they make gamblers out of the most cautious of men.

My brother was no exception. Rono released me from my cell to test his vampire theory. He offered to have me be his military advisor because he needed me to fight his war. The king didn't have many options. It was either come up with a way to investigate Paderok or send me out to gather information. Time was of the essence. If Paderok was giving information to the Diefetians, it could jeopardize our plans for the war. Paderok needed to be confirmed as a spy sooner rather than later.

"My brother can save his usual brutality for the Diefetians. Am I right, Bowv?" Rono asked, turning to me.

"I can," I confirmed.

"Then I see no problem with it as long as Paderok remains unharmed," Rono said.

"I'll do my best," I promised.

"I need more than that, Bowv," my brother said.

"I don't know the exact circumstances I will find myself in," I told him. "For all we know, he could have a conspirator waiting to attack anyone asking questions about him."

"Then be careful," ordered the king.

"He'll kill Paderok!" cried Chancellor Marilok

"My brother is a murder chancellor; everyone knows it. He made it no secret he killed our father, and he has committed some of the most heinous crimes the Continent has seen. Bowv is a killer through and through.

"However, he is not an impulsive killer, and I have no doubt he has grown his public image to be one of a bloodthirsty animal lacking in self-control to sow fear in the minds of kings and peasants alike," rebuked the king.

"Father is right, chancellor. When we were sent to stop the Diefetian force, he analyzed the situation, formed a plan, and struck. My uncle is anything but impulsive," Jorn backed his father up.

The chancellor fell silent and nodded his head in agreement.

"I better get going then," I said, leaving the room.

Chapter Seven

I WENT TO A TAVERN ON THE EASTERN SIDE OF TOWN, having to snake through streets and the occasional back alley to get there. When I saw buildings with boarded windows, the paint on them chipping and peeling, and the occasional circular indentation where a mace, the favorited weapon of the local gangs, had bludgeoned an exterior wall, I knew I was approaching my destination.

I walked up the wavy tavern steps. Small gaps between the boards showed the barren dirt below them. When I got to the door, the only evidence it was painted was two faded gray patches, one at the top and the other at the bottom.

The bottom edge of the door was not parallel to the ground; rather, it was angled down with its top hinge breaking away from the frame, and the bottom right corner was nearly on the floor. It gave a creak and a scraping sound as it opened, and I entered the tavern.

Inside were some of the most powerful criminals in the city: smugglers, heads of gangs, thieves, and racketeers. As I walked up to the bar, a few heads turned to investigate who I was. No one said anything, but hands moved towards weapons, their owners once calm and relaxed, not wide-eyed and tense. The bartender looked at me more closely, studying me to figure out who I was, when a familiar voice shouted my name. I turned around to see someone I hoped would be there.

"Daelfon," I said, turning around to greet the scoundrel who had a scar running down the length of his left cheek.

"What brings you to this part of town?" he asked.

"I need information," I told him.

"Then I'm your man for a small price," he said.

"You'll be well rewarded. I need you to tell me about one of the king's courtiers, Paderok," I requested.

"What about him?" asked Daelfon.

"He goes on a walk every day, early in the morning. I need to know if he is meeting anyone," I explained.

"Why is a courtier important to you?" he asked.

"It's none of your business. Do you know anything or not?" I asked.

"It is my business, considering you are working for the king," Daelfon explained.

"All I'm doing is helping him fight the war against the Diefetians. Salroon had one of his men try to kill me after I refused to give him something he insists belongs to him. If I was helping my brother reduce crime, I would have barricaded the exits, poured pitch around the building, then set the place on fire," I said.

"You would have," Daelfon said with a grim tone. "I don't know much about Paderok, but he stops at a trader's shop on the south side of town."

"Who owns the shop?" I asked.

"An old man, a Diefetian who immigrated here during your father's reign. I don't know much other than that. I don't even have your name for you," Daelfon informed me.

"Thanks for the information," I said, giving him six pieces of silver.

"With pleasure," he said.

I exited the tavern and walked back to the palace, thinking if anyone else could give me information on Paderok or the Diefetian trader. One person came to mind. I headed back towards the palace and continued down the street to Glendeo's inn.

In my Father's day, the old man watched the king's associates and foreign visitors. I hoped he kept the habit. Walking into the inn, I found the old man sweeping the floor.

"Back for the night?" he asked.

"The sun is just setting," I pointed out.

"Then what do you want?" he asked.

"Know anything about my brother's courtier Paderok?" I asked.

"He goes for a walk each morning," said the innkeeper.

"Which direction does he head?" I asked.

"Heads to the south side of the city," he answered.

"Does he bring anything with him?" I asked.

"Nothing from what I've seen," Glendeo answered.

"Interesting. Does he have anything with him when he returns?" I asked.

"Not that I can tell," Glendeo answered.

"Thank you. I better get back to the palace," I said.

"Aren't you forgetting something?" asked the innkeeper.

I gave him four pieces of silver. "I trust this takes care of my tab."

"It does and more," confirmed Glendeo.

I left the inn and returned to the palace, where the setting sun was casting long shadows in the street. Knowing that Rono would not leave his throne until I came back with information, I headed straight to the throne room. As expected, my brother was there, and Hydela was talking to him.

"It's almost dark, and he's not back. Face it, Bowv saw an opportunity to escape, and he took it," she said.

"Escape? I didn't know I was in chains," I said as I walked towards them, a smug grin adorned my face.

"He's back, just as I knew he would be. Now, if you excuse us, love, we have sensitive matters to discuss, the type that few people should know about," Rono told his wife.

Hydela turned, and she shot me a sour look before leaving the room.

"How did you know I would be back?" I asked.

"You said it yourself: Salroon wants you dead, and the safest place for you to be is around an army," my brother told me.

"Good point," I said.

"What did you find out?" asked the king.

"Paderok travels to the south side and visits a Diefetian shopkeeper," I said.

"What do we know about this Diefetian?" he asked.

"He's supposedly been here since Father's reign," I said.

"A long time," commented my brother. "Though any connections with Diefet could still be strong if he's kept in contact with people in the country."

"Depends on who he knew before he left," I countered.

"Very true," agreed my brother. "But we need more to go on, and you can't follow Paderok around; he'll think you want to kill you."

"I could break into the Diefetian's house and see what I can find," I proposed.

"That could tip both of them off," Rono pointed out.

"Marilok thought Paderok was stealing papers from his office. We could set a trap and catch him red-handed," I proposed.

"We could, though it will take some time," Rono said, then thought about it. "Come back tomorrow, and we will talk about it more."

"There is something else," I said.

"What is it?" the king asked.

"According to Glendeo, Paderok doesn't take anything on his walks," I said.

"And Chancellor Marilok told us that Paderok takes a bag with him," Rono said.

"That he did," I said.

"Either the Chancellor misremembered or lied to us," the king concluded.

"Yes," I agreed.

"Looks like we may have to investigate the Chancellor after all," he said. "If he is the spy, it could mean he lied about the missing papers."

Rono turned in for the night, and I returned to the inn. I found Glendeo once again sweeping the room, his regular evening routine. There was not much to sweep, considering Ilkon and I were his only guests. The old man probably just needed something to do.

Glendeo was never one to sit still when he was younger, having been responsible for the inn and my training. In those days, the inn was always full, with most guests being foreign diplomats and royal couriers from other kingdoms. After I finished my morning training, I always wondered why people chose to stay there with the noise.

Glendeo would return to the inn after training me to help his customers, greeting each with a smile and apologizing for the noise. He would explain how he was in the army, and an old friend asked him to train his son. The innkeeper always failed to mention that his old friend was the king. I must have had a nostalgic look since Glendeo asked me what I was thinking about.

"About how busy this place was when I was young and how it is empty now," I answered.

"War will do that, especially with Diefet. No one in their right mind wants to stay in the capital of the kingdom Salroon is at war with," he explained.

"I am crazy," I agreed.

"That's not what I was implying," Glendeo clarified.

"Don't lie to yourself," I told him.

"That would make your associate just as crazy," said the innkeeper.

"Ilkon's still here?" I asked.

"Not currently. He said something about needing to check something. He should be back any minute," informed Glendeo.

"What was he doing?" I asked.

"He said to tell you he was looking into the matter about Diefet," Glendeo told me.

"Good," I said.

"It's about vampires, isn't it?" the old warrior guested.

"It is," I confirmed.

"So, who is he?" he asked.

"A heretic who believes the Protectorate Temple has covered up the existence of vampires. His order hunts them down," I explained.

"I'm surprised your brother talked to him," Glendeo said.

"Considering he is going on about vampires, I'm not too surprised," I told him. "And he's the one who believes vampires are more than stories."

"You killed three men who did not bleed, and you still insist vampires are just stories," he said, amazed.

"Life's full of strangeness," I said.

"Yes, but men with fangs who don't bleed when stabbed fit the descriptions of vampires to the tee," countered the old man.

"Descriptions that no one can prove were based on events that happened," I pointed out.

He sighed. "Forget it. You're as stubborn as your father."

"I am," I said, then walked over and handed him a few pieces of silver. "When Ilkon returns, tell him I want to talk to him. Consider the silver an advance payment for the room."

"Will do," he said, and I walked to my room.

About an hour later, I heard a knock on my door.

"Come in," I said, and Ilkon entered.

"You wanted to see me," he said.

"Yes, he told me you were looking into the matter we discussed with my brother," I said.

"I have," he confirmed.

"Well, what did you find out?" I asked.

"My order suspects that vampires make up most of the Diefetian court and its military hierarchy," he informed me.

"Assuming vampires are real," I said.

He laughed. "For someone who has killed three, 'assuming' is a strong word."

"Vampires existing doesn't sit well with my atheism, something people don't seem to understand," I told him.

"It would look like your atheism doesn't align with the facts at hand," counter Ilkon.

I laughed. "You're a quick one."

"You have to be when the Temple of the Protectorate wants you dead," he said.

"I thought they stopped burning heretics," I said.

"They did, but now they chop off our heads and bury us in unmarked graves," the heretic informed me.

"I haven't heard of any executions, though," I told him.

"They do them at night and aren't public," Ilkon said.

"The Temple is trying to make it look like there are no heretics," I reasoned.

"Exactly," he agreed.

"And how many of you are there?" I asked.

"I don't know," he admitted.

"You don't know?" I repeated.

"It's called the Heretical Temple, but it is not like the Temple of the Protectorate. We aren't a united body, so it is difficult to know how many of us there are," he told me.

"So, the different sects don't communicate with one another," I guessed.

"Yes. There is no need to communicate with one another, considering each sect holds separate beliefs," explained Ilkon.

"Separate beliefs like what?" I asked.

"Some sects hold similar beliefs to the Protectorate Temple but differ on key issues. Take my order as an example. We have most Temple beliefs, but we believe vampires were never eradicated, and we continue to hunt them. Once all the vampires are killed, we'll disband and merge into the Temple.

"Other sects hold much more radical beliefs, such as there being one true god and each member of the Protectorate is an aspect the god uses to communicate with people since we could not understand the god if he spoke in his true form," Ilkon answered.

"Then why is your order hunted down?" I asked.

"Because the Temple denies that vampires still exist, they preach that they were all killed by Frood the Half-god and his successors in the Vampiric Wars. My order believes certain members of the Temple have been covering up the fact vampires still walk the Continent," Ilkon informed me.

"And you believe them to be vampires," I concluded.

"Yes," confirmed Ilkon. "But we haven't found any hard evidence yet."

"Why is that?" I asked.

"The only proof of someone being a vampire is that they don't bleed when stabbed," the vampire expert explained.

"Sounds pretty simple," I said.

"In theory, yes, but not in practice for obvious reasons," reassured Ilkon.

"Maybe it's because vampires aren't real," I suggested.

"Yet you killed three," countered Ilkon.

"Believe what you wish," I said.

"How's the war going?" he asked, abandoning any hope of persuading me.

"By now, the Diefetian army we sent packing should almost be at Eshtar's border if they come back," I guessed.

"You don't know for certain?" he asked.

"I don't know. We haven't heard anything about the enemy's movements," I told him.

"I see," he said.

"I think that is all we needed to talk about. In the morning, I'll tell my brother what you have told me," I said.

Ilkon wished me goodnight and left the room to return to his. I stayed up a while to think about what he said. The thought of vampires making up most of the Diefetian court and military hierarchy was unbelievable, though I knew Rono would believe it. I was more concerned about the Diefetian army.

Rono was caught off guard by the siege at Gregoros, having no clue the enemy had crossed into his territory and had only a fraction of his small army mustered. If Ilkon's claims were valid and vampires were as deadly as the old tales say, the war would be bloodier than I thought, and the odds would be stacked against us even more.

Both were of little concern to me; after all, I was sure that my brother, Glendeo, and Ilkon were letting their imaginations run wild. Stories are a powerful force; I knew this better than anyone else. Many times, I had spread stories about how I eradicated whole villages, leaving no survivors, and people believed it. However, they had never heard of the village's name before or questioned how word got out if there were no survivors.

When people believe you are going to burn their homes and slaughter them without remorse, they will hand over whatever it is that you want. Some of the atrocities they thought I committed were real, but the most terrifying ones did not play out on the stage of history but in the theater of their minds.

I thought the tale of vampires was similar. That night, I thought the origin myth of vampires must have spawned in a similar fashion. I believed there were no such things as gods and demons, but there were empires back then.

What I thought happened was that one empire conquered the Continent, and there was peace for multiple generations. The opportunistic priests contributed that peace to the people's piety and how the gods couldn't help but grant them prosperity.

Then I imagined some disaster hit, a famine, earthquake, or drought placing a great strain on the empire, and the emperor in question went to the temple his ancestors built. He confronted the gods, seeking an answer to his people's suffering. A priest turned to the emperor and reassured him it was some righteous act by the gods. At this point, the emperor wouldn't have paid much attention to the priest and issued an ultimatum to the gods: undue the burden of his people, or the temple would be destroyed.

Perhaps the emperor waited a few days before he returned to the temple, his rage growing with each hour without a miracle. His faith in the gods diminished with every report that told him more people, the most pious in history, were experiencing a breed of suffering that only the gods could relieve. Maybe it was rage, desperation, the loss of faith, or the love of his people that compelled the emperor to go to the temple and demand immortality from the gods.

And the "curse," I thought, was nothing more than the continual pain of the people of the empire. The vampire tale, I reasoned, was nothing than lies spread by priests who couldn't handle one simple truth: the gods aren't real.

Chapter Eight

EARLY IN THE MORNING, while the rising sun cast an orange-yellow hue onto the faint blue sky, I got up and headed towards the palace. Walking into the throne room, I found my sleep-deprived brother sitting on his throne, barely able to keep his head up.

"You've looked better," I said.

"And you were never the empathetic type," mumbled the king.

"Do we have more problems, or have the current ones been enough to keep you up all night?"

"Unempathetic and pragmatic to an insulting point. I'm starting to wonder why I let the palace be open to you at all hours," my weary brother stated.

"Because it's a perk that comes with being your military advisor. Seeing your only sibling first thing in the morning that's just a bonus," I said, grinning.

"Getting back your question," Rono said, ignoring my slight. "The answer is we have a new problem."

"What's going on?" I asked.

"I got news from the west. A Diefetian force is besieging Tuldum," he informed me.

"How many men?" I asked.

"Reports say about a thousand," Rono said.

"And how many men are defending?" I asked.

"A couple hundred, maybe four hundred at the most, judging from the last report I got from the general stationed there," the king answered.

"So Salroon doesn't want us getting help," I concluded.

"How so?" my brother asked.

"Both Gregoros and Tuldum's roads lead out of Eshtar. If Salroon gets control of both, he can cut off your communication and trade with other countries," I explained.

"But why go through all the trouble when he has the numbers to crush?" the king wondered.

"Because Salroon doesn't want the sword leaving the country," I said, reminding my brother of what caused this mess. "And he can't afford to waste too many men in this war while he has others he is fighting. If I'm right and Salroon is trying to lock down Eshtar, he will try to take Swendufen in the south."

"Then what do we do?" he asked. "I don't have enough men to send to all the cities."

"You don't need to," I told him.

My brother looked at me with a puzzled look.

"Send some men you can spare to bolster Swendufen's garrison since we know it's likely a target. We have already been gathering some for Gregoros, so send supplies to help them resist a siege: food, weapons, and building materials to better their defenses. Salroon's objective is to close the borders to make sure you don't call for help and the sword doesn't leave the country," I explained.

"How are we going to destroy the armies? If Salroon is on our borders, and we take all our forces to engage with one of his besieging armies, wouldn't he end one siege, walk right into my undefended capital, and declare victory?" my brother asked.

"We don't need to destroy the armies. We need to keep the borders open, which is why you are going to send me to break the siege," I said.

"You and who else? The two hundred men you took to Gregoros?" inquired the king.

"No. It was pure luck that most of those men made it out alive," I said.

"Who then?" he asked.

"Considering you have the surviving members of my bandit clan locked up..." I began.

"No," he denied.

"They are better fighters than any of your soldiers and excel at fighting against superior forces and evading those forces," I explained. "It's as if they were made for this purpose."

"No," he said sternly.

"Don't be stupid, brother! This is the best thing to do, and you know it," I said.

"Be stupid!" he cried. "Be stupid enough to release what is left of your sadistic band of killers. Don't try to play me, Bowv; I know exactly what you are doing. Remember, the only reason I don't have you thrown back into a cell and execute you is because I don't have anyone else capable of helping me fight this war."

I smiled.

"Why in the gods' names are you smiling?" he said.

"I'm smiling because that type of conviction will get you through this war," I told him.

"You and your damn tests, just like Father. How are you planning to defeat the Diefetian armies, and what do you need to do it?" he asked.

"I don't know yet. As for what I need, I need the equivalent of my bandit clan or a small army. No one on the Continent has the former, and you can't spare the latter. You suggested the two hundred men I took to Gregoros, but none of them are veteran campaigners, so two hundred would only slow me down when I need to move fast.

"I'm explaining my thinking here so you don't think I am crazy. Give me a quarter of the men I took to Gregoros," I answered in a way that I hoped would remove any shock Rono had.

"Fifty men!" he said in shock.

I sighed. "Yes, fifty men."

"Against a thousand?" he asked puzzled.

"You are overlooking something important," I told the king.

"And what is that?" Rono asked.

"I'm the one commanding them," I pointed out.

"No. Figure out another way. I will not have you torturing people while acting as my advisor," Rono forbade.

"Who said anything about torture?" I asked.

"I know how you operate," he said.

"I won't need to torture anyone," I assured him.

He still looked a bit puzzled, but he could tell I was being serious, and after a moment's pause, he spoke. "Fine then. The men that you took to Gregoros are at barracks. Pick fifty of them; by then, I will have gathered supplies for you to take."

"Sounds good," I said.

"And I will have Jorn meet you at the barracks," he added.

"As you wish, brother, just don't complain to me if the boy dies," I said.

"I'm sure you can keep him alive," he told me.

"We will see," I said as I exited the throne room. "And keep an eye on that problem you had me look into. That can cause more trouble than any army."

"SO WHERE ARE WE HEADING," Billen asked, who I managed to persuade to accompany me again as we walked to the barracks.

"To Tuldum to break a siege," I said.

"With fifty men?" he said.

I turned and looked at my old friend. "You act as if we haven't done crazier things," I said.

"Crazier things? Since when did we ever go up against an army with fifty barely trained men?" he asked.

"With Jorn, you, and myself, it's a bit more than fifty," I pointed out.

"It's not much of a difference," he flatly said.

"Don't underestimate yourself like Billen," I responded.

"You shouldn't make light of this Bowv," he said.

"I'm not," I said. "After all we have been through, I thought you would have a bit more trust in me."

"When you were leading the most ferocious bandit clan on the Continent, it was a lot easier for me to trust you. Now, you are proposing we take fifty poorly trained men to stop an army of a thousand, all of whom probably have seen combat. I have seen you beaten the odds before, Bowv, but this is insanity," he explained.

"Then why bother coming? You could stay in your shop and make weapons and armor for the war and not come with me on a suicide mission," I pointed out.

"Someone has to make sure you don't sneak off and resume banditry," Billen said.

"There's more to it than that," I sensed. "But that'll suffice for now."

We arrived at the barracks, and Jorn was waiting for us outside. His eyes lit up, and he smiled as he greeted the blacksmith.

"Billen, will you be joining us?" asked my nephew.

"I will be Prince Jorn," assured Billen.

"You sound surprised," I noted.

"I am. I don't see a reason for Billen to rejoin us; he has a shop to run and was reluctant to join us the first time," my nephew said.

"Someone needs to keep an eye on your uncle," my old friend said.

"Why did you take up smithing anyway?" Jorn asked him. "From what I have heard of my uncle's bandit clan, you could have retired with the wealth of a nobleman."

"He could have if he wanted to," I agreed.

"I could have, and as Bowv is suggesting, would have let me. But when a man starts a new life, it's better if he isn't anchored to his old one. It threatens to drown him in the dark depths," Billen answered.

"This new life must include helping the kingdom. Otherwise, you wouldn't have agreed to join us again," concluded the youngest of our group, getting the information out of Billen only minutes ago he didn't want to tell me.

"You would be correct," affirmed Billen, almost as if he was thinking the same thing. He then turned to me and said, "He's a thinker."

"Just like his father," I agreed.

"I would have said like you," Billen said.

Our conversation ended there as I turned and opened the door to the barracks, deciding we had wasted enough time chit-chatting, and walked into the barracks. The barracks was a cluster of four one-roomed buildings. Each had a row of bunks on both sides of the room. At the end of each bunk was a decent-sized wooden chest for its occupants to store their gear.

At the end of the line of bunks, there was a weapons rack holding spears and swords alike.

During my father's reign, the four buildings were referred to as "Barracks One" since there were five other clusters of barracks around the city, each comprised of four long and narrow buildings. When Rono was elevated to the throne, he pursued a policy of peace and trade, reasoning he didn't need four barracks, only one. Of the five barracks operational during my father's reign, only one was still in use. One barracks is not enough to defend a besieging city, something I hoped my brother didn't have to learn the hard way.

When I abdicated, I told myself I would never be a part of the kingdom again. But absolutes conflict with my pragmatic nature. The truth was I needed Rono as much as he needed me. Beyond the reasoning I gave Rono, the truth was that Salroon was the most capable conqueror the Continent had known since the Wretched King.

If Diefet shallowed the Continent, then Salroon's power would be unmatched, and he would have the resources to hunt bandits. It wouldn't matter how many men I would have in my clan if Salroon could afford to send a hundred times more men to hunt me without worrying about borders. I would be done for. I could fight Salroon as a bandit or while he was at war with my brother. It was an easy decision to make.

Half the men I took to Gregoros were housed in the building we were in, and the other half were housed in one of the adjacent buildings that made up Barracks One. When we entered, Lieutenant Halerod was talking to one of the men whom I recognized but never learned his name.

I didn't bother to learn any of their names because I believed at least half of them would die at Gregoros. No doubt Rono thought it was the work of the gods how we completed our mission with minimum casualties and not the great stroke of fortune it was. I knew none of the men Rono gave me would be a match for a Diefetian soldier, and this time around, Billen and I would need to teach the men more than just how to hide in the woods.

When Halerod finished talking, he turned to face us. "I hear we're setting out for Tuldum," he said.

"Yes, we are," I confirmed.

"With just fifty men?" he asked, though it was a question he knew the answer to but didn't like the answer.

"Fifty men is all we need, Lieutenant," I assured him. "If we had any more men, then we would be even slower than we need to be."

The Lieutenant gave me a puzzled look.

"That means we must move fast and get to Tuldum before the city is taken. If we take too many men, we'll move slower than a tortoise. We need to take fifty or fewer men," I said.

"Of course, these men aren't the best fighters either," Halerod reminded me, though it was far from necessary.

"Oh, we'll take care of that on the road," Billen said with a smile.

"How are we going to defeat an army that outnumbers our small band?" the lieutenant asked.

"We will see once we get to Tuldum," I told him.

"So, we have no plan," concluded the lieutenant with a look of desperation.

I turned to Billen. "I think the lieutenant and I need to have a conversation outside. You and Jorn stay here and make sure the men are ready to move in ten minutes."

"Will do," Billen said.

Once Halerod and I had exited the building, we walked down the street. When I said I needed to talk with Halerod, fear filled the man's eyes. With each step we took down the street, he became jumpier and had an ever-increasing amount of sweat streaking down his brow. I stopped and turned to him.

The look on his face was one I had seen countless times. Terror consumed his eyes, from the pupils to the irises. His mouth formed a contorted mess of worry, and his cheeks appeared to sink straight down as if pulled by miniature weights. It was the look of a man who feared death and believed he was about to die.

"If I wanted you dead, you would already be dead," I told him.

The lieutenant visibly relaxed, yet he retained the posture of a spooked deer frozen in place. How this cowardly man became a lieutenant when he was not used to being within five feet of danger was beyond me. Halerod was the type of man my father would have used as arrow fodder.

Father's philosophy was that if you had a soldier in need of courage, you sent them into a situation with slim chances of survival. If the man survived, a beautiful metamorphosis would occur, and he would transform from a scared, emotional wreck who became paralyzed when combat began into a brave warrior with a newfound respect for his martial abilities. If death cut this astounding transformation short, then Father would say he was better off since he wasn't made to be a soldier.

"You don't like me," I continued. "And you believe I'm a criminal who should be executed for his crimes, not put in command. You think taking fifty men to lift a siege is a crazy idea, but you are too terrified to say that to my face because you think I will kill you if you do. Am I right?"

Halerod slowly nodded his head.

"Of course I am," I said. "And you don't think our odds aren't good either."

"No," Halerod admitted.

"Then tell that to my face before the men," I told him. "They have the same doubts as you and need to see you bring them to me. Otherwise, they will stop looking to you as a leader."

Halerod's face went from fear to puzzlement as he tried to understand how I knew this was the correct course of action.

"Remember Halerod, I was a soldier before I was a bandit. I was trained by the greatest warrior in my father's army. I was trained by my father, the Wretched King, one of the greatest military minds the Continent has seen in the art of war. When most kids were starting their apprenticeships, I was campaigning.

"I know what I'm doing. If you have doubts, the men under your command must hear them. Though I am in command, you are their lieutenant. They have the same doubts—it's obvious—but as their lieutenant, you need to address these doubts, and they need to see you address them. Understand?" I asked.

"I do," he said and was more relaxed.

"So, we are going back to the barracks, and that's exactly what you will do," I told him.

He nodded, and then we began to walk back to the barracks. For the entirety of the brief journey, Halerod was silent. We climbed the steps to the barracks, and when I opened the door, a slow, deep creak greeted us. All the men were lined up with their travel packs on, something that I thought would take longer, thinking that Billen had lost his touch, but I was pleasantly surprised.

Two lines of twenty-five men shot down the room, facing each other. I don't know if they were volunteers, though knowing Billen, I would guess the former. The soldiers who weren't joining us were in their bunks.

Billen was at the head of the line to the right, and Jorn was at the front to my left. Both men were facing the door, waiting for Halerod and me to return. The first building of Barracks One, looked like a proper barracks, and the men within it looked like the professional soldiers they were supposed to be. I would have smiled if I knew them better and wasn't confident most would return to their gods, not to the barracks.

"Are we ready to head out?" I asked Billen.

"Does it look like we're not?" he asked with a smirk.

I turned to Halerod. "What do you think, lieutenant?" I asked.

"Sir...," he began.

"Don't call me 'sir' lieutenant. Save it for when you address your prince. I'm an advisor to the King, not a superior officer. I'm no gentleman either," I corrected.

"Of course," he said. "I agree the men look ready, but perhaps we should take a minute to reflect on the nature of our mission."

"As I informed you, the mission is simple: break the siege at Tuldum," I said. "I've already explained this to you."

"Yes," he said. "But I, and I expect everyone else, well maybe not Billen, have concerns about the odds of our mission and how we are supposed to break a siege with just fifty men."

I looked around the room to witness a sea of nods. The nods of men on the bunks were far more definitive than those lined up. It never ceases to amaze me how much more honest people become when they are not in a position where there could be consequences for expressing their opinions.

"Fine," I said, adding annoyance to my voice so the men didn't know I told Halerod to bring this up. "By a show of hands, how many of you thought our mission to Gregoros would be successful?" I asked.

I scanned each line and the bunks, and there was an unsurprising lack of raised hands.

"And how many of you thought you would survive that mission?" I asked.

Not one of them dared to raise their hand.

"How many of you have heard a story about how my bandit clan was about to be captured and there was no possible way escape, only to hear shortly after we did escape?"

Fifty hands slowly made their way into the air.

"And how many of you have heard a story of how when I was serving under my father, the Wretched King, I turned a losing battle into a victory?" I asked my final question.

Again, fifty hands went into the air.

"If any of you think those stories are fictional, I hope our exploits at Gregoros have convinced you otherwise," I told them. "And if that is not evidence enough, the fact my brother, your king, believes I can beat the horrible odds Eshtar finds herself against should be sufficient evidence.

But I won't lie; the odds of your survival are not good. It's not what you want to hear, but that's the case. So, to increase your survival odds, Billen and I will be training you as we travel, and hopefully, we can shape you into an acceptable fighting force by the time we get to Tuldum."

"That's it?" a soldier in the back asked.

"Yes, it is," I said. "Now, let's get going. Our supplies should be ready for pick up."

Chapter Nine

WE PICKED UP THE SUPPLIES then immediately started our week's long journey. As promised, Billen and I trained the men. The training was not what they expected. Billen and I spent an hour drilling them each day, but the training continued when we were marching. We marched in two parrel lines of twenty-seven, with Billen and Halerod leading the two lines, and Jorn and I were in the back of the lines

The men all carried a look of suspicion as if they expected me to draw my sword and cut them down where they stood. And a jitteriness possessed them whenever I was near. This was nothing new. They all acted this way since the day we embarked for Gregoros.

I didn't notice it as much when we marched to Gregoros because they had just met me, and fear was a natural response. If they followed orders, I didn't mind it too much, but I had hoped after Gregoros, they would be more comfortable around me.

Jorn pulled me aside that night and asked about the spy problem.

"Your father will take care of it," I said. "He can be crafty when he needs to be."

"What about the vampires?" the young prince asked.

"Don't worry about stories," I told him.

"How can you dismiss them as stories when you killed three of them?" my nephew asked confounded.

"I killed three alleged vampires," I told him. "But I'm far more open to the suggestion vampires are real than I was before your father locked me up in a cell."

"Does that mean you are open to the possibility of the gods being real?" he asked.

"No," I said.

"Don't even bother my prince. You're more likely to attend my funeral than get your uncle to admit to the existence of the Protectorate," Billen said, walking over.

"If your silly Protectorate was real, then I should have been killed a long time ago. You, of all people, know that," I said, looking straight into his eyes.

"That may be true if they didn't have another purpose for you," counter the blacksmith.

"Must be an important one since when I open my hands, rivers of blood pour from them," I said.

"I think it will be," Billen said.

I grunted, ending the conversation there. The next day, we continued our march, with me drilling military theories into the men's heads. We had made our way into the Hendrill Forest, where the trees stood closer, and the leaves grew thicker and bigger than in the Ventillor.

Despite the forest's thickness, it could not hide its secrets from me. Out of the corner of my eye, I caught movement in the tree line, and Billen shot me a look to say he had seen the same thing. Our hands fell to our weapons, expecting trouble.

Then, our path was blocked by a single man standing in the middle of the road. He wore no armor; instead, he wore a tunic and trousers that didn't tightly cling to his muscular body and left him comfortable whether traveling, working, or fighting. A short sword hung on his hip, and he stood upright with his arms calmly crossed in the front. His hair was dark brown and ran down past his shoulders. A smile came across his angular face, and his brown eyes lit up when I walked to meet him.

"You must be Bowv. Just the man I was looking for," he said.

"Who are you?" I asked.

"I am Ilonek, a servant of King Salroon," he answered.

"I suppose you want the sword," I guessed.

"My king does," he replied.

"It's not for sale," I said.

"I know. A fight is what I want," the now smiling Diefetian said.

"One against fifty hardly seems fair," I replied.

"Just me and you," he said.

"Why would I agree to that when I can just have my men charge you down?" I asked.

"Because mine will riddle them with arrows," he said.

With that cue, thirty Diefetian arches emerged from the forest on each side of the road, bows already in hand and arrows notched. I had marched my warband straight into an ambush and had no archers to counter the enemy's. Before we left, Rono said he couldn't send any with us because he needed archers to defend Kiholp in case of a siege. I laughed.

"There must be a reason you want to fight me since you've just given up the element of surprise," I deduced.

"I want to avenge Ambassador Zimkoo and Lords Leernu and Gaenic, all of whom you murdered," Ilonek explained, the fires of hate lighting up his eyes.

"I didn't murder Gaenic; we fought, and I was the victor. The other two I murdered," I clarified

"Do you accept then?" asked the Diefetian.

"If your men drop their bows and promise not to attack after I kill you," I said.

"Fair enough," Ilonek said. "Men, drop your bows; if Bowv is the victor, then your orders are to withdraw."

After I saw the Diefetians drop their bows, I drew *Hueik,* and he drew his short sword. After glancing at his blade's length, I knew *Hueik* was longer. I wasn't surprised when he closed in, attempting to negate my advantage of having a longer weapon. I let him. Gaenic was an exceptional fighter, and I wanted to see if Ilonek was the same.

Sensing an opening, he thrust towards my chest, which I swatted aside with *Hueik* to the left. Ilonek recovered within an instant and jabbed at my leg closest to him. I parried low and swept my sword at his leg right after the parry. Ilonek hopped back and feinted a thrust to his chest; then, as he was about to block it, I arched *Hueik* around his arm and then cut sideways towards his ribs. But Ilonek was too fast and rotated his sword, pointing its tip down. Our swords clashed again.

Pulling my sword back, I returned to my guard, and Ilonek did the same. He went on the offensive. He approached me not with the hectic rush of a novice but with the calm, calculated footwork of a master. The

Diefetian did a series of thrusts and cuts so smoothly I couldn't register when one attack ended and the other began.

I parried. When he stopped his assault, mine began. My arms moved with a tempest's furry, my strikes moved with the force of a tsunami, yet my opponent's defense was steadfast and unyielding as a mountain. During our exchange, he had worked his way closer to me, where my longer sword struggled to keep up with his nimble short sword.

I attacked viciously, needing to drive him back. I attacked his center body. He parried. I swung my sword to the side in a cut. He blocked. I feinted a few times, then struck at his head. I felt my sword crash into his. Undeterred, I continued my attack.

I worked my sword fast, striking with speed and recovering just as quickly when my blade met his. Thrust and cut all were blocked. Strikes high, low, and to the center were all parried. Feints did nothing. With each failed attack, Ilonek would move closer.

Ilonek wore the face of a stoic warrior and moved his sword with calculated purpose. But his eyes told a different story. In his eyes, flames of vengeance danced alongside those of fury. When I stopped attacking and needed to come up with a better plan, a wicked grin worked its way across Ilonek's face, and the fire in his eyes burned brighter. He attacked.

Like the rush of a thunderstorm's torrential downpour came his strikes. I worked my sword furiously to keep up, sweat pouring down my brow. Too busy blocking the Diefetian's attacks to strike out with *Hueik,* I kicked out with my back leg. The Diefetian hopped back before my foot could hit his body. Now, with more room, I attacked.

I thrust to his chest, then heard the ring of a perfect parry. I swung my sword up briefly, intending to cut at his head. When Ilonek raised his short blade to block, I dipped mine down at the last moment, landing a blow on the side of his body, and felt *Hueik* nick a rib.

Ilonek's jaw clenched, and his eyes widened as if I had struck him with a hot poker. The Diefetian flicked his sword towards my chest. Years of experience told me he was feigning an attack. I was ready when he diverted his blade at the last second towards my stomach.

Instead of blocking, I stepped back, swung my sword in a downward arch, and my blade cut an opening in the back of his shin. I smiled. Ilonek would bleed out in a matter of minutes. But no blood poured from the Diefetian's wound. When I looked up at his face it was in anguish. Seizing the opportunity, I quickly closed and thrust *Hueik* towards his chest.

Metal rang against metal as Ilonek managed to bring his sword around to block mine. I disengaged my sword from his and gave a lightning-fast stab at his face. He parried my attack, and we stepped back out of each other's range.

Neither of us moved for several moments. Instead, we stared at each other, analyzing the other's guard, trying to find an opening. Ilonek moved first. Closing the distance between us with the speed of a rabbit, the Diefetian rushed me. A less experienced fighter would have been caught off guard, but I was far from inexperienced. After we moved away from each other, I knew if I didn't do anything, there was a chance Ilonek, who had the shorter sword, would.

So, when the Diefetian thrust his blade toward my stomach, I was ready. *Huik* met my enemy's sword as I blocked his attack. As he pulled his sword away from mine, Ilonek arched his sword around, threatening to land a cut on the side of my body below my ribs.

I pivoted so that I was now perpendicular to my adversary and fell back as I did, creating more room to use my longer sword. As Ilonek's sword sliced through the air, his back was now towards me. I took advantage of this new angle, got closer to him, and delivered a thrust, aiming for his back.

It should have worked. There was no possible way he could have seen me. But with battle-hardened instincts, Ilonek turned around and intercepted my strike. Not wanting to give up my momentum, I probed his defenses with a series of feints. No matter where I struck, high, low, or to his center, no gaps in his guard appeared.

I increased my speed, but Ilonek recognized the feints for what they were. The Diefetian only bothered to block when the feints came in too close and evaded the rest. I switched to combinations of feints and attacks as I threaded the two together into a delicate, martial tapestry.

I didn't let up; instead, I increased my speed. Ilonek was like a phantom I couldn't touch as he continued to evade and block. Then I saw an opening. The Diefetian had brought his sword too far to the left after he had blocked one of my cuts. Before Ilonek could recover, I quickly thrust my sword through his chest.

As I pulled the sword from the body, its moonlight color, unblemished by blood, gave off a glimmer, brightening the blade more than it should have in daylight. I wish I could say that I was shocked, but at that point, I had already seen this phenomenon three times before. I would have been grateful Rono was not with me to spew stories about vampires if I hadn't remembered Billen and Jorn would.

The thought briefly passed as I returned to the problem at hand: being surrounded by Diefetian archers. When I looked up from the blade, I was shocked to see the Diefetians had stuck to their word and had melted back into the forest. The lieutenant, Billen, and my nephew came rushing up to me.

"I can't believe they're gone," Halerod said.

"They may not be," Billen informed him.

"No, they're gone. They went back into the forest as soon as Ilonek fell," refuted Jorn.

"That doesn't mean they won't come back and fill us with arrows," Billen argued.

"No, they're gone," I assured Billen.

"We wouldn't be gone. Either we would hide or circle back," my old friend said.

"We didn't have anyone to report to," I told him.

"Report to?" a confused Halerod asked.

"Bandits don't report to kings," I informed the lieutenant.

"You think they have gone off to report to Salroon," Jorn guessed.

"Yes," I confirmed. "Or one of his commanders."

"Why would they do that? If they wanted the sword, they could have let loose a volley, killed you, and retrieved it," Billen argued.

"Our men would be on top of them before they notched another arrow," I said.

"And risk losing the sword in the fray," Jorn concluded.

"Precisely," I said. "And if I am right, then they have to report another one of Salroon's... whatever Ilonek was... is dead."

"The word would be 'vampire,'" Billen said.

"If it is, then vampires aren't all what they are made out to be," I remarked.

"Easy to say when you have the Sword of the Gods," Billen refuted.

"Shouldn't we be going?" asked a concerned Halerod. "The Diefetians could be getting reinforcements."

"Yes, we should. Let's get the men moving," I ordered, and within a few minutes, we were back on the march towards Tuldum.

Chapter Ten

DURING NORMAL CIRCUMSTANCES, there's not much for a traveler to look at when they gaze upon the city of Tuldum. The city lies on the border of the western frontier and provides a needed stop for travelers and caravans to enter Eshtar. The city saw a good deal of coin flowing through it, enough to keep its citizens well-fed, clothed, and housed. Like Travelios, where visitors could witness the city's beautiful arches before even entering it, one could witness Tuldum's claim to fame from the road: the city's wall, the only thing slowing the besieging army down.

The Araekian walls of Tuldum had only been around for four generations but were famed throughout the Continent as impenetrable. Constructed by King Araek, my grandfather, the fifty-foot-tall and twenty-foot-wide walls were worthy of an imperial city, not some tiny frontier city. But Tuldum was Eshtar's capital when my grandfather ruled. His grandfather, Towol. had lost most of Eshtar to a Bendilli invasion and was killed in a subsequent battle.

Despite this, my great-great-grandfather stopped the Bendilli from conquering all of Eshtar. His son Lormto managed to build up enough wealth through trade while playing a dangerous diplomatic game with the Bendilli to keep what fragile peace his father made, that his son, Araek, had enough gold to pay for the massive walls. The walls were both an impenetrable obstacle from an invading force and a refuge for a retreating army.

King Araek took back a kingdom thought to be lost and will forever be known as the Reclaimer. After the foreigners were driven out, my father came into power. Growing up during a war made him a great fighter and an even greater general. It was said that if Father had been around to command when the war was declared, the Bendilli would have been repelled in months. Not to diminish my grandfather's ability, but my father was a master of war before his twenty-fifth birthday, fighting four dozen battles before that time.

My father's rule promised peace. But, the citizens of Tuldum would have to wait until my brother took the throne for them to know peace for more than a couple of years. I held the city's mayor hostage once after I murdered the Wretched King. My brother's men had caught up to me in Tuldum, and I needed to do something to buy time while I thought of an escape plan. Besides the one mayoral kidnapping, Tuldum's citizens were lucky enough to experience more than two decades of peace.

But the war had come to Tuldum once again. When Billen and I were scouting, what we saw looked like what we saw at Gregoros. A Diefetian army had surrounded the city, so no matter which direction one's eyes glazed, they were bound to find an invader's tent. Unlike Gregoros, scaling ladders were spread throughout the camp, along with three siege towers constructed on the city's northern, western, and eastern sides.

Just by looking, I knew there were far more soldiers than the original one thousand, the reports said. Judging from the number of tents I counted, I estimated there were three thousand Diefetians. The positive was the presence of a medical tent filled with a few occupants, meaning the Diefetians had tried an assault and were repelled.

Amongst the sea of tents, the Diefetian commander stood out. The illuminated, dirty steel and iron was the shining gold-plated armor of the Diefetian commander. The armor covered him from head to toe, marking him as a noble but also as one who had likely bought his command and wasn't competent.

I've fought enough haughty nobles to know that may not have been the case. Either he bought his command, or he was a noble so confident in his skills that he chose to wear such expensive armor because he thought he couldn't be killed and stripped of it.

A haughty general is easier to best than an incompetent one. Incompetency breeds unpredictability, while arrogance is always predictable. Forever, arrogant commanders march their men forward to seize victory, never considering they have underestimated their enemy and the path to victory they see is an enticing trap they have walked into.

Judging by the order of the camp and the well-built siege towers, the Diefetian commander was far from incompetent. I gave a nod to Billen, and we headed back to camp.

We found the camp exactly as we left it: quiet and peaceful. I headed for my tent and told Billen to gather Jorn and Halerod, who would then meet me there. We were outside my tent a few minutes later, discussing what to do next.

"We can't break the siege!" exclaimed Halerod after I told him and Jorn the situation. "We don't have enough men."

"Some would say we didn't have enough men at Gregoros," Billen rebutted.

"We at least had more men then than we do now," the lieutenant pointed out.

"And that's not going to stop us," my nephew said. "If Tuldum falls, then Eshtar gets cut off from the western part of the Continent."

"The prince is right. Not to mention the loss of morale if we lose our most well-defended city," Billen added.

"Their commander is the arrogant type," I said.

"Why do you say that?" asked Jorn.

"And how is that important?" Halerod asked.

"He was wearing golden-plated armor," I said, answering the first question. "And it's fortunate for us because we have a good idea of how he will react to what we decide to do."

"What are we going to do?" asked Jorn.

"That's what we are here to figure out," Billen said. "And I wager your uncle already has a plan."

"I do," I confirmed.

"We can't defeat an army of three thousand," Halerod said.

"We don't have to," I said.

"What do you mean we don't have to?" asked Jorn.

"We are here to break a siege, not to crush an army," I clarified.

"Without doing anything criminal," Jorn was quick to remind me.

"I'm not proposing anything criminal; I'm proposing deception," I said.

"What do you mean, Bowv?" Billen asked.

"I say we let the Diefetians think they have taken the city," I said.

"Make them think they have taken the city?" Halerod asked, puzzled. "How is that going to help us?"

"Aren't we here to prevent the city from falling?" Jorn asked.

"If the enemy walks through the gates and we are still in control, has the city really fallen?" I asked.

"Bowv, you're not proposing..." began Billen.

"I am," I confirmed.

"It barely worked in Grisedom," argued Billen.

"It worked there, and it'll work here," I said.

"We had more men," Billen pushed back.

"And the enemy outnumbers us more than they do now," I reminded him.

"The king will not be pleased," Billen said.

"My brother ordered me not to commit any crimes and to break this siege. I am following his orders to the letter. Deception and trickery aren't crimes in war. How could he possibly be mad?" I asked.

Billen fell silent and shook his head.

"What happened in Grisedom?" Jorn asked.

"We had taken the city and demanded payment from the Hunderian emperor to leave. The emperor didn't take kindly to us holding one of his cities hostage and refused to pay. When a Hunderian army ten times the size of our bandit clan surrounded the city and began a siege, there was nowhere to hide, nor to run," I explained.

"Then Bowv came up with the idea of faking a surrender and letting the army into the city. They thought they had victory in their hands until he sprung his trap," Billen continued for me.

"What trap?" the prince asked.

"I managed to convince the officers to meet me to accept my surrender, nothing out of the ordinary. They didn't know that they were walking into an ambush," I said. "They were all shocked when my men sprang out and killed them."

"But that was just the officers. What about the rest of the army?" Jorn asked.

"Chaos erupted after soldiers found the officers dead. I had some of my men act as civilians and spread rumors throughout the city we had slipped out during the confusion. Enough reports made it to the soldiers that whoever was in charge decided they needed to leave the city and began a pursuit. When the last soldiers filed out of the city gates, we came out of our hiding spots, packed up what loot we had taken from the city, and headed in the opposite direction of the army that was hunting us," I recalled.

"You want to do something similar here? How? We are not even in the city," Halerod pointed out.

"Murdering an enemy officer violates the king's orders," Billen pointed out.

"We aren't in contact with anyone in the city," Jorn added.

"We don't need to be," I said.

"What do you mean, Bowv?" Billen said, looking as confused as Halerod was.

"This will be like Grisedom because there will be a fake surrender. We need to do is convince the Diefetian commander we are an advanced force, and I am here to break the siege," I explained.

"How does that help?' Jorn asked.

"It means that the Diefetians will be looking for the rest of an army that doesn't exist," Billen said, understanding where I was going.

"And the Diefetians will leave the siege in order not to be attacked in the rear," Jorn concluded.

"Exactly," I said.

"You are going to break a siege by bluffing? How will you convince the Diefetians there is an army coming?" asked Halerod.

"By surrendering to the Diefetian commander," I answered.

"You plan to have us all captured to break a siege. Are you crazy?" Halerod asked.

"He is," confirmed Billen. "But you would be surprised how often crazy works."

"We can capture him and use him as a bargaining tool to make the rest of the army leave," concluded Jorn.

"That's the plan," I said.

"But my father wants us to stay within the bounds of the law. I fail to see how kidnapping an enemy officer is legal or a false surrender," Jorn interjected.

"He's an army commander, not a civilian. It's well within the Laws of War to take him prisoner," I explained. "And false surrender isn't covered in the Laws."

"It's a gray area, and you know it," Billen argued.

"Last time I checked gray areas, whose legality needs to be determined. They can be dubbed either legal or illegal by a judge. But, since a judge, or in this case, my brother, hasn't expressly said false surrender isn't banned in the Temple's Laws of War, I would say it's legal until proven otherwise," I argued.

"How isn't kidnapping banned in the Laws?" Jorn asked.

"The Laws permit the capture of enemy combatants, and the enemy commander is a combatant," I said.

"Your uncle is correct, my prince. I'm afraid he has the two of you beaten," Halerod said.

"What about *Hueik*?" Billen asked.

"What about it?" I asked.

"The Diefetians are going to disarm us. We can't let the Sword of the Gods fall into the hands of a vampire," he elaborated.

"Billen, it's a fancy sword, not some divine weapon," I said.

"He has a point," Jorn chimed in. "Even if you believe this talk about vampires and divine weapons is nonsense, you already have admitted Salroon believes it."

"It's either you give Jorn or the lieutenant the sword, we alter the plan, or we come up with a new one," Billen said. "Else, we risk giving the Diefetian king what he wants."

I thought it over for a minute. They were right, but giving the sword to someone else was too risky. Halerod and Jorn couldn't fight off one of Salroon's lackeys if they came for the sword. I needed to alter the plan.

"You're right," I admitted. "I can't go into the Diefetian camp when I know they will disarm me."

"Thank the gods," Halerod said.

"Don't speak too soon, lieutenant," Billen cautioned. "The plan's not dead yet."

"You're right, it isn't," I said with a grin. "The original plan is too risky. It's easier to pretend to give the Diefetians what they want, the sword, while informing them that an army is only a few days away."

"You'll pretend to be turning traitor so that they don't disarm you," Jorn put it together.

"Yes, and I will say I want a meeting with Salroon to hand over the sword personally and to smooth things out between the two of us," I said.

"Will they buy it?" Jorn asked.

"They will, my prince. It is all too realistic of a situation. I would say Bowv would have intended to do just as he described if Leernu hadn't tried to kill him. Your uncle doesn't need the protection of an army, despite what he says. He is helping your father and the kingdom because it gives him the best chance of killing Salroon," Billen said in the truth.

"Here, I was mistaken. I could fool you, old friend," I said.

"You never could," Billen reminded me.

"That's what you think," I said with a mischievous grin.

"You're okay with the plan?" Jorn asked Billen.

"I am. Your uncle and I have done similar things before," Billen answered.

"I am not surprised," Halerod mumbled.

"You shouldn't be lieutenant," Billen said. "And if you think things will get less crazy as the war goes on, think again. Bowv wants everyone to think he became the most successful bandit on the Continent because of fear alone. But no one ever mentions his incredible ability to find ways out of impossible situations."

I dismissed them, and they went back to their tents.

Chapter Elven

WE ALL WOKE UP THE NEXT DAY, assembled the men, and told them the full plan: Billen and I would convince the Diefetian commander to lift the siege so that Rono would believe the mission was accomplished and I was still loyal.

This would give Billen and me time to meet with Salroon before Rono learned about our "betrayal." I was debating either killing the Diefetian commander or kidnapping him to use him as leverage in future negotiations, but I kept this a secret. I was leaning toward the second because Billen wouldn't go along with murder.

There was a time he would have without question, but the man had changed since he began to live an honest life. Though I was confident, I could convince him of the kidnapping. If I killed the Diefetian commander in the process of kidnapping him, then that would not be murder; it was a kidnapping gone wrong.

I told the men the plan and informed them Jorn and Halerod would be in charge while I was gone. After giving some final instructions to Jorn and Halerod, Billen and I packed up and headed straight toward the enemy camp. Running into two Diefetian sentries posted around their camp didn't take long.

We acted surprised when they ordered us to stop and approached with weapons drawn because Billen and I had already noted their patrol patterns. They demanded to know who we were, and I sprung the plan into action.

"I'm Bowv," I said and saw fear creep into both of their eyes. "I am the military advisor to the King of Eshtar, sent here as the head of an army to lift the siege. Take us to your commander."

"Why?" asked one sentry.

"I have a proposition for him," I said.

"What type of proposition?" asked the other.

"The type he wants to hear about," I said with a dangerous edge to my voice.

"You'll have to surrender your weapons," said the sentry on my left.

"Now, why would we do that?' I asked. "Your commander is surrounded by an army. What could we possibly do to harm him? If we meet with your commander unarmed, then we look weak, and that's not good for negotiating. So, if you're telling us that we have to look weak to negotiate, then we might as well kill you and find your commander ourselves."

The two sentries glanced at each other, coming to a silent agreement on what to do, and then one of them motioned for us to come along. With the sentries leading us, we walked in silence, layered with the tension formed by suspicion and mistrust, towards the Diefetian camp. As we walked towards the center of the camp, we were followed by the wandering eyes of soldiers.

I noticed the Diefetian commander about a hundred feet away, wearing his ridiculous gold-plated armor without a helmet. He was in the camp's center, giving orders to a soldier. The two sentries approached and snapped to attention.

"General," one of the sentries said.

"What is it? Who are they?" barked the general.

"We caught them coming into the camp's perimeter," the sentry said, and I suppressed a grin. "One claims to be Bowv and the acting military advisor to King Rono. He says he's in command of an army and has a proposition for you."

The general turned towards me and gave me a hateful glare. "You're Bowv?" he asked.

"Yes," I said.

"The Terror of the Continent?" the general asked.

"I am," I affirmed.

"The man who killed Lord Gaenic, Ambassador Zimkoo, and Lord Leernu?" the general asked, hate building within his eyes and seeping into his tone.

"All dead by my hand," I told the general, and the hate in his eyes burned brighter. "And I killed a guy named Ilonek, too."

The general didn't react to Ilonek's name, but he turned towards his sentries when he saw we were armed. The hate in his eyes was replaced by rage. "This man claims to be the Terror of the Continent, and you two didn't take away their weapons?" he asked, his face something between a dumbfounded look and an angry one.

The sentries stood still and silent like two children being scolded by their father.

"It's my fault. They demanded my friend and I disarm, but I convinced them otherwise," I told the general

"I see," the general said, though he didn't break his condemning glare.

"Shall we get to business? General…"

"Nilomek," he filled in. "And I don't see the point. Within the week, I will take the city."

His statement about taking the city within a week, though he had the Araekian Walls to deal with, verified my judgment of him.

"You don't see the point," I said with a laugh. "Of course, you don't. I haven't explained anything yet."

The general sighed.

"You have nothing to offer. I have Tuldum surrounded. If my men can't take the walls by force, then I will starve the city into submission. What could you possibly offer me?" he asked.

"You nothing," I said, and Nilomek looked at me like I was stupid.

"You approach me with a proposition, but it's not for me?" Nilomek asked, looking at me as if I were crazy.

"Yes," I confirmed.

"Why are you here then?" the Diefetian asked. The irritation in his voice was as clear as a siren.

"I have a proposition for your king," I clarified.

"Then why are we talking?" he asked.

"Because I need someone to take me to him," I said.

"And you want that to be me?" he asked.

"Yes," I said.

"What do I get out of this?" he asked.

"The location of an Estaran army that is on its way to end the siege," I answered.

"There is no army," Nilomek told me. It wasn't the answer that I wanted to hear.

"'There is no army,' the general says. How would you know that when you're in the middle of a siege?" I asked.

"Because if the entire Estaran army came to lift the siege, then its number would only be equal to mine," Nilomek said with a smile.

"Fine, there's no army," I admitted, abandoning the plan. I wasn't concerned he knew the size of our entire army. There was a spy in the palace, and Salroon was known for seizing up the enemy's strength before launching an invasion. "But I have something your king wants." And with that, I drew *Hueik*.

"Hmmm," hummed the general, then speaking to the sentries, ordered, "Kill them both," and they both drew their swords.

My plan was a considerable risk to take. Getting captured and then trying to convince the enemy's general there was an army creeping up behind him while trying to negotiate a meeting with his king was a plan with low odds of success. Add convincing the Diefetians Billen and me we were turning traitors, and you get a plan forged from the fires of desperation. But considering he knew who I was, Nilomek ordering two sentries to seize our weapons was stupid.

The two sentries must have thought the same because caution weighed down their steps as they approached. Billen chose to wait until the sentry was about a yard away before he drew his sword, and even then, he did not strike. Billen, his guard raised, waited for the Diefetian to make the first move. I had already approached my opponent.

I launched a series of attacks that overwhelmed the Diefetian's guard and placed a surgical cut on his sword hand, causing him to drop the weapon. Billen performed a similar technique, though he waited for his opponent to launch an attack and countered with a disarming strike.

I turned to General Nilomek and asked, "Now, are you willing to listen?"

We had drawn attention to ourselves, and soldiers came to see the ruckus. Many of them had their armor on and their weapons drawn. We must have come when they were preparing another attack on the walls. The others must have been assigned camp duties because they wore standard uniforms.

"I am not," Nilomek said after looking around at the nearby soldiers.

"Fine," I said. "But the sword was not the only part of the offer," I said.

"Really? Do tell me the rest of your generous offer," prompted General Nilomek.

"Kiholp," I said, taking a gamble.

Nilomek thought about it for a minute, then thought better about it. "No, Bowv," he said. "My king nor myself do not need you to open the gates to Kiholp. We will take the city even if the whole Eshtaran army is in it," Then he ordered his men to kill us and to take the sword.

I started to laugh, which drew puzzled looks from everyone around me, including Billen. "Kill us," I said, then continued to laugh.

"You think that you can kill us after we just disarmed two of your men in less than ten seconds? Have you forgotten who I am, who you dare risk your men against? I am the Terror of the Continent," I yelled the last part, and the closest soldiers approaching us slowed down.

"If you wish to risk someone's life, then why not risk your own?" And as if acting as one, the Diefetians stopped their advance and stood still for a moment. I looked around the huddled mass of armored men and could see a few head nods, along with the faces of men accepting the logic they had just heard.

"What's it going to be Nilomek? You waste your men's lives, or you face me yourself? Surely, you want to be the one to avenge your comrades? Or do you believe that you can't beat me, even with your army around you?" I asked.

The last line proved to be intolerable for the general. In one controlled yet furious motion, Nilomek drew his sword, one roughly the same length as *Hueik*, and advanced towards me with the steady pace and footwork of an expert fighter. I drew *Hueik* and calmly moved towards my opponent.

With the speed of a cheetah, Nilomek thrust his sword down low to my left thigh, though he did not put his full force behind it. Recognizing the feign for what it was, I stepped out of the way, and as the Diefetian ushered in his true attack, a thrust to my torso, the air rang with the sound of clashing metal as my sword met his. The general pulled back into his guard, and I did likewise, wanting to see what he was capable of.

The soldiers had formed a large circle around us, giving us plenty of room to move around. The nearest soldier was twenty feet from me. I didn't need to wait long for the general to begin his next assault. Within seconds of reestablishing his guard, my opponent was back on the move, rapidly entering striking distance.

A series of attacks followed: a sideways slash that, if landed, would have cut open my stomach, followed by a thrust to my face, which in turn transformed into a downward, arcing cut circling over my shoulder and threatening to land on my arm. I made him miss each attack by a fraction of an inch, and when his sword was arching down towards my arm, I raised *Hueik* and blocked it.

After his failed assault, the general hastily raised his guard. I waited and looked for a gap in his guard. When none appeared, I moved forward. Nilomek fell back with each step I took, his guard never wavering.

My sword darted towards his stomach like a thunderbolt. I didn't see any gaps in his armor, but if I only attacked his unarmored head, I would be predictable. I needed to attack other parts of the body so that he would move his sword away from his head, giving me an opening to go in for the kill. And for all Nilomek knew, I did see a chink in his armor, and he couldn't risk not defending against my attacks even if they weren't to the head. With the same quickness, Nilomek parried and slashed out with his sword. I stepped back. The tip of his sword was just a few inches away as it moved past my stomach.

With a viper's speed, I stepped forward and stabbed at his exposed chest to angle the stab upwards to pierce his neck. The Diefetian whipped his sword back around, and the ring of clashing metal filled the air. His sword harmlessly knocked *Hueik* to the side.

Nilomek brought his sword up and sent it pummeling down, intending to chop open my skull. I jumped back as the general's sword came crashing down. Having missed me, he quickly raised his guard just in time to block my returning thrust. He countered with a thrust of his own, aimed at my sternum. I whipped *Hueik* around to parry, then rapidly brought it up over my right shoulder and swung down at an angle, aiming for Nilomek's exposed head.

Before my blade could crack open his skull, the general darted out of my reach. I had to be quick if I wanted to get into striking range of him. With the speed of a lion, I moved in, but the general proved to be a speedy gazelle. Before my feet had landed, Nilomek had moved out of striking distance. I tried again, moving faster than before, but the nimble general was too fast for me.

Knowing I couldn't get close to Nilomek and he would evade me until I was worn down, I decided to change tactics. As I looked at Nilomek, standing a couple of feet from me, his gold-plated armor was glittering in the sun, taunting me with the protection it provided Nilomek. But the gleaming armor, the wall that I would need to ascend to achieve victory, also served as a reminder. I stood still and lowered my weapon.

Hueik's tip touched the ground, daring the general to stop evading me and start fighting. I could feel the eyes of the surrounding Diefetian soldiers on me, and I knew their thoughts. Some thought I was crazy for standing, and others thought I was bold to challenge their leader in such a brazen fashion.

But their focus didn't stay on me forever. I felt their eyes move off me and lock onto their general. Anticipation thickened the air as they waited, their eyes glued to their general, a single question on their mind: would he accept my challenge?

Nilomek stood there. The general stared at me, hate beaming from his eyes. A snarl pulled the corner of his mouth upwards, distorting his cheek. Feeling the eyes of his men on him, Nilomek walked towards me, and his soldiers cheered.

Each step was calm and purposeful as he approached with his sword down. Only a warrior confident in his abilities could have walked towards me, the Terror of the Continent, a known master of the blade, with such control over his body and emotions.

Nilomek may have given up his advantage by coming to me after I refused to go to him, but the general was not doing so because he cracked under the pressure of his men. I only needed to look at the rage which dominated his eyes.

I let Nilomek get within striking distance of me. Not wanting the general to go back to dodging my attacks, I let the Diefetian strike first. His blade flashed forward into a thrust aimed at my upper stomach. The clash of metal against metal ran out as my sword met his before it could pierce my stomach. The Diefetian recovered quickly and rapidly put up a guard. I had to be patient; if I struck too soon, Nilomek could return to dodging my attacks.

After a few moments of waiting, the general struck again, this time with a convincing feint at my torso, which was then redirected to my leading leg. A great strength was put behind the attack, causing his body to come forward. Not wanting to tip off my enemy, I suppressed a smile. I lowered *Hueik* down for a block. The ring of metal rang out once again. Our blades were locked together. Seizing the initiative, I pulled my blade away before the Diefetian could.

I began a series of attacks. Thrusts followed cuts as I worked my blade with killing intent. Nilomek defended against my first three attacks, and I was astounded when he deflected the fourth and the fifth, which are when most people don't survive past three. But on the sixth, *Hueik* sliced across his exposed neck.

I expected blood to pour out of the general's neck. Yet there was no blood. Shock and confusion were written on the faces of the Diefetian soldiers around me. Billen nodded his head as if he wasn't surprised. Billen must have figured Nilomek for a vampire, something I didn't even consider.

Looking back, it makes sense. Nilomek was mad at me for killing three vampires, and it would have been four, though I suspect the general didn't believe me about Ilonek. Hindsight makes everything obvious, but, like Billen, I was not shocked to learn Nilomek's true nature. What surprised me was *Hueik* glowed, though this time it was a definite glow, not a faint one.

While looking at the now glowing sword, Nilomek raised his guard. Moments before, he held his sword proudly and stable, and his stance was as grounded as a mighty tree. But then his sword shook in his once firm grasp, and he rocked back and forth—the tell-tale sway of someone trying to keep conscious. I don't know how the general was still alive at that point.

With labored steps, the Diefetian general moved towards me, but on the fourth, he fell over dead.

Silence fell over the whole camp. Later, I learned that all the soldiers had heard what was happening and tried to watch the fight. I doubt all three thousand soldiers watched; that's impossible outside an arena. But they all formed a circle. The officers pulled rank to get to the front, and they would tell the guys behind them what was going on, and they would tell the guys that were behind them, and so on, until the ones in the back who couldn't see anything found out what was going on.

I looked at the general's corpse, then up to the Diefetians surrounding me. "You didn't know, did you?" I yelled. "You didn't know what he was. The looks of disbelief say it all. I'm surprised but not shocked. All those 'men' your general mentioned before the fight: Gaenic, Leernu, and Zimkoo, and the one I mentioned, Ilonek, I killed them all, and they didn't bleed either.

"They all had a set of fangs, too, and I bet if we examine the corpse of your general, he'll have some. Now, you all know who I am. I am Bowv, the Terror of the Continent, and you know I dismiss any talk of gods or demons as nonsense. Yet, even I, a staunch atheist, must admit the obvious: your general, along with the four individuals I named, were vampires."

No one objected or refuted what I said. They all stared down at Nilomek's corpse, looking at the physical proof that lay before their eyes. How couldn't they? Those at the front of the line witnessed their general die a mortal wound but did not bleed in the process.

It was the stuff of legends and fairy tales, and they saw it all play out before their own eyes. Who wouldn't be speechless? It should have been impossible; the ground should have been blood-laden. Instead, the stainless ground silently supported the weight of a soulless body that wasn't human in life.

"Who's in charge now?" I asked and looked around to find Nilomek's second in command.

A man stepped forward, a colonel guarding by his armor, "I...I am," he stuttered.

"You're a colonel?" I guessed.

"Yes," he confirmed.

"Good. Check your general's teeth. See if there are two sets of fangs in there," I ordered.

The colonel nodded his head and went over to the corpse. After squatting down next to the head of what was once General Nilomek, the colonel carefully opened the jaw with one hand and used the other to move the lips. After mere moments, the colonel pulled his hands back and shot straight back up, his eyes widened.

"There were fangs, weren't there," Billen chimed in.

The colonel nodded his head.

"Your general was a vampire," Billen said, addressing the crowd of Diefetian soldiers. "For those of us who know the Sacred Texts, we know that vampires cannot be killed like normal men. To kill one, you need to piece its heart, cut off its head, or burn it. Yet, my companion here did none of those things.

"He struck a wound that would have killed a normal man, but not a vampire. Only one weapon can kill a vampire as if he were a man: *Hueik,* the Sword of the Gods. Look at his glowing blade. It is the Sword of the Gods."

Their eyes fell upon my illuminated blade, and I saw an opportunity to do what Billen and I had come to do. Some battles are won by crushing the enemy army, others by routing them, and others are won not by deeds but by words. My father had taught me the differences between all three at a young age, and I knew this battle, this siege, would be broken not by sword or spear but with words

"I don't know what reason your king gave for this war," I said. "Perhaps he said it would be a glorious conquest of another land. But as soldiers, men confronted by grim truths of war, you recognize the lies of a king. Do you want to know the real reason you have trekked across most of the Continent? The reason you are so far from the land you call home? The reason you are separated from your families? Why you lives put at risk?

"You are looking at it! Salroon wants the sword. Before the war broke out, he sent Lord Leernu to find it, who tried to buy it from me and then threatened a fight if I did not hand the weapon over. I killed him. Then your king sent an ambassador, Zimkoo, to demand that my brother order me to hand the sword over, threatening war if he did not. I killed the ambassador for his threat, and war was declared.

"That's where you fit into this. Why aren't you besieging Eshtar's capital? It's the quickest way to a swift victory. Take Kiholp, and the war is won. Yet, your armies are sent to take border cities because your king does not want a swift victory. He wants the sword, and he doesn't have the decency to travel all this way and take it himself. Instead, he wastes your time and endangers your lives to gain possession of what he covets. Tell me, soldiers of Diefet, will you stand for this?"

Acting as one, the Diefetians let out a thunderous roar. Of course, they weren't. It is one thing for a soldier to answer his king's call for war when that call is for the good of the realm. But, when a king sends an army to do what he is capable of, then mutiny and rebellion are legitimate courses of action. Needing to break the siege, I was ready to settle for either.

"Are you going to stay here continuing to fight a battle, one that you now know your king himself can do it himself?" I asked. Yet again, a thunderous roar rang out from the Diefetian soldiers.

"Your general lies dead. There is no one here who will force you to continue to do the bidding of a cowardly king!" A cheer erupted from the surrounding soldiers.

"Then begone. Show King Salroon that the soldiers of Diefet refuse to be his errant boys. That Diefetian blood will not be wasted in a war, whose objective could be fulfilled if the Diefetian king was willing to come out of his palace to retrieve what he covets." A final roar came from the Diefetian soldiers, now fully turned against their king. They dispersed and walked back to their tents, many removing pieces of their armor.

I waved the colonel over to me. "Make sure your men leave the country in an orderly fashion. No raiding or looting. I suggest you assemble them later and figure out some story to tell once you return to friendly lands. When you do, make sure this message gets to King Salroon: 'If you want the sword, come and get it yourself.' Understood?' He nodded his head.

"Good," I said. "And I don't think I need to remind you that I am capable of wiping out your entire army, no matter the size of my force if I find you marching back towards Tuldum, do I?" With a terrified look, he shook his head, then walked away, and Billen came up to me.

"That didn't go according to plan," my old friend said.

"It seldom does," I reminded him.

"No, it doesn't," he agreed.

"I'm going to have to tell my brother about my latest kill," I told him.

"And how you managed to break the siege," Billen added.

"I doubt if he will believe me," I remarked.

"He'll believe you," Billen reassured me. "He knows you can be as deadly with your words as you are with a blade."

"A fair point. We should stick around until we know for sure the army is leaving," I suggested.

"That would be wise," he agreed.

It didn't take long. After Billen and I had finished our conversation, we saw the camp being taken down with the colonel who was now in charge overseeing it. The entire Diefetian camp was broken down within a few hours, and the army departed. I almost couldn't believe it. A duel and a little persuasion were all it took to break a siege. It was remarkable.

After shadowing the Diefetians to see if they were leaving, Billen and I headed back to our camp. When we walked into the center of the camp, the sun was beginning to set; the men gave us varying looks of confusion, which included Jorn and Halerod, whom we found in the center of the camp.

"What went wrong?" a concerned Jorn asked.

"The plan failed. The Diefetian general knew the size of our entire army. When I told him that an army was on its way to attack him, he didn't believe me," I explained.

"Then you failed to break the siege," the lieutenant concluded.

"The plan failed, but we didn't," clarified Billen.

"The siege has been broken then," Jorn said.

"It has been," Billen informed them.

"How?" asked Halerod.

"Billen and I got captured by some sentries. I tried to convince the Diefetian general about an army coming to break the siege, but as I said, I wasn't successful. Then, the general ordered the sentries to capture us; we disarmed them in seconds. I challenged their general to a fight, killed him, and persuaded the rest of the rest of the army to leave the country," I said.

"How did you do that?" my nephew asked.

"By turning them against their king. I told them that Salroon wanted the sword and said he sent them across the Continent to die because he didn't want to do it himself," I explained.

"That worked?" Jorn asked. He couldn't keep the surprise from his voice.

"For now. If they realize that Salroon may not just want the sword but wants to conquer Eshtar, they may be back," Billen pointed out.

"If Salroon wants to conquer Eshtar more than he wants the sword, he would have taken Kiholp by now," I countered.

"We should still be prepared just in case," argued Billen.

"What are we going to do if they come back? We are still outnumbered," Halerod asked.

"He has a point," Billen said, turning to me. "Even if it's not the same army that comes, Salroon will send another to besiege the city."

"Either way, we will have time to prepare," I said.

"We could fortify the city more," Jorn proposed.

"How?" I asked.

"The walls are some of the largest on the Continent, so we can't do much there, but we could dig a trench around the city, making it more difficult to scale the walls with ladders or siege towers," he suggested.

"It could help," Billen agreed.

"We could do something similar for the other border cities," I said.

"We will have to coordinate with the king," Billen stated.

"We should go back to Kiholp," Jorn said.

"What happens if the Diefetian army does turn around?" Halerod asked. "The city will be doomed, and we will be halfway across the country."

"Their general is dead, and their morale is poor; I doubt they will be back," I said.

"He's got a point," Billen said.

"Yes, and what can we do? We only have fifty men. If we go back to the capital, we can check to see if the rest of the army has been mobilized. We can do much more if the Diefetians return if we have a force to match theirs," Jorn argued.

"Good point," conceded BIllen.

"Back to Kiholp then," Halerod said.

"We will break camp in the morning," I said, then told everyone to get some sleep.

When I walked back to my tent, all I thought about was how to fight a war with three thousand men, the same size as the Diefetian army I had convinced to leave. Add that to the thousand which besieged Gregoros, and Salroon could field at least a thousand more men than us. Most of the Diefetian soldiers were experienced, having been fighting half of the Continent for the last several years, while Eshtar's soldiers were ill-trained, and the odds became suicidal.

If my forces were equally trained, I could win a war against a more enormous army. Fighting with inferior numbers was one of Father's earliest lessons, a lesson I put well to use during my bandit days when my clan was outnumbered by our pursuers. In both cases, I often had the superior trained force, but now I had the inferior one. My brother expected me to give him a miracle.

How someone as sensible as my brother could have let the Eshtaran army shrink to such a minuscule size is a mystery to me. Rono did the right thing, ending the wars the Wretched King was fighting with diplomacy and then pursuing a foreign policy of peace and trade. But after the Wretched King's reign, many countries were bitter towards Eshtar, and plenty still considered themselves Eshtar's enemies. It would have made sense to keep a modestly sized army if only to deter attack.

The war dominated my thoughts before I fell asleep, yet it did not dominate my dreams. I stood alone and unarmed on a field lit by a full moon. A misty darkness surrounded the edges of the field, obscuring my vision and preventing me from looking further past the field.

Soon, five men emerged from the murk to surround me: Lords Gaenic and Leernu, Ambassador Zimkoo, Ilonek, and General Nilomek. They all appeared as they did in life, except their eyes glowed crimson. At first, they all formed a line in front of me, with Gaenic to my far left, Leernu next to him, Zimkoo in the middle, Ilonek at Leernu's side, and Nilomek to my far right.

Gaenic took a step forward and addressed me, though I couldn't understand the language he spoke. It didn't sound like anything spoken on the Continent. Seeing my confusion, Gaenic switched to my native tongue.

"You have managed to kill five of us and know our true nature," the dead lord spoke. "Yet, you do not understand what you have done, what you will face." Then he stepped back, and Leernu moved forward.

"This is not the war that you think it is, Bowv," Leernu told me. "Your enemy is not who you presume it to be." Then he, too, stepped back into line, and Zimkoo stepped forward.

"You struck me down in cold blood, and I was not the first," spoke the ambassador. "Who would have ever thought a murderer would be chosen?" He returned to his place between Leernu and Ilonek, the latter steeped towards me.

"You escaped my trap. But not even someone as resourceful as you can stop what is coming. The time is near; the promise will be fulfilled," Ilonek said, then moved back between Zimkoo and Nilomek, the latter of whom stepped forward.

"My army routs back to Diefet because of your persuasion, but not even your silver tongue can get Fate to release you from her chains," the general said, rejoining the line.

After all five specters had given their speeches, they turned their backs toward me and, in unison, began to walk back toward the darkness from which they had come. They were almost back to the safety of the dark when the moon lit up brighter than the sun, and a beam of light struck the five of them, disintegrating them to ash. The moon dimmed and crawled across the sky, eventually sinking beneath the horizon.

There was no source of light, and I felt the darkness expand and move towards me. The sun began to crawl up from the horizon, and I felt its warmth, but the darkness contracted. As the sun rose, eventually taking the highest point in the sky, the darkness withered away until there was no more.

Thirteen stones stood erect along the edges of the field; each was about a foot high and shaped like an arch. There was no mistake that they were gravestones. I walked up towards one, whose inscription was in a language I couldn't understand, but certain symbols I did recognize, though I couldn't remember from where. When I began to remember, I woke up.

I got dressed and left my tent about an hour past dawn. I was happy to see that the men were up and eating breakfast in the center of the camp. I walked over and told them to meet me in front of my tent in five minutes. When they got to my tent, Billen asked what was going on.

"I had a dream last night," I said.

I shared the whole dream with them, from standing alone in the field illuminated by the moon to the sun rising and the gravestones at the end. Everyone agreed the red eyes were signs that the five dead men were vampires. But no one made much sense out of the dream; besides, the dead vampires told me something big was happening, and it was more important than the war. Billen thought the moon and the light shot from it was *Hueik,* but he couldn't understand anything else. Neither could Jorn nor Halerod.

"Looks like it's a mystery," Jorn concluded.

"I don't think it was a dream," Billen told me.

"What do you mean?" I asked. "What else could it be?"

"A vision," my old friend said.

"It can't be a vision because I was asleep," I said.

"He's right," Jorn chimed in. "The visions priests come onto them when they are awake, never when they are asleep."

"That's for priests," argued Billen. "And your uncle is far from being a priest. But you are right. When the gods bestow visions on priests, they are always awake. However, for everyone else, the gods use dreams to convey their messages. The Sacred Texts tell of numerous people the gods chose to deliver a message or to perform a specific action. Frood the Half-god is the most famous and, for us, the most important."

"What do you mean he's the most important?" I asked.

"Because Frood was the first one chosen by the gods to wield *Hueik,*" explained Billen. "And they revealed it to him in a dream. In your dream, Zimkoo mentioned you, a murderer, was chosen."

I laughed. "Billen, you know my crimes. If the gods are real, and if they are righteous and just as I have heard all my life, then they would punish me, not choose me to be their agent."

"The gods can find use for anyone, even the most undeserving," Billen said.

"Put that ridiculous Temple propaganda out of your mind and think! If the Protectorate is real, and they have chosen me to kill vampires, then they must not be just," I countered. "We can discuss this more on the road back to Kiholp."

I ordered the camp to be packed up, and within two hours, we were traveling back to the capital. I dispatched a messenger to Tuldum to inform the city of what happened, advise them to build a trench around the city, and inform them of possible resupply and the chance the enemy may be back at their gates sooner than they thought.

Billen's suggestion that we coordinate with my brother on such matters was a good idea, but it would have been a waste of time if Rono had done what I had suggested anyway. I knew my brother would think Tuldum digging a trench and getting resupplied were good ideas, so there was no point in going back to the capital and having him order it.

While I would have to wait for Rono to authorize the resupply, I wasn't going to waste time traveling back to the capital to tell Rono to order a trench dug around Tuldum and then have a messenger travel to Tuldum to give the city's mayor the message to construct a trench. It was much easier for me to send the messenger, and it would give the garrison at Tuldum more time to finish the trench because the Diefetians would attempt to capture the city again

As we trudged back to the capital, Billen tried to convince me that the gods had chosen me as their champion. I told him he was wrong, and I was sure my brother, for once, would agree with me.

But Billen didn't give up. He kept pressing the issue. While Billen and I debated, we weren't paying attention to the road as well as we should have. I should have ignored Billen, but I couldn't. At that point, I believed in vampires. It was impossible not to. I had killed five "men" with fangs who didn't bleed. I had to let go of my disbelief and accept the existence of vampires; otherwise, I wouldn't be able to understand the whole nature of my enemy.

The gods, though, were another matter. I could see with my own two eyes vampires existed, but I couldn't say the same for the gods. If anything, vampires confirmed my atheism. If the gods lived, they couldn't allow abominations like vampires to exist. I knew Billen and my brother would insist that Hueik was evidence of the gods' existence.

But that argument was weak. Never had I seen a god forge a sword before, but plenty of times, I've witnessed a blacksmith make one. Therefore, I believe a man forged *Hueik* and not a god.

To my surprise, Billen didn't make this argument, but he still insisted the gods were real because I had killed vampires, and it drove me over the edge. Believing the gods couldn't exist in the same world vampires did and sick of hearing "gods" and "vampires" in the same sentence, my sole focus became debating Billen. I was too focused because instead of surveying the area around us, as I had been trained to do since I was a child, I was too busy coming up with arguments and counterarguments.

In contrast, most of the men appeared to be on alert, scanning the road and the forest for the enemy. I preferred them being on edge since we walked straight into Ilonek's ambush on the road to Tuldum, and it meant I could devote all my attention to debating Billen.

But we were the group's veterans who knew better than to let a debate take our focus off the road. In my defense, Billen refused to drop the subject matter, though that's not an excuse. I was in charge and should have ordered Billen to stop. We were the only two who could thoroughly scan the tree line, yet we were too caught up in our debate to do so.

No one saw the archers. The first arrows were shot from the tree line and buried into various body parts. Having an experienced ear for the moans and cries of battle, I guessed those first few arrows killed two and wounded five. I let out a string of curses as rage filled me from head to toe.

The archers had to be the same ones who were a part of Ilonek's ambush and must have been ordered to watch the road from Tuldum to Kiholp to ensure we wouldn't make it back if we managed to break the siege. It had been a decade at least since I was caught off guard by the same enemy. While I wanted to chop off the heads of my men for not seeing the archers, I became angrier as I realized it was my fault.

I was on campaign with city guards, not the experienced soldiers I led as a prince. I was the one in charge and should have stopped debating Billen. Father's words echoed in my head: "A commander does not blame his men for his mistakes. You will fail; it is initiable, but when you do, move past it quickly."

I barked for the men to raise their shields. If they had been experienced soldiers, they would have done it on their own, but they weren't. The men weren't accustomed to combat, and most stood still as the arrows flew out of the surrounding forest. Even after I had shouted, some of them still were frozen.

The arrows found their marks, and bodies fell. I heard cries of pain from survivable wounds and the cries of the dying. That time, I couldn't tell how many there were of each as they were drowned out by the thuds of arrows slamming into shields.

I didn't have a shield. An arrow zipped past my cheek, and another buried itself in the ground next to me with a thud. I scanned the tree line to find where the archers were. They were lined up on both sides of the road. I could see the heads of the Diefetian arrows, a bit of their bows, and the hands gripping them. Leaves and branches obscured the rest of their bodies.

I considered splitting the men into two groups and having each group rush a line of archers. It may have worked if I commanded veteran troops who could move fast with their shields up. Then, I realized I had been spoiled as a commander when it came to the quality of my troops. In the Eshtaran army, I had access to some of the Continent's most battle-hardened soldiers. In my bandit days, I recruited skilled fighters and drilled them so much that my bandit clan became an elite fighting force. Before I had agreed to become my brother's military advisor, I had never fought with a force comprised of inexperienced troops.

I heard another cry as an arrow found its mark, and I cleared my thoughts. If I didn't think of something quickly, we would all be dead in minutes.

I knew rushing the archers was suicidal since the men didn't have the discipline to remain in formation as they charged the archers. My men would break and become easy targets for the archers. The Diefetians had us beat; we had to retreat.

I shouted to fall back. More arrows found their marks, but this time, I heard more arrows slamming into shields than I did cries of pain. My men kept their shields up and tried to stay close together as they walked backward on the road towards Tuldum. I spotted Billen, one arm with a shield strapped to it and with his other hand dragging a wounded soldier, who had an arrow in his thigh. Billen must have taken the shield from the soldier because the smith had only brought a sword on campaign.

The Diefetians honed in on Billen like the weak link he was. Arrows zipped all around Billen; one flew over his head, missing by inches; another landed where his foot was a moment ago, and another soared by his side. So many arrows slammed into Billen's shield that I was amazed the man could still hold the thing up. I shouted for Billen to leave the man behind. There was no point in Billen getting killed when the Diefetians would just take the man captive.

Billen turned his head toward me and we locked eyes. Never had I seen a man look with such disgust before. Not wanting to divert his attention from the deadly arrows for too long, Billen held my gaze for a moment or two, but the intensity of his look made it feel as if it lasted for hours. Billen always possessed a stark determination whenever it came to completing a mission. Yet, as he looked at me while dragging the wounded soldier, there was something more than sheer willpower giving Billen strength.

I didn't stand around thinking what it was. I walked towards Billen and the wounded soldier, knowing the only thing that would stop the archers from aiming at the two of them would be to give them another target. More arrows zipped past me before I got within a yard of Billen. As one passed over me, I could feel the wind it created move my hair.

While being bait, I noticed the rest of my men, who weren't riddled with arrows, were coming towards Billen. I shouted for the men to form a defensive circle around Billen and the soldier. The rang of arrows hitting shields had drowned out my voice. I shouted again. No one heard me. I was going to shout again when I heard Jorn echo my orders to the men. Soon, we had a defensive perimeter around Billen and the soldier.

Jorn was next to Halerod, who was shouting for the men to hold formation and keep their shields up. Quickly, I looked to see if any of them still had their supplies, and three of them did. A plan began to form in my mind.

I ordered some soldiers to get down on one knee, continuing to hold their shields, while the others stood up and held their shields above the men who were kneeling, providing our full bodies with protection. Once this was done, I got to work. The standard Eshtaran army cooking supplies include a ration of cooking oil, a cloth to clean any pots and pans, flint-and-steel, and two animal skin canteens.

More arrows came soaring out of the forest and came smashing into shields. Commandeering cooking oil from one soldier who had it and another's flint and steel, I emptied both of my canteens and filled them with cooking oil. Halerod, who put together what I was doing, volunteered his washing cloths and his extra canteen, which I promptly filled with oil.

I dunked a cloth into an oil-filled canteen, let it soak for a moment, pulled it out, and then did the same for the other. I heard arrows hit their mark. I heard the thuds of arrows on shields and two cries of pain as arrows pierced flesh. My hands began to move faster. I tied a knot at the bottom of each cloth, small enough so that the rest could stick out of the canteen's top but large enough that the cloths would stay in the canteens. I was finished as the next heavy wave of arrows came.

One of the first things an Eshtaran soldier learns is never to let his cooking oil burn. It isn't a high-quality cooking oil like the Hunderians provide their armies with. When Hunderian cooking oil burns, it burns without smoke and doesn't smell. The Eshtaran cooking is the complete opposite. When it burns, it's accompanied by a cloud of thick smoke and a strong, nasty smell.

The Diefetians kept shooting their arrows, and I heard shields absorb their impact and a few more cries of pain. Despite the screams of agony, our defense held. I told the men what we were about to do and where to go. As I used the flint and steel to ignite one of the cloths sticking out of one of the oil-filled canteens, I ordered Halerod to assign men to drag or carry our wounded. The Diefetians remained relentless in firing their arrows as a spark spawned from the flint-and-steel landed on the cloth and ignited a small flame. Quickly, the flame grew, and I gave the order.

Two soldiers facing one side of the forest removed their shields, giving me an opening. Spotting the Diefetians in the thicket of trees, I aimed and threw the canteen. It soared towards the enemy, leaving a trail of smoke and a disgusting smell behind it. The men took up their positions again, but no arrows came from that side of the forest.

Hurrying, I began work on lighting the second canteen's cloth. Arrows continued to fly out of the other side of the forest, resulting in numerous thuds and one cry. I heard Halerod ask who was hit and how bad. A soldier answered and reassured the lieutenant he was fine. Striking the flint-and-steel with urgency, a spark finally was made and landed on the cloth igniting it.

I gave the order. Two soldiers moved out of the way, giving me an opening to throw the canteen. Scanning the tree line, I spotted the Diefetians and threw the canteen. It arched towards them, leaving a trail of smoke behind and a pungent smell like its twin. After waiting a few moments for the smoke to spread, I ordered to break the formation and begin the retreat.

The protective shield ring broke, and the men Halerod had assigned to the wounded were quickly dragging them, carrying them, or holding them up and having them lean on them as they hopped on one leg. We should have left the wounded behind since we needed to withdraw before the smoke disappeared. But Billen wasn't going to let that happen, and he was too valuable an asset to leave behind and be captured.

The obvious and stupid move would have been to get as far down the road as we could before night fell. Instead, we melded into the forest, where we could hide from the Diefetians. The only problem was that moving with wounded men through the woods slowed us down to a snail's pace.

I decided we didn't need to go too deep in the forest. The Diefetians had the advantage because they were archers, and we moved slowly. If we had stayed on the road, they would have riddled us with arrows. But the forest trees would grant us cover from arrows.

We filed into the woods, with men helping to carry whoever could not walk. After staggering through the woods for hours, I ordered everyone to rest. Those who were carrying the wounded were breathing heavily and struggling to keep their eyes open. We placed the wounded in the most comfortable spot we could find, and everyone else sat down on the forest floor to rest. I looked around and counted how many of us made it out.

Including Jorn, Halerod, Billen, and myself, we had fifty-four men before the ambush. Now we had thirty-six. I didn't know how many of the seventeen were dead or were wounded and left behind, but it didn't matter.

The Diefetians had wiped out about a third of my force, not including the six wounded, we managed to drag with us. I only had thirty men, including myself, who could fight.

Before the ambush, we couldn't afford a direct fight; now, a confrontation would be suicidal. We needed to make it back to Kiholp without encountering any Diefetians. We needed to stick to the forest cover to have any chance of making it back to the capital without encountering more Diefetian soldiers.

We didn't have any medics with us. Billen and I were the only ones who knew how to get arrows out of people, dress a wound, and wrap a bandage. Jorn asked me how I knew all this and if Father had made me do some medical training when I was young. I laughed and said when I was young, I had to go to medical tents, count the wounded, the dead, the fatally wounded, and those wounded so badly they would have to be discharged from the army and sent home because they couldn't find anymore, then report.

I would be in the medical tents for hours, and I saw the medics and the healers assisting them in their work. After seeing so many wounds get dressed and bandaged, it's hard not to pick up on the procedure. The same applied to pulling arrows out of people. Whenever I went into a medical tent, someone was getting an arrow taken out of them.

I was never squeamish around blood when I was young, but it wouldn't have mattered. I would have had to learn to bear the sight of blood, like the medics and healers, because my job required me to. The job also required me to look at horrible wounds without reacting. There are few things in life so haunting as looking at a soldier with a deep slash on his face, where a sword just missed his eye, and blood running down half of his face.

A face slash would give the soldier a scar once it healed, and if worse came to worse, then they would be missing an eye, though I rarely saw that. The wounds soldiers died of the most were by far stomach wounds. Often, the ones with gaping wounds in their stomach were dead before they were brought to the medical tents.

There was one soldier I saw whose stomach was opened wide by a sword, and his guts were falling out. I marked him as fatally wounded and continued with my rounds. By the time I came back, the soldier was lying on a cot, his guts having been put back into his stomach and had stitches across his stomach.

By the time I was fourteen, I must have seen all the possible wounds a battlefield could produce and knew which were survivable and which were fatal. Looking around at our six wounded sprawled out across the forest floor, I knew they would all pull through. But about half of them wouldn't be ready to fight for some time. Two were hit in the shoulder, one in the arm, and I had to pull arrows out of three thighs. On top of not being able to fight, the men with thigh wounds needed help to walk, and whoever was helping them wasn't going to be fighting.

After I treated the last wounded, Billen approached me with a clenched jaw, narrowed eyes, and scrunched eyebrows. Both of his hands were clenched in a fist.

"If you're going to use those fists, you better not miss," I warned him.

"We should go for a walk," he said through clenched teeth and waved for me to follow him.

We walked through the forest in silence, stepping over tree roots that had broken through the ground and ducking beneath branches. When we were far enough from the camp, Billen stopped and faced me. The blacksmith opened his mouth and unleashed a tempest on me.

"How in the gods' names could you tell me to leave the man I was carrying? For the seven years I was a part of your bandit clan, never once did you tell anyone to leave a wounded man behind, and we were the scum of the Continent, villains who deserved whatever fate we received if we were captured. But now, after I have agreed to accompany you while you lead soldiers fighting for their country's survival in a desperate war, you tell me to leave a wounded man behind. What's wrong with you, Bowv?

"These men are fighting against the odds to defend their kingdom. They don't deserve to be left wounded on the battlefield. I've seen you fight through swarms of enemies to rescue a clan member, a criminal, yet today, you wanted me to leave a wounded man behind. Why?"

"Because these men aren't criminals," I said and watched as the anger drained from Billen's face to be replaced with confusion. His fists unraveled.

"What?" he asked. His jaw was slackened, his eyebrows raised, and his eyes wide.

"Criminals get tortured and executed when caught. Soldiers get captured and ransomed back to their army or are exchanged as prisoners," I explained.

I went on, "A lesson my father taught me was if you find yourself in a position where your army is threatened to be wiped out, you cannot afford to evacuate the wound. Your charge as a commander is to save your army and trust your enemy will take prisoners of war and members of the Temple will come and treat them. If the wounded die, it is the gods' decision, not yours as a commander."

Billen fell silent. He began to say something in response, then stopped just as he began to open his mouth. Then he closed it, taking the time to think of what I had just said and to come up with a rebuttal. I stood there with my hands clasped and resting on my stomach, waiting to see what he would come up with, but no rebuttal came.

"While you are a great warrior and old friend and have survived fights where less skilled men would have died, this is the first time you are fighting a war. You know a little about war since whenever the clan found itself in a precarious position, you've witnessed me rely on my experiences as a soldier to get us out of those situations. But waging war is what I was brought up to do, so on campaign when I order you to do something keep that in mind.

"I know war as both an art and the death struggle that it is. You don't. You know how to fight as a bandit but know nothing about the subtleties of war and the brutal calculous of commanding an army. I wouldn't have had to explain myself if you did, old friend. You would have known as a commander that my responsibility was to evacuate the able-bodied and trust that the Diefetians would have abided by the Laws of War, taken the wounded captive, and treated them as best as they could. Or have members of the Temple do it, as the Diefetians always do, even under Salroon.

"You think I am fighting this war because I want Salroon dead for authorizing my death. Fair enough. But as my brother's military advisor, have I acted as a bandit? I could have snuck off and killed Ilonek if I wanted to, but I didn't because I am in a position where I have to be a soldier else

Eshtar becomes the latest Diefetian providence and Salroon frees up more resources to hunt me down.

"I know it's difficult for you to stop thinking of me as a bandit, but you need to stop. I am a soldier, nothing more, nothing less. If you can't comprehend that, then you jeopardize whatever mission we're sent on and the lives of the men I lead. If that's the case, tell me now, so when we get back to Kiholp, you can help the war effort by resuming blacksmithing and leaving the fighting to me," I said, the intensity clear in my voice.

"You're right. I haven't fought any wars, and you have. If I had, I might have understood your reasoning when you told me to leave Kalrel," he admitted.

"Who's Kalrel?" I asked without thinking. As soon as the question left my lips, I knew the answer.

"The wounded man I was pulling. You still haven't learned any of the men's names, have you?" asked the smith.

"I think that's obvious," I told him.

"Why?" he asked. "You knew every member of the clan even when we were a hundred strong."

"I recruited most of those men myself," I reminded him.

"That's not an answer," he pointed out. "You can tell the others whatever you like, Bowv, but I've known you too long. You're making a decision not to learn the men's names, whether it's a conscious one or not."

"Why should I bother? They likely won't survive this war," I answered, but as I said it, I knew there was more to it than that. Billen did, too; he was looking at me, but he didn't press the issue. I don't know why, but after staring at me for a while, he nodded and said we should get back to camp.

Silence was our companion as we walked back to camp. As we walked back, I realized the real reason I didn't learn any of the men's names. But as soon as it revealed itself to me, I dismissed it, sending it back into hiding, trying to convince myself I gave Billen the real reason I didn't bother learning any of the men's names. With truth comes pain, and at that moment, I didn't want to deal with the pain, so I buried the truth and decided to lie to myself. Both were things I had a lot of practice at.

Chapter Twelve

A S WE WALKED INTO CAMP, we noticed the tents were already pitched, including the small medical tent we had brought. In my mind, I credited Halerod for ordering the tents to be set up but cursed the fool for the campfire roaring away in the center. I walked up to the flame with a clenched jaw and hands balled into fists. The soldiers sitting around the campfire jumped up and scurried off like rabbits when they saw me approach.

No one dared stop me as I kicked dirt onto the fire. It took several minutes for me to extinguish the flames, but that was for the best. By the time I smothered the fire, I was no longer angry. I called everyone to gather around, and soon, I was facing everyone who was able to stand.

"You all did well setting up camp so fast," I said. "But why would you think it was a good idea to light a campfire when the enemy is looking for us?"

Some men looked down; others just stood there speechless. No one spoke. What would they say? They knew they had put us in danger. Why they thought lighting a campfire was a good idea after we were ambushed is something I didn't know was due to inexperience or stupidity.

"From now on until we reach Kiholp, I want you all to have one thing on your minds: we are being hunted, and if you fail to act like it, I can assure you that you won't make it back to Kiholp alive," I told them and saw a small sea of nodding heads. What I didn't tell them was I was as liable to kill them if they continued to make such stupid decisions. Since everyone was assembled, I turned to Halerod and told him to set up a watch and assign people to look after the wounded, then went to set up my tent.

While setting up my tent, Jorn offered to help since the sun was setting, but I declined. Jorn didn't go away. I could feel him standing there watching me.

I sighed. "What is it you really want?"

"Does it get easier?" my nephew asked with a shaky voice.

"I need more, kid," I said as I continued to set up my tent.

"Seeing people get killed," he softly said.

"Why are you asking me?" I asked.

"You're my uncle," the prince answered.

"Kid, I've just met you what about a month ago? Before your father told me who you were, I thought you were a courtier, so being your uncle doesn't count for much other than asking me questions about the past as you've been doing," I told him.

"Oh," an embarrassed Jorn said, and he began to walk away.

"Where are you going?" I asked. "Didn't your father teach you not to walk away until you get a proper answer? Or did my brother forget to teach you that lesson?"

I heard Jorn walk back. I had already finished setting up the tent and told him to sit by the entrance. He did, and I took a seat right down next to him.

"I remember asking your grandfather the same thing when he took me on campaign for the first time. It was after the Battle of Weiks Pass. The Bendilli were already pushed out of Eshtar by that time, and the war was over when your grandfather took his armies deep into their territory and defeated army after army. But our dear Bendilli neighbors are stubborn people, and saying they don't hold grudges is laughable.

"So, when there were reports of a large Bendilli army heading for the border years after a peace treaty was signed, no one was surprised. The quickest way to get into Eshtar from Bendill is Weiks Pass through the Illeri Mountains. The Illeri are not the largest mountains on the Continent, far from it, nor are they challenging to traverse, but hiking over mountains will always slow an army down no matter their height.

"No doubt hoping if they were fast enough, they would catch us off guard. The Bendilli chose the quickest route: Weiks Pass. Unfortunately for them, your grandfather suspected the Bendilli wouldn't take their defeat well and, when they were strong enough, attack Eshtar again.

"Our army was assembled at the Pass, blocking it off and patiently waiting for the Bendilli when their advance guard was spotted. When they saw us, they quickly turned around, no doubt going to tell their commanders we were blocking the exit.

"It was the sensible thing to do since your grandfather had blocked the mouth of the pass. About three thousand spearmen bunched between the edges of the Pass, creating a thicket of eight-foot-long spears. Along with their spear, each man was armed with a sword. Instead of the standard Eshtaran shield, which was round, protected most of the torso, and allowed for a reasonable degree of maneuverability, they were equipped with long rectangular shields.

"The bottom of the rectangular shield could rest on the ground and still provide the user protection until the end of their neck. With the rectangular shields, men could be lined up next to each other with their shields touching and using their spears overhead, or the men could be lined up with enough space between them to use their spears at their side.

"The first row of spearmen was arranged with small gaps between them, while the lines behind them were locked shield to shield and had to use their spears over their shields so the first row's spears were pointing straight out and could thrust at the center of the enemy soldier's body and the row behind them could attack from above.

"Archers were behind the spearmen with orders to fire on the approaching Bendilli, but those weren't the only archers. As a precaution, your grandfather put some archers in the mountains on each side of the pass. They had orders to fire only if the Bendilli found a way to break our lines. If that happened, then arrows coming from both sides of the pass would create enough distraction for the spearmen to regroup or begin to retreat. If a retreat was needed, the cavalry would be in a position to stall the enemy.

"The Bendilli should have turned back once they learned we were waiting for them, but they didn't. I don't know who gave the order to attack a general or their king, but it was one of the dumbest military decisions in the history of the Continent. Wave after wave of Bendilli soldiers were thrown against our spearmen. In droves, they came, and in droves, they were killed.

"After the Bendilli finally gave up, their dead numbered over two thousand. We could have made a wall of corpses to block the entrance to the pass. The ground at the entrance of the pass was painted red with blood. When the sun's rays came running across the mountaintops, they did not rest on the ground but bounced off, creating a glimmer as beautiful as it was morbid.

"The night after the battle, I asked your grandfather how he dealt with all the death. He told me that no man will live forever and to remember that after a battle. We aren't gods kid, we die, and sometimes death comes slowly, but other times it doesn't.

"People don't like it when death comes in droves because they can't escape back into their disillusion that they can't die. When people are facing a large amount of death, they are forced to stare the truth about their mortality in the face and can't escape it.

"Your grandfather taught me not to be afraid of death, to accept it as a natural process, and when men are being killed all around you, not to be disoriented. Their time has come, as yours will come one day. As the dead have passed from this life to the next, so will you."

The sun was setting by the time I finished talking. Jorn didn't say anything for a while; he just sat there thinking about my answer. Whether he found it helpful or not, I didn't know. With this morbid talk over, I was reminded though my brother told me to keep his son alive after the ambush, I knew his chances of survival had dropped.

The men I had, especially Jorn, whose military training I had to provide while we were on the march, weren't experienced enough to survive being hunted down by a better trained and determined enemy. Add the enemy's advantage in numbers to that, and it was suicidal for me to take a group of soldiers outside of a walled city.

I was about to suggest Jorn go back to his tent before it got completely dark, but he spoke before I could. "How do you deal with killing?" he asked.

"I'm the Terror of the Continent. You're assuming I've got a conscience," I said. "Besides, I don't think you killed anyone at Gregoros. Did you?"

He shook his head. "But it's what you're training me to do, and we're fighting a war. It's bound to happen eventually. Could you tell me how you dealt with it as a soldier?" he asked.

I let out a laugh. I had to give the boy credit. If his father had shown he was capable of such basic foresight, then he wouldn't have needed me to fight his war for him.

"How did I deal with killing? First, I didn't make the mistake of not thinking about it. I've seen soldiers bury what they did, and if they didn't snap, then they didn't like to talk about the war. When you kill in war, it's different than murder. Some philosophers and scholars disagree with that, but they haven't done either. I've killed in war, and I've murdered; they're similar acts but aren't the same. The outcomes are the same, but situations and mindsets are different; if anyone else tells you otherwise, they haven't done both.

"In war, you're nothing more than a cog in the machine. You're the one doing the killing, but you aren't the one who started the war, and you're not the one who dictates where your army marches. Your job is to follow orders and to fight, and fighting involves killing.

"It's something you must accept as your job and nothing more. If you are a king, you must fight the wars you started. Otherwise, you are dodging the consequences of your actions, and no one, noble or peasant, will respect you.

"Now murder, on the other hand. It's all your decisions. You decide who to kill, where to kill them, and how to do it. And you don't want your victim fighting back. In war, you fight the guy in front of you. Maybe you intend to kill him, or maybe you don't, but it's either you're getting stabbed or he is."

"I was hoping for a more optimistic answer," my nephew said.

"There's nothing optimistic about war, kid," I told him. "Now go back to your tent and get some sleep before it gets too dark to see."

Jorn nodded and walked off in the direction of his tent. Deciding it was best if I did the same, I opened the flap of my tent and went to sleep. As sleep fell over me like a gentle rain, I wondered if we would return to Kiholp. Only one successful ambush by a small number of archers was needed to thin our ranks. Knowing the archers, or some other Diefetian force, would come again, I thought of what we could do to prevent being surprised again, then stopped as my weighted eyes closed and sleep overtook me.

Chapter Thirteen

WHEN DAWN'S FIRST LIGHT made its way through the maze of branches and leaves to shine on the forest floor, I was already up, dressed, and ordering the men to break camp. With verbal encouragement to make them move faster, we marched through the forest within an hour after dawn. Wearing grumpy faces and dark circles under their eyes, the men marched forward with the sluggishness of people unaccustomed to sleeping on the hard forest floor and then having to wake up early the next day.

The thick forest made it difficult to walk in the two columns we had been in while traveling on the road. We marched in four loose and different lines, with Jorn, Halerod, Billen, and myself being the heads of the lines. The wounded and the men who were carrying them were immediately behind us or as close as they could be with the trees in the way. Then, behind them were the able-bodied.

I called for a stop around noon so the men could rest and eat lunch. Before everyone was done eating, I ordered the camp to be broken down so we could begin moving again. The men who hadn't finished eating expressed their unhappiness on their faces, but I didn't care how they felt. The longer we remained in one spot, the higher the chance the Diefetians would find us.

There was silence when we were back, ducking underneath tree branches and carefully stepping over roots that broke through the forest floor, though I didn't ban talking while we marched. The absence of conversation was natural, and in its absence were tense, wide-eyed men carefully scanning their surroundings.

An hour before sunset, I stopped the men and ordered camp to be set up. The forest had gotten thicker than the area where we had made our first camp, but there still was room to set up the tents and ensure the wounded had a comfortable spot. Without a medic or a healer, Billen took it upon himself to look after the wounded.

There was no shortage of bandages and other medical supplies because each Eshtaran soldier carries some as a part of their kit, though it wasn't always that way. Father had made the change because he wanted to decrease supply lines and was sick of seeing soldiers die of treatable wounds just because medical supplies had run out.

After I had called for a rest and watched Billen change the bandage of a wounded soldier, Halerod walked over to me. The lieutenant wore his usual concerned look whenever he was going to ask me a question.

"What's your concern?" I asked.

"How did you know it was a concern?" the lieutenant asked.

"Your facial expression gives it away," I told him.

"If I were better at hiding my emotions, then I would have been a diplomat or a spy and not a soldier," Halerod noted.

"What's your concern," I repeated, not bothering to hide the annoyance in my voice.

"We've been marching in the forest for two days now, and it occurred to me that we are going deeper into the forest and not trying to get back on the road to return to the capital. I understand we are making sure we lose the Diefetians if they are on our trail, but shouldn't we be trying to get back to the road by now?" he asked.

"A fair question, lieutenant," I told him. "Whenever a determined enemy pursues you, you must make it difficult for them to find you and get to you."

"Of course, but don't we also have to get back to the capital to inform the king about our success?" Halerod asked.

"Yes, we do, but if you were the Diefetians, what would you do, knowing we needed to get back to Kiholp to do so?" I asked him.

"I would watch the roads to Kiholp and have men ready to intercept you," Halerod answered.

"And do you think, lieutenant, there will be more or less small groups of Diefetian soldiers like the archers who ambushed us, watching the roads waiting to spot us?" I asked.

"More," he said.

Halerod was a good lieutenant in the sense he knew all the soldiers under him, could keep the men in line, kept order in the camp as well as his senses in battle, and knew when to follow a superior's orders and when to voice his opinion. But the man wasn't promoted beyond lieutenant because he couldn't think about the larger picture.

"This is why we aren't going to be sticking to the roads anymore lieutenant until Kiholp's walls are in our site and cavalry can be sent out to assist us if the Diefetians do decide to attack us so close to the capital," I said.

"Understood, I'll go tell the men we won't be seeing any roads for a while," Halerod said, then walked away.

"And inform the men I will be stopping by their tents in the morning," I told him.

"For inspections?" a confused Halerod asked.

"No, to learn their names. Regardless of not being a part of the army and just an advisor, we all know I am the de facto commander, and a commander needs to know the soldiers he's leader," I explained.

"You know they're terrified of you. Many of them hate you," he informed me.

"I know. Those who hate me have a good reason for it. If they don't fear me then they're stupid," I said and dismissed him.

Halerod walked over to the nearest group of soldiers to inform them I would be stopping by. If our situation allowed us to have a fire, then I would have talked to the men that night so they weren't nervous before going to sleep. But our enemies did not permit us such luxuries. Just before dawn broke, I was outside of a tent talking to the first soldier of the morning.

Hunder was his name and he was twenty years old. Terror burned in his eyes as bright as torchlight at night. Worry pushed around his voice, unbalancing his pitch, and providing for frequent stops as he struggled to let the words out of his mouth. He was from Kiholp and had joined the army because his father and grandfather were both soldiers. When I said it sounded like he didn't have a choice in the matter, the young soldier nodded his head.

Then there was Pendol. The man was at least a decade older than Hundar, was from Eshtar's southeastern countryside, and became a soldier so he wouldn't have to be a farmer for the rest of his life. While the man was tense when speaking to me, he didn't stutter or trip over his words. Nor did he act upon the hatred which shone through his eyes.

Hundar and Pendol were bookends and everyone else fell between them. Hundar was the youngest of the group and Pendol was the oldest. Some soldiers could talk to me a bit better than Hundar, while others approached Pendol's level of calm. Many of them were from cities, but few were from the capital, while others grew up in more rural areas, but not as remote as Pendol was from. Despite the small size of the Esharan army, it still managed to find recruits from all over the kingdom.

While all of them, in one way or another, showed their fear of me, I could feel the hatred most of them had towards me. I could tell whose family member or friend I killed or whose village I sacked or extorted because their hatred formed a thick aura around them. To their credit, they all remained professional.

It takes a great deal of self-control and discipline for a man to look at another who he knows has done him great harm and not throw a punch at him, let alone refrain from saying something unpleasant. I was surprised.

When I was done talking to all of them, including the wounded, who were surprised to see me since I didn't tell Halerod I planned to talk to them, we were back marching through the woods towards Kiholp. As we traveled, there were no signs of the Diefetians pursuing us. Whether that meant they couldn't determine where we went, had given up their pursuit, or were close by.

I didn't know which but decided a little paranoia wouldn't hurt in case it was the latter. Two days later, I lifted the ban on the campfire since we had traveled far from the spot of the ambush and there still was no sign of the Diefetians.

With the wounded, we were moving slower, and I expected it would take us more than a week to reach Kiholp. I hoped my brother wouldn't do anything foolish until he got word from Tuldum or had a credible report of our deaths. If I had trekked more than a week through a forest and found out my brother had surrendered, I would not have been furious like a lion whose prey had escaped.

We made it out of the forest on the eighth day and the flat plains of central Eshtar sprawled out before us. We didn't run into trouble. Under normal circumstances, the journey from the forest edge to the capital city would have taken two days with the number of people in our group. But we had wounded who still couldn't move without the aid of another, so I expected us to reach Kiholp in four days. Even though we were so close to the capital, I was far more nervous about this stretch of the journey than any other.

The forest slows one down, but that is the price you pay to be hidden by it. The plains offer quick, unhindered movement at the cost of being visible for miles around. On the fourth day, I knew we would be within sight of the city walls and if the Diefetians did choose to attack us, my brother could send out cavalry to rescue us. For the other three days, the Diefetians could attack and we would have nowhere to hide and no hope of reinforcements coming to save us.

"At least here, we can see for miles and will know if we're being pursued," Billen said, reading my mind.

"I don't think it matters if we know we are *currently* being pursued since we know Salroon has his soldiers hunting for the sword," I said.

"So, we are going to assume someone is after us," Billen concluded. "I thought soldering would be different from banditry."

"You would be surprised how much they have in common," I said.

"That's not a pleasant thought," my old friend said.

"The truth rarely is," I said.

"Only if you accept the grim truths of life," Billen assured me.

"Grim truths are the only truths," I told him.

"That's a lie Bowv and you know it," he argued.

"And you're being foolish," I countered.

Billen let out a laugh. "Well, who's the fool in this case? There are two painters, both equal in skill and ability, who can paint anything. One painter decides he has had enough of painting with a full pallet, and rejects the lighter hues deciding to paint only with darker ones, while the other painter continues to paint with a full pallet. Who's the fool?"

"I see your point, but the painter who paints with a full pallet is the fool," I answered.

"Why?" the blacksmith asked.

"Because the world may be filled with colors, but that doesn't mean each color reflects the truth of the world. The painter who paints with the darker hues recognizes the true nature of this world: one of hardship, pain, and misery. Because the painter with a full pallet doesn't recognize the nature of the world: the sunny, happy place it appears to be is an illusion. When he paints with bright colors he chooses to believe a lie making him not only a fool, but a naïve one," I explained.

"But even if this world is harsh and everything which says it isn't is a lie, then doesn't a painter need a full pallet to paint both the truth and the lie?" Billen asked.

"I suppose he would," I answered.

"Then wouldn't the lie be a part of the truth of the world?" he questioned.

"It would," I conceded.

"Then what makes you think it is a lie and not simply another truth of this world?" he asked.

"Because I have suffered in this life and have lived a happy life," I said. "Happiness is always replaced by suffering, so suffering must be the truth of this world and happiness must be the lie which is stripped away," I said.

"What a horrible way to look at the world," Jorn said as he approached us.

"You and Halerod are supposed to be in the front of the lines," I said.

"I'm here to let you know we haven't seen any signs of the enemy up ahead," Jorn said. "Now what is all this talk about suffering and happiness?"

"I am trying to convince your uncle that the world is not just filled with pain and suffering," Billen explained.

"It sounds like you aren't doing a good job then," Jorn told him.

"He isn't. I can't understand how after all the crimes Billen has committed, he believes suffering is not the true nature of the world," I said.

"I know too well the horrors of this world and the suffering they can cause. You know my crimes and you know them well. Unlike you, though, Bowv, I'm not foolish enough to believe the world has pain and suffering in it because that's the way it is. While I believe the gods occasionally intercede, the truth of this world is our actions make it what it is.

"It's why the painter who paints with dark colors is the fool because he does not realize this and the truth that while people are capable of atrocities their nature is to be good. Yes, I have caused suffering in this world, but I've also decided to do some good in it.

"I didn't take in my apprentice Sevent because the kid needed a job. I gave him the job because his parents died of the plague five years ago and he couldn't find a job despite being a hardworking kid. I chose to help him, though there have been plenty of times in my life I have chosen to bring people pain," Billen argued.

"I agree," Jorn said.

"We already had this conversation when you left the clan. Do you think it's a good idea to rehash old arguments when the Diefetians could be right behind us?" I asked Billen, not bothering to hide the annoyance in my voice.

"Considering Prince Jorn hasn't heard your argument before, I think so," he said.

"And I would like to hear the rest of your argument," Jorn said.

"Fine. Billen says suffering is not the natural state of the world because we choose to make one another suffer. I'll admit it is a good argument, but one which fails to understand the nature of man. Yes, we may choose not to harm others, but you two haven't realized the fundamental nature of people is to harm one another.

"The choice to not inflict pain onto others is at the core of human nature. It takes constant work to maintain and can be torn like a coat. Civil society is a perfect example of this. People work hard to have a functioning society. They get jobs, pay their taxes, follow the laws, and don't inflict harm on one another.

"Then something happens: disease, famine, war, or a natural disaster. The catastrophe strips away the illusion of civility, and then people revert to their base nature. A once thriving society becomes a wasteland of people hurting one another to survive. Civil society was created in the first place to escape this natural hell.

"The natural, savage nature of man is always there underneath the delicate layer of civilization. I chose to accept human nature and cease pretending we are something we are not. Billen made that choice, but now he has chosen to reenter the illusion. And stories of benevolent and just gods have been invented to make rejecting one's true nature easier," I explained.

"That's a depressing way to look at the world," Jorn concluded.

"It is," agreed Billen.

"Now, that's enough debating philosophy, it's getting dark and we need to make camp," I said.

They nodded their heads and walked away. While the tents were being set up, I went around asking people whether they saw any signs of the Diefetians. No one reported anything, but I suspected the Diefetian archers who had ambushed us were good at hiding their tracks. If that were the case, then the signs of them following us would have been subtle and not noticeable to my men.

A part of me was relieved no one reported anything since I knew on the plains, there was no natural cover if we were barraged by arrows. Another part of me was skeptical. I knew Salroon knew I had the sword and he wasn't going to stop trying to get it just because I escaped an ambush. More Diefetians would come the only question was whether they would come before we got back to Kiholp or after.

Then there was the question of which Diefetians would come. Would Salroon send his archers after they had failed, a vampire or another group of soldiers? Fearing the worst, that night, I talked with Billen, trying to guess who Salroon would send and whether we should take the time to set up some defenses around camp or just hope we were close enough to the city that we could make it there before the Diefetians caught up.

I told Billen no one had seen any signs of the Diefetians, but he agreed that didn't mean we weren't still being followed. We talked about whether we had been followed for an hour. If we were, then by who and how could we defend the camp against a possible attack? Though we agreed we likely weren't being followed, we disagreed on whether to set up defenses around the perimeter of the camp.

Billen wanted to dig ditches, but I was against it, arguing that the longer it would take us to reach Kiholp, the more exposed we would be. Billen disagreed, stating that we didn't see the Diefetian archers before they attacked and that the same could happen before we reached Kiholp.

I told him we were no longer in the forest and there was no place for the Diefetians to hide from us. Billen agreed.

The next few days were uneventful and knowing we could afford to slow down a bit being so close to the city I decided to continue Jorn's training. Not having done any training since the day of the ambush Jorn was rusty. Everything Jorn did, whether it was an attack or getting back to his guard, wasn't as fast or as strong as before the ambush. Every time Jorn tried to tighten his guard, he could only hold it there for a minute or two before he lost strength and dropped his shield a bit.

To motivate him to keep his shield up, I took a stick and began prodding at him whenever his shield dropped, creating a gap in his guard. Within a minute, I had landed the stick on his chest ten times. Each time I hit Jorn, his mouth would bend into a scowl.

We went on for half an hour. While Jorn was exhausted he did his best to keep his shield up by his chest, but he couldn't hold it up for that long. If he was in a shield wall of spearmen it would have gotten him killed, but fortunately, all he had to contest with was being poked by a stick.

When I ended the training, I didn't know how many times my stick landed on Jorn's chest. I lost track after fifty. Jorn had complained about how long it lasted, which was a way for him to vent out his annoyance about getting poked so many times. I laughed and told him when I was younger Glendeo would have me do the same drill for at least two hours. Knowing from personal experience how the smallest of gaps in defense can lead to death, I stuck with this drill until we got back to Kiholp.

By the time we were a two-day march from the city Jorn's stamina had increased and was managing to keep his shield up for longer. That morning, I scored forty-two hits on him, which while was a death sentence in combat, was progress nonetheless. The rest of the day was as uneventful as it was during the other days we traveled on the plains. Like the other days, I ordered the camp to be made a distance from the road, hoping the cover of the night's darkness would hide our presence from any passerbyes.

The watch was set and I settled down in my tent for a peaceful night's rest. We all were sleeping better on the flat ground of the plains compared to when we were sleeping on the bumpy forest floor where no matter where you pitched your tent you couldn't avoid the sticks scattered all across the forest's surface. I must have slept only a few hours before I heard a sound that forced me out of my tent with my weapon drawn.

Horse's hooves slamming into the ground, sounding like thunder, got closer and closer. I cursed myself for not taking Billen's advice about the ditches, then wondered how we didn't spot the cavalry sooner. We should have seen the Diefetians coming towards us. Somehow, they had remained hidden on a landscape with nothing to hide them.

I yelled for the men to get out of their tents and arm themselves. They all came rushing out, spears in hand. Some had managed to equip their helmets but the only armor most of them had was their shields. When all of them were out I began to bark orders. I assigned men to bring the wounded into the center of the camp and told everyone else to make a tight circle around them where they would stand shoulder to shoulder, backs facing the wounded, shields raised and spears pointed outwards.

I was a part of the circle with *Hueik* drawn, looking back at the way we came, away from Kiholp. It wasn't the best position for me to be in considering a sword can't be thrust at a horse as well as a spear can and I didn't have a shield. But I needed to see the enemy.

This circle of spears would have been enough to make most cavalry units on the Continent hesitate before attempting an attack, but Diefetian cavalrymen were above their peers. Famed for being the most skilled and daring light cavalry on the Continent, the Diefetians were expert horsemen who could maneuver their steads with pinpoint precision. For most of history, the Diefetian cavalry was victorious whenever they took the field, and if the battle was a loss for the Diefetian army, their cavalry would often still complete their objectives.

Despite only wearing a simple breastplate and no other armor, the Diefetians weren't afraid to come riding into a body of infantry. There were stories of Diefetian cavalry performing a frontal charge on a line of spearmen and breaking the line.

I had authorized a campfire that night, and it was close enough for us to offer some light, but it wasn't bright enough for us to see far away from the camp. The pounding of the horses' hooves grew louder and louder until the first rider like a specter emerged from the darkness. Everything was black: the horse, the rider's clothes, his thin metal breastplate, the cowl covering his face. Even his lance shaft was painted black. A bloodred scorpion, the symbol of the Kingdom of Diefet, on the middle of each of their breastplates stood out amongst the black garb.

Two more riders emerged from the depths of the dark, then three, then four more. None carried a torch or a lantern. The moon was trapped behind clouds that night, and the stars that weren't couldn't have provided enough light for the Diefetians to see. Yet, there were ten Diefetian cavalrymen charging towards us, lances lowered, undaunted by the sight of our spears.

The rider in the lead was charging straight at us. His stead rushed him forward bringing him closer and closer. When he was perhaps twenty feet away it was clear I was his intended target, a good choice considering my weapon and lack of a shield. I ordered the two soldiers next to me to aim their spears at the oncoming rider. They did so with speed and the spears moved towards me as if they were going to touch and make an inverted *V* but didn't touch, leaving enough room to fit a charging horse between the spearheads.

Undismayed by the sight of two spears ready to impale him, the Diefetian stayed his course. Within moments the blackened rider was five feet away from the tips of the spears. I ordered the two men to thrust with their spears knowing the Diefetian would be within range. But at the last second, something happened. As my men were pulling back their spears for the thrust, the horseman spurred his horse forward and increased his speed. When my men's attacks were finished the spearheads ran into each other and the clang of metal rang out across the plains.

The Diefetian rider, who was supposed to have been skewered was now in the space between the two spears inside the inverted *V*. I raised *Hueik* and extended my arm bringing the tip of my sword to be aligned with the horse's left eye. The Diefetians may have had exceptional skill when it came to riding horses but their horses were still horses. Blinders are put on horses so they are forced to look ahead and not get distracted or unsettled by their surroundings.

But when you point the tip of a sword at the eye of a horse, the blinders prevent the horse from taking its eyes off the impending danger. The horse abruptly stopped its charge. With the force of all the momentum it was building up in its charge, it went back on its hind legs, violently throwing its rider from the saddle and sending him soaring towards the other side of the spear circle. My soldiers retracted their spears as the horse's forelegs shot up from the ground, unleashing a whine as it did, then dropped its feet and ran off in the other direction.

I didn't hear the Diefetian's neck snap, but I had seen enough cavalrymen fall from their horses to know that it did. Seeing what happened to the first rider did not deter the rest of the horsemen. Other cavalrymen were charging towards us, but this time I was not their intended target. Instead, the horsemen were charging towards someone who was on my right side.

I turned to look who it was and saw Billen had come out of the protective circle, challenging the Diefetians to strike him down. The blacksmith stood straight, his shield lowered in a natural manner so it was against the side of his body not in front, and his spear pointing down with its tip resting on the ground.

One cavalryman accepted Billen's challenge and spurred his horse on ahead of his companions. As the horse carried its rider closer and closer to Billen, the trotting of its hooves was loud enough to drown out the loudest of yells. The former bandit stood there waiting.

The rider aimed his lance at the center of Billen's chest. There were thirty feet between the two, then twenty then ten. Billen had done nothing, yet he was within range of being struck by the lance. I wanted to scream for him to do something, but it wouldn't matter, Billen wouldn't have been able to hear me over the trotting of all the hooves. He was going to die and I knew it.

Then I saw Billen smile. As the Diefetian thrusted his lance, Billen with inhuman speed and the strength only someone who'd spent years at a forge hammering metal could manage, flicked his spear up from the ground and hit its shaft against the shaft of the incoming lance. The cavalryman's weapon was knocked to his left into the air, missing the blacksmith. Having created his opening, Billen quickly turned his body to the side so his shoulders were parallel with the horse's head and tail and he was facing its left flank.

As the horse's head was beginning to pass him, the blacksmith raised his shield. The horse continued to run straight past Billen, the rider knowing Billen couldn't use his spear at such a short range, kept his horse on the same course choosing to ride past Billen. When the horseman's left leg became lined up with Billen's torso, the blacksmith struck. In one crisp and fluent motion, Billen smashed his shield into the rider's leg, causing the man to unleash a cry of pain that could be heard over the drumming of the horses' hooves. The now wounded Diefetian slouched in his saddle and with what little control he could exert over his mount he rode away from us back into the black night he emerged from.

The eight remaining Deifetians weren't willing to attack with the same boldness as their two companions had and chose to circle us instead. They rode just outside the reach of our spears looking for weakness as they went. After the second lap, I saw one of the Diefetians shoot out toward us and heard one of my soldiers let out a wail as the horseman's lance found its mark. I yelled for the men to tighten the circle before the Diefetians could exploit the gap. Within moments our circle had shrunk and the gap closed.

The men didn't need any motivation or instruction from me. Everyone knew if the circle broke, we would all be dead. Two more Diefetians rushed in. One's horse whined as it stopped before it could meet the thrust of a spear. The other's lance found its mark forcing me to order the circle to shrink once more.

The Diefetians continued to circle us. Another rider broke off from the group and launched an attack, only to be thwarted by spears. Then two more came. Both were repelled and a horse was cut by the side of a spearhead. Several more attacks came within quick secession of each other. Much to my surprise all were defended against.

Having repelled them multiple times, the Diefetians made one final circle and rode off into the night, back in the direction they came from. As I watched the enemy disappear into the night, Billen walked up beside me. He and I were accustomed to having to defend against waves of enemies. The others were all wide-eyed and held their shields up, refusing to believe the enemy had just left.

"One injured and one dead," the smith reported.

"Who?" I asked.

"Sendrol is dead and Hiltrek is wounded," he informed me.

"Sendrol, he was young," I commented.

"Twenty-two," Billen said.

"And he was from Kiholp," I remembered.

"He was," my old friend confirmed with a smile.

"See to Hiltrek's wounds and tell Halerod to get someone to gather Sendrol's body. It shouldn't decompose too much until we reach the city. We'll bring it along so he can have a proper burial," I said.

"I'm sure his family will appreciate that," Billen said.

"They will. Now, go see to our wounded man," I said and began to walk away towards the dead body of the Diefetian who was thrown from his horse.

In all my years of warfare and being hunted by every army on the Continent, I had never seen nor heard of soldiers, cavalry especially, who could navigate a moonless night without any light source. As skilled as Diefetian soldiers were on horseback, no group of cavalrymen should have been able to rush at us without carrying lanterns or torches to see.

The greater mystery was how the Diefetians managed to get close to us without revealing their position. While ten men isn't a large cavalry force, it would have been enough to be visible on the plains, especially during the day. It was as if they had appeared out of thin air. The idea didn't unsettle me because I thought the possibility was ridiculous, but it would unsettle everyone else with the possible exception of Billen.

As I walked over to the cavalryman's corpse, I thought about what foolish explanation the men would give for the enemy's appearance. There would be more reasonable explanations, such as the Diefetians being trained to ride in near-complete darkness, but I knew there would be more fantastical explanations.

Since I was young, I've witnessed how superstitious soldiers can be. When Father took me on a campaign for the first time, I wasn't surprised to see men praying to the Protectorate to survive the next battle. When men are faced with death, it is only natural that they ask their gods for an extension of life.

I was surprised to see small rituals being performed around the camp unconnected to any god. There was an entire section whose soldiers were convinced if they waved a bird of prey's feather, it didn't matter which one since I saw hawk, eagle, and falcon feathers, outside of their tent, then disease would be warded off. I asked where the ritual had come from and someone told me a story about a Hunderian soldier who had performed the ritual while on campaign and was the only member of his army not to fall ill when the plague hit their camp.

Then there was superstitious behavior that divided the camp. Should one sharpen his weapon in or outside of his tent? The men who said in thought it was good luck to do so, though no one was quite sure why, while those who said outside believed sharpening your weapon outside of the tent allowed the sun and open air to strengthen the weapon's metal. How was a mystery, but I have vivid memories of veterans, many who wore scars from their previous campaigns on their faces, looking me in the eye and assuring me it was true.

That was the infantry though, the cavalry could be just as superstitious, if not more so. Which side of the horse should a rider be on when they saddle their mount? I discovered that if a horseman saddled his horse on the right, his mount would be calmer in battle. But if the horse were saddled on the left, then it would be cowardly. Others believed if a horseman saddled his mount on the right of the horse, the beast would be stubborn and move slower than its rider wanted, but if saddled on the left it would go as fast as it could when spurred on. It didn't matter they were contradictory beliefs; I was assured they both were true.

But I learned the archers were the most superstitious people in the army. Half of the archers informed me the only way to wax a bowstring was after it was strung onto the bow, otherwise your arrows would never find their mark. Why? I was told that's how it worked. The other half assured me you needed to wax the bowstring while it was off the bow because otherwise, your bow might break in battle.

What type of leather a quiver should be made of was a topic as sensitive as it was superstitious. A leather quiver made from cowhide was thought to grant the archer more strength, one from sheepskin was believed to make the archer stealthier and was favored by rangers and scouts, and a quiver made from goatskin was believed to offer some vague magical protection. Archers would frequently debate quivers, bowstrings, and other superstitions I won't bother to mention.

But those are all superstitions regarding a soldier's everyday life. I can remember numerous times when there was news of the supposed supernatural that got the entire army riled up. If an enemy had managed to defeat a superior force, then it must have been because of bad luck, not superior planning. Or an army got lost while it was marching to its destination because it went through cursed lands, not because the maps they relied on weren't accurate.

Or there was an enemy who could not be defeated, so maybe he had the war god's sword or had a magical amulet which made him and his army unbeatable. Never was it because the enemy general was a brilliant tactician or that the enemy was better trained. Nope. It must have been because of the gods, magic, luck, or a combination of all three.

So, when I was looking down at the corpse of the Diefetian who was thrown from his horse, I knew if I didn't find an explanation for the Diefetians' sudden appearance, then I would be hearing the men talk about how magic was the reason we couldn't see them before they attacked. Both I didn't want to hear.

The body was on its back and one might have mistaken the deceased rider as someone sleeping had it not been for the unnatural position of the neck and head. I had seen the corpses of people thrown off from their horses before and when I first looked at the dead Deifetian for a moment I thought he might still be alive.

Crouching down, leaning in closer, and moving my torch closer to the body, I began to take a closer look. The dead man's clothes were made of cotton dyed black and the breastplate was made of steel painted black. I pulled back the bottom lip and brought the torch as close to the head as I could. I examined the teeth, which were all normal and not unusually pointy.

"Vampire?" I heard Jorn ask as he approached me from behind.

"No. Our dead cavalryman here doesn't have any fangs," I answered.

"Then how did they manage to see us on a moonless night?" the prince asked.

"It could have been the campfire," I said.

"The campfire may have given up our position, but it wouldn't have provided enough light to ride a horse on a night like this. And the tents would have blocked much of the light from the fire," argued my nephew.

"A good point, which is why there has to be something else going on here," I told him.

"What do you think that is?" he asked. "And who were they?"

"What it is, I don't know, but judging by how they fought, they were some of Salroon's elite horsemen," I said. "Though I've never heard of any group of Diefetian cavalry riding in near pitch black without any light sources."

"And appeared out of thin air," Jorn added.

"They didn't do that. Somehow, they got the jump on us," I said.

"While we were several days march into the plains? It would have been impossible not to have seen them coming," he argued.

"Another good point," I conceded.

"So how did they do it?" he asked.

"I don't know right now, but we'll see in the morning," I told him.

"In the morning," he repeated inquisitively.

"Yes, in the morning, when the sun is up, we can see the tracks the horses made and follow them," I said, then told Jorn I was going to sleep, and he should do the same. As I walked to my tent, the questions still lingered, but there was nothing more I could do at night, so I opened the flap of my tent, laid down, and drifted off to sleep.

Chapter Fourteen

BEFORE DAWN COULD CAST ITS FIRST LIGHT, I was awake and walked over to the general direction from where we saw the Diefetians come. After scouring around, I found the first section of ground beaten by horses' trotting hooves. As expected, the tracks came from behind us, towards the forest, and implied the Diefetians had been following us.

I began to follow the tracks, which was easy since the Diefetians rode close together, and the aftermath of ten horses moving as a group isn't something that can be missed. I followed the tracks for about ten minutes before they ended. Figuring that there must be more, I scanned the ground around me to see where the trail picked up again, but it didn't. The tracks had come to a stop.

It looked like the Diefetians had materialized from the night and galloped towards our camp. But that was impossible. Men do not appear out of nowhere. As I was thinking about how the Diefetians could have hidden their tracks, Billen walked beside me.

"Where are the rest of the tracks?" the smith asked.

"If you can figure that out, I'll give you a pot of gold," I said.

"You can't find them?" he asked.

"No. I've searched in all directions, but from what I can tell, this is the end of the trail," I told him.

"But that's impossible," the smith said.

"I was just thinking the same thing. I don't know how they would have gotten so close without any of us seeing them, then take the time to cover any portion of their tracks, let along the tracks farthest away from us. It doesn't make any sense," I said.

"It doesn't," he agreed.

"If I don't come up with a reasonable explanation, rumors of how the Diefetians can appear from the shadows will flood the city once we get back. Considering how desperate the war already is, I don't want rumors like those going around," I explained.

"No, we wouldn't want that," Billen agreed. "Have you checked the body's teeth?"

"I have, and there were no fangs, so at least there won't be talk of vampires circling the city," I said with relief. "If I have to deal with commoners talking about vampires while walking through the streets of Kiholp, I'll kill someone."

"I thought you were more open to the existence of vampires," Billen said and gave me a puzzled look.

"That doesn't mean I want to hear about vampires wherever I go," I told him.

"Fair enough," he said. "Though if our dead rider wasn't a vampire, then why do the tracks start so close to our camp?"

"Right now, I don't have an answer," I said, still looking around for clues as we spoke.

"Could be magic," Billen said.

"Magic?" I asked. "The Temple doesn't even believe in magic. Magic is said to have died out a millennium ago."

"What else could it be?" questioned the smith. "If some of the Diefetians are vampires, which we know they are, then what's to say they don't have access to magic."

"Because magic isn't real," I said.

"You said the same thing about vampires, and then you killed a few of them," he pointed out.

"That's different," I argued.

"It's not, and you know it," Billen pushed back.

I let out a grunt. Billen was making logical sense, but that didn't mean I had to like it or that his assumptions were correct. "Then where have all the mages been in the last thousand years?" I asked.

"They would keep their existence hidden like the vampires," Billen answered.

"Why would a mage work with vampires?" I questioned.

"Money, a common goal, a shared enemy," Billen offered up possible reasons. "Or maybe the vampires have a mage amongst them."

"If that's true, it will make killing Salroon harder," I said through gritted teeth.

"And make winning the war harder," he added.

"That too," I said.

"Anyways, I'm sure no number of mages will prevent you from killing Salroon," he reassured me.

"No, they won't if they are real," I said. "I don't know how the Diefetians got so close to us, but it's concerning no matter the explanation. Let's get back to camp and into the city just in case our late-night visitors pay us another visit."

Billen nodded his head, and we got back to the camp. Once we were back within a half hour, we were back on the road, marching towards the capital. To my surprise, no one spoke about the attack as we walked towards Kiholp's imposing grey walls. There would be plenty of chatter debating how the Diefetians had appeared so suddenly, but there wasn't. The men were marching in complete silence.

I was fine with this since it meant I didn't have to listen to implausible theories about how the Diefetians could magically teleport or how they weren't men but ghostly specters who emerged from the night's darkness. There were no such theories, though, and I wondered why. I got my answer when I looked at the faces of the nearby soldiers. Each soldier was wide-eyed and had a blank look on their face. I should have realized it sooner.

They weren't coming up with theories about the Diefetians because they were in shock. We were taken by surprise twice in a period over two weeks, and they didn't know how to cope with the trauma. Instead of taking their minds off what happened by theorizing how ten horsemen had attacked us on the open plains without being spotted, they marched, still trying to process what had just happened.

I figured it was best if I didn't say anything. They needed time to process what had happened, and me talking to them wouldn't have done any good. Before we set out, they all knew the odds of the war weren't good, but I got the feeling then, after suffering from two surprise attacks and barely escaping, that the men were no longer just aware of the odds but were coming to appreciate what they meant.

The abstract was becoming concrete, and I wouldn't interfere with the process. If they continued to know what the odds were and did not comprehend them, then there was a higher chance they would die because they wouldn't take the war as seriously as they should.

An hour before the sun fully set, we arrived in the city. Halerod led the men back to the barracks, Billen headed back to his shop, and Jorn and I headed for the palace. We didn't talk as we walked. Jorn knew I didn't want to discuss how ten horsemen could get the jump on us, so he wasn't his typical inquisitive self. When we got within sight of the palace, I told him I would do the talking. He gave a weak nod, and we walked through the palace doors; the two guards posted outside gave a slight bow to their prince as we entered.

When we entered, a servant recognized us and told us Rono wanted us to meet him in the throne room. Though my brother wasn't in the throne room, the servant told us he would inform Rono of our arrival. Thanking the servant, Jorn and I walked to the throne room and began our wait. It wasn't long before my brother came walking into the throne room, a father's concern for his son in his eyes. The concern disappeared when he saw Jorn.

"What happened?" the king asked. "We were expecting you back almost a week ago."

"We were ambushed by archers on the road from Tuldum. Then, last night, we were attacked by Diefetian cavalry," I answered.

My brother's face paled. "Last night? No one on the walls reported seeing any signs of cavalry."

"Nor did we," I said. "This morning, I went out to find the horses' tracks to see where the Diefetians came from. I found the tracks, but they ended close to the camp."

"That's impossible," my brother softly said.

"It is. I don't know how they pulled it off," I admitted.

"If they can get that close to you on the open plains without being seen...." Rono trailed off, no doubt thinking about its implications for the war.

"It could be disastrous," I said, describing what he was thinking. "But I don't think the cavalry group who attacked us last night were a part of a regular unit."

"You mean they were…"

"No," I cut him off before he could say "vampire." "I had checked the corpse of the rider I killed, and there were no fangs."

"That's a relief," my brother said, giving a quiet thanks to the gods. "How many casualties?"

"In total, thirteen dead, and I don't remember how many are wounded. Some wounded have healed since the archer ambush, so I don't know the exact number. I would guess the current number is around half a dozen. I had Billen take care of the wounded, but I didn't get an exact number before he returned to his shop," I explained.

"Billen was taking care of the wounded? I wouldn't have expected that," Rono said.

"I required everyone in my clan to learn how to treat wounds," I told him. "I treated some arrow wounds myself."

"Even more surprising. But, getting back to the matter at hand. Even though your attackers might not have been an elite unit, I'm still concerned they got so close to the city without anyone on the walls spotting them," the king said.

"And there's the matter of how they managed to see in near pitch black," Jorn added.

"What are you talking about?" his father questioned.

"The Diefetians didn't carry torches or lanterns," I answered.

"It was a moonless night; the stars alone aren't bright enough to provide enough light to ride a horse," Rono said.

"You would think so. But our attackers managed to ride their mounts. It would have been an awesome spectacle to watch had they not been trying to kill us," I commented.

"I don't know what to say. How are we supposed to defend against an enemy who can attack from horseback in the darkness of night and make it look like they came out of nowhere?" he wondered. I had never seen my brother so worried before. In those few minutes of conversation, he aged a decade.

"That's for me to worry about, not you, brother," I told him.

Nervousness turned into anger. "Of course, I need to worry about it. For the Protectorate's sake, I am the king!"

"You are a king who was wise enough to get a military advisor to worry about these things for you because you know you are out of your area of expertise," I clarified.

Rono sighed. "You're right. I'll let you worry about it." Then he turned to Jorn. "You're all set, son. Get some rest; you need it. Once you have, see your mother and siblings; they have been worried sick."

Jorn gave a dreary nod and, with labored steps, walked out of the throne room.

"I've never seen him that tired before," Rono said once Jorn was gone.

"War will do that to you. You remember how I was when I returned home after my first campaign," I reminded him.

"I do, but Jorn wasn't like that when you returned from Gregoros," he pointed out.

"That's because the mission went as smoothly as possible. We arrived before the city fell and did minimal fighting, which I made sure Jorn wasn't doing because the boy would have gotten killed, and we weren't attacked on the way there or on the way back.

"This time, though, we were surprised on the way to Tuldum; a vampire surrounded us with his archers. I managed to get him to agree to a duel, and I won. Billen and I did the fighting once we got to Tuldum. Long story short, the general was a vampire, and I killed him.

"Then we got attacked by the same archers and had to trek through the forest to ensure we weren't being followed. Once we were a day away from the city, we were attacked by night," I explained the contrast between the two missions.

"I hadn't considered that," the king said.

"Just make sure to give him some space. He needs time to process what happened, not just time to rest his body," I said. "Speaking of rest, I need some. I'll be at the inn if you need me."

But I wouldn't get any rest. When I walked into the inn, Glendeo was waiting for me and wanted an update on the war. I gave him one, albeit brief, but when I got to the end and talked about the cavalry attack, I asked him if he had heard of anything like that before. Glendeo might not have been as active for long as my father was, but the old soldier was well-known among veterans.

Time and time again, Glendeo opened the doors of his small inn to former soldiers and their families who needed a place to stay, whether a natural disaster destroyed their house or they needed a place to stay until the father found work.

Some had sold their house and were hoping to purchase a new one but got the money stolen before they could buy it. Others had a family member die, inherited their home, and decide to move their family into it, only to arrive and have a court order them not to move in because their siblings were disputing their inheritance.

It didn't matter what happened. If a fellow veteran was in Kiholp and needed a place to stay, Glendeo would welcome them with open arms and let them stay in the inn for free until they and their families got back on their feet.

Glendeo would talk with them about life in the army, and the conversation would ultimately turn to the wars each had fought in. This made Glendeo an encyclopedia of recent Eshtaran military history. If anyone knew about stories of Diefetian cavalrymen being able to ride with precision and finesse on a moonless night without lanterns, it would be him.

"I've never heard anything like that before," the old soldier said.

"Are you sure?" I asked.

"No, and if I did, it probably would have been a story about you," he told me.

"Thanks for the compliment," I said.

"The rider wasn't a vampire?" he asked.

"No, I checked the corpse. There weren't any fangs," I told him.

"Still, it might be a good idea to ask Ilkon if he's heard anything like it before," he said. "While the riders might not have been vampires, that doesn't mean they didn't have something to do with it."

"I will. Is he still here?" I asked.

"He's in his room," the innkeeper said.

Within ten minutes, I had found Ilkon, and for the third time that day, I told someone what had happened since I had left. I asked him if he had heard of anything like the cavalry attack.

"Hmm," he hummed. "Where to begin? Do I answer your question first or tell you some information I've learned."

"Answer my question first, and then you can tell me what you've learned," I instructed.

"Fair enough. I've heard stories about vampires being able to enchant armor with magical properties, such as giving the wearer the ability to see in the dark. These items are rare, but it's not uncommon for vampires to give enchanted armor to their henchmen. It's possible similar artifacts could explain how they got so close to you without you seeing them from a distance or why the tracks stopped, though I can't be sure," he said.

"At least you explained one thing," I said. "What did you want to tell me."

"All the vampires you killed, including Nilomek and Ilonek, were keshgus, elite vampire warriors. Since you told me you killed Lord Gaenic, I asked one of my order's hunters to send a list of known keshgus. Every vampire you've killed has been on the list," he told me.

"I've been killing their elite, good," I said.

"Yes, even Zimkoo was a keshgu, and I suspect the ambassador would have put up a fight if he was armed," guessed the heretic.

"And if he didn't think he was safe in the palace," I said.

"That too," Ilkon agreed.

"You mentioned hunters," I said. "If the Diefetians have an abundance of keshgus, then why aren't they doing anything?"

"I don't know. I'm a scholar, and the hunters keep to themselves for the most part," he admitted.

"Did the list indicate if the Diefetians have any more keshgus?" I asked.

"No," he answered. "We only know the identity of a few keshgus, and we don't know how many there are, so it's hard to tell how many the Diefetians might have."

"Thanks for the information," I said and left. I walked towards my room, wondering about how many keshgus there were.

As much as I would have liked to ignore all the vampire talk and dismiss it as nonsense while clinging to my belief that vampires weren't real, I was never one to let my stubbornness turn me into a fool. I had killed multiple men who did not bleed and who had fangs for teeth. Whether I liked it or not, vampires were my enemies, and only the stupid or suicidal ignore their enemy's nature.

As I opened the door to my room, I stopped thinking about how many keshgus there were. It mattered to Ilkon and his sect, but it didn't matter to me. I wasn't in a millennia-long struggle against creatures created by a demon. No, I didn't care about that. I cared about killing Salroon and figuring out how many more keshgus the Diefetian king had because the more he had, the harder it would be to kill him.

And what did it mean for the war? I doubted Salroon would waste keshgus fighting the Eshtaran army and instead use them to recover the sword. But we would have to be careful if the vampires were supplying small groups of Diefetian soldiers with enchanted armor. I knew if Billen and I hadn't been there when the Diefetian horsemen attacked, then Halerod and the men would have been slaughtered to a man.

If Salroon had more tricks like enchanted armor, fighting the war would be much more difficult. Staying in Kiholp wasn't an option because I was the only capable commander my brother had, and if I stayed in the capital, Salroon would know where the sword was and would besiege the city. There was no way the city could survive a siege, not with how few men there were. Knowing I needed sleep and wouldn't solve these problems tonight, I cleared my mind, got in bed, and drifted off to sleep.

Chapter Fifteen

I T WAS AN HOUR PAST DAWN when I had woken up, dressed, and walked into the inn's lobby. Glendeo was waiting around in the lobby. He asked if Ilkon knew anything about the mysterious riders. I said he did, then told the innkeeper what the heretic told me.

"Vampires making enchanted armor. I would have remembered that one if I heard it before," he said. "Anyways, a messenger from the palace came in about half an hour ago and said the king wanted to see you as soon as possible."

"I figured," I said as I put some pieces of silver down on the counter to pay my tab. Glendeo thanked me as I exited. Minutes later, I stood in the throne room waiting for my brother. Then, I noticed Rono had a different throne than Father's.

Father's throne, like the palace, was a symbol of power. The Wretched King's throne was made of wood, lacked any elaborate carvings, and didn't have a cushion. It was a simple wooden chair, which was more significant than average and whose back extended up further.

My brother getting rid of our father's throne wasn't an unusual action to take. Eshtaran history, and the Continent's, was filled with new kings replacing their predecessor's throne. But where my father had taken the design of his throne to one extreme, my brother took it to another.

Cushions were on the throne's seat and armrests, which at the ends were carved to resemble olives. The throne's back didn't have a cushion, but the silhouette of the Eshtaran deer was carved into the headrest. The legs glittered with gold, but they were no doubt gilded wood. It was a throne with a message, one that was true until the war broke out.

I wondered why I hadn't noticed before, though looking back, being in charge of a war consumes one's thoughts.

"I was wondering when you were going to realize I changed out the thrones," my brother said as he walked into the room.

"I've been busy," I said. "But it suits you. Father's old throne wouldn't."

"That's why I got rid of it, though I moved it to a different room," he said.

"Which one?" I asked.

"You'll see in due time," he assured me. "Now, I have some bad news."

"That's the only type you have since you released me," I remarked.

"That's not true; you've been giving me good news," he complimented. "But the bad news is I haven't made much progress with the spy problem. Neither the chancellor nor Paderok has been seen doing anything suspicious, which is concerning because I think the spy told the Diefetians where you were going."

"What makes you so sure?" I asked. "After Gregoros, we signaled our intent to lift any sieges on the border. The enemy could have guessed I would be going to Tuldum and would have taken the most direct route not to waste time."

"Official documents relating to the war have gone missing, including some letters I have been sending to mayors, only to be found again a day or two later," the king informed me.

"As if they were copied," I said.

"Exactly," my brother agreed. "One of the documents was the report from Tuldum informing me about the siege, and I noted that I sent you there."

"If they are being taken, copied, then returned, it means your spy isn't a professional one," I deduced.

"Why is that?" Rono asked.

"Because a professional spy would have copied the documents without needing to take them," I said.

"We were right then to guess someone close to me is spying for the enemy," he concluded.

"Yes, we are," I concurred. "Was that everything you needed to tell me?"

"No. What are the chances the cavalrymen who attacked you are still around?" the king asked.

"Depends whether they were ordered to follow me. If they were, then they should be somewhere near the city, waiting for me to leave," I said

"If they were, do you think you could find them?" he asked.

"Most likely, though I don't know if I could get close to them, even at night," I said.

"I don't want a fight. I want to know if any of them are by the city," my brother said. "If they are, it could mean an army isn't far behind."

"Good point," I said. "I'll need a small group to do it, twenty men. Billen, Halerod, Jorn, and myself included.

"How long will you be gone?" he asked.

"A week, maybe two. There are not too many places to hide near the city, but considering they seemingly appeared out of nowhere, we'll have to search thoroughly," I said.

"I'll leave you to it then," the king dismissed me.

An hour passed, and I walked out of Kiholp's gates with Billen, Halerod, Jorn, and sixteen men from the barracks. Each was from the group we took to Gregoros since the men we took to Tuldum needed the rest. Each man was equipped with a spear, a shield, and a sword, though Jorn didn't know how to use one.

Billen had brought me a shield, which I had accepted, but I had turned down his offer of a spear. I was more than capable of taking on cavalry with only a sword if it came to that. But I would have been stupid if I had refused the shield, knowing we were trying to find cavalry.

We searched for a week and a half and found no sign of Diefetians. We left no stone unturned at each possible hiding spot and searched every tree and bush. Our mysterious horsemen were nowhere to be found. Not at the small hill a couple of miles from the eastern gate, the beginning of the Ventillor Forest, and the old ruins of an ancient, crumbling fortress in the south.

We traveled and searched in silence. I didn't want the Diefetians, if they were there, to be alerted to our presence. But I lifted the talking ban once we had searched through the ruins, our last location, and avoided several stones tumbling down at our heads.

On the way back to Kiholp, I resumed Jorn's training. I had stopped it again because of the need for silence. The conclusion of our search provided the perfect opportunity to continue the boy's training. As before, the training sessions were held in the morning. Considering we were attacked by cavalry and archers, I thought it best to perform drills to teach him how to defend against such enemies.

"You will learn to hate archers and cavalry if you don't already. Archers are a nuance at best if they don't manage to shoot an arrow into you. If an arrow goes into you but doesn't kill you, it will give you excruciating pain. You'll hate cavalry, especially well-trained cavalry like the Diefetians, because it's unfair for a man on horseback to fight one who isn't," I said.

"Isn't a war about taking an advantage, even if it's unfair?" he asked me, and I smiled.

"It is, which is why I am going to train you to be unfair to cavalry," I said. "But first, let's begin with archers."

I told Jorn to take his shield, walk two hundred steps away from me, and be ready to block with it. When he got into position, I took a stone from the ground, and with an exaggerated motion so Jorn could see what I was doing, I threw the stone towards him.

As the stone soared through the air, Jorn realized it was coming at his head and quickly lifted his shield to protect himself. I heard a cling as the stone bounced off the shield. Before he could lower his shield, I had already picked up another stone and threw it. Then another one and another one, until a handful of rocks soared towards the young prince.

The small volley of rocks soared through the air, rushing towards Jorn's head. The young prince was smart enough not to drop his shield. I heard a chorus of clings as the stones smashed into his shield. My nephew held his shield up for a few moments after the last stone clashed against his shield, then proceeded to lower it, causation slowing down his movement. I walked up to him.

"Good, I thought you would have dropped your guard after the first stone," I complimented him.

"You didn't tell me you were going to do that," he said, unable to mask the annoyance in his voice.

"Archers don't tell you they are going to attack. They just do," I told him.

"I thought this was training. You could have told me what the drill was," he argued, his tone turning from annoyance to frustration. "You could have hit me in the head."

"You figured it out," I said. "I didn't try to hide what I was doing. You read my movements, inferred what I was about to do, and reacted accordingly, as I knew you were smart enough to do."

"Fair point," mumbled the prince.

"It was a simple exercise, and you performed well," I assured him. "Now stop your mumbling. You had enough common sense to keep your shield up even though, from what you saw, you could have thought I was only going to throw one stone. Assuming you know how many arrows are coming your way is the fastest way to get killed by archers."

"But I can't keep my shield up forever either," Jorn said.

"No, you can't. Either your arm will give out from all the arrows smashing into it, or one of them will be in you. You must think of something while arrows are peppering you. Look to your sides while keeping your shield up; see if you can find a way out. Or rally some men and attack the archers' position," I told him.

"That's it?" asked the young man.

"Yes," I said, then proceeded to instruct him on how to hold his shield to defend against a cavalry lance, how to stand so the force of the impact wouldn't knock him down, and how to thrust a spear into a horse so it wouldn't get stuck.

I drilled Jorn for hours. There was nothing to do about archers other than to keep your shield up and assault them when the opportunity presented itself. Cavalry was a different matter though. Skill was needed, and it needed to be drilled in through countless hours of repetition. As I watched Jorn perform thrust after thrust, sweat pouring down his reddened face as I listed the best points to stab on a horse and its rider, I hoped he could get enough practice before he needed to put the training to good use.

As we returned to the city, Jorn asked me about my childhood, the Wretched King, what Eshtar was like before he was born, the wars I fought in or observed, and what his father was like growing up. I answered the best that I could, but it wasn't enough.

As Jorn asked his endless questions, I knew my brother didn't talk much about the past with the boy, and I couldn't blame him. The Wretched King's and my actions made the past challenging to talk about for my brother. What was my brother supposed to tell his son about the good parts before our father became the Wretched King? Recalling those memories would only stir up the bad ones; some memories are better buried.

Besides, how do you explain two good men turning bad? You don't, nor do you try, because while you think you might know why, you don't know for sure. Rono might have guessed why Father became the Wretched King and I the Terror of the Continent, but he didn't know for sure. It would be easier for Rono not to relive the pain of the past and then drive himself crazy to understand why the Wretched King or I did what we did.

And my brother wouldn't understand why I abdicated the throne. He never would because he didn't see what I had seen. The harsh nature of this world and its brutality was something Rono didn't witness because he wasn't a soldier, and it was something I worked hard to keep him from when we were younger. The last part I decided was something Jorn didn't need to know because, like Rono, there were sections of the past I didn't want to relive either.

But despite his insatiable appetite for learning about the past, Jorn was equally dedicated to his training. I suspected it was because he wanted to learn how to fight, but his father had prohibited it. Perhaps my brother was worried his son would end up like me.

I kept my lessons to the spear because it was his weapon at the time, teaching him how to fight individually and as a part of a group. While I did this, Billen would drill the men, and they were improving but still were no match for the average Diefetian soldier. If we got in another direct fight and were outnumbered, they would be slaughtered or run.

After the morning training was finished and we were back on the march, Jorn would begin his questioning. I can't tell whether this was because the boy was warming up to me or because he wanted to distract the men, who often overheard our conversations, from all the talk about vampires. If it was the latter, my nephew proved more perceptive than I thought he was.

When we were a few days march from Kiholp, I asked Jorn why he was asking me all these questions, not Rono.

"Father doesn't talk about the past much," my nephew told me, confirming my suspicions.

"Of course, he doesn't," I said. "He didn't like what your grandfather had become. None of us did."

"So, he wasn't always the Wretched King?" Jorn asked.

"No, he wasn't," I said. "Once, he believed in fighting for peace, not conquest. Remember, Eshtar was invaded under his grandfather's reign, and there was fighting for generations while we drove the Bendilli from our lands. Eshtar was taken back, but the wars still waged on. He wanted to finish those wars and give the Eshtaran people peace. He also let the nobility have some say over the kingdom's affairs, which was unheard of in those days."

"What happened then?" asked Jorn.

"Your grandmother died, and he fell into a deep depression," I told him. "By then, we had already driven the Bendilli out of our lands, invaded their countries, and won the war, but your grandfather wanted more. I don't think the wars were just for conquest, at least at first, because the first few wars were against the Bendilli and their allies. Neither had come to the negotiating table after they were driven out of Eshtar, so more fighting was needed until they would agree to peace. The later wars were for conquest."

"Sounds like he was hurting from the loss of his wife and used revenge as an excuse to bring pain to others," Jorn said.

"Perhaps," I said. "Perhaps not."

"Was this about when he became a more ruthless ruler?" asked Jorn.

"I suppose so. He started to ignore the nobility and began making laws without their input. Years later, when the nobles became resistant to these changes, the accusations of treason started," I answered.

"What were you doing?" he asked.

"Keeping my head down and waiting for your grandfather to deploy me to some front. We were at war with almost the whole Continent at this time," I said.

"You didn't fight against him when he was executing nobles for treason?" he asked accusatively.

"You assume all of them were innocent," I said. "Your grandfather was able to make the first few accusations because he had evidence those nobles were conspiring with our enemies. After that, the evidence became scarcer, and the accusations became baseless, but no one dared speak out against the Wretched King."

"Sounds like he took advantage of an opportunity to rid the kingdom of any nobles that disagreed with him," Jorn concluded.

"Precisely," I said as we marched on.

"What was Father doing during all of this?" he asked.

"The Wretched King had him studying diplomacy and administration," I said. "Sometimes, he was out of the country visiting a foreign court."

"You mentioned that before when I asked why Father wasn't trained to fight," he remembered.

"Yes, though I didn't tell you I studied both when I was younger, though I didn't take to it as well as your father," I admitted.

"That's not to say your uncle can't be diplomatic," Billen chimed in. "He can when the situation calls for it."

"An interesting claim, considering he has killed an ambassador," Jorn said.

"We witnessed his diplomacy with the Diefetian army around Tuldum," Billen claimed

"That was persuasion, not diplomacy," I said.

"Diplomacy is gaining victory through words, not violence," Billen pointed out.

"You're forgetting I killed their general before I attempted persuasion. What's this sudden boasting about my diplomatic skills, anyways?" I asked Billen. "I'm a military advisor, not a diplomatic one."

"Because you keep implying that King Rono is the only diplomatic one out of the two of you, and I know better. I think it's a good time to tell Prince Jorn about our run-in with the Hushta Unkae," Billen said.

"Hushta Unkae? Who are they?" Jorn asked, not well-versed in the Continent's criminal underworld.

"A group of assassins who trace their origins back centuries. They are the best in the business," I explained.

"They are among the few boogiemen besides Bowv that keep nobles and kings up at night. Once, a group of nobles banded together and hired them to kill your uncle," Billen explained.

"I thought it was the whole clan," I said.

"No, the contract was on just your head. Remember, they told us when we caught up to them," the blacksmith recalled.

"Ah, yes, that's right. Fortor wasn't too happy about that," I remembered.

"No, he wasn't," Billen agreed.

"Who's Fortor?" Jorn asked.

"A bandit who wasn't happy his reputation wasn't great enough to have someone hire the Continent's premier assassins to kill him," I explained.

"He sounds crazy," Jorn said.

"He was crazy, violent, arrogant, and short-tempered," Billen elaborated.

"Sounds like a liability," Jorn said.

"He would have been if he wasn't one of the best fighters in the clan," I explained.

"But why would nobles hire assassins to kill you?" Jorn asked.

"I had large-scale extortion rackets undermining their ability to pay taxes," I answered.

"What happened when the Hushta Unkae found you?" he asked.

"Your uncle killed the first three that were sent," Billen answered for me. "Which, before he did, it was unheard of for anyone to manage to kill one Hushta assassin."

"Killing assassins isn't diplomatic," noted Jorn.

"By this time, Bowv realized that the Hushta would not rest until he was dead or until he made it too costly for them to continue the contract. When the fourth assassin was sent, your uncle laid a trap and captured him. Bowv told the assassin he would release him if he delivered a message to the Hushta leaders; there were only two then. The message was to meet him at a tavern in Derceilum, where they could discuss the contract," Billen said.

"Did they try to kill Uncle at the tavern?" Jorn asked.

"They tried," I said. "I had the clan trickle into the tavern throughout the day in case the Hushta had people watching the building. They were armed with small crossbows, so when the Hustha leaders tried to succeed where their acolytes failed, a few crossbow bolts flew over their heads. They realized they were outnumbered and were more than eager to enter negotiations," I said.

"Clever," Jorn said.

"Yes, it was," Billen agreed.

"I asked what it would take for them to remove my contract," I said, getting back to the story.

"They said that they never take away a contract. I told them pursuing this contract would result in many of their assassins meeting an end. They told me that they could train more. I said if they wanted to be that persistent, then I would treat the contract for what it was: war. They assured me the Hushta Unkae were capable of fighting a war.

"I told them we could start now and ordered my men to fill them with crossbow bolts. The two head assassins cut me off before I could finish, wanting to negotiate after all."

"Funny how leaders stop talking tough when it's their lives on the line and not someone else's," Billen commented with distaste.

"Yes, it is," I agreed. "The two Hushta leaders were open to the idea I could negotiate the contract on my head. I told the head assassins I understood that whoever placed the bounty on my head must have paid a lot of money, and I didn't want to see them lose that money.

"I proposed I pay for the contract in full, plus fifty percent more in exchange for the contract being removed. They asked if I wanted the names of the people who hired them. I told them I could find out on my own, and I understood that if they told me, it would be bad for business, and I didn't want them to suffer financially because of me. They accepted."

"How much did the nobles pay to have you killed?" asked Jorn.

"Ten talents of gold," I answered.

"And you ended up paying fifteen talents of gold," Jorn said.

"Yes," I confirmed.

"You had fifteen talents of gold," he said with awe.

"Why does that surprise you?' I asked. "I was the richest bandit on the Continent, probably still am, though the banditry has been put on hold."

"I know, but you say fifteen talents of gold as if it were nothing," my nephew clarified.

"I would have been willing to pay anything because I knew that whoever paid for the contract would have enough wealth for me to take," I explained.

"What did you do to the noblemen who paid for the hit?" he asked.

"He killed them, then robbed them," BIllen said. "What else do you think he did?"

"Were they all a part of one court?" Jorn asked.

"They were scattered all across the Continent, but that didn't stop me," I said. "Their corpses were all found with their tongues cut out and replaced with a note with 'This is what happens when you try to kill the Terror,' written on it."

"When your uncle wants someone dead, he's a force of nature," Billen told Jorn. "Something which Salroon will soon learn."

"Yes, he will," I said, the intensity in my voice as clear as a lion's roar.

Everyone fell silent after I said that, and I was fine with it. Like the previous group, I learned their names and where they were from, and they began to look less terrified of me. But after Billen's comment, the soldiers returned to being tense around me, albeit nowhere like before.

I don't know what Billen was thinking, starting off the conversation with my diplomatic skills and then ending it with how I am a force of nature when I want someone dead. I couldn't figure out why he did it. There had to be a reason because Billen was never loose with his words. The blacksmith was trying to do something, though I was clueless about what it was.

When night fell, I asked him about it. When I asked, my old friend smiled and said he was surprised. I didn't understand what he was doing, but I could figure it out. I insisted he tell me, but he refused, saying I would figure it out eventually. I knew I wouldn't get an answer from him, so I went to my tent and slept.

The next day, after the morning's training, Jorn resumed questioning. We were about a day from the capital, and the time for him to ask me questions ended. Perhaps it was this scarcity, or perhaps he was inspired by Billen's comments the other day, but whatever the reason, Jorn's questions were centered around me and the wars I fought in during his grandfather's reign.

I asked him why he wanted to hear about the wars. I knew Rono had given him a rigorous education when he was younger, not as rigorous as the one the Wretched King gave Rono and I, but still, Jorn was more educated than most other princes on the Continent.

"I know what is taught," my nephew told me. "But you were there. You experienced it. From what I understand, you are the only Eshtaran commander from that time period still alive."

"That's right. Your father mentioned plague killed any experienced generals he had," I recalled. However, I did not mention that I killed all the other experienced generals after Rono sent them to arrest.

"So, you are the only link I have to the wars," he said. "I want to know if the histories are true."

"Fine," I said. "But only pick one war for today since there won't be time to talk about more than one in a day. In those days, we were at war with most of the Continent. How your grandfather was able to fight that many wars still amazes me."

Jorn thought about it, then asked me what the earliest war I could remember where I was a combatant, not just an observer, was.

"The War of the Triad," I said. "The only war I fought in, besides this one, which your grandfather didn't start."

"But the histories say that he started it," Jorn said.

I let out a big laugh, which shocked those around us. They had never heard the Terror of the Continent, the monster they heard commit atrocity after atrocity, laugh before. But I did, and I couldn't stop for a full minute.

"I started the war..." I said and gave another chuckle. "Someone told you my father started the War of the Triad..." I said and laughed again.

"Why is that so funny?" Jorn asked.

"Because..." I said, then let out another laugh. "Your grandfather entered the war a full month after the conflict started. How could he possibly have started a war in which he wasn't an original combatant? What lunatic told you the Wretched King started the War of the Triad?"

"My tutors did," he informed me.

"Your father, at least, should know better. He was old enough to remember when the war started," I said, shaking my head.

"How old was he?" Jorn asked.

"Rono was about eleven when the war started," I said.

"And how old were you?" he asked.

"Fourteen," I said.

"And your father sent you off to fight in a war?" he asked, horrified.

"No, I was sixteen when I first fought in a battle," I corrected. "Though he did take me on campaign starting when I was around eleven, possibly ten. In those days, Eshtar was still fighting the Bendilli and their allies. I was an observer for the first two years of the War of the Triad."

"What was it like?" Jorn asked.

I fell silent. Memories I thought were long buried rose to the surface of my mind like a vengeful corpse rising from its grave. "I saw combat for the first time. Killed my first man."

"Weren't you taken on campaign before this though?" he asked me.

"I was, so I was used to the hardships of campaigning and the sounds of battle," I answered. "But, before the War of the Triad, your grandfather kept me well out of harm's way, thinking that I was not ready for combat."

"What changed?" asked Jorn.

"He thought I was old enough to at least be around the fighting," I told him.

"How long did you fight in the war?" Jorn asked.

"I fought until the end. In total, it was about three years," I said. "Though that's not counting the two years of observation."

"So, you were nineteen when the war ended," Jorn did the math.

"Roughly," I said.

"And what did you do in the war besides fight? Did you command?" he asked.

"Did your tutors mention me when they taught you about the war?" I asked, not believing the boy's tutors could leave him this ignorant.

"They didn't mention you," he admitted.

"How long did they spend teaching you about the war?" I asked.

"We covered it for a whole week," Jorn informed me.

I let out another laugh. "Your tutors told you the Wretched King started the war, even though he couldn't have. And they didn't mention me, one of the key generals during the war. If I didn't know any better, I would say someone was trying to rewrite history," I said.

"So, you did have a command?" Jorn asked, though his tone made it feel halfway between a question and a statement.

"Have a command? By the war's end, the Wretched King gave me command of half the Eshtaran army!" I told him. "I was second in rank only to the king, and before that, I had control over an entire theater of war."

"Which theater?" he asked.

"The difficult one," I said.

"Which was?" he asked.

"The Swadonilic Theater. It was the first campaign I would win. I hope your father didn't pay too much for those tutors since it's apparent that they didn't teach you anything meaningful about the war," I said.

"But you didn't start as a general," Jorn noted.

"No, like I said, I was an observer at first, but I became a general during the war. While your grandfather let me fight once I was sixteen, he didn't give me a command right away, and when he did, it wasn't commanding half of the army. The more I think about it, I fell into command," I said.

"What do you mean you 'fell' into it?" a confused Jorn asked.

"There was chaos during a battle, more so than the usual type. The guy in charge, along with his second in command, died; everyone else was losing their heads, and I started giving orders," I clarified.

"What battle was this?" he asked.

"The Battle of Odfret," I said.

"It ended up being a rout," Jorn recalled.

"It was for those of us who weren't massacred. The enemy had engaged our forces in the front and managed to attack us in the rear, cutting off our line of retreat," I said.

"I can see how that would be chaotic," Jorn said.

"It was. You don't know the true meaning of anarchy until you witness the breakdown of a well-organized and disciplined fighting force," I told him.

"How did it become a rout and not a slaughter?" the prince asked.

"The commander, his second, and the rest of the highest-ranking officers were in the back when the enemy attacked in the rear. After a messenger told us that we were under attack from the back, there were no other messengers from the rear.

"The officers may have still been alive, but it didn't matter because everyone in the front assumed that they were dead. Without orders coming in from the rear and an enemy attacking from the front, things began to break down. People didn't know what to do. Not wanting to die, I started to give orders," I said.

"And they listened," Jorn said.

"Of course, they listened; I was their prince," I told him.

"How did you get out of there?" my nephew asked.

"By cutting a bloody path through their lines," I told him. "I guessed the Rushide had split their forces to attack us both in the front and the rear, and we were being attacked by one army, not two. I was right. It took some effort, but once we concentrated on the attack in the front, the Rushide broke," I recalled.

"Was this when you first killed a man?" he asked.

"It was," I confirmed. "He was a Rushide soldier, five years my senior, maybe. When I pulled my spear from his throat and watched the blood flow out of the wound, I didn't have time to process what had happened until the battle was over.

"The only two things on my mind were survival and breaking free from the enemy's trap with as many soldiers as I could manage. It wasn't until the next day when we had put some distance between ourselves and the Rushide, that I could process what I had done. I became sick to my stomach, my hands began to tremble, and nightmares plagued me for a week."

Jorn began to ask another question, but I told him that would be it for the rest of the day. He could continue questioning the next day until we got back to the capital, so long as the subject matter was about the War of the Triad. He agreed.

For the last day of the march, the Jorn asked me questions of a mixed sort. Sometimes, he would ask about my experience in the war; sometimes, he would ask about the war in a broader context, such as the strategic decisions made or the political implications of the war; and other times, he was curious about his grandfather and the actions he made throughout the war. By the time we had reached Kiholp, I was confident I had undone most of the damage the boy's tutors did.

Chapter Sixteen

WE PASSED THROUGH KIHOLP'S GATES. We left the men at the barracks, parted ways with Billen, and Jorn and I returned to the palace. As we approached the Stone Palace, the four guards outside were standing alongside two Diefetian royal guards. Jorn turned and gave me a look, silently asking me what we should do. I began to walk towards the palace entrance and waved for him to follow me.

I ignored the Diefetians, and Jorn followed my lead. Once inside the palace, we saw it was teeming with Diefetian royal guards. I counted and found out the foreigners outnumbered the native guards at least two to one. Concern smashed into me like a falling anvil.

Why Rono let them in is beyond my comprehension. Knowing my brother, diplomacy had something to do with it, but diplomacy sometimes overrides common sense, and this was a prime example. The Diefetians could have quickly taken control of the palace if they wanted to, then the war would have been over.

Again, Jorn looked at me. I walked towards the throne room, and my nephew followed. We heard Rono's and another man's voices as we approached the throne room. Both were calm and neither was yelling, but you could tell by both their strained tones the conversation's topic was a heavy one. I didn't recognize the stranger's voice, but I knew exactly who he was from what I overheard.

"Salroon!" I beamed as I first laid eyes on the Diefetian king. "What a pleasant surprise. I sure hope you're not making threats or demands to my dear brother. If you are, I should inform you that it didn't turn out well for the last guy who did. He wound up a corpse."

The Diefetian king was not impressed nor amused. He wore an ordinary soldier's simple shirt and trousers, which were beaten and torn. He had the tanned skin of a native Diefetian along with light brown hair cut short to the scalp in the Diefetian army style. Two types of kings exist: those who send their soldiers off to war and those who go to war alongside them. My father was the latter, and Salroon's clothes dubbed him the same.

The Diefetian king's brown eyes were sharp with intelligence and reflected the soul of a cunning, cold, and calculating man. They were the eyes of a general well acquainted with war, one you did not want to have as your enemy. Looking at Salroon, I knew he didn't have his guards storm the palace because he knew while he could take the palace and take the royal family hostage as a means to end the war, it wouldn't get him what he wanted.

Salroon did not want to end the war; he knew his army could easily win. He wanted *Hueik and* needed to deal with me to get it. I wouldn't care if Salroon held my brother and his family hostage. We all knew it, so he couldn't use them as leverage to force me to give up the sword.

While I measured Salroon up, he was doing the same. I will never know what he thought about me. Salroon had spies, and it was impossible he didn't know I was Rono's advisor and broke the sieges at Gregoros and Tuldum and was the one who killed five vampires. Having gotten ambushed by archers and attacked at night by cavalry, I knew Salroon had already deemed me a threat on the battlefield. At that moment, I suspected he was determining if I would be a threat in a duel.

"Is that a threat, Bowv?" the Diefetian king asked.

"You know it was, so why waste your breath asking?" I asked.

"I will speak with both of you later," Rono told Jorn and me. You are dismissed."

Jorn turned around to walk out of the throne room but stopped when he realized I wasn't.

"You can dismiss your son, but you have no authority over me, brother. I am the eldest, and you surrendered any sovereignty over me when you declared me an outlaw," I told him.

Rono sighed, knowing I was right. My brother could have argued I was his military advisor and technically was a part of his court, so he had the authority to kick me out of his throne room. But in Eshtar, military advisors are viewed as contractors or mercenaries and can refuse a king's request to become an advisor without repercussion. As such, they weren't considered part of the king's court.

"I do not mind Bowv's presence," Salroon spoke up. "I'm sure we'll address Bowv's actions concerning several dead members of my court anyway."

"Most of whom you sent to kill me," I remarked.

"But I believe we were discussing the possibility of opening peace talks before your brother arrived," Salroon continued.

"We were," Rono confirmed. "Though, I remain skeptical of your motivations and your intentions."

"My intentions are peace and obtaining what rightfully belongs to me," declared Salroon.

"The sword," I said.

"Which I bestowed upon Lord Gaenic for his service to the kingdom, and considering he has no living kin, it is mine by rights," the Diefetian king said. From what Ilkon told us, this was a lie. If the heretic's information was accurate, Gaenic already had the sword centuries before Salroon ascended to the throne.

"What, I give you the sword, and Eshtar is spared? You are in the process of conquering the Continent and expect us to believe you will uphold the peace once you have the sword?" I asked.

"I have never broken a peace treaty," claimed Salroon.

"You have yet to sign one," I pointed out.

"I cannot order my brother to hand over the sword," Rono interjected. "First, as he already pointed out, I don't hold any power over him. Second, even if I did have such authority over him, he would do as he wanted anyways."

"I'm sure we could come to an agreement," Salroon said.

"Perhaps, but I would need time to convene with my brother in private," Rono told the Diefetian king. "As you have already seen, he can be quite difficult to deal with."

"I understand," Salroon said.

"Then allow one of my servants to show you to a room so you can rest while Bowv and I talk. I'm sure you are tired from your travels," Rono said and summoned a servant.

"You are a gracious host," Salroon told Rono, then followed the servant whom Rono summoned out of the throne room, flanked by his royal guards.

I waited a few minutes before speaking, wanting to make sure that they were gone. "When did he arrive?" I asked.

"An hour or two before you and Jorn returned," my brother answered.

"How many Diefetian guards are in the palace?" I asked.

"Far more than mine," the king informed me.

"By the look of him, Salroon's been fighting his wars. He could have already been in the country or was already on the way," I reasoned.

"Could be either," Rono agreed. "He could have already been here organizing the war and searching for the sword, or he was already on the way to try to convince me to give him the sword."

"Or to kill me," I said.

"Possibly," Rono agreed. "But, what about the Diefetian cavalry who attacked you coming back from Tuldum? Did you manage to find them?"

"No sign of them," I answered. "I wonder what road Salroon took because we didn't see him on the road."

"Hmm. Interesting, I would have thought you would have seen him," Rono said. "I don't know which gate he came in."

"What are we going to do about Salroon?" I asked.

"*I* am going to try to negotiate peace," the king informed me.

"Peace? There will be no peace until he conquers the Continent," I said

"That is a risk I am willing to take," he said. "It's better odds than trying to fight the war when all Eshtar has is a small, inexperienced army. Salroon has been reasonable so far. Perhaps peace is possible."

"He's been reasonable, brother, because he thought you could give him the sword. Now that he knows you can't give him what he wants, he won't be so reasonable," I argued.

"I have to try Bowv. Eshtar is not the fighting force it was under, Father," countered Rono.

"Because you let it be," I said.

"I wouldn't be placing blame, brother," he said, anger infecting his tone. "I did not abandon the kingdom for a life of crime."

"You're right. I wasn't king," I said. "You have been king for the last twenty years. I wasn't the one who left Eshtar vulnerable. That was you. I was not the one who was unprepared for war when it was clear to everyone that Salroon wanted to conquer the entire Continent.

"You can blame me, Rono, for not sitting on the throne all you want. It doesn't change the fact that Eshtar is about to be conquered because *you* have been in charge all these years. Not me. You can blame me for the pain and death my crimes have caused, but don't blame me for your poor choices, brother. It does not befit a king to do so."

I didn't wait for him to respond. Instead, I began walking out of the room. Rono asked where I was going, and I told him I wouldn't be sticking around when I knew I had an item Salroon was willing to kill for.

"Are you finished as my advisor?" he asked.

"No," I told him as I left the throne room.

It's funny, now that I look back at our exchange. Rono was a believer in the gods and, consequently, vampires, while I was a vehement denier of the gods and had reluctantly accepted the existence of vampires.

To Rono, Salroon surrounded himself with demonically created monsters, yet he thought he could negotiate with the Diefetian king, knowing he was most likely a vampire. You would think that I would advocate for peace negotiations. Yet, the roles were the reverse.

Maybe Father was to blame for taking me off to war and sending Rono to be trained as a diplomat. I wound up with a soldier's skepticism, while Rono got the hope of a diplomat. It wouldn't be the first time our father influenced us beyond the grave. But I think it's because I knew what Salroon was, which caused me to be skeptical of his willingness to negotiate peace.

The only difference between Salroon and myself was when Salroon cut somebody's throat, he would say it was for the betterment of Diefet. If he wanted to take over a country for conquest's sake, he had to insist that Diefet needed more land or that the government was a dangerous enemy, and few would question the ensuing slaughter. When I got bloodied, I didn't have those excuses. I took something because I wanted it and was a criminal for it.

When you're a killer with a crown, people don't want to see you for what you are. He wouldn't have been called a despot if my father had stopped at expansive conquest and left the nobles alone instead of executing them. Instead, people would have called him a great king.

I knew Rono was being foolish, but he made it clear that he wouldn't listen to me. At that moment, I could have walked away. No, I should have walked away, considering how delusional my brother was being. I was Rono's advisor, and he didn't even consider my suggestion, which was in his right, but it was during a situation where the danger could not be more apparent to see.

I could have started my bandit clan again, and it would have been easy. I just needed to break the survivors of my clan out of prison and tell the right people I was looking for recruits; then, I would have been back in operation in no time. The wars going on would have provided an excellent opportunity to do some robbing.

I don't know why I didn't. Instead, I found myself walking down the street to an all too familiar inn to talk to someone I thought could persuade my brother to see reason. I opened the door and found Glendeo behind the counter.

"I take it you're coming from the palace," he said.

"I am," I confirmed.

"I never thought Rono could be this stupid," he said, and I wasn't surprised the old man knew what was going on.

"A desperate man clinging onto hope is not stupid. Foolish, yes, but not stupid," I said. Though Glendeo was a cynical old soldier, calling Rono stupid was not entirely accurate.

Did my brother make a stupid decision to let Salroon enter the palace accompanied by so many guards? Yes, and it was ridiculous. But in Rono's eyes, he was taking a calculated risk; one, if it paid off, would get Eshtar out of the precarious situation she found herself in.

"He could have fooled me," Glendeo said. The bitterness in his voice was not mistakable.

"Is Ilkon still here?" I asked.

"He is. The last time I checked, he was still in his room. Why?" Glendeo asked.

"Because he is the only one who can persuade Rono not to make peace," I answered truthfully.

"Why do you care?" pressed the old man.

"A man's got to look out for his younger brother," I said.

"You expect me to believe that?" he asked.

"No, but it's the only answer I got," I said. "I wasn't planning on coming here in the first place. I was going to skip town, then come back when I got news the Diefetians left."

"Hmm," Glendeo hummed. "Well, go and talk to Ilkon. I don't know why you think he can talk some reason into your brother, but I hope you can get him to do it. Gods know the king's not going to listen to you."

"Hopefully, or else the crown may fall to me again," I said.

"And we all know how much you don't want that," Glendeo commented as I walked towards Ilkon's room.

Once at the heretic's room, I knocked. He asked who it was, and I told him it was me. Ilkon said to come in, so I opened the door and found him studying a scroll at his desk. He looked up and asked me the reason for my visit.

"What are the odds that Salroon is a vampire?" I asked.

The question took him aback somewhat, but after a few moments of deep thought, he said it was possible. When I told him I killed two more bloodless Diefetians since my last visit, he then revised his answer and said relatively high.

"Why do you ask?" he questioned.

"Because Salroon showed up at the palace, and my brother, in the hopes of possibly securing peace, foolishly let him and his royal guards in," I explained.

"That's concerning, but what does this have to do with me?" he asked, the inflection of his voice pointed to his confusion.

"My brother is not listening to reason," I said. "But if someone credible could convince him of the possibility that Salroon's a vampire, my brother, devoted to the Protectorate as he is, would begin to listen to reason."

"And you think that's me?" asked Ilkon. "Why would you think he'll listen to me? You killed a handful of vampires already, and the king isn't listening to you, so why would he listen to me?" He had a fair point.

"Because you are a believer, and I am not," I told him. "Rono knows I don't believe in the gods, and I was skeptical about the existence of vampires, so he won't believe I am sincere. If you do it, there is a good chance you can get him to realize how much danger he's putting himself, his family, and the kingdom in."

"You want me to persuade the king that Salroon is a vampire just because the Diefetian king is associated with vampires? Would King Rono even be persuaded without hard evidence?" asked the heretic.

"I am sure you can do it," I reassured him.

"I don't know," Ilkon said.

"Look, all the alleged vampires I killed took orders from Salroon, right? Why wouldn't Saloon also be a vampire? Does your sect know of any instances where vampires followed and took orders from a mortal man?" I asked.

"I can't think of any, and I have read the Sacred Texts and our histories many times over," he admitted.

"Then all you have to do is tell Rono that," I said.

"How are you going to get me to the king?" Ilkon asked. "If people figure out who I am, it won't look good for the king's pious image."

"I will get you a soldier's uniform, armor, and a weapon and tell him that we have something to report," I told him.

"Isn't impersonating a soldier illegal?" asked Ilkon.

"You ask as if I care," I said.

"I don't want to hang for it," he said.

"The punishment is beheading," I corrected.

"I don't want that either," Ilkon said with a horrified expression.

"It's not illegal if I make you a soldier," I said.

"You can do that?" he asked.

"I am still a member of the royal family. I abdicated the throne, but my brother never stripped me of my titles. Though he should have when he named me an outlaw, he didn't. Maybe he thought he didn't need to because I abdicated. Regardless of his reasoning, I am still a prince of Eshtar who can accept recruits into the Eshtaran army," I explained.

"It wouldn't be illegal then," Ilkon concluded.

"And I would have the power to dismiss you from the army after we return from the palace," I said.

"Okay, I'll do it. But, how are you going to get me a uniform, a weapon, and armor?" he asked.

"I'll go to the barracks and ask to borrow a uniform. I have a friend who is a blacksmith, from whom I can get a breastplate and a weapon," I answered.

Ilkon agreed, and I headed to the barracks to get him a uniform. As I walked into the barracks, I found Halerod, who had a look of surprise on his face that quickly faded into dread. He asked why I was there, and I told him I needed a uniform. Judging by his reaction, I think he thought I had two heads.

"Why do you need a uniform?" asked the lieutenant. "You're an advisor, not a soldier."

"I didn't say it was for me," I told him.

"Then who is it for?" he asked.

"A recruit," I answered truthfully. "Though I just need to borrow it for a couple of hours because he is going to be discharged by the end of the day."

"That sounds suspicious," Halerod said.

"If I needed it for illegal activities, I have other ways of procuring a uniform," I admitted. "My brother is making a serious mistake, and I need to get someone in the palace to help him see the error of his ways without drawing too much attention. That's why I need the uniform."

"I'm not sure if I believe you," Halerod said.

"Halerod, we both know that I have no qualms about stealing a uniform or killing a soldier to get one," I said. "I didn't have to come here and ask you for one, but here I am. If you say no, that's fine. I will find another legal way to get a uniform: coming back with my nephew and ordering you to hand one over."

"Fine," Halerod said as if he wasn't still terrified of me and wouldn't fold if I got a bit rough with him. "You can borrow my spare."

"Appreciated Lieutenant. If all goes well, I will have it back by nightfall," I promised him.

"And if all doesn't go well?" Halerod asked, worry visible in his eyes.

"Best not to dwell on those things, Lieutenant," I told him after he handed me his spare uniform. I walked out and headed for Billen's shop.

When I entered Billen's shop, his apprentice was at the counter. He called for Billen when he saw me come in. A few moments later, Billen walked down the hallway towards the front of the shop.

"Back so soon," he said.

"I need to borrow a breastplate," I said.

"For you?" he asked.

"No," I said. "But for someone about my height and weight."

"You know these things need to fit properly to work, right?" he asked.

"Just estimate, it's urgent," I ordered. "And I need a dagger, something a soldier would carry when walking around without any armor."

"I can do that for a price," he said.

"It's going to sit on a hip for an hour or two, not see combat," I argued.

"Then consider it a rental fee," he said.

"I don't have the time for this," I complained, placing a gold piece on the counter. "Just get them."

"It's that urgent," he said.

"It is, so I would appreciate it if you hurried up," I told him.

"Alright," he said, then reached down behind the counter and brought out a dagger of the same style and length regulated by the Eshtaran army, which he placed on the countertop. It was what I wanted to see. He then went down the hall and grabbed a standard breastplate.

"Thank you," I said, taking the dagger and breastplate from the counter.

"Whatever it is, good luck," Billen said.

"I might just need some of that," I said as I exited the shop.

When I returned to the inn, Glendeo asked what the uniform, breastplate, and dagger were for. I told him he would see me in a few minutes, then went over and knocked on Ilkon's door. The heretic opened, and I handed him the gear. I told him to get changed.

A few minutes later, Ilkon walked out of his room, wearing the standard black pants and green shirt of the Eshtaran army and wearing the breastplate. The pants and front of the shirt had no design, but on the back was the Eshtaran deer.

"Are you ready?" I asked.

"No," he admitted.

"You look like a soldier, and that's all we need," I said, not caring whether he was ready. "Let's get moving."

He followed me into the lobby, where we found Glendeo. The old man was still by the counter, standing with his hands crossed over his stomach, looking towards Ilkon's room. When he saw the heretic emerge looking like a soldier, he sighed.

"I know you don't respect the law, Bowv," the old soldier began. "But could you at least respect the concept of serving one's country?"

"That's what I forgot," I said, turning to Ilkon. "Just say yes to the following questions, so we make this legal, and Glendeo doesn't throw the knife he keeps under the counter at my head. Remember, I'll discharge you after you convince my brother of his stupidity."

"Okay," Ilkon agreed, though it sounded like a question.

"Only a member of the royal family or an officer of appropriate rank can accept recruits into the army," objected Glendeo, guessing what I was planning to do.

"My brother never got around to stripping me of my titles or rank," I said.

"He didn't strip you of either?" a flabbergasted Glendeo asked.

"No, he didn't because he was obsessed with capturing then executing me. Now, Ilkon, do you swear to defend our home, the Kingdom of Eshtar, with your life?" I asked.

"I do," he answered.

"Do you swear to be her people's shield in times of war?" I asked.

"Yes," the heretic said.

"And do you swear loyalty to Eshtar's king, to never raise an arm against him, to defend him, and to answer his call to war when the time comes?" I gave the final question of the oath.

"I do," Ilkon said.

"Then, by my rights as Prince of Eshtar, I accept you as a soldier of the Eshtaran Army. May you serve the kingdom, whether as a sword or shield," I recited the last bit of formality that made Ilkon a soldier.

"I am surprised you remember all the lines," Glendeo chimed in.

"With enough repetition, the mind won't forget anything," I remarked, remembering how often my father had made me recite them. At one point, I couldn't eat dinner until I had recited the lines without error.

"I remember a time when you took the oath seriously. You lived by it," the old soldier said.

"I remember those times well," I told the veteran. "I was a foolish and idealistic boy who didn't comprehend what the world was. It was a time of naivety and ignorance, and both were taken from me on the battlefield. Now, I do not have time to argue with you about the oath or what war is. I need to get our friend here to the palace before the consequences of my brother's stupid decision begin to unfold."

I could see it in Glendeo's eyes that he wanted to argue with me, but for once, the old dog bit his tongue. I gestured to Ilkon, and we headed out of the inn. Then, we began the short walk to the palace. Ilkon was tense as we walked, and his stride was quick as if he knew he was doing something he wasn't supposed to be doing and wanted to get it over with. I told him to relax, telling him everything was fine since neither of us had broken any laws, nor were we about to.

After I said that, he relaxed his posture, and his stride slowed. I told Ilkon to follow my lead when we got to the palace gates. The guards recognized me, and we were let in without any problem from the Eshtaran or the Diefetian guards. As we walked into the palace, we headed straight to the throne room. I had no idea whether Rono would be there, but I figured it was the best place to try to find him. My brother was there and alone, except for a few guards.

"Back so soon?" the king asked, and it looked like he was about to say something else. He stopped midway when he saw who I was accompanied by and what he was wearing.

"I am, and I believe my companion has valuable information for you," I answered. "To be discussed in private, of course."

"Of course, guards leave the room and ensure no one enters," the king ordered. After the guards had left the room and Rono looked around to make sure there weren't any servants in the room with us, he resumed talking. "This is risky even for you, Bowv, not to mention having our friend here impersonate a soldier is illegal."

"It's not illegal. You never stripped me of my titles, so like it or not, brother, I am still a prince of Eshtar, which means I have the power to accept recruits into the army. He would have caused suspicion from your guests and everyone else in the palace if he didn't come here without a soldier's uniform," I defended my actions.

"Be that as it may, though, why have you brought him here?" Rono asked. "Honestly, I don't see how this benefits you."

"Not everything has to benefit me, brother. I'm a bandit, not a nobleman. And in this case, it benefits you more than it does me. You see, our friend here has something very important to tell you," I said.

"I believe there is a good chance that King Salroon is a vampire," Ilkon said.

"Of course you do. Every vampire Bowv has killed has been close to him or a member of his court. I doubt that vampires would take orders from a mortal man," Rono reasoned.

"Then you can't make a deal with him," I said. "Your faith does not permit it."

"You are not the one to lecture me about what my faith does or does not permit!" Rono snapped.

"But our friend here can," I said, turning to Ilkon and ignoring my brother's outburst. "Am I right or wrong? Can someone who firmly believes in the Protectorate and their laws make a deal with a man we are certain is a vampire?"

"It is possible, but it would also be inconsistent with that person's beliefs because they would be negotiating with an enemy of the Protectorate," explained Ilkon.

"Yet, the gods have stated they wish kings to end wars peacefully whenever possible," countered Rono.

"What makes you think Salroon will be willing to agree to peace when you cannot give him what he wants?" I asked.

"He hasn't done anything rash while he's been here. Perhaps he will be willing to settle for something other than the sword," Rono argued.

"What else might that be, brother, the Eshtaran throne?" I asked, and anger swept across Rono's face, and he snapped.

"Out of the two of us, I have remained loyal to the kingdom. I haven't abandoned my responsibilities to the kingdom or its people. You are the one who killed Father, your king, jeopardizing the stability of the realm, then decided not to wear the crown. Do not speak to me about harming the kingdom when you have caused enough harm to it," he said with a raised voice full of anger.

"That's all true, Your Majesty," Ilkon interrupted our exchange. "But it does not change the fact as a devoted believer in the Protectorate and someone who has concluded King Salroon is most likely a vampire, then negotiating with him, even if it is for peace, is something you shouldn't do."

"And what would you two have me do? Continue a war Eshtar cannot fight?" asked the king. "Bowv you are a brilliant general, but not even you can pull this off."

"But the gods can," Ilkon spoke. "Your Majesty, you must admit it is more than coincidental that your brother kills a vampire who just so happened to have the Sword of the Gods. Then, shortly after you managed to capture Bowv, a miracle, and before you ordered Bowv to be executed, you learned that he may have killed a vampire wielding the Sword of the Gods. You asked him to take you to the corpse and then the sword. By doing so, you come across several other vampires your brother killed."

"What are you saying?" Rono asked.

"Perhaps you find yourself fighting this war and that your brother finds himself in possession of *Hueik* because the gods have chosen both of you to eliminate a vampire threat," elaborated the heretic. As soon as Ikon said that, I knew he would persuade Rono.

Rono fell silent. He knew Ilkon had him in a bind; there was no way out. For Rono to deny that the gods had a hand in how events had turned out would be to deny the existence of the gods entirely, something that was impossible for him to do.

My brother may have been taking a long shot by wanting to negotiate with Salroon, but that noble intention fell beneath his piety. Before Rono was a king, he was a man of faith, something instilled in him by our mother. It was that faith Ilkon was appealing to, something I couldn't do with any credibility. Ilkon had Rono backed into a mental corner. I was not surprised when Rono was about to speak but was caught off guard when Jorn entered the room.

"Father," he said.

"This better be urgent; we were in the middle of something important," Rono told him.

"The guards have reported that Salroon has left the palace," reported the prince.

"Left the palace," echoed the king. "Did he take his guards?"

"He did," confirmed Jorn.

"You two don't need to persuade me any longer," Rono said. "Looks like you were right, Bowv; Salroon wasn't going to make peace."

"This isn't good," I said. "Salroon must have been close by when he arrived earlier today, and judging by his clothes; we know he has been fighting the wars himself. He could be returning to his army or in the city performing sabotage with his guards."

"Like the barracks or a supply warehouse," Jorn said.

"And those guards could be vampires," added Ilkon as if things couldn't get worse.

"Which one is the most likely Bowv?" Rono asked.

"Considering Salroon wants *Hueik,* I would wager he has an army, or at least a sizable force nearby, to try to take the city in the hopes of cutting me off from escape," I said.

"How nearby? How much time do we have?" Rono asked.

"It depends. It could be a week or a couple of days," I said. "Though that's assuming he is bringing an army."

"What are we going to do if that happens?" Rono asked.

"I don't know what you are going to do. But I am going to kill Salroon," I told him.

"I will not have you murder a king when you are my advisor!" exclaimed Rono.

"So, murdering the ambassador was okay? We know Salroon is surrounded by at least a couple dozen royal guards and is most likely heading back to an army. I can assure you there will be no murder. We know the Diefetian king is a fighter; he won't stand still when I draw my blade, so calm yourself," I lectured my younger brother.

"Could you track him?" Jorn asked.

"Track Salroon? What for? He could be at Kihlop's gates in a matter of days at the most," I told my nephew.

"Assuming he is not still in the city trying to perform sabotage," Ilkon said.

"I don't think he would still be in the city," Jorn said.

"Why is that?" I asked.

"Because there is not much to sabotage besides supply warehouses or the barracks," the prince said. "But they didn't seem to have the numbers for that. The only other thing that would keep them in the city is the chance to take the sword."

"The sword would be a good reason to stay in the city," I admitted. "But we are not certain they have left the city. All we know is they left the palace."

"Then we need to find out because if they are still in the city, Salroon will come for the sword, and we can't risk him getting his hands on *Hueik*," Rono decided. "Bowv, take Jorn to each of the city gates and ask the guards if our visitors have left the city."

"And if we find out that they didn't?" I asked.

"Return to the palace, and we will discuss our next steps. In the meantime, since the war is still going on, I will check to see if the rest of the army is close," he said, dismissing us.

By this time, the sun had set, and the pitch black of night had consumed the city, forcing us to take a torch while we exited the palace. The palace had always been well stocked with torches and lanterns; as a child, it seemed we had an infinite supply of both. You don't have to worry about fires when your palace is made of stone.

As we stepped out of the palace, the warm glow of the torches dimly lit up the roads enough that we could see the cobblestone they were made of and about fifteen or twenty feet in front of us. Considering that the Diefetians might still be in the city, I would have liked the torches to illuminate the dark streets more.

Except for the occasional candle in the window or a group of city guards or soldiers passing us, everything in about a twenty-foot radius was covered in impenetrable darkness, the perfect environment for an enemy to lay in wait. Jorn must have had the same thoughts as me because whenever my nephew heard footsteps in the distance, he would turn his head like a deer, which heard a predator's footsteps towards the direction they originated in, and he would increase his grip on the torch.

I knew better. There would be plenty of people out in Kiholp at night; it was the capital of a country at war. Messengers would be sent to and from the palace regardless of what hour it was, and a few soldiers would accompany the ordinary city guards who patrolled the streets at night to bolster the number of men on patrol.

If Saloon or his guard were still in the city and looking to attack us, then they wouldn't hide on the edges of the street like a group of thugs waiting for a victim to mug. No, if they were still in the city, they would have likely laid a trap for us, not a simple ambush in the streets where a nearby patrol would join the fray. I wasn't concerned about a fight; I was concerned with being followed.

Salroon could have left the city to recruit an army and left some of his guards here to watch our response. This would have given the Diefetian king insight into our next move, making repulsing an attack on the city more difficult.

When we got to the first gate, the northern one, the guards were standing in their usual spots watching for anyone who wanted to leave the city during the night, which was once typical for them because there was always a steady flow of merchants and traders in and out of the city, no matter the hour. But the bustling trade that saw Kiholp and other Eshtaran cities prosper diminished almost to the point of vanishment after the invasion, no doubt leaving the gate guards with boredom as a near constant companion, something that makes guard duty a dreadful experience.

When we approached the gate, a glimmer appeared in the guards' eyes, which appears when a man who has been bored for hours receives a sense of purpose. Being assigned to guard duty while I was younger, I knew the jolt of excitement they were feeling all too well. The guards recognized Jorn, and all six gave their prince a short bow as he approached. They didn't recognize me, which was fine since I wanted them focused on Salroon.

But if I thought Salroon had bribed them or they were working with him, I would happily disclose my identity to motivate them to tell us the truth. I told Jorn before we got within hearing range of the guards that he would be asking the questions.

"Why me?" he asked.

"Because they don't look like they know who I am," I said. "Which we want to keep secret if we can until we may need to entice the truth out of them."

"So, you think they are working with the Diefetians," Jorn concluded.

"It is a possibility," I answered. "We'll see how they respond to your questions."

The guards responded well to Jorn's questions. They admitted they knew Salroon and his guards were in the city, but they didn't enter through the north gate or exit through it. Jorn looked at me to see if I was satisfied with their answers, and I gave him a nod. We began the walk to the western gate, where the same events played out.

Jorn asked about the Diefetians, and the guards told us they didn't enter through their gate, nor did they leave through it. On our walk to the southern gate, the last gate we needed to visit, this pattern broke. The guards told us that Salroon and his men did enter through the city at the southern gate, but they had yet to see the Diefetians again.

Jorn turned and looked at me, worry on his face. I thanked the guards for their time and motioned for Jorn to follow me. Once we got out of earshot of the guards, my nephew told me his conclusion: Salroon and his bodyguards were still in the city.

"Perhaps," I said.

"What does it mean?" he asked. "They couldn't have gotten out of the city without being caught by a city guard or a soldier."

"What is possible and what you think is possible are two separate things," I informed him. "One of the first lessons your grandfather taught me about war was this: if you wish to do something without being harassed by the enemy, then do something he thinks is impossible."

"They may have gotten out of the city then. But how?" the young prince wondered as we walked back to the palace.

"How do you think they could have escaped the city?" I asked.

"Walking out of the gate or climbing over the walls," he said.

"Then those might be your answers," I told him.

"But the gate guards didn't say they saw Salroon and his guards exit the city, and the walls are too high to climb," he protested.

"What guards knew what the group of Diefetians looked like," I asked.

"Only the southern gate guards," Jorn answered.

"Which leaves three whole other gates where the guards haven't seen our distinguished visitors, which they could exit as one group or several groups wearing clothes which didn't reveal their identities," I explained.

"Sounds like you have firsthand experience in these matters," Jorn commented.

"Of course I do. Ninety percent of the time, if you don't raise suspicion, you can walk out of a city without being harassed by the guards. For instance, after I killed Leernu in Travelios, we left the body there. I told your father we needed to get out of the city before the guards started to investigate, if they did bother to investigate. We didn't give the guards any reason to be suspicious towards us, and as we left, they didn't give us any problems," I said.

"Father told me about that," Jorn said. "Anyways, what is our next move?"

"We go back to the palace and wait," I said.

"For what?" he asked.

"For news that Salroon is on his way back with an army or for whatever he did in the city, if he did do something, to be discovered," I told him.

"That's it? We wait, that isn't a proactive strategy," Jorn said.

"Of course, we will be collecting as much information as we can while we wait, but you're right; it's not a proactive strategy," I admitted. "But we can't attack an enemy when we don't know where he is. We can only sit and wait until Salroon reveals his hand."

"What happens if Salroon returns with an army and besieges the city?" Jorn asked.

"Then I'll need to get creative because we can't withstand a siege," I said

The walk back to the palace was uneventful, though Jorn was still seeing enemies in every shadow, and in each alleyway we passed, he would tense up, expecting an ambush. For me, it was a calm walk by torchlight through the city. Though my guard was up, it always was, but I didn't have the anticipation that Jorn had. Instead, I had caution paired with readiness.

Could Salroon and his guards have emerged from the walls of darkness, which touched everything the light of our torches could not reach? Yes, they could have. But Jorn thought it was a certainty, even though, at this point, we didn't know if the Diefetians were still in the city, which made him far jumpier than I was on the way back to the palace. When we reached the palace, we immediately went straight to the throne room, where Rono awaited us.

"Has Salroon left the city?" he asked.

"He could have. The Diefetians came through the southern gate, and the guards there claimed that Salroon and his party hadn't returned to that gate," I informed him.

"Then they could still be in the city," Rono said.

"Or they went out a different gate than they came in," I said. "Or several other possibilities, including scaling the walls, tunnels, bribes, and threats."

"You don't trust the southern gate guards," stated my brother.

"I don't trust any gate guard. Bribes and threats aside, they aren't known to be an observant bunch," I told him.

"You would know how easy it is to sneak out of a city," he said.

"I do, and it's simple, especially if people aren't looking for you," I said, stressing the last bit.

"What should we do?" he asked.

"He wants to wait," Jorn answered for me.

"Wait," Rono said and gave a questioning look.

"It's the situation we're in, brother, reacting to Salroon's next move. He has more information on us than we have about him. We could spend resources gathering information to determine if Salroon has left the city, but we can't plan our next move until he reveals his next move or we figure out what it is," I explained.

"I see," Rono said. "That's not what I wanted to hear. What would Salroon do if he was still in the city?"

"Try and get the sword or sabotage the war effort," I said. "Those are the two most likely things."

"You have to worry about one, and I have to worry about the other," Rono concluded.

"Indeed," I said.

"What's the likelihood that Salroon left the city and is on his way here with an army?" asked the king.

"High, since we have no hard evidence Salroon is still in the city," I said. "I advise sending out some scouts if those do exist in your army, to see if they can come across a Diefetian force coming this way," I advise.

"And if Salroon comes back with an army? What then?" my brother asked.

"I get creative and see if I can get Salroon to fight me," I answered.

"Which you will not," Rono sternly said. "The fate of the war depends on your survival."

"Salroon can't kill me, and once he is dead, the war will be over," I argued.

"Until his successor takes over," countered Rono.

"Which would take weeks. The Diefetian army's head would be severed, and while Salroon's successor is being crowned, his generals will be jockeying for power," I refuted.

"By seeing which one of them can take the most Eshtaran territory," the king said.

"Father," Jorn interrupted. "If Salroon does turn out to be a vampire, then he is too dangerous to be left alive. I don't think it is a coincidence that Uncle Bowv came across the Sword of the Gods just before you managed to capture him. Then a war broke out with a king who we suspect is a vampire."

"Ilkon has already expressed the same opinion," Jorn's father informed him. "I am having him look into the possibility that Saloon is a vampire."

"We already agreed that Salroon was a vampire," I said.

"We agreed that it was probable, but I want to be certain. That's what Ilkon is searching for now: certainty," Rono said.

"If Salroon does attack, we may get that certainty sooner than we think," commented Jorn.

"I'm sure he will attack," I said.

"And what are we going to do? We can't resist a siege," the king said.

"Remember, brother, early in the war, we talked about the one advantage we have: the sword. We know Salroon wants it. He has said that to our faces, which means we can control him," I said.

"What do you mean control him?" Jorn asked.

"He will go to wherever the sword is," I said. "If we move the sword, then Salroon and the Diefetians will follow."

"You just said the ball was in Salroon's court," Rono pointed out.

"It is," I said, "We can't do much until we know whether or not he is bringing an army to our front door. When we know his intentions, we can derail them by moving Hueik, and then we can counterattack."

"Where would we move the sword to? Salroon has most of the Continent under his control," asked Rono.

"The Desolate Lands," I said.

"Bowv, you can't be serious," Rono said.

"I am. It's a location outside Salroon's grip and the perfect place to wear down an army," I said.

"An army?" Jorn asked.

"If we can convince Salroon to send an army after me," I said.

"Brother, don't be ridiculous," insisted Rono.

"A 3,000-strong inexperienced army against who knows how many thousands of veteran Diefetian soldiers. My plan isn't more ridiculous than the odds we're currently facing," I said.

"It is a feasible plan, at least," Jorn interjected.

"Maybe as a backup plan," Rono said.

"Brother, where's the army? Are all the 3,000 soldiers even in the city?" I asked.

"They are," confirmed Rono.

"It's just enough men to defend the capital in a siege," Jorn stated.

"You're right," I told my nephew. "If we take them out of the city, then we will lose the city."

"Then what do we do?" Rono asked.

"My plan, that's what we do. I know you don't like it, but we need to see what Salroon has in store for us before we can do anything since we can't fight an enemy we can't find," I told him.

"We will discuss this more in the morning," Rono said, dismissing the both of us.

I left the throne room and exited the palace. As I began the short walk back to Glendeo's inn, I wondered what I could do with 3,000 soldiers. As I walked into the inn, I asked if Ilkon was still there, and the innkeeper confirmed he was.

Earlier, the heretic told Glendeo to expect many scrolls to be delivered to the inn and to notify him when they arrived. Taking this to mean Ilkon hadn't gotten a chance to investigate Salroon in earnest, I decided not to take the time to stop by his room. There wasn't a good reason to do so late at night when he had no information for me. Instead, I bade Glendeo a good night and headed towards my room.

As I lay on my bed, I again considered leaving and assembling a new bandit clan. But only for a moment before I returned to the problem. I don't know why I didn't decide to abandon Rono and leave him to solve the problems that were a consequence of his poor decisions.

At first, I agreed to be his military advisor because I knew Salroon would keep sending men after me, and being around an army would offer some protection. But when Rono told me the size of the Eshtaran army, I knew I could get more protection if I restarted my bandit clan, though I would have to do some recruiting than stay as a quasi-member of the Estaran military.

Looking back, maybe I didn't decide to leave because it felt good working with my brother. Maybe it was because deep down inside, I regretted abdicating, and I was seeking reconciliation by helping the kingdom in one of its darkest hours. Maybe I started to grow attached to my nephew and his endless questions.

As an older brother, I may have felt I had to help my younger brother out of a tough spot, but at the time, all that wasn't at the forefront of my mind. I wanted Salroon dead, and helping my brother gave me the best chance of killing the Diefetian King.

When sleep finally came over me, so did the past. My dreams thrust me back into the War of the Triad, reliving the battle of Odfret. I could feel the weight of my armor and the heft of my spear in my hand. Despite being an observer, Father had me in armor and armed in case I did need to fight. The ringing of metal, mixed with the moans of the dying, creates a harmonious tone one can only experience on a battlefield, casting a spell of surrealness over those who hear it.

A messenger from the rear informed us the enemy had attacked us from behind, news we didn't want to hear when the enemy was already pushing our front lines back. I wasn't in charge; Father had paired me with a colonel to see what it was like to command a battle. I wasn't supposed to fight, and I wasn't supposed to give orders. I was supposed to be a watcher, not a combatant.

Everything changed when an arrow barrage killed the colonel and his second in command, and then the messengers from the rear, where the general and his staff were, stopped coming. The enemy kept moving closer, pushing our front lines further and further back. Ten soldiers fell for every foot the enemy gained. Our lines started to wave, then broke.

What was once the organized fighting of two neat phalanxes struggling against one another became small groups of the enemy honing in and slaughtering isolated Eshtaran soldiers who weren't fast enough to pull back. The casualties mounted as the seconds passed. Eshtaran soldiers darted past me, and unless something were done, a full rout would ensue.

The ones who weren't retreating and weren't being attacked were staring at me, looking for me to tell them what to do. They shouldn't have had. My father hadn't given me command over anyone yet, and the whole army knew it. But with the commanding officers dead, someone had to give orders. Why not the prince?

The soldiers looked at me and saw the son of a warrior-king. They didn't know this was the first time I witnessed a battle up close; they didn't know an unnerving fear was rushing through my veins like a stampede of stallions threatening to paralyze me or my stomach had twisted into a Gordian knot.

The men looked at me as if I were a military genius like my father. They didn't know that for a thousand heartbeats, a small voice telling me to survive was the only semblance of tactical brilliance that formed in my head.

I yelled for the men to regroup on me. My voice was shaky when I did; the panic hadn't yet subsided in me, and I believed none of them would obey. But those who weren't fighting approached me and began reconstructing our broken line. Our line grew as Eshtaran soldiers still trapped in the group melee vanquished their adversaries and fled to the relative protection of our newly formed line.

I knew we couldn't beat them. The Rushide had more men, and with no messengers from the rear, I knew the rear was either dead or in retreat. I saw the enemy walk towards us and knew I had to act fast, or else our lines would break again, and we would be slaughtered. I didn't have enough men to flank the enemy, and after a few brief moments of thought, I came to a dreadful conclusion: we would have to break their line.

I left the formation and made my way to the middle of the line. Taking my place at the phalanx's center, I ordered the soldiers to my left and right to slant the line to form an inverted V, with me as the top point. Then, I gave the order to move forward.

As we approached the enemy, panic built up as fast as sweat poured down my face. I hoped we could puncture the middle of their line with our newly formed wedge, and it would break, giving us a chance to escape and march back to camp. Even if the enemy bent their line to match ours, I hoped we could still break out if we kept moving forward and kept up the pressure.

Being at the front, the only protection I had was my shield. As I walked forward with heavy, determined steps, I realized I would be in stabbing range for three enemy spearmen until the two soldiers behind me got close enough to engage. My heart began to race, yet I continued my slow, intentional walk

A spear was thrust at me. As my eye caught the glimmer of its head, the fear of death pushed adrenaline through my veins. Acting on instincts drilled into me by Glendeo, I brought up my shield to defend myself before any recognition of danger formed in my mind as the spear hit my shield. With abnormal speed, I lowered my shield, raised my spear, and, with no target in mind, thrust my weapon forward. The sharpened spear tip ripped through the Rushide soldier's throat. Sprinkles of blood splashed out of his throat as he dropped dead to the ground.

It was the first time I had ever killed anyone. I froze. My arms began to shake so much I couldn't control my shield or spear. I nearly dropped both. I saw an object out of the left corner of my eye gleaming in the sunlight.

With my mind failing to process the danger I was in, my body acted independently of my mind as I raised my shield and blocked the spear just in time. The force from the spear's impact transferred from the shield and moved through my arm. The jolt it caused was the reminder I needed of where I was and the danger I was in.

By that time, the two men behind me had engaged the enemy. The Rushide didn't have the time to fill the hole in their line I caused. With the space still empty, I pressed forward, treading over the corpse of the man I had killed moments ago. I continued to move forward. Sometimes, my spear would strike the enemy soldier's shield. Sometimes, it would strike their flesh, and they would fall to the ground, wounded or dead.

It took an hour of hard fighting, but the Rushide were pushed back, and their line broke. Not wanting to give them time to regroup, I ordered a retreat. Once we escaped, I led my men back to the main army camp. It was a three-day march without food.

We must have looked half-dead when we arrived at camp. I didn't know if we lost anyone when we punctured the Rushide line, but none of us died on the way back to camp. When the camp sentries spotted us, they yelled for surgeons and rushed to us. A guard approached me, and I collapsed into his arms. If it weren't a dream, I would have woken up in the surgeon's tent with the fatigue and headache only three days without food can cause.

Instead, I woke up in my bed in my room at Glendeo's inn with the bright light of day shining through the window. I've heard about people reliving memories in their dreams, but it was a first for me. I blamed Jorn and his questions.

I got out of bed and went to find Ilkon. I needed to know if the heretic made any process of proving that Salroon was a vampire. I walked down the hall to Ilkon's room and knocked on his door.

Ilkon said, "Come in," and I entered. The room's floor had become a sea of scrolls, and there were so many. Ilkon had a clear path from his desk to the door, and it branched off about a quarter of the way to the door towards his bed. Despite the number of scrolls on the ground, chaos did not reign.

Each scroll was laid horizontally, with one end pointed to the end of the room where the desk was while the other pointed to its entrance. The scrolls were pushed up against one another so much I needed to squint to see if there was any space between them. Each scroll was tied with a colored ribbon, either green, blue, or yellow. I couldn't begin to imagine how long it took to organize all of them.

"I take your silence to mean you're impressed by my organizational skills," Ilkon said, not bothering to look up from the scroll he was reading. I had never seen a man surrounded by so many scrolls before.

"I am," I said. "How goes the search?"

"About as well as a hunt where your hound is too busy sleeping to track your quarry," he said. "I can't find any indication that Salroon is a vampire."

"Where have you been looking?" I asked, still frustrated that Rono had the heretic searching for proof when it was almost a certainty the Diefetian king was a vampire.

"The scrolls in red are from my order's archives. We compile notes on any suspected vampire. If the suspected vampire is tied to a government, we compile notes from various sources, not just through observation. The blue are copies of Diefetan biographies on their kings, the green are copies from any author who was, or still is, close to Salroon and wrote about him, and the yellow are gifts from King Rono, they hold spy reports on Diefet and its king," he explained.

"I didn't know my brother was spying on Salroon," I said.

"No one was except him and the spies he sent," Ilkon said.

"It sounds like you've got enough information to determine if Salroon is a vampire. What's the trouble then?" I asked.

"My order watched Salroon from afar since we couldn't get close to the king. What prompted us to observe the Diefetian king was a hunch from one of our most senior members, a man renowned for uncovering vampires. The initial investigation didn't find much, and we ceased observing Salroon, so those scrolls don't possess much useful information," Ilkon explained.

"What about the others?" I asked.

"The scrolls written by people who were, or still are, close to Salroon had to be published with Salroon's approval, and if any of the authors knew about Salroon being a vampire, then they wouldn't include it in their work. I have the biographies of the Diefetian kings to see if there may have been other kings who could have been vampires, but again, they had to be approved by the king to be published. The spy reports from King Rono are perhaps the most useful due to their recency, but the spies were looking for information that didn't concern Salroon being a vampire," Ilkon listed.

"Like whether he would invade Eshtar," I said.

"Precisely, and it appears that the king's spies concluded he wouldn't," summarized Ilkon.

"How unfortunate," I grimly said.

"It's like the king carefully approached a horse only to be kicked in the face," the heretic observed.

"Yes, it is," I agreed with a laugh.

"But other than Salroon's plans for invasion, the spies didn't gather any useful information that would help me," Ilkon informed me. "Are you alright? You look exhausted."

"I didn't sleep well," I told him.

"Bad dreams?" asked the heretic.

"The worst kind," I said.

"Nightmares?" he asked.

"No, the kind where you relive the past," I clarified.

"What did you relive?" Ilkon asked. His tone and inflection revealed he was more interested than I thought.

"Nothing important," I said.

"Yet, I heard from Prince Jorn you had another dream on the road back to Kiholp," he said.

"Why do you care?" I asked.

"Certain traditions say *Hueik* is not merely a weapon forged by the gods but acts as a medium for the Protectorate so that they may communicate with their chosen," he explained.

"Yet another myth for me to ignore," I said.

"Like vampires?" the heretic smugly asked.

"Your point is noted, though that does not mean your other point is correct," I said.

"Perhaps, much like how you killed a vampire without realizing it, the gods are sending you messages," he argued.

"If the gods sent me messages, their purpose would be clearer. Urging me to believe and repent," I gave an argument of my own.

"Perhaps," he said. "As much I would like to argue this further, I have work to do. Come see me if you wish to talk about your dreams."

"No promises," I said and turned to walk down the narrow pass between scrolls Ilkon had made. I walked down the hall to the inn's lobby and headed for the exit. Glendeo was behind the counter.

"Dreams, eh?" the old man said loud enough so I could hear him. I was standing in front of the inn's door with my hand on the knob when he said it. I turned around towards him.

"Here I thought your hearing was going," I said. "And you weren't spying on your guests anymore."

"I haven't been a spy since your brother took the throne," the innkeeper claimed. "But that doesn't mean I don't overhear my guest,"

"Which is the polite way of saying you eavesdrop," I accused. "Same thing as spying, as far as I am concerned."

"Fine, I was eavesdropping. I want to make sure you won't do anything rash in my inn," he admitted. "Now, what's this about dreams?"

"Why do you care?" I asked. "As I recall, you didn't want to give me a room in the first place."

"If those dreams are about past battles, it could mean your mental state isn't stable. I've known men to relive wars in their sleep, and their minds snap. They can't distinguish past from present; some are so bad they end up killing their loved ones while they dream of the war," the old soldier said.

"I've had two," I said, knowing Glendeo wouldn't relent until I answered him. "The one last night was what you described. I was reliving the Battle of Odfret. The first one was different; it was on the trip back to Kiholp from Tuldum; I don't know what it was."

"What was the first one like?" he asked, and I described my first dream to him in detail. I told him about everything: the darkness, the moon, the tombstones. As I detailed the dream, Glendeo had a puzzled look on his face. I wasn't sure if it was because he was trying to decipher the dream or thought the whole thing strange. When I was done with my descriptions, he still had the look on his face.

"What do you think they mean?" he asked.

"I don't know about the first one, but I must have had the second on because I stirred up some old memories talking to Jorn about the War of the Triad," I said.

"When was that?" Glendeo asked.

"About a day ago, when we were returning to Kiholp. The boy wanted a history lesson," I said.

"That could explain the second dream but not the first one," he agreed. "What did Ilkon think about the first dream?"

"I didn't tell him any details, though he told me he was willing to discuss them again," I answered.

"Maybe you should because I can't make heads or tails of it," the old warrior suggested.

"Nor can anyone else. Perhaps I'll talk to him about it later, but right now, I should get to the palace to see if we know if Salroon is still in the city," I said.

"I won't keep you then," Glendeo dismissed me.

I exited the inn and began the short walk to the palace. I couldn't get my first dream out of my head on the way. What did the darkness mean? Why was it closing in on me? What did the moon represent? What were the gravestones at the end? It was obvious that the five dead suspected vampires were vampires, but that was the only thing that made sense.

And why did I have the dream? I told Jorn about the Battle of Odfret a few days before my second dream. Was Ilkon right? Did the gods provide me with the dreams because I possessed their sword?

I wasn't ready to answer those questions. I didn't want to admit the gods existed and didn't want to experience what Glendeo described. I didn't have to worry about the gods possibly providing me with *Hueik* because I had already arrived at the palace and switched my focus back to fighting the war.

As I entered, I walked past the two guards stationed in front, and I could tell they were anxious. I guessed Rono didn't hear anything about Salroon, or at least didn't tell the guards what he knew. I went straight to the throne room and was surprised to find the throne empty except for Jorn.

"Where's your father?" I asked.

"Follow me. He's upstairs," Jorn instructed.

Jorn walked past me, and I followed him out of the throne room into the hallway, which had alternating silk banners depicting the Eshtaran deer or a symbol for a member of the Protectorate. No other decorations adorned the walls unless you count unlit lanterns.

I followed Jorn to what I knew to be the southern side of the palace, where there was a flight of stairs. I had a suspicion as to where we were going. Still, I wasn't quite sure because I thought Rono would have renovated the upper floors of the palace to his specifications, which meant repurposing and redecorating rooms in a stone palace.

I followed Jorn down another hall that was barren of decorative banners. I was surprised since its barren state implied Rono had kept the hallway like Father had. Then I realized Rono didn't change much in the first-floor hallway; he just swapped Father's old banners for ones made from silk and added a lot more.

I followed Jorn down the hallway, passing so many doors it felt like we passed one every third step. Finally, after passing what must have been a couple of dozen doors, Jorn stopped in front of one and gave a knock. I heard Rono say, "Enter," Jorn opened the door, and we walked in.

The room wasn't large, but it didn't need to be since there were never more than five people in it. In the center of the room was a table with maps covering it and scrolls, both rolled up and opened, which occupied the edges of the maps. The maps were made of forun, a rare material more durable than a scroll. Each map depicted Eshtar.

One map was of Eshtar's geography, another was a political map showing the territories within the country, and the final one was another political map. However, it had numbers scrawled on it, along with a series of red lines and arrows. There were no chairs around the table; Rono was standing and leaning over the table with both hands on it.

About five feet from the table was my father's old throne, a silent, wooden reminder of the past. Rono had told me he had moved the seat to another room. I didn't expect the other room to be the war room, but it made perfect sense.

"I can't imagine how much dust must have been in here," I said, thinking about how little the room had changed since Father's reign. Even the table was the same. Sure, the maps and the notes on the maps changed, but they always did.

"You don't give me enough credit," Rono said. "I've been in here more often than you would think."

"Considering that this is a war room, and this is your first war, I doubt it," I told him.

"True, but I have used this room before," he insisted.

"To hide from annoying diplomats," I guessed.

"To track your movements," the king revealed.

"A personal war then," I said.

"You could say that," my brother agreed.

"Speaking about movements," I said. "Any word on Salroon's movements?"

"No," he informed me. "And it concerns me."

"Chances are he is coming back with an army to besiege the city," I said.

"He could very well be," Rono agreed.

"What are we going to do? We can't hold out in a siege," Jorn chimed in.

"We can't. So, I need to see if I can come to a diplomatic solution," Rono said.

"Brother, don't be a fool. If Salroon wanted a diplomatic solution to the war, he wouldn't have left the palace," I argued.

"He's right," Jorn told his father.

"It's all I can do," Rono claimed. "If it does come down to a siege, then we know it will end in defeat for us."

"He won't settle for anything except for the sword," I said. "That is assuming he's not planning to backstab you after he has it."

"What other choice do I have?" the king asked.

"The option I recommended. If Salroon shows up with an army, I lead him and his army on a chase," I said. "Preferably to a place where attrition will wither away his army, and the Desolate Plains are the best grounds for that."

"I can't allow that," Rono said.

"You don't trust me, do you ?" I asked. "You trust me to be your advisor, to train your son and command him in war, and to break two sieges. But you don't trust me enough to let me travel freely without having a rough idea of my movements."

"It's not that…" Rono began.

"Now's not the time to stop being honest with me, brother. We both know you can't hurt my feelings," I urged him.

"For the time being, I do trust you, Bowv, though not completely; I would be a fool to do so," Rono said. "But I don't trust your plan. It leaves too much to chance."

"I understand the plan is risky, but it is far better than a siege," I said.

"And if you die and Salroon gets the sword? Not only will he come back here and level the city, but the Sword of the Gods will fall into the hands of a monster," he said.

"The sword's already in the hands of a monster," I told him.

"An actual monster, Bowv," my brother clarified.

"You called me a monster before," I reminded him. "The day you stuck me in that cell, screamed it at the top of your lungs. Don't you remember that? If you don't, surely you'll remember the time you called me a monster after I killed Father."

"I'm talking about the stuff of nightmares," Rono argued.

"I am the Terror of the Continent, Killer of Kings. I have monopolized the nightmares of emperors, peasants, and everyone in between. I am a monster," I said.

"Gods forbid you take a blow to your ego," my brother exclaimed. "When I say 'monster,' I am talking about a demon-created abomination."

Jorn, who looked very unsettled as Rono and I had our heated exchange, decided it was a good idea to steer the conversation back on track. "So," he said. "What if we faked it?"

"Faked what?" Rono asked.

"The chase. What if we faked it?" Jorn asked again.

"Then we risk Salroon finding out that he is on a wild goose chase, then turning around to lay siege to the city," Rono argued.

"But what if we used the sword as a lure? We could use it to get Salroon and his army to follow us, then lead the Diefetians to a place where we can trap them," suggested the youngest member of our group.

"It could work if we pick our ground right, but we risk his troops breaking our lines. We would need to even out the odds even more," I said.

"By doing what?" asked the king.

"Attacking the enemy's supply lines, poisoning their wells, night raids," I informed him.

"That's not honorable," Rono told me.

"There's no honor in war, only death," I said.

"A pleasant thought," Jorn said.

"But it comes from a grizzled veteran," Rono pointed out. "It would be unwise to ignore it."

"I am shocked to hear you say that," I said.

"I have never seen a battlefield, though I believe that will be changing soon, and you have seen plenty, perhaps too many," he said.

"But is Salroon coming with an army?" Jorn asked, once again changing the topic. No doubt he was uncomfortable with the conversation's current tone.

"We don't know," admitted Rono.

"Then what are we going to do?" the prince asked.

"I sent out scouts to see if an army is marching our way to besiege the city," the king answered.

"Do you even have scouts? Not one of the soldiers you sent with us to Gregoros and Tuldum was a scout," I asked.

"There are scouts in the Estaran army, Bowv," my brother reassured me. "That's how I knew where the enemy was besieging."

"Are there some in the capital?" I asked.

"Of course. I may be inexperienced in war, but I am not stupid," he said.

"Then why haven't you sent them out sooner?" questioned Jorn.

"Because your uncle was right: Salroon could have still been in the city. I only have a few scouts here; I didn't want to waste them trying to find an army that may not have been there initially," the king explained.

"Have you sent out the scouts or not?" I asked.

"I just sent a messenger with orders about ten minutes before both of you arrived," the king informed us.

"Good," I said. "But you should reconsider Jorn's suggestion."

"And ignore the fact the Diefetians have the better-trained army while I do?" Rono asked.

"We just need to survive long enough for me to kill Salroon, not murder brother, since the Diefetian king will join his men in battle. The rest of the army should route once I kill him in battle. And Salroon's death may give you the chance to find a diplomatic solution to the war," I explained.

"Sounds too simple," Rono said.

"The best plans are," I told him.

"Wouldn't Salroon's successor hunt you down after you kill him?" asked my nephew.

"If I murdered him, then yes. But this will be on the field of battle, supposed honorable combat. I would be responsible for his death, but it would reflect poorly on Salroon's successor if he took vengeance when Salroon was killed in battle," I explained. "The Kingdom of Diefet will be in a crisis after their king dies. Salroon's successor will have to worry about all the wars his predecessor started and controlling an army sprawled across the Continent."

"Much like I had to do when you killed Father," Rono interjected.

"But you could pursue vengeance. Salroon's successor won't be able to," I said.

"I like to think I was pursuing justice," Rono argued.

"Which isn't much different from vengeance," I said.

"I beg to disagree," the king stated.

"Then you are being disingenuous with yourself," I insisted.

"We can argue this later," Rono said. "It would be best if we moved on and discussed picking a battlefield if a Diefetian army does come."

"Fine," I agreed.

"Where do you think we should fight the Diefetians?" Rono asked me.

"Ideally, I would want a place close to the city so we could have somewhere to retreat," I said. "But there's no terrain by the city which will give us that advantage. Plains surrounds us, and I doubt we could make it to the forest with Diefetian calvary chasing us."

"So, we have to go further out and risk losing the entire army," Rono said, reading my mind.

"Unfortunately," I said.

"How far away from the city are you thinking?" he asked.

"I don't know," I admitted. "It would depend on what direction the Diefetians approached from."

"And we need the scouting reports to tell us that," Jorn realized.

"We do, but I would guess that since Salroon came into the city via the south gate, the army would be coming from the south," I said.

"If they come from the south, where would you suggest we fight them?" asked Rono.

"Near Lake Viltder, if they are that far. They may be that far, considering we didn't stumble on a Diefetian army while searching around the city for the cavalry," I said. "And we'll need to find a spot to get the Diefetian army's rear to the lake."

"How would we do that?" Jorn asked.

"We could get lucky and catch them marching past the lake at the right angle," I told him.

"You can't rely on luck," Rono said.

"You're starting to sound like Father," I told him.

"How do we get their backs to the lake?" Rono asked.

"We persuade them to make camp by the lake," I said.

"And how do we do that?" Jorn asked.

"By making sure there's no other clean water source around them," I said.

"We are not poisoning wells," the king said.

"We don't have to poison them for a long time, brother; we just need to make the Diefetians believe they can't drink the water," I said.

"That doesn't make any sense," Jorn said.

"There's a chemical that lasts only a few days in water. If we use this poison on any wells near the lake, then the Diefetians won't know which wells are poisoned, and they will make camp by the nearest source of fresh water," I explained.

"Is this chemical deadly?" Rono asked.

"Not at all. It induces vomiting and fatigue," I answered.

"Doesn't sound poisonous," Jorn said.

"In high doses, it can kill a man," I informed him.

"And if it is the substance that I am thinking about, it is illegal," Rono said.

"Serpetum is not illegal," I said.

"Yes, it is," the king informed me.

"Since when?" I asked.

"About two years ago," Rono told me.

"It's not even that deadly. You have to give twenty times the normal dosage for it to kill a man. Surgeons have used it for centuries," I protested.

"It killed a nobleman's son," Rono said.

"Probably because some quack gave him too much," I said. "Which is hardly an excuse to ban the substance."

"Fortunately, Father did not make it illegal for surgeons to possess it, so we should be able to obtain some," Jorn said.

"Good, and maybe we can include something more potent," I suggested.

"Brother, we are not risking villagers' lives," Rono insisted.

"They can evacuate their villages; they will already do so when they see Salroon's army coming. What's the harm of adding something more potent into the wells to slow down the Diefetians?" I asked.

"Because when the war is over, the villages can't use those wells without getting sick," argued the king.

"You can rebuild," I said.

"We won't use Serpetum or any other toxic chemical," Rono said with a tone of finality.

I was about to argue when we heard a knock at the door. It was a messenger. He quickly entered, bowed to his king, handed Rono a scroll, and whispered something in his ear. An inquisitive look crossed my brother's face, and the messenger bowed again and left the room. Rono undid the scroll and began to read; surprise popped onto his face.

"What is it?" I asked.

"It's a message from Salroon," he answered.

"What does it say?" Jorn asked.

"It says he will duel Bowv for the sword," Rono told us.

"Any peace offers mentioned?" I asked.

"No, but Salroon is proposing you two duel for the sword. If he wins, he takes *Hueik* and withdraws his armies from Eshtar," Rono informed us.

"And if he loses the duel?" I ask.

"There's no mention of what happens if he loses," the king said.

"Where's the duel? When is it? Is it to the death?" I asked.

"Salroon says to meet him outside the city's south gate at dawn tomorrow, and the duel is to the death," my brother answered.

"Looks like he was still in the city or at least nearby," Jorn commented.

"Then I will be there," I said.

"This could be a trap," Jorn pointed out.

"It most certainly is," Rono said. "And I don't like the idea of you, Bowv, willingly walking into a trap."

"I'll be the only one at risk," I said.

"No, the whole kingdom would be at risk since you are the only one capable of fighting this war," Rono pushed back.

"It's better than waiting for Salroon to besiege the city," I argued.

"Not if we lose the war!" Rono said, raising his voice. "If you die, the war is over, and Diefet conquers Eshtar."

"I think he is right, Father," Jorn interrupted us. "If he can kill Salroon, the war will end."

"And if Salroon kills him, a vampire will have the Sword of the Gods," Rono countered.

"Is that better than letting the war continue and have Kiholp burn?" Jorn asked.

"If Bowv dies, then we will lose control of the one weapon that makes killing vampires easier, and we don't know how many there are or what they are planning," argued the king.

"Lord Gaenic was a vampire, and the world didn't end because he had *Hueik*," I reasoned.

Rono turned to face me, his eyes glowing with seriousness, "Can you win?"

"What type of a question is that, brother?" I asked. "Of course, I can win."

"And if it's a trap?" Rono pressed.

"Then I will need to get myself out of it," I said. "And I don't think I have to remind you that getting out of traps is a specialty of mine."

Rono dropped his graze to the table, and silence filled the room. The king's eyes were darting back and forth from the different maps, only stopping briefly to land on key numbers or locations, then shot across the map to other important information. When this erratic behavior ended, Rono tilted his head and stared at the wall across the room. Silence filled the stone room as the Eshtaran king stood still and weighed his options. He had the emotionless expression of a man operated by the cold, efficient gears of reason and logic.

Whole minutes passed as Rono decided what was best for the kingdom. I knew he had a point. If I died, no one else could fight the war. I didn't care since I knew I could beat Salroon, and my concern wasn't for the kingdom. No, my only concern was killing the Diefetian king in a way that wouldn't cause his successor to seek retribution.

Rono, though, had to think about the kingdom when making a major decision. In this case, it was a decision no one could have predicted he would need to make. Who could have predicted that the Wretched King's youngest son would determine Eshtar's fate with one decision? Only a true prophet could predict that the decision would involve the son who abandoned the kingdom, dueling a foreign king to the death.

"I will allow it," Rono said, breaking the silence. "Though I do not like the idea of you walking into a trap."

"I've walked into plenty before, and it helps when you know you're walking into one," I assured him.

"Then it's decided. All we have to do is wait for dawn," declared the king.

"I'll be at the inn if you need me, and I'll see if Glendeo knows anything about how Salroon fights," I said.

"Why would he know that?" Rono asked.

"Because he's a nosy innkeeper, that's why," I told him.

"Father, if it's okay with you, I would like to go with him," Jorn said.

"Why?" his father asked.

"The boy wants another history lesson," I predicted, and Jorn gave an affirmative shrug.

"Very well then, but don't ask your uncle too many questions. I won't have you tiring him out before the duel," Rono said, dismissing us.

We left the room, and I told Jorn he couldn't start asking questions until we got to the inn. I didn't want to be battered with questions about the past while I was walking through my childhood home. The emotions attached to memories are far harder to keep at bay when your physical surroundings don't trigger memories.

Much to my enjoyment, we walked down the stone hallways of the palace without my nephew asking a single question about his grandfather, his father when he was young, or myself when I was growing up. The silence held as we exited the palace and began the short walk down the street to Glendeo's inn. After we entered, greeted Glendeo, and sat at a table in the lobby, Jorn began asking his questions.

"Why do you want to kill Salroon?" my nephew started with an unexpected question.

"Do you remember what Billen and I told you about the Hushta Unkae?" I answered with a question of my own.

"A group of nobles paid them to kill you. You killed several of the assassins they sent and brokered a peace," he recalled.

"You did what?" Glendeo asked in astonishment.

"You heard him, and it was years ago," I said, ignoring the old man. "Why do you think I did that?"

"You didn't want to die," my nephew answered.

"Of course not. But I did it because they needed to learn no one tries to kill me and gets away with it," I explained. "I only needed to kill a few of their assassins, then persuade the leaders to give up the contract, not the names of the noblemen because the Hushta Unkae's reputation depended on them not disclosing the names of their clients."

"So, you ended the Husta Unkae contract to kill you so you could kill the people who hired them to kill you," Jorn reasoned.

"Precisely," I said.

"And Salroon was willing to kill you and Father when he sent Leernu to receive the sword, so you want him dead for it," my nephew further reasoned.

"Right on the money," I confirmed.

"That's the only reason you were willing to put aside your differences with Father and agree to become his military advisor?" he asked.

"Pretty much," I told him.

"You are going to kill Salroon and be done with the kingdom?" he asked.

"Of course he is," Glendeo said, injecting into the conversation. "Bowv doesn't want to be a part of the kingdom. If he did, your father would not be on the throne."

"There's your answer," I told Jorn.

"What about your dream?" Jorn asked.

"It's irrelevant," I said.

"I have yet to hear about this dream," Ilkon said, walking into the lobby. "Though I suspect we are talking about different dreams."

"You had more than one?" Jorn asked.

"I had one about the Battle of Odfred, the battle you asked me about on the road. I relived it in my dreams," I explained.

"But that doesn't tell me anything about the first one," Ilkon protested.

"No, it doesn't," I agreed.

"You should tell him. He may be able to make sense of it," Jorn said.

And so, I did. I recalled everything from my first dream to them, from standing in the field surrounded by the murky darkness to the end, where the darkness dissipated, and how I was left looking at the gravestones at the end of it all.

"What do you think?" I asked.

"I think you have killed a lot of vampires," Glendeo said.

"We already knew that," Ilkon said.

"What do you think, Ilkon?" Jorn asked.

"I think it wasn't a coincidence your uncle came across the Sword of the Gods," the heretic said.

"That's what Billen told him," Jorn agreed.

"If the gods chose a murderer as a champion, then they chose poorly," I said.

"They chose perfectly," Ilkon argued.

"How so?" I asked. "Why would the Protectorate appoint a murderer as their chosen? It goes against everything they are supposed to stand for."

"To kill vampires," the heretic reasoned.

"Ridiculous," I claimed.

"He has a point," Glendeo said.

"Of course he does," I admitted. "But it doesn't make it less ridiculous."

Ilkon ignored my insult and said he couldn't decode all of the dreams for me, insisting the gods never send straightforward messages, which I thought was suspiciously convenient for the priesthood. How wrong I was. Ilkon deciphered the darkness as the presence of vampires and connected the moon to *Hueik* since the sword was said to have been forged from a sliver of the moon. But the heretic couldn't make sense of anything else in the dream other than suggesting the vampires were alluding to something more significant than the war.

"What could be bigger than a war for a kingdom?' Jorn wondered.

"It doesn't matter," I said. "At dawn, it will be all over when I drive my blade into Salroon's chest. Now, if you excuse me, I need to get some sleep." Standing up from the table, I went to my room to sleep and got a dreamless night's rest.

Chapter Seventeen

I GOT UP ABOUT AN HOUR BEFORE DAWN, attached *Hueik* to my hip, and began my journey to the southern gate. I had dueled plenty of times, often when one member of my bandit clan challenged me for its leadership. Those always ended with the challenger's eyeless head mounted on a stick in the center of camp. I would always order the challenger's eyes to be removed before the head was mounted on a stake. I like the symbolism: they were blind to the fact they couldn't beat me, and I was the better leader of the clan.

It never happened often, but someone would always forget about the last guy who challenged me and then end up suffering the same fate. Though it wasn't an everyday occurrence, it happened enough times that my dueling skills weren't permitted to get too rusty. I knew Salroon was far more capable than the wannabes in my clan, but I wasn't too worried. Glendeo's training saved me time and time again, and I knew it wouldn't let me down.

I was anxious as I walked down the city streets with a torch, steadily working toward the southern gate. It wasn't the anxiety that stemmed from being unconfident. I was sure I would walk away from the duel victorious while Salroon would be a corpse. No, what I was anxious about finally getting a chance to kill Salroon. The Diefetian King had given his underlings authorization to kill me, and I wanted to feel the hilt of my sword slam into his chest after the blade pierced through.

I didn't care about Eshtar, and I didn't care about Diefet if Salroon died. I wanted blood. The duel could end the war, but that was irrelevant to me. I wanted the whole Continent to be reminded of what happens when someone tries to kill me. When I got to the south gate, I found a crowd waiting for me. Rono, Jorn, Billen, Glendeo, and Ilkon were all loitering around, holding torches, and awaiting my arrival. I figured out why Rono and Jorn were there but wondered why Billen, Glendeo, and Ilkon showed up.

"I thought we both agreed this was going to be a trap," I said to my brother as I walked up to the five of them.

"It most certainly will be a trap," Rono stated. "But we all wanted to see the duel."

"I suspect the old man's here to see if his training has lasted all these years," I said.

"I am," Glendeo confirmed.

"I don't suppose you all have a plan for when Salroon springs his trap?" I asked.

"We do not," Billen answered.

"Well, I wasn't expecting you to," I said.

"So, what are we going to do when Salroon moves?" Jorn asked.

"We will do what is best for the kingdom," Rono said.

"So, you'll surrender," I said.

"We will do what is best for the kingdom," my brother repeated.

I looked straight at my brother, right into his eyes. "Don't give up so easily," I told him. "Father, for all his faults, knew it was a king's job to fight no matter the odds, especially if he is the king of Eshtar. Is Salroon here?"

"Not yet," Billen said, so we waited.

As we waited for the guards on the wall to announce that Salroon was approaching, the tensity in the air rivaled the thickness of the five-foot city walls we were standing by. Jorn, the youngest and most restless of our group, made a few half-hearted attempts at starting a conversation, but none of us were willing to take the bait. Between these intermittent attempts at breaking down the walls of silence, Glendeo would complain about his feet or back.

After some time, the sun rose high enough from the horizon, illuminating our surroundings so we no longer needed torches. Soon after dawn's break, we heard the guards on the walls shout they spotted Salroon. Rono ordered them to open the gate, and within moments, we heard the creaking of wood and the movement of chains as the guards operated the wheel, which lifted the iron gate off the ground. I was impressed it took them less than a minute to lift the gate. With the gate up, we walked out of the city.

I could see Salroon walking along the road with five members of his royal guard walking behind him, each carrying a spear and a shield with a sword attached to the hip. They were about ten minutes out, and as they continued walking toward the city, I was scanning the horizon, looking for additional Diefetians. There were none, and I wondered what Salroon's trap was. There was no sign of a trap, though, which in hindsight should have concerned me, but I was too focused on killing Salroon to be paranoid.

As Salroon got closer and closer to the southern gate, I could see that he did not wear the regalia of a king but the durable and plain clothes of a soldier. Yet, the Diefetian king had an aura of majesty around him. The way Salroon walked had the grace and air of a king and the tone of an army on the march. Each foot was put down and lifted back up with the discipline and mechanical motion of a man who had been a soldier for most of his life.

The Deifetian king's walk was a portal to the past since Father had an identical walk. But I didn't allow myself to dwell on the similarity. What would be the point? Father and Salroon were warrior-kings, and I suspect I would have walked the same if I had kept the throne.

Deciding that Salroon was close enough, I walked outside the gate and onto the road. Rono, Jorn, Billen, and Glendeo moved behind me. I don't know what they were planning on doing if I lost. Rono and Ilkon were useless in the fight, Jorn was a little more than useless, and Glendeo was years past his prime. Billen was the only one out of the group who could last in a fight. Maybe that's why Rono brought him. Glendeo, Ilkon, and Jorn probably came to see the duel.

Identical to Salroon and his guards, the four of them walked behind me. Judging by the message that Salroon wanted to duel outside the southern gate, I didn't walk far. It was a good spot for a duel with even ground, and the sun wouldn't be in our eyes. But being a good location for a duel didn't mean a trap couldn't be sprung. Salroon had entered through the south gate when he arrived in Kiholp, which allowed him to lay a trap if he already had the duel in mind, which I expected was what he had done.

When Salroon came to the palace and offered Rono peace for the sword, the Diefetian knew it was a long shot when I wasn't factored in and an impossibility when I was, but it cost Salroon so little to ask, and if successful, he would get what he desired. It may have been a long shot, but it was sensible.

But Salroon knew Rono wouldn't agree to peace if it meant Salroon got *Hueik*, so he needed a backup plan: the duel. Once Salroon came across the land outside the southern gate, he knew he had a location for a future duel and laid some trap. That's what I thought.

Minutes later, I was face to face with the man I wanted dead more than anything else in the world. He looked straight at me with the raised gate behind me. The raised gate gave Salroon a glimpse of the city. The gate's frame acted like a picture frame surrounding the piece of the city just behind it. I stood back towards the city walls, looking out at the meandering road and the opening of flat land, which stood at the feet of a sprawling forest. Salroon stood there, his guards about ten feet back from him, standing tall with his hands by his sides and a stoic look on his face.

"I will give you one last chance to hand over the sword," the Diefetian king said.

"We should discuss the terms of the duel," I said.

Salroon smiled, "I propose a fight to the death. If I win, I take the sword; if you win, I make peace with Eshtar."

"And your successor, or any member of your court or your family or army, cannot seek vengeance for your death," I proposed.

"I will agree to that," Salroon said. But you are confident that you'll win, Bowv. Do you want to make a proposal that involves you losing?"

"I won't lose," I assured him.

"Then I accept the terms," Salroon said.

"As do I," I agreed.

We approached each other, and Salroon drew his standard Diefetian army sword roughly the same length as *Hueik*. As Salroon pulled back into a high guard, I drew *Hueik* from its scabbard and took up a low guard. Salroon moved closer. His guard remained steady as he did, then swung his sword at my ribs.

I brought Hueik up within a heartbeat and heard metal cling on metal. I feinted at his chest, then flicked my strike toward the king's head, but Salroon didn't take my bait and raised his sword to block my attack. Our swords met, and I stepped out of his attacking range, dropping back into a low guard.

"You have my respect, Bowv. Lord Gaenic was one of the best swordsmen on the Continent," Salroon said.

I responded with an offensive. I struck low and high, thrusted, and cut. Each attack was faster than the winds of a hurricane, fueled by the desire to see Salroon dead. Yet, Salroon blocked each attack with the delicacy and effectiveness of a master. Failing to land a single blow on the Diefetian, I pulled back, this time to a high guard right before Salroon began his attack.

The Diefetian attacked slowly at first, slow enough that I had more than enough time to counter them. Usually, I wouldn't have paid any mind to such attacks, but as I raised my sword to block each attack, I caught several glimpses of Salroon's eyes. They were cold and calculating. He was using simple and slow attacks to control the timing of the duel so he could study how I moved with little risk. It was in that instance I began to respect Salroon.

After the king finished his last attack, I pulled back, once again getting out of his range, but this time choosing to come up into a high guard. "You're good, Salroon," I admitted. "But I will kill you."

"We will see about that," the king answered as if he were responding to a boasting child.

Before the words were out of his mouth, Salroon was closing the gap, and within moments, he thrust his sword low, striking at my leg underneath *Hueik*, but this time, it had the speed of an attack meant to hit its target. I dropped *Hueik* down to meet the king's blade. Less than a second later, I felt the blades connect. I tried to knock Salroon's sword to the side, then followed up with an upward thrust to his stomach. But I didn't manage to knock Salroon's blade far enough.

The Diefetian whipped his sword back to block my attack. The force of our blades slamming into one another sent shockwaves down my arm. Moving with speed, I pulled back to a middle guard as Salroon transitioned from a block to a counter. The king raised his sword over his head, then whipped it down with the intent of splitting my head wide open.

Rapidly, I raised my sword over my head to block, and the Diefetian's sword slammed into mine. Straining my arm, I strengthened my defense by pushing my sword against his. My arm began to shake. Sensing that he could break through my block, Salroon began to push down harder with his sword.

Suddenly, the pushing stopped as Salroon's sword separated from *Hueik*. Someone less skilled would have pressed an attack once they felt the tension release. Not me. Well-honed instincts kept me from attacking, telling me to be on guard because my adversary had not completed his attack. When Salroon arched his sword down and to his right, hoping to strike at my ribs, I swung *Hueik* around to block. Our weapons clashed, and we withdrew from each other's striking range, returning to guard as we did.

"I'm almost regretting that we agreed to duel to the death," Salroon said. "The Continent has so few great warriors nowadays."

"You aren't going to win," I said.

"I will win Bowv. I wouldn't have suggested a duel if I didn't know I would win," the king said smiling, then muttered some words under his breath, words I couldn't understand. For a moment, Salroon's eyes flash red. I could feel *Hueik* grow cold in my hand.

I didn't have time to process the change as Salroon rushed towards me. Ignoring my sword freezing in my hand, I held my guard, ready to defend against Salroon's attack. The Diefetian king moved significantly faster than he was moving before and reached me well before I thought he would. Now close enough, Salroon began a series of fast strikes with inhuman speed.

I knew Salroon was a vampire, but no other vampire I had fought moved that quickly. Salroon's attacks all blurred together. Instincts drilled into me by Glendeo and honed during war saved me as my body performed the proper blocks before my mind could register what Salroon's attack was.

I expected Salroon to exhaust himself and pull back. Instead, the Diefetian pressed his attack, moving even faster than before. I struggled to defend against the king's onslaught. Each time I felt his sword clash with *Hueik,* my sword arm weakened, and my fingers, numb from holding an almost freezing sword, threatened to drop the blade.

As I defended, I noticed mist forming around us, though minutes ago, I could make out Salroon and his guards walking on the road from a far distance. My sword arm burned as I kept up with Salroon's offensive. The mist began to thicken.

The king's assault did not stop, and I could feel exhaustion sweeping over me, and sweat was pouring down my face. I began to feel a pulling sensation as if some distant destination was calling to me. I could hear Glendeo shout something to me, but his voice sounded faint and distant. My guard collapsed, and I felt Salroon's blade pierce my right thigh. Pain shot throughout my leg as I fell to the ground.

The mist thickened so much that it threatened to block out the sun. Beyond the pain, I felt a tug towards somewhere, but I didn't know where. Despite lying on the ground, I still gripped *Hueik,* ready to fight until death. Salroon approached, not noticing the mist had formed a wall around us.

"I told you this was a fight you couldn't win, Bowv," Salroon said as he walked towards me.

The mist thickened even more, becoming as dense as a mountain. The pain in my leg subsided, and I felt like I was moving despite still being on the ground.

Finally, Salroon took notice of the mist around us. "Impossible," Salroon said, almost in awe.

I began to lose consciousness.

"You chose *him*!" the king shouted. "The man who committed patricide and regicide in one act. The Terror of the Continent! You chose him, of all people?"

"I have," a deep, ancient voice answered.

The blackness of unconsciousness threatened to overtake me completely.

"You can't!" protested the vampire.

"I can," the voice repeated in the same tone.

I lost consciousness.

Chapter Eighteen

WHEN I AWOKE, I DIDN'T KNOW WHERE I WAS. I wasn't out in front of the southern gate; I knew that much. I couldn't feel the pain in my leg anymore, and when I looked down at it, there was no wound. *Hueik* was no longer in my hand. Instead, the sword was resting in its scabbard.

I was in a small room with a high ceiling. Its walls were a dim grey except for the two large doors in front of me. They looked like solid gold, though they were most likely gilded. I looked around the room for clues to where I was, and there were none. The golden doors were huge, but they were absent of decorations and handles. The hinges provided the only clue that they were doors and not walls.

"You're not dead," a man behind me said. His monotone voice had an uneasy steadiness to it.

I turned to face a man dressed in a black shirt and pants who was not there before. He was pale as a corpse. The blackness of his clothes was accented with an aura of finality.

"Of course, I'm not dead. Where am I?" I asked.

"Ah, that's the question, isn't it?" the stranger said. "Where are you, Bowv, Terror of the Continent?"

"You know who I am? Then you know it would be wise for you to give me an answer," I said.

"Ah, but I can't. If you want answers, you'll have to walk through those doors," the man informed me.

"And why can't you tell me where I am?" I asked, annoyance clear in my voice.

"Because you're not dead," answered the stranger.

"Fine," I said, the annoyance in my voice turning into frustration. "How do I open the doors? There are no handles."

"Draw *Hueik* by the doors, and they'll open for you," the stranger answered.

"That doesn't make any sense," I said.

"It makes perfect sense to me," the pale man replied.

For a moment, I debated whether I should kill him but decided against it because he was the only one who could tell me where I was.

"You couldn't even if you tried," the man said with a smile, though his eyes only had the subtlest glimmer of life.

"Do what?" I asked.

"Kill me," he answered.

"Many men have said the same thing before I ended their life," I told him.

"Men," the stranger said, then let out a soft chuckle. "Just draw the sword by the doors, Bowv. It's an easy thing to do. Do you want to know where you are and how you got here? The answers are beyond those doors."

I wanted to kill the man for his smugness. As my blood began to boil and my hand reached for *Hueik*, I studied the man. Beyond the mask of his pale skin lay an assuredness that was as strong and sturdy as stone. The man truly believed I couldn't kill him.

"Just open the doors," the stranger said, reading my mind. "They're probably getting impatient. And when they get impatient, one of them blames me."

I wondered who he was talking about. Was he referring to his superiors? How many of them were there? Whoever they were, they were expecting me, but why did they put me in this room, not the room beyond the golden doors?

As I thought about the answers to these questions, my frustration with the stranger subsided, and I began to remember my duel with Salroon. I remembered the mist, feeling like I was moving away, and Salroon seemingly yelling to no one before I lost consciousness. But I didn't remember anyone there but Salroon, so how did I end up where I was?

"Just get on with it," urged the pale man, impatience managing to seep through his voice without breaking his monotone.

Needing answers, I walked towards the two golden doors, taking slow steps at first with my hand on *Hueik* in case the pale-skinned man decided to attack me. He didn't. Instead, he stood there with his arms crossed, his expression suggesting he was a busy man and I was wasting his time.

Considering he had wasted my time with his shallow answers, I was okay with wasting his. When I stood before the doors, I noticed they weren't just absent decoration but were perfectly smooth, as if someone had taken a roller to remove any bumps in the metal. I had never seen anything like it before. It was so simple, but its perfection demanded the onlooker stare at it in awe.

As I stood there wondering how someone could have done this, my hand vibrated, still wrapped around my sword's handle. Alarmed, I pulled my hand away, and *Hueik* began to shake in its scabbard. I looked down at the sword, and it shook harder and faster. Soon, the weapon shook so much that the blade threatened to shake out of its scabbard. I shot my hand back down to stabilize the sword.

When my hand wrapped around *Hueik*'s handle, the shaking stopped. I froze, my mind trying to process what had happened. I turned around to see if the pale man in black had anything to do with it, but there was no one else in the room. I wondered how the man had gotten into the room since there was no way into the room save for the golden doors.

I ignored the stranger vanishing because I didn't have an explanation for it, and in the end, it wasn't that important. What was important was that I no longer had to deal with the man and his refusal to answer my questions. I drew *Hueik*. The massive doors swung open away from me as if a giant had pushed them open.

I walked into a room with white marble flooring, and what I found before me caused me to think I was hallucinating. I stood in a semicircle of nine thrones, each occupied by a figure. To my left sat a bearded man with muscular arms wearing a blacksmith's apron with a hammer on his lap. To the smith's left was a man wearing a sailor's clothes. Nets decorated his throne, and its armrests were carved into the shape of dolphins.

Next to the sailor sat a mature woman who had the soft, loving look of a mother. Sitting next to the mother was a young, beautiful woman with long flowing hair who wore a dress that fitted her figure well. To her left, and in the middle of the semicircle, sat an imposing man wearing a gold crown decorated in its center with the scales of justice.

To the king's left was another muscular man, but unlike the smith, he had the figure of a soldier accompanied by a scar running down the right side of his face. A spear rested against the right side of his throne, and a shield was on the left.

Besides the soldier, another woman wore a long dress covered in artistic designs. She sat there twirling a paintbrush as if she had something on her mind she wanted to paint but had to be at her throne instead.

Adjacent to the artist sat an older man dressed in a scholar's long, heavy, brown robes. The legs of his throne were carved to be hourglasses, and the man sat there reading a scroll. Finally, to my far right, and occupying the other end of the semicircle, sat a man wearing the simple grey shirt and pants of a healer with herbs growing on the sides of his throne.

Dread washed over me as I knew where I was: the Hall of the Protectorate. This meant I wasn't just standing before the nine gods to be judged; it meant I was dead.

"You're not dead, Bowv," the king in the middle spoke, who was Numveron, the god of righteousness, justice, and order. The king of the gods and leader of the Protectorate. "I thought I told Tolunfie to tell you that."

"He's seen enough war to know he's not dead," the soldier, Pafix, the god of war, said.

"That's true," agreed the scholar, Wusneric, the god of wisdom.

"We are not here to talk about the past but rather the future," Numveron reminded them.

"Well, you should just get on with it and tell the man. He looks like he's lost a sea right now," the sailor, Kalrekos, god of the seas and patron to sailors, chimed in.

"What do you think he's doing?" asked Junyl, the goddess of motherhood. "He's just standing there."

"It wouldn't be a proper meeting without it taking ten minutes to say why we are here," complained the smith, who was Aeruno, god of craftsmen.

"That's what makes these things exciting," the young woman, Heques, the goddess of beauty, argued.

"And incredibly inefficient," a voice to my far right said. It belonged to the healer, Xaretgriu the god who wards off disease.

"I find there's a nice flow to our meetings," the artist chimed in, and I turned my head to look at her, Ferjera, the goddess of the arts.

Numveron cleared his throat, a clear indication for the gods to put their commentaries to an end. "Do you know why you are here, Bowv?" the leader of the Protectorate asked.

I couldn't speak. How could I? The Protectorate, the very thing I spent most of my adult life denying, mocking, and arguing against its existence, was sitting right before my eyes. My whole worldview shattered like a clay pot dropped from a great height.

Religion, the thing I had cast aside and condemned as valueless, I now had to contend with. The crimes I had committed throughout the past two decades, all the thefts, blackmailing, pillaging, arson, torture, kidnappings, and murders, all of which I had committed believing there would be no divine repercussion because gods who weren't real can't punish, I saw now in a new perspective.

My entire life since I killed the Wretched King was flipped upside down. I stood there frozen as my mind ran rugged, desperately trying to process everything. I heard the gods converse amongst themselves, but I couldn't hear what they said. I barely registered that they were there at all. The next thing I knew, I saw Xaretgriu before me and felt the god's gentle hand on my head. The thoughts flooding my mind dissipated. Xaretgriu walked back to his throne as if he had done nothing and sat back down.

"Thank you Xaretgriu," Numveron said. "Now, do you know why you are here, Bowv?"

"*Hueik*," I said.

"Yes, but there's more to it than that," said the king of the gods.

"Vampires," I said.

"Not just the vampires, but their master, the demon Allemar," the god of justice specified.

For the second time that day, I stood still. I had already accepted the existence of vampires. It's hard to deny something exists when you keep killing it, though it was a struggle to admit it openly. Nor could I continue to deny the existence of the gods since I was standing before them.

But my mind struggled to accept the reality that if the gods and vampires exist, then so would the demon said to have created vampires. The logic was simple, yet I stood there. This time, my mind wasn't working as hard as it was moments before because I never gave demons too much thought.

I didn't enter as deep of shock as I did earlier. When I heard one of the gods suggest Xaretgriu heal me again, I came to, shaking my head in denial. Not only were the gods real, but so were demons. I couldn't dismiss it all as a hallucination caused by me slowly bleeding out from the wound Salroon gave me. But I couldn't, not when I felt Xaretgriu's hand on my head earlier.

"I told you it would be too much for him," Xaretgriu told Numveron.

"He's not still in shock, is he?" Numveron asked.

"No, he's come out of it," the healer assured the king.

"Then why isn't he talking?" asked Kalrekos.

"Probably because we haven't given him a chance to," said Xaretgriu, and the rest of the gods fell silent, then turned their attention towards me.

I knew I had to say something, or else they would think Xaretgriu was wrong, and I was still in shock. "You want me to fight a demon?" I asked, disbelief filling my voice.

"Not directly, of course, that would be suicidal," Numveron said. "We need you to stop Salroon and his vampiric lot by killing them, thus severing their ties to Allemar and weakening the demon's influence in your realm."

"So, this is a proxy war. The vampires are Allemar's proxies, and I would be yours," I said.

"Precisely," Numveron confirmed.

"No," I said. "I want Salroon dead, but I won't fight against a demon. I don't care for your war. Find someone else."

"Son," this time it was Pafix who spoke. "We didn't choose you. If Numveron had his way, then this would be a judgment, and you would be unanimously damned for your crimes. The reason you're still alive and aren't being sent to an afterlife full of suffering is because the *sword* chose you, not us."

"That's ridiculous," I scoffed.

"What is ridiculous is that the weapon we all created, albeit Aeruno forged it, chose *you*, the Terror of the Continent, to wield it after you liberated it from Lord Gaenic," Numveron said.

"You see, the sword was built to be an instrument of our will, but after I forged it, we realized it was not going to the person we selected to be our champion," Aeruno explained. "We can charge the sword to seek someone out to be our chosen, but we cannot tell the sword whom to choose."

"Then how did a vampire come to possess it?" I asked, anticipating another nonsensical answer.

"We don't know," admitted Wusneric. "Our guess is Lord Gaenic killed the previous owner, and the sword did not deem anyone else fit to wield it."

I laughed at the absurdity of it all. The Protectorate created a weapon to kill vampires but didn't know how a vampire came across it. It was as if I was living in a comedy one of the playwrights had written. And they said the *sword* got to choose the person to be the *gods'* champion. If the gods losing track of their divine weapon wasn't humorous, then the gods not being able to pick their own champion certainly was. If this were revealed to me earlier in life, then I would never have believed in the gods in the first place.

"I told you he wouldn't take it seriously," Junyl said to Numveron, her tone rang with annoyance.

"Can you blame him? We just told him a sword chose him," asked Ferjera.

"He's a soldier at heart. Of course, he doesn't believe a *sword* could be sentient," argued Pafix.

"Enough!" Numveron shouted, his voice ringing across the room and echoing off the pristine marble floors.

As the sound waves washed over me, I felt as if I were in a storm. My body jolted as if I just heard an unexpected thunderclap as the god's voice hit me with the force of a hurricane's wind. I stopped laughing. Silence had conquered the room. The other eight gods stood still, eyes locked on Numveron. Not one of them dared to move.

The king of the gods sat there, his right arm resting on his throne, his left elbow placed on top of the left armrest, and the rest pointed up where his hand supported his downward tilting head. The expression on the god's face was one of frustration and exhaustion. Before he became the Wretched King, Father had often worn the same expression during his monthly meetings with his advisors.

Each meeting began with the advisors making one suggestion to Father. Some suggestions dealt with foreign policy, others domestic, which inevitably were tied in with the nobility, and others would be minor, such as palace decorations, when court should be held, and who should organize a festival. At least once during each meeting, a look of frustration and exhaustion would appear on Father's face. As I remembered how Father looked during those meetings, the king of the gods looked all too human.

"Believe what you will, Bowv. I doubt if you will believe what is happening to you right now. But the sword has chosen you as the best person to kill vampires. We don't know why, but it has. Regardless of whether you believe *Hueik* has chosen you, you are already on a path where you are trying to kill Salroon, who will no doubt send more of his vampiric henchmen after you since we pulled you from the duel at Hueik's urging, mind you.

"I was happy leaving you to die. It doesn't matter what you believe; circumstance has already put you on the course we want," Numveron explained, then looked at me, expecting me to respond.

"I want Salroon dead. I don't care about all this talk of vampires and a demon. If anyone gets in my way, I will kill them. If that means I have to fight a hoard of vampires along the way, then so be it. If my actions somehow benefit you, then good for you, but it's irrelevant to me," I said.

"This selfishness and arrogance cost you the duel with Salroon. You didn't care about Eshtar or helping your brother. Nor did you care about the threat vampires pose to the Continent. All you cared about was killing Salroon because he authorized one of his minions to kill you if you didn't give up the sword," observed the king of the gods.

"Vengeance has gotten me farther than belief in any of you has," I said.

"Can we send him back now?" asked Junyl. "He's more of a hindrance than an aid."

"We can, though I'm considering stripping him of the sword," Numveron answered.

"You can't, and you know it," Aeruno interjected. "The sword has chosen, and there is no going back. I know you don't like who the blade has chosen, but it has yet to be wrong."

"I fear this may become its first error," Numveron told the god of smiths.

"If it is, then we can't do anything about it. The die is cast," Aeruno told him.

"Aeruno's right. There's nothing for us to do except trust that the sword has picked the right man for the job," Pafix backed up Aeruno.

"I was only speaking what was on my mind. I know both of you are right, but that doesn't mean I have to like it," their leader said.

"Can we conclude then?" Heques asked.

"We can," Numveron said, then waved his hand, and everything went black.

Chapter Nineteen

I WOKE UP IN MY BED AT GLENDEO'S INN. Immediately, I looked down at my thigh to see if the wound was healed. There wasn't even a scar, the very thing I didn't want to see. *Hueik* was lying in its scabbard right next to me. I grabbed the sword, attached it to my hip, got out of bed, and opened the door. I didn't want to think about what just happened. Either the whole thing was a hallucination, or the gods were real, and I just got evidence to show they were useless.

If the Protectorate was real and concerned about vampires threatening the Continent, why didn't they act? The Protectorate wasn't protecting. Instead, they were passing that responsibility off to someone else.

No, something else, not even a person, who then turns over the responsibility to someone else. Did I believe a sword chose me as the gods' champion? No, of course not. I killed Lord Gaenic, hid the sword, then took Rono to the corpse and then to the sword a short time later. There was no way the sword "chose" me.

Walking down the hallway to the lobby, I had one thing on my mind: how to kill Salroon. I didn't know what the Diefetian king did in the duel, but whatever he did wouldn't work again. Outright murder was an option, but my pride was wounded. I wanted another chance at facing Salroon one-on-one. The Diefetian had cheated somehow; I was sure of it, but I had to think of my reputation. Even losing a duel where the opponent cheated looks bad.

I found Glendeo sweeping the lobby, but it wasn't the normal type of sweeping where he scrutinized each section of the floor to ensure it met his near-impossible standards of cleanliness. No, as the old warrior dragged his broom across the floor, he would stop for a moment as if reflecting, then proceed with his half-hearted attempt at cleaning, permitting the broom to wander wherever it wished. Several times, he would go to sweep a spot, then realize he had already cleaned that spot and pulled the broom back. The normally astute innkeeper failed to register my footsteps as I approached. I had never seen the old man like this: gloomy and despairing.

"Did my brother lose the war?" I asked as I walked into the lobby.

The old man stopped his meandering sweeping and stood still for a moment. He stood there, frozen with his hands glued to the broom's handle, looking straight towards the empty lobby. I never knew Glendeo to be a man easily surprised.

When I was younger, I witnessed him not even flinch when people came rushing through the door of the inn heralding some bad news, or the time when a patron was thrown through a door of a room, or when the building next to the inn broke out in flames when he was training me in the courtyard. In each case, the innkeeper stopped what he was doing and turned his head as if someone had called his name to see what was going on.

Nor did he ever act surprised when Father would have him over for dinner at the palace and he informed his old friend about an unexpected political betrayal or that a country declared war on Eshtar. Glendeo would slowly nod as if to say, "This is how the world works, after all." I only saw the old warrior mad when I killed the Wretched King. I had never seen a man so mad in my life, and I doubt I ever will again.

I waited a few moments, but the old man wasn't turning around. "I thought you wanted me dead," I said, figuring that was what all the fuss was about.

The broom dropped. Once the wooden handle connected with the floor, I heard a small thud. Glendeo started to turn around. The innkeeper was so slow a tortoise could have moved with more speed. Finally, the old man completed his rotation and faced me. His expression was one of shock, and he stared, not believing his own eyes.

"Your brother thought you were dead," Glendeo said.

"That's understandable," I said. "But that implies you didn't."

"I didn't know what to think. We all saw Salroon stab you in the thigh, then you both were consumed by mist. We heard Salroon screaming something, though none of us could make out what he was saying.

"Then the mist dissipated, and you had vanished. Salroon didn't say anything, though he looked like he wanted to kill someone. He barked at his guards to follow him and then headed back down the same road they had arrived on."

"Interesting," I said. I had suspected that Salroon would have insisted he won the duel, and he managed to kill me.

But the more I thought about it, the less it made sense. Salroon wanted the sword, which was the purpose of the duel, so if he claimed to have killed me and didn't have *Hueik*. It wouldn't have made sense for him to claim he killed me without being able to show he had *Hueik*. It wouldn't have gained him anything, and he would have to explain the mist, something he wasn't responsible for, and what he was shouting.

However, I wondered why the Diefetian king withdrew. Was he assembling an army to besiege the capital, or did he leave to begin to hunt me down? Saloon's words before I was transported replayed in my mind. Clearly, Salroon was yelling about me being chosen, so he knew that the gods had whisked me off somewhere. But what was he doing in response?

"What happened?" Glendeo asked.

"I don't know exactly," I gave an honest answer.

"You don't know?" the old man asked.

"Mist suddenly formed around us, and then something crazy happened. That's all I know," I told him.

"What's the crazy part?" Glendeo asked.

"You wouldn't believe me even if I told you," I said.

"I don't think I would," he said. "But regardless, your brother thinks you're dead, so if you're going to tell anyone about what happened, you could do it when you're at the palace."

"I thought he wanted me dead, too," I said.

"He does. Same as me," the old man admitted. "But I think King Rono wants you dead. He has to make you pay for killing your father and the other crimes you have committed. Your brother Rono, now that's a different story. I don't think he wants to see you dead; you're his older brother, after all, and no man wants to see his brother dead, regardless of what he has done."

"And what about you?" I asked

"You know my opinion," the old warrior said.

"I thought I did, but you were gloomy when I walked into the room," I said.

The old veteran gave a dismissive grunt.

Knowing all the conversation I would get from the old man, I walked out of the inn and headed towards the palace. I began the short walk down the street when I saw Jorn walking towards the inn. My nephew froze as if to check his mind wasn't playing any tricks on him.

"It's me," I said as I walked towards him.

"We thought you were dead!" the young prince exclaimed. "Well, everyone except for Billen."

"I should have figured. Billen knows not to count me out unless I'm cold and dead," I commented.

"To be fair, Glendeo wasn't sure at first if you were dead or not," Jorn said. "He was debating it for a few days."

"A few days!" I exclaimed. "How long has it been since the duel?"

"A little over a week. Nine days, I think," answered Jorn.

"What about the war?" I asked.

"The Diefetians haven't marched near a city as far as we can tell," the prince informed me.

"What about Salroon?" I asked.

"Haven't heard from him since the duel. When that strange mist disappeared, he gathered his men and walked straight back the way they came," Jorn said.

"What has your father been doing?" I asked.

"Not much. He thought you were dead and didn't take it well," Jorn told me.

"That's because he knows he doesn't have anyone else to fight the war for him. Eshtar is doomed without me," I said.

"How can you say that?" he asked.

"Say what?" I asked.

"Father took your death hard because of the effect it would have on the war and the kingdom," my nephew said. "You're his brother."

I put a hand on his shoulder. "Kid," I said. "Your father will never forgive me for what I've done, and he shouldn't. When he had me in that cell, we both knew he was going to execute me. And I've killed so many people I deserve to hang more than once.

"Your father doesn't care for me. But he's always cared about Eshtar, even when he was younger. It's what makes him such a good king. I felt I could abdicate partially because I've never cared for the kingdom as much as he does. If your father was unsettled by the thought of me dead, it was because he needed me to help the kingdom, that's it."

With that said, I told him I should go see his father. Jorn told me Rono was in the war room. I thanked him and told him to stop by the inn and ask Glendeo if Ilkon was still there. Then, I headed to Billen's shop to tell the smith he was right and that I was still alive. After giving me a nod, my nephew started to walk in one direction and me in the other.

I never paid attention to what was between the palace and the inn before. When I was younger, I was always in a hurry to get to the inn for training because Glendeo would have me run five laps around the courtyard for each minute I was late. The walk from the palace to the inn was short, but I had tunnel vision each morning. I ignored everything along my path that could distract me and make me late.

But, as I traveled, what I cast aside before now jumped out in front of me as if demanding retribution for the years I had passed them by without notice. There were houses, compact two-story buildings made of brick with terracotta titles making up the roofs. Father had decreed all buildings within a certain radius of the palace had to be built out of brick and have terracotta roofing.

The reasoning was the same as the palace being made of stone: to make the buildings fireproof in case a besieging army tried to set fire to the city. Father ended up starting a trend since, by the time I was a teenager, almost all the homes in Kiholp were made from brick and topped with terracotta roofing.

The first floor of some houses acted as stops, and wooden signs painted with the shop's name were hung on the houses' outside walls. When I passed by, people were entering and exiting, though not many. War doesn't stop commerce but decreases it and transfers what it does not destroy to kings and their armies, always with increased prices.

I didn't pass any inns, though. Father had made sure there were no inns closer to the palace than Glendeo's to ensure that visiting diplomats who weren't invited to or didn't want to stay at the palace would make the logical choice and stay at the closest inn. Either way, whether they were at the palace or Glendeo's inn, Father would have someone watching them.

What I saw, and would never have seen when I was younger, were boarded-up houses. Their owners must have done the math and realized that Eshtar did not stand much of a chance against Diefet. They packed up, boarded, and left the city, seeking refuge elsewhere.

Father had given out land close to the palace to reward his veterans like he did with Glendeo, so I wasn't surprised to see the boarded-up houses where, in a minority, those men wouldn't dare leave the country they fought for, but everyone else would.

The more I thought about it, the more I realized the boarded-up houses were what should have been. Glendeo was old and most of the men Father gave land to around the palace should have been dead. Large swaths of the city should have been boarded up as their inhabitants fled from the war. Everyone knew the Diefetian army was far more formidable than the Eshtaran army, despite not knowing how severally the latter was outnumbered. While Eshtar had not seen war in a generation, maybe even two, Dietfet, for the last decade, was in the process of conquering the Continent.

Everyone knew that Diefet was likely to win. Yet plenty of people stayed in their homes and kept their shops open. I figured it was because they must not have had anywhere else to go. They were ships trapped at sea during a storm because there was no safe harbor to make port.

I was wrong. Something far more powerful was at work than men making harsh survival calculations. After the war, I found out people didn't evacuate because they trusted their king to end the war.

When I reached the palace, I recognized two of the four guards at the door. The first one on my left was shocked as I approached the door, and his expression melted into disappointment. The other guard across from him smiled and had victory in his eye—disappointment accompanied by a look of triumph, the sure sign of a bet's conclusion. I reasoned the wager was about whether I was dead, though I don't know how much time needed to pass before I was considered dead.

I ignored them both as I entered and headed straight to the war room. What to tell Rono? I didn't have an answer, but I would need one soon. And I wondered what would happen if I told Rono the truth. Would he believe me? Or would he insist that I was lying?

The fact the gods were real and I had spoken to them was irrelevant. I had dismissed the possibility of hallucinating because neither Glendeo nor Jorn mentioned anyone taking me back to the inn after the duel. If I hadn't been teleported somewhere else, Salroon would have killed me.

Salroon left without saying anything about the duel, as if he knew it needed to be finished later. The more I thought about it, the more I realized I had to tell Rono the truth, whether he believed me or not.

But if he believed me, I would have to admit to my brother I was no longer an atheist. I would admit to Rono the gods were real, but I hated them. And I did hate them. The Protectorate wasn't doing anything about the vampire menace. Their definition of "doing something" was having the sword they made choose someone to deal with the problem for them.

And they did nothing to stop my father from becoming the Wretched King or me from becoming the Terror of the Continent, let alone punish us for our crimes. My only opinion about the gods as I walked to the war room was that they were useless. If I had given the matter more thought, I would have admitted they weren't entirely useless because they intervened during the duel and saved my life.

When I stood in front of the door to the war room, I was confident my new beliefs would be as divisive as my old atheism. The door was wooden, and I hadn't noticed that the last time I was there. While Father was alive, some were made from wood, but doors to important rooms, like the war room, were made of stone to prevent eavesdropping since wood does not block sound as well as stone. Rono must have replaced all the stone doors.

When he was younger, he would always complain that the stone doors were too heavy to open, though Father had hired master masons to build them, and they did so in a way that the doors would glide open with such smoothness a child could open them with ease. But my brother always said the stone doors were too heavy, and I suspect it was because he had a hard time, for whatever reason, opening them. My thoughts ended as my hand reached for the doorknob, and I opened the war to the war room.

Rono was standing in front of the table, still covered in maps. One of his courtiers stood beside him, looking down at the maps. My brother's face was painted with a grim look. Not even bothering to turn to the man beside him, Rono mumbled something. The man stood there and gave a weak nod, humoring his king.

I thought I recognized the man, but I was unsure where I did. Either way, he must have been someone my brother relied on, or Rono would not have let him in the war room in the first place, let alone permit him to see information important for the war. When I thought of it, I didn't know why Rono was in there in the first place. Based on what Jorn and Glendeo told me, Salroon hadn't done anything since the duel. Rono must have been trying to plan a way to defend Kiholp against a Diefetian siege.

"If you are doing what I think you are doing, just stop. There's no point; the Diefetians have far more men than we do, and they can make siege engines to scale the walls or break them down. There's little you can do to defend against a siege besides stocking up on supplies," I said.

"You're alive," my brother said with a look of disbelief.

"I have to say, I'm disappointed in you. I ran into Jorn coming here, and the boy said only Billen thought I was still alive. I had expected you and Glendeo to have more faith in me. Particularly the old man, since he trained me," I told him.

"How?" he asked. "How in the gods' names' did you escape?"

"That's a tale to tell when I have you all in the same room because none of you will believe it when I tell it," I said.

Rono stared at me, trying to determine whether I was telling the truth. My brother still didn't trust me, a testament to his good judgment. I never expected Rono to trust me because he made me his military advisor. After a few moments of scrutinizing me, Rono decided that I was being truthful and told me we would get everyone together in the war room so I could tell them all what had happened.

"Glendeo's inn would be best," I recommended. "No need for the old man to climb all those steps to get up here."

"Right, he isn't as mobile as he used to be," Rono said and gave a slow nod to indicate he knew I suggested the inn so that we could include Ilkon in the conversation.

"Jorn told me that Salroon hasn't made any moves since the duel," I said.

"After you vanished, Salroon gathered his men, and they left the same way they came," Rono informed me. "There have been no reports on any Diefetian army, not even of one marching."

"How long has it been like this?" I asked.

"Since the duel," answered the king.

"Are your scouts all dead?" I asked.

"No, they have been reporting in," the man beside my brother said.

"Bowv, this is Paderok, my courtier. Do you remember him? You met when I told you I assigned him to investigate the spy matter," Rono asked.

"I do remember him," I said, recalling the look of terror he gave me when we were outside the throne room. I then wondered what he was doing there since he was a suspected spy. Rono likely wanted to keep a suspected spy close to him, though I don't know what my brother was doing, letting a suspected spy help plan the city's defense.

"He's been helping me plan how to withstand a siege," Rono added.

"What about the spy problem?" I asked.

"It's complicated," Paderok said. "I managed to identify a few suspected spies within the court, the chancellor included, but we still can't prove any of them to be spies."

"But you think they are," I said.

"There are hints that they are, but there is nothing solid for me to order their arrest," the king elaborated.

"There's a war going on. You don't need an excuse to lock them up if you suspect them of being spies," I argued.

"You would be right, brother, but we have so little against them. It would look like I was locking them up without evidence," explained Rono.

"Then why do you suspect them of being spies when you have little evidence that they are?" I asked, confused.

"They have broken their normal routines in ways that make it appear they are in secret communication with someone," Paderok said.

"Then get your hands on one of these secret communications, and you can arrest them without starting a riot," I said.

"That's what Paderok is working on now," Rono confirmed.

"We might not have time to deal with them if Salroon shows up at the gates with an army," I commented.

"No, we won't," my brother agreed. "What do you think Salroon is doing?"

"I think he's looking for me because he still wants the sword," I said. "If there are any spies, they'll tell him I am here. Then, who knows what he is going to do? Though I think the best bet would be for him to march on Kiholp if his spies tell him I am still in the city."

"And you'll still be in the city?" the king asked.

"I don't know," I admitted. "But I need to tell you and the others about what happened. After I do, I will decide if I am staying."

"Fair enough," Rono said. "You should go see Billen. He'll want to know he was right."

"Jorn should be at his shop telling him that right now. I told him to go tell Billen I was alive after I ran into him coming out of the inn," I said.

"I should have known you would go see Glendeo before you came here," my brother said with disappointment. I didn't want to tell him I woke up at the inn. That would cause him to ask too many questions, the type I didn't want to answer around Paderok, not when there was a chance he was the spy.

"When we are at the inn, I will tell all of you the full story," I told him.

"Then let's get to the inn," Rono said.

"Let's go then," I said, exiting the room.

As I left, I could hear Rono give a set of instructions to Paderok before he followed me, and I concluded Rono didn't think he was the spy. It could have been that Rono was giving Paderok orders because he suspected Paderok was the spy and didn't want to tip him off. If that was the case, Rono did a great job of it since Rono looked like a king talking to one of his most trusted advisors.

I strolled down the hallway, allowing my brother to catch up with me, which he did, walking up beside me. As we walked, we didn't talk. Rono knew that I wouldn't tell him anything without Jorn, Billen, Glendeo, and

Ilkon present. There was no point in describing what had happened more than once when I could tell them what had happened as a group.

Once I told my story, inevitably, the conversation would turn to whether I still believed the gods were not real. I didn't want to get into that with Rono because I didn't even know if he, or any of them, would believe me. The person's opinion I wanted the most was Ilkon's.

However, I decided what had happened was real. But if Ilkon told me there wasn't any tradition of *Hueik* choosing champions for the gods, then it would mean I could have been hallucinating all along, though there would still be unanswered questions. Why did Salroon withdraw after the duel? How did my wound heal? Why didn't Salroon kill me? How didn't Glendeo know I was in the inn when I woke up? Who had brought me back to the inn in the first place?

There was a time in my life when I would have wanted it all to be an illusion. But as I walked through the palace alongside Rono, I realized I didn't want to prove it was an illusion because of the unanswered questions. I felt that the answers to those questions if there were any, would tell me the world was a far stranger than I had ever thought.

Before I knew it, we were heading for Glendeo's inn. I hoped we didn't have to go tracking Jorn and Billen down since I wanted to get this over as soon as possible. If Salroon's spies managed to get word to the Diefetian king that I was still in the city, he would make his move, and we wouldn't have time to react if Rono and I were searching for Jorn and Billen.

My worries disappeared when we entered the inn and saw Jorn and Billen in the lobby talking to Glendeo. The only person who we needed to find was the heretic. All three of them turned towards us as we entered.

"I knew you weren't dead," Billen said as we got closer.

"Why?" I asked.

"The lack of a body gave it away," my old friend said, and after he said it, I wondered why people had thought I was dead in the first place.

I turned around the room and looked at the other four, "How come he's the only one to put that together?"

"I was on the fence," Glendeo told me.

"Which just makes it worse," I said. "Who's on the fence about someone being dead when a body has not been found? It's either there's a body, and he's dead, or there's no body, and he's probably still alive. There's no room for middle ground."

"We saw you get stabbed in the thigh," the old man protested.

"You know that's not necessarily fatal. You've been stabbed in the thigh four times," I reminded him.

The old vet let out a grunt.

"But you disappeared in a cloud of mist," Jorn said, attempting to come to Glendeo's aid.

"Why would that kill me?" I asked.

"Salroon could have teleported you to somewhere you would instantly die, like in the middle of a volcano," my nephew argued.

I turned and faced my brother, "See what those philosophy tutors do? They teach people to argue absurd things."

"If you paid attention to the tutors Father gave us, you would know he is making a logical argument, though it's a poor one given his assumptions," Rono explained.

"I think I was the only 'tutor,' if you could call me that, your brother ever paid attention to," Glendeo said.

"That's not the point. The point is out of four of you, the only one who concluded I wasn't dead was Billen," I said, then turned towards Rono again. "What's your excuse for thinking I was dead?"

"I didn't know where my brother was and didn't see him alive," answered Rono. "Which is just as logical as assuming you're alive because there's no dead body."

"Fair point," I admitted. "Glendeo is Ilkon still here?"

"He is," answered the innkeeper.

"Is anyone else?" I asked.

"No, business has been slow with the war," Glendeo said.

"Good, then let's get Ilkon in here," I said. I yelled for the heretic to join us. A few minutes later, he walked down the hallway into the lobby.

"And here I thought you were dead," the heretic said.

"Why did you think he was dead?" Jorn asked.

"Because Glendeo thought he was dead," Ilkon said.

"He was on the fence about it," Billen said, triggering another grunt from the old soldier.

"How can you be on the fence about someone being dead when there's nobody? Wouldn't that mean they're alive?" Ilkon asked.

"Enough!" Glendeo cried, then turned towards me. "Are you going to tell us what happened, or are we going to stand here all day debating which of us was the most foolish?"

The room fell silent, and I told them what had happened—everything from the mist surrounding Salroon and me during the duel to feeling like I was being carried away somewhere to Salroon shouting about me being chosen. While I did, everyone in the room looked puzzled as they attempted to connect the dots and figure out what happened before I continued. Everyone except for Ilkon, the heretic, had a knowing smile on his face. He knew what I would say next from the little information I had given them.

I moved on to tell them about how I woke up in an empty room with my thigh healed, the pale man who had appeared from nowhere, and using *Hueik* to open the massive golden doors. At this point, I could tell Rono knew what I would say next.

My pious brother no doubt recognized the pale man in black as the god of death and the golden doors as the Doors to Judgement, but Jorn, Billen, and Glendeo still looked as if they were trying to make sense of it all. Their expressions soon turned to shock when I described what lay beyond the golden doors: all nine gods of the Protectorate sitting on their thrones, arranged in a semicircle.

I could remember the gods' opening remarks, but I didn't remember much. I gave them the revelation the gods did not choose me and wanted to condemn me, but the *sword* did, to fight against vampires and their demonic master. Then I ended it with me, once again, getting surrounded by mist and waking up in my room in the inn.

When I finished, the room erupted into a fury of conversation. In the tempest of words, I could hear an "I told you" from Billen, referencing when he told me the gods could use me to kill. Glendeo was talking to Jorn, claiming that I must have hallucinated all of it because a sword choosing someone on behalf of the gods was the most absurd thing he had ever heard. Ilkon and Rono both had decided I was telling the truth and were discussing the demon Allemar and how large the vampire threat was.

The chatter continued for several minutes while I stood there waiting for the conversations to die down. There was little point in cutting their discussions off short when doing so would stop them from fully forming opinions, the very thing I wanted to hear from Ilkon. After a few minutes, the voices subsided, and silence took over the room.

"I don't buy it. You want me to think that the Sword of the Gods chose you, the Terror of the Continent, to be the Protectorate's champion? Are you sure Salroon didn't hit you in your head?" Glendeo asked.

"It's not hard to believe that the sword would choose him. After all, who's better at killing than Bowv," Billen argued.

"But it could have chosen someone with a more honorable background, not the man who murdered his father and then became the Continent's most infamous bandit. For the gods' sake, how many people has Bowv killed? How many people has he exploited? How many has he tortured? How many settlements has he raised to the ground or butchered outright?" asked the old soldier.

"Remember who you are speaking to, old man. Out of everyone in this room, I don't need to be reminded of Bowv's crimes because I was there for many of them. But I think that's why the sword chose Bowv. He doesn't care if he kills and will kill anyone, nobility and monarchs included. To fulfill the Protectorate's desire to kill vampires, one needs to be comfortable with killing people attached to governments.

"Nearly all, if not all, of the vampires Bowv has killed were members of the Diefetian court, a part of the Diefetian army, or in Ambassador Zimkoo's case, an official of Diefet's government. We can't forget that Salroon is a king, and the gods want him dead. An honorable man would have no concerns about killing a vampire, but striking down a king, something which has been taboo since ancient times, would give him hesitation.

"Chances are you're not going to find a warrior with honor willing to commit regicide. It's better to get someone who already has committed regicide, on more than one occasion, I remind you, to face Salroon," Billen explained.

"But choosing an atheist? How do you explain that?" Jorn asked.

"It doesn't matter. Bowv is, or was, an atheist. We don't know if he still is since he hasn't given us his opinion on his experience. But the gods didn't choose him. The sword chose him. Bowv may have spent years denying the existence of the gods, but he's never denied that swords exist," argued Billen. "*Hueik* is a sword, not a god. It doesn't care if Bowv is an atheist."

"When did you get so good at arguing?" I asked Billen.

"After I left the clan, I tried being a theologian before settling on blacksmithing. It's one of the reasons King Rono granted me a pardon," my old friend answered.

I turned to my brother, "I should have known you gave him the pardon and not some lower official."

"Fortunately, he didn't like theology as much as he thought he would and opened his smithy. Since the war began, he and his apprentice have proved invaluable at supplying weapons and armor," Rono said.

"Anything to support the kingdom, my king," Billen said.

"Enough about justifying what I told you all. I asked Ilkon to join us to see if it's real," I said, then turned to the heretic. "Is it?"

"I suspect you already know the answer," Ilkon said with a small smile. "But I would need you to clarify what you mean by 'if,' considering the amount of information you just told us."

"The sword choosing people and not the gods, is that real?" I asked.

"Yes, though the Temple has decried it as heresy," Ilkon answered. "Though I must admit my order did, too, at one point. I will need to write a report to ensure we do not change our opinions again."

"That's what I thought you would say," I muttered.

"Does this mean you're a believer now, Bowv?" Rono asked.

"It does, but it doesn't mean I hold a favorable opinion of the gods. They couldn't be bothered to pick their champion themselves. Instead, they let a sword do it," I said.

"They didn't stop the Wretched King, and they sure haven't stopped me from committing atrocity after atrocity. And after I die, they'll have the audacity to judge me for it. Yes, brother, the gods are real. I'll openly admit it since I can't deny it any longer, but I will also hate them openly."

The room fell silent. Ilkon dropped his eyes to the floor, and Glendeo shifted his stance. Jorn stood there, glancing around the room to avoid eye contact. Although Rono was the most fervent in his faith, he nodded as if he expected me to take this stance. I wasn't surprised. Out of them all, my brother knew me the best. He couldn't have been shocked when I said I hated the gods.

Looking back, I think I didn't say anything new. It might have been a revelation to those in the room with me, but as I reflect on my life, I realize I didn't jump straight into atheism. I hated the gods for what happened to my mother, but I still believed in them. It wasn't until I went to war, witnessed its horrors, and watched my father become the Wretched King that I began to think the Protectorate was just a story men told themselves to give them hope, shielding them from the wickedness of this world.

Silence took over the room again for what felt like hours, but it was only a few minutes. Glendeo drove it out when he suggested we all go about our business. He reminded us there was a war that Rono needed to fight, Billen had a shop to return to, Ilkon had a report to write, and he had an inn to run.

Everyone nodded, and the four men went their separate ways. No one bothered to talk to me except the king. My brother told me Jorn still had more questions to ask me, and he would appreciate it if I said the young prince more about the wars I fought in.

Rono also mentioned it might teach the boy about strategy and tactics. Despite the request about Jorn, I knew my brother was asking because he thought I needed some rest after what I had been through. I didn't need rest, and my wound was healed, so there was nothing to rest. I sensed my brother was trying to keep me preoccupied while he figured out a way to keep me protected from anyone Salroon sent for the sword.

Rono didn't dare suggest I needed protection, though. He knew I would scoff at the idea, let alone admit I needed protection. My reputation as the Terror of the Continent wasn't enough to have any vampires shaking in their boots, but my reputation as a fighter should have been enough protection.

And it was impossible for Salroon not to have heard about how I dealt with the Hushta Unkae. I wondered how many vampires Salroon could afford to send to try and kill me. Indeed, there weren't as many vampires as Husta assassins.

I reasoned the number was low since I killed almost half a dozen of them. If hundreds of vampires were running around the Continent, then people wouldn't believe they were a myth, and priests like Ilkon wouldn't be labeled as heretics. No, Salroon wouldn't try an assassination attempt. I had already killed too many vampires, though I knew there was no purpose in trying to convince my brother of that.

The room cleared out, and I was left alone with Jorn in the lobby. Not wanting to stand any longer, I motioned him to follow me and then sat at the nearest table. The lobby felt bigger than it was because there were only four small tables in the room. They were close to the front desk, flanked by a hallway on either side.

When I was young, I asked Glendeo why he didn't have more tables in the lobby, and the innkeeper said he didn't want anyone loitering around for long. Being young, I accepted the answer, though when I was older, I realized there were too few tables because the old soldier wanted a clear line of sight to the doorway in case trouble came knocking. And, of course, to keep track of the foreign diplomats, Father wanted to be watched.

"What do you want to know?" I asked Jorn as we sat down.

"I want to know more about the War of the Triad," my nephew answered.

"What about it?" I asked

"What happened after the Battle of Odfret?" he asked. "Did Grandfather give you a command?"

"No, he didn't give me a command," I said.

"Then what happened?" the young prince asked.

I stopped a moment as memories long buried made their way to the front of my mind, along with the pain of who was their companion. I began the story.

"All of us who had survived the battle trekked for three days to the camp where your grandfather commanded our forces—three days without food and little water. When the camp's sentries spotted us, each of us was ten pounds thinner, and there were a couple of us whose cheeks were beginning to sink in or whose skin was tightening around the ribs. I don't know how many of us there were, perhaps a couple dozen. We didn't lose anyone to thirst or hunger along the way, though I thought many of them wouldn't make it.

"When we arrived, we were rushed to the medical tents, where the surgeons treated us with small amounts of food and water. Fearing that some of us were on the verge of death, the surgeons prohibited us from sleeping and assigned three aids to keep us awake by any means. In fairness, they were right to fear losing some of us, but that didn't mean I didn't want to muster the energy and find a knife to stab the aid who would poke or shake me whenever he thought I was falling asleep.

"Since our conditions were that bad, the medics kept us in the medical tent for a few days, but your grandfather needed to know what happened at Odfet, so on the second day, he came into the tent for a visit. When he entered the tent, I heard him ask the surgeon in charge of us to take him to the highest-ranking soldier.

"The surgeon complied, but when they approached my bed, which was a low table the length of a man with a thick blanket covering its top to add some comfort, Father thanked the surgeon for taking him to his son, then reiterated that he wanted the highest-ranking soldier, not the prince who was an observer of the battle.

"The surgeon informed his king there were no officers, and I was the one the men followed when they came into camp. Your grandfather thanked the surgeon again and, after the surgeon walked off, rebuked me for not following his orders without giving me a chance to explain what had happened. Father went on for ten minutes explaining how I was not ready to lead.

"Finally, he calmed down. He wasn't always like that. When your father and I were younger, your grandfather could control his temper and was never mad if someone didn't follow his orders if the outcome was acceptable. Those days were long gone, though, and I was dealing with the Wretched King, even though your grandfather didn't have that name yet.

"When his beratement ended, and I got the chance to tell him about what happened at the battle, I had to endure a rapid and thorough line of questioning from your grandfather. I answered all the questions that I could, but there were a few questions, like what happened to a specific officer, that I couldn't answer. There were so many questions that I was driven to exhaustion, so much so the surgeon in charge had to tell Father to cease.

"Your grandfather did so, but not without an argument. Though the surgeon got his way, one did not tell the Wretched King what he could not do. The same surgeon was executed months later for trumped-up charges of medical malpractice, but Father got away with it. People told themselves that it was the war getting to him, that under normal circumstances, he would have just barred the surgeon from the medical tents, which was the standard way of dealing with these things.

"There was little talk in the camp of the charges being fraudulent since officers and enlisted men alike never considered that their righteous king would charge an innocent man with a crime as an excuse to execute him. I knew better, as did every other survivor from the Battle of Odfret.

"We knew it was murder via execution. It was the first one, and there were more as the war continued. After the war, the unjustified executions made their way from the frontlines to Eshtar and its nobility. The name 'The Wretched King' was coined."

"Did you speak out?" Jorn asked.

"About the execution? Yes, I approached Father about it. The surgeon did nothing wrong. He told his king to stop endangering his patient. That's it," I said.

"How did that go?" my nephew asked.

"He chewed my head off. At this point in the war, he had given me command. It was nothing difficult. I commanded a support force for General Furderak. As punishment for protesting and 'insubordination,' I was relieved of my command and was given command of a force in the Swadonilic Mountains fighting the Jilldues," I informed him.

"Why was it a punishment?" he asked.

"Because the Jilldues were a guerilla force, not a proper army. We all would have avoided the Swadonilics altogether, but the Jilldues were a member of the Triad and, in my opinion, their strongest warriors. Keep in mind I fought both the Eschlee and the Rushide," I said.

"Most historians disagree with you," my nephew informed me. "The common view is the Eschlee were the most formidable."

"On paper, yes, The Eschlee had renowned infantry and were masters of logistics and supplies. I remember one battle where they supplied their archers with a steady stream of arrows until the battle was finished. The battle went on for a full day. I still don't know how they did it.

"Though the formidable reputation of their infantry was shattered during the war. There were countless times when the slightest dent in their line was enough to break it. But the Jilldues, they wouldn't stop the assault until you were good and bloodied if you weren't already dead.

"And you never knew when they would appear, but they would appear screaming at the top of their lungs as they descended the mountainside, popped out from behind boulders your scouts said were searched, or in rare cases, climbed up from a cliff to attack your rear. When they screamed, it was terrifying and paralyzed the most hardened soldiers," I said, yet again debunking the nonsense of scholars.

"Sounds like a certain bandit lord I've heard of," Jorn observed.

"Who do you think I learned from?" I asked. "You're probably the first to make that connection, and I wouldn't be surprised, considering what your tutors have taught you about the war. The Jillues taught me how to hide, to wait for the prime time to strike, and the value of being feared on the battlefield, though the Wretched King taught me the value of having people fear your presence."

"Can you tell me some specifics? Maybe a battle you fought against them? And how did you defeat them?" the prince asked.

"I'll tell you about the whole campaign," I said and began a tale full of pain, death, and the hard truths only war can teach a man.

Chapter Twenty

WHILE COMMANDING General Furderak's supporting force, I made few important decisions except when I had to bail him out of trouble. Furderak outranked me, so though I oversaw a separate force, it was an extension of Furderak's force.

It wasn't until I arrived to take over the force in the Swadonilics that I had a true independent command. I told you I was sent there as punishment, and that became clear when the man who was to become my second in command informed me the previous five commanders were all killed by the Jilldues.

But I don't think punishment was the sole reason the Wretched King sent me. While commanding Furderak's support force, I pulled the general from a few tight spots. Your grandfather wanted to see if I could do the same in the Swadonilics because the Jilldues were winning.

Supply lines were being cut, whole platoons of men were being slaughtered to a man, and, as I said, the last five commanders in charge were killed. Morale was also nonexistent. When I first inspected the small army, the men's clothes were tattered and torn, their weapons and armor poorly kept, and defeat shined in their eyes brighter than any star.

It was no surprise to learn that desertion was through the roof, and we had yet to win a single engagement in months. It was the worst state I have ever seen an army in, regardless of size. The will to fight wasn't there, which shouldn't have been the case.

Eshtar entered the war to defend our neighbor and tributary state, Kwendol, a young country at the time, and didn't survive the war even though it was on the winning side. We had the moral high ground; we were helping a neighboring country defend itself from the aggression of the Triad. You wouldn't have been able to tell this with the indifferent tone of officers, the downward gaze of the foot soldiers, and the slouch of defeat which plagued both.

And there was a dreadful lack of urgency. Whenever I gave an order, the men would carry it out as if it didn't matter because nothing mattered since they thought we were all good as dead. A part of me wanted to start hanging people just so that the men would fear me instead of the Jilldues.

Queel, who became my second in command, advised against it. He pointed out that executions could drive what little morale we had into nonexistence, increase desertions, and lead to mutiny. Queel was a good man, willing to perform his duties but always tempered with compassion and sympathy.

It was because of Queel there was some sense of caring within the small army, and without him, there would have been far more desertions than there were. By taking Queel's suggestions, I was able to turn around morale and stem the flow of desertion.

They were all common-sense changes that past commanders should have changed if they had half a brain: more extended scouting missions, not senselessly marching through the mountains without a tangible objective, and improving camp defenses when we were in the mountains. When I enacted these changes, morale doubled across the 4,000-strong army.

4,000 may appear to be a big number for operating in the mountains where armies are constricted, but the Swadonilics are the most unique mountains on the Continents. They aren't the largest in terms of altitude, but the mountain range is unique for the flat sections on each mountain, as if parts of the mountains were formed by stacking plateaus on top of each other.

Throughout the mountains, boulders of all shapes and trees, which got smaller and smaller as you ascended the mountains, filled these flat sections. This provided hiding spots for the Jilldue to set up ambushes.

The campaign was fought in the mountains, but the Jilldue civilian population didn't live there. Instead, they made their homes on the base of the mountains, where there was fertile land for crops and flat land where cities and towns could be built. Early in the war, we had captured the towns and the cities.

From what I understand, it was an easy conquest, and the Jillduen army didn't put up much of a fight. Instead, they raided our supply lines and attacked our lines of communication, essentially isolating us from the rest of the Eshtaran army and forcing us to follow them into the mountains, where they could easily pick us off.

Whenever we got reinforcements, you would think they would be for fighting in the mountains, but they were sent to the cities and towns to reinforce the garrisons there. Someone up the chain of command, perhaps your grandfather, decided that the cities and towns were more strategically important than the Jilldue fighters and were worried about the Jilldues taking them back. Whoever they were, they made the mistake of confusing territorial gains with victory.

I understood that we needed to crush the Jilldue fighters to achieve victory, not hold their cities and towns. Holding cities and towns had strategic value, but it was offset by the cost of having some of our forces search for the enemy in the Swadonilics and be bled dry in the process.

Before I took command, the army used the occupied towns and cities as bases, leaving a small force to counter raids. Then, the rest of the army was split up and assigned different parts to hunt down the Jilldue in different sections of the mountains. The problem was that the Jilldue switched from the hunted to the hunters. Too many times, whole squads were ambushed, surrounded, and killed by a man.

A soldier can deal with the clash of two armies; there's clarity in it, even when witnessing this world's barbarity. When the armies camp across from each other and lines are formed, even the most inexperienced foot soldier knows what will take place. It's impossible not to know.

But, when hunting a dangerous foe in the mountains, one who has proven he can attack from anywhere and scale the sheer mountain cliffs to do so, clarity is replaced with paranoia. You begin to see enemies behind every boulder and hiding in every tree. It's the type of paranoia that leaves a soldier on constant alert since he knows that a dropped guard means certain death while chipping away at his sanity as the ever-present tension threatens to break his mind before the paranoia completes its slow execution.

I didn't comprehend the mental toll of such a fight at first, and not having a better plan, I decided to keep sending out patrols for the first few weeks of my command. It was a mistake. In those weeks, the Jilldue killed up to half of every patrol we sent out. The men who survived staggered back, starving and wounded.

I accompanied a few patrols the second and third weeks after I took command. The enemy was spotted twice before they began their attack. We would hike through a section of the mountains to get to a spot where scouting reports had indicated an enemy presence.

You never knew when you were safe from a Jilldue attack. The moment you walked through a city gate, your guard was raised, and your eyes began to see enemies in every hiding spot your mind could fathom.

On my first patrol, no one dared talk, not wanting to alert the enemy to our location. When I asked them about previous engagements, the officers began scanning their surroundings with greater speed, as if the Jilldue were some breed of dog that could hone in on the sound of our voices.

Reaching the section of the mountains mentioned in the scouting report took days of marching. When we reached it, we had hiked a section not too high up on the mountain, and the spot was closer to its base than its peak. No one saw any sign of the Jilldue. We were still marching when the first Jillduen arrow pierced the throat of the soldier marching in front of me.

As he dropped to the ground, giving off a blood-filled choking sound as he did. Drops of his warm blood fell on my face. I gave the order for the men to form ranks. No one heard me. I was drowned out by dozens of savaged war cries that were collectively louder than a thunderclap. My men froze, becoming sitting ducks for the enemy's arrows. At that moment, when I saw soldier after soldier fall to the enemy's arrows, I understood why patrols were coming back with up to seventy percent losses or were wiped out completely.

Over the death-inspiring screams, I continued to shout to my men to form up and raise their shields. Some heard me, and I heard the ring of shields as arrows slammed into them, and my soldiers snapped back into reality. Most didn't, though.

Along with the ringing of shields, I heard cries of pain and the last noises of dying men, which my mind had a hard time registering as human, as the Jillduen arrows pierced the flesh of my men. I'm sure several arrows were stopped by armor, but in battle, you ignore such details unless your armor saved your life. As a commander, all you see are men that can still fight. You ignore the scratches on their armor or the blood on their weapon. All you see is an able-bodied soldier.

The initial arrow barrage didn't leave too many men standing, but the enemy didn't end there. The Jilldue are ferocious fighters who revel in close combat. With more war cries, our ambushers charged forward with their infamous handheld war axes and short swords designed for hacking apart limbs.

It would have been suicidal if I had managed to get most of my men into a defensive formation, but there was no chance that I could. The sight of the screaming, charging enemy paralyzed my men. Even the ones who managed to raise their shields and block the arrows were standing there with terror dominating their eyes.

The rest of that day is a blur, filled with the barbaric battle cries of the Jilldue and the sanguine screams of men getting their limbs chopped off. The Jilldue warriors came for me. They always sent a group to attack the officer in charge if they could find him. I had a standard arming sword and began to parry ax and short sword alike in a flurry of movements as I was surrounded and attacked by five Jilldue.

The first one came in with an ax swing for my head. Rapidly, I raised my sword to meet his weapon. My blade caught his weapon's shaft just below its blade. Smoothly, I detached my weapon from his and rotated my wrist almost completely around. My blade bit deep into his flesh, and the Jilldue dropped his ax.

Two of his comrades, armed with short swords, rushed me to prevent me from delivering a killing blow. One lunged and thrust at my chest. He was fast but sloppy. I don't know what he was aiming for: my stomach or chest. I parried his thrust with minimal effort, deflecting his sword to my right side, and since his attack was reckless, his left shoulder followed his sword. Seizing the opportunity, I sent my sword ramming through his gut.

In one motion, I drew my blade from the dying Jilldue's gut and pivoted just in time to defend against the third's attack. The other warrior raised his sword, arching it down at my head. The instincts Glendeo instilled in me saved my life as my body raised my sword in defense without a thought crossing my mind.

A clang rang out as our weapons collided. The impact staggered my enemy back. Quickly, he got his footing and raised his guard. The Jilldue whose arm I wounded was nowhere to be seen. That left me, his friend, and two others hanging back, waiting for an opportunity to strike.

I didn't give them one. Approaching the Jilldue who attacked me, I began an assault of my own. In a series of strikes, I put my enemy on the defensive. Knowing his two friends would take my assault as an opportunity to attack me while my focus was elsewhere, I sped up my attacks. My opponent couldn't keep up, and when I found a hole in his guard, I finished him off with a slash to the throat, and he fell to the ground dead.

I spun around to face the other two. Despite having killed two of their comrades and wounded another, they were not intimated. One wielded an ax, and the other a sword. If their swords weren't so short, it would have made sense for the one with a sword to approach me, attacking while keeping his distance then pressing an attack when he thought his partner could get close to me without being noticed.

But I had the longer sword, so both needed to get in close to strike. They knew this, and acting as one, they approached me from the sides, hoping I couldn't defend against two attackers simultaneously. They were wrong.

The one on my left reached me first. He was the one with the sword and the taller of the two, so he was moments ahead of his partner. He struck low at my legs. It was a sincere attack, though he was shocked when I blocked it, stepped forward, and pivoted my body. My sword arm swung from pointing towards him towards his partner, elbowed him in his stomach, and blocked his partner's ax nearly the exact moment my elbow connected with his stomach.

I attacked the one with the ax. Shocked by my speed in blocking his attack, his guard was sloppy. I easily broke it and ended the fight with my sword, ramming through his chest. As he dropped dead to the ground, I turned back around to deal with the other one. He held his sword up on guard.

His face was calm, but his constrictive grip on his sword told another story. Striking faster than when I fought the other four, I pressed the Jilldue's guard hard. In a matter of seconds, it broke. His life ended as I ran him through with my sword.

With my fifth attacker dead, the Jilldue pulled back and vanished as fast as they appeared. However, my prowess was not the reason for the Jilldues' withdrawal. A third of my patrol was dead on the ground. The Jilldue had done their jobs, so they had left.

I would learn that the Jilldue culture values a dead enemy more than a wounded one. We all stood there with our weapons at the ready, waiting in case the enemy returned for another strike. They didn't, and after waiting for what felt like hours, I ordered a march back to the city.

We weren't hindered on the way back, and the other patrols I accompanied in the following weeks weren't attacked. But the anxiety of waiting for a Jilldue attack filled the soldiers when on patrol. I respected the Jilldue as fighters that they feared them. It should have been the other way around.

We were the ones who captured their cities and towns. They were the ones who fled to the mountains to hide. On paper, they would be scared, but the mighty soldiers of Eshtar, arguably the best on the Continent in those days, were the ones who were scared.

That first patrol convinced me sending patrols to hunt the enemy was futile. Victory would come when the Jilldue laid down their arms, and at the rate they were killing us, that wasn't going to happen anytime soon.

When I returned to the city, I brought the highest-ranking officers into my war room to discuss a new strategy. Queel suggested we lure the Jilldue out into a proper battle, though no one had any ideas on how to do that. Another officer, Frenston, suggested we cease all patrols and continue to occupy the cities and towns.

It was a sensible plan. We were marching out to the Jilldue to fight, and with his plan, the Jillue would come to us. The flaw was that if we held up in the cities and towns, the Jilldue would continue raiding unless we could successfully defend against their raids, and then we would be back patrolling the mountains.

Then there was the plan proposed by Hiltole, who grew up with my father and served in the army when Eshtar was reclaimed. Hiltole suggested we torch all the cities and towns and then withdraw entirely, leaving the Jilldue soldiers to come down from the mountains to rebuild, taking them out of the war.

There were several other ideas, but those were the three main ones. I wanted to study the enemy more before I enacted a new strategy. I decided to decrease the number of patrols, but I would go on most of them to study the enemy by fighting them. The Jilldue must have realized this because the enemy did not attack each patrol I accompanied.

I don't know if they knew who I was, but few officers in the Eshtaran army could have defeated five men in an ambush as I had. Perhaps it was the paranoia, but more than once on the patrols, I could feel dozens of pairs of eyes watching me. The Jilldue were watching us and could have attacked if they wished to.

They didn't, though, robbing me of the chance to study them and forcing me to settle for secondhand information from battle reports and questioning survivors. I didn't learn much. Most of the information was useless. But I did find out the Jilldue targeted officers if they could find them. It was interesting to learn, considering their main goal was to kill as many of us as they could, and men often retreat when they see their commanders killed.

As I read more reports, I realized that Jilldue never used up all their arrows. When they managed to kill the officers in charge of the patrol, causing a retreat, they would fire the remainder of their arrows at the fleeing survivors, something I would have experienced firsthand if the Jilldue weren't the ones who retreated on the first patrol I accompanied.

The Jilldue's bloodlust, marital prowess, and hit-and-run tactics combined to make the most challenging campaign I've ever fought. Queel was a big reason we emerged victorious. If he wasn't my second, I couldn't turned around the campaign. He was a good strategist and tactician, not an expert in logistics.

But Queel was a master of something most commanders lack: diplomacy. Most commanders and officers are good at discipline. When an enlisted man does something wrong, he's reprimanded, or when a midlevel officer messes up a plan, he's removed from command. Many don't know how to reason, negotiate, listen with sincerity to grievances, and seek resolutions. Queel could because he cared about people.

When there was trouble in the ranks, the soldiers would always settle down after Queel talked to them. I can't think of a man who fought harder for the men around him or would jump faster into danger to save a wounded or surrounded comrade than Queel. In my life, I've only known a few good men, and Queel was one of them.

Queel advocated luring the Jilldue into an open battle, though no one knew how. That changed when we got word from our spies that the Jilldue forces were gathering to vote on who would become their new general. Their old general was dead, a stroke of good luck considering we didn't kill him, and I couldn't tell you what did. Some said it was old age, others illness, while a few people claimed he was killed by one of the many beasts in the mountains.

It was the opportunity we were looking for. His death meant we didn't have to lure the Jilldues into a fight since all the Jillduen warriors would be assembling to vote on a new general, as was their tradition. Thanks to my spies, I knew where they were gathering and when. Fortune herself had given us a golden opportunity to get the battle we wanted or, at the very least, get the jump on the Jilldue for a change.

The plan was to get to the location shortly after the Jilldue, then attack when they least suspected. It didn't work. Someone must have tipped off the Jilldue because, by the time we had arrived at the part of the mountain where the meeting was taking place, they had already chosen a new general and were waiting for our arrival, though we didn't know it.

We expected a thriving camp filled with enemy soldiers, but what we found was an abandoned one with ash forming dozens of circles on the ground where roaring flames once provided the Jilldue with islands of warmth in the sea, which was the frigid air of the Swadonilics.

The scouts found the empty camp first after I sent them out to estimate the enemy's numbers and observe the camp's defenses. I wanted to know if we could attack the Jilldue in their camp or if we needed to wait when they were on the move, and if that was the case, what possible routes they could take. When the scouts reported the camp was abandoned and there was no sign of the Jilldue, I should have known something was wrong.

But after weeks of frustration dealing with an enemy of phantoms who appeared from thin air, killing half of our patrols and then vanishing, I didn't think something was wrong. All I saw was a missed opportunity, one that could have defeated the Jilldue and ended the campaign.

When some officer, a colonel, I think, pointed out it was getting late and proposed we take over the abandoned Jilldue camp instead of making our own, I thought it was a great idea. I wanted to hunt down the Jilldue, and I couldn't think of a better place to begin than their old camp, so I ordered my men to make camp.

The camp was in a flat spot, had a few boulders on its edge, and had fewer trees than the average, but enough to hide the camp from prying eyes, but few enough to provide enough open space to pitch tents. What I should have been thinking was there were enough trees to prevent us from forming ranks.

The Jilldue attacked that night. They had moved in complete silence as they surrounded our camp, then, as loud as roaring lions, they broke the silence with their war cry and rushed out from their hiding spots. The sentries were the first to fall, hacked apart by axes and swords as the Jilldue tsunami rushed over them.

Having heard the war cry, my men rushed from bed, grabbed their weapons, and exited their tents, ready to fight for their lives. Unarmored, they were exposed, and scores fell to the arrows—the Jilldue, sensing weakness, unleashed barrage after barrage. Queel didn't hesitate.

Within moments of the first arrows hitting, he was organizing men to pull the wounded to safety while also looking for a defensible position to hold, hoping to rally the men and push the Jilldue back. I was looking right at him, thankful I had brought him along, when an arrow pierced his skull.

I screamed as his corpse dropped to the ground. Queel was the best of us. The brutality of war had not wiped away his compassion. I never served alongside an officer who cared more about the army he was in and the men in it than Queel. It's why the man was so good at logistics; he couldn't stand seeing his men ill-supplied. Nor have I served with anyone who cared so much about the enemy civilians.

When a problem was stirring with the Jillduen civilians in occupied towns or cities, all I had to do was send Queel to talk to them. Things didn't settle down because he had a silver tongue and could persuade the locals that their problems weren't important. Queel cared about them.

Many nights, I hosted him in my tent, arguing over the issues the Jillduen civilians had raised. Queel argued as hard for them as he did for our men. In part, it was because he knew if the issues weren't resolved, then we would have bigger problems on our hands, but mainly because he was a humanitarian at heart.

You could tell by the passion in his voice he couldn't stand to see people being treated poorly though he was not soft. When Queel knew he had to send his men into battle, the man never hesitated, knowing a soldier's job wasn't to stay safe in the barracks. He fought hard, but when it was time to make peace, he would be the most reasonable person in the negotiations. He did not want to hurt the surrendering party more than necessary to ensure a lasting peace, whether it was one man surrendering or a group.

On the rare occasion that we defeated the enemy, any Jilldue who surrendered always sought Queel out because he gave the fairest terms. If he had been born fifteen hundred years earlier, we would have called him the Last of the Inamors, the great and honorable people who forged a near-eternal empire.

By the time Queel's body hit the ground, I was in a rage. During my morning training sessions, Glendeo would lecture me about how a warrior needed to have a clear head and master his emotions, not let them master him. A warrior consumed by emotion is reckless, one who doesn't see he is walking into a trap. Those same lessons were stressed by my father when I accompanied him on campaign.

At that moment, I was the opposite of their ideal warrior. Rage filled me. My attacks were quicker than lightning and had the strength of a charging bull. No single Jilldue could match me. I fought three enemies one on one. They all fell within seconds. Furry filling my veins, I sought more enemies to sate my thirst for blood and vengeance.

I sought out groups of Jilldue, locating them with the focused vision of a hawk. Once I spotted them, I ran toward them with the speed of a cheetah. I threw myself at them, becoming a flurry of attacks and parries, my body acting with the fluidity of a river while having the power of the roaring waves of the sea.

Group after group of Jilldue fell to my blade. My mind didn't register my body's movements. Rage was my mind's sole occupant, fury my body's guide. Axes and swords failed to hit me as I whipped my sword around for parries, delivering quick killing blows, all while dodging attacks from three or more enemies. I remember the look of fear on the Jilldues' eyes and how there was one less pair of terrified eyes with each strike I gave.

What anyone else was doing in the battle was beyond me. I jumped from Jilldue group to Jilldue group, killing them all with near supernatural speed. I remember dropping a group of Jilldue when someone began shouting my name. I saw one of my officers standing a few feet away from me.

He told me the enemy was gone. I asked him how, and he told me to look around. I did. Around me laid scores of dead Jilldue. My sword was dripping with blood, and my clothes were soaked in it, so much so that they stuck to my skin.

The rage left me, but the need for vengeance still burned, though it would have to wait to be quenched. I ordered the officer to see the wounded while I gathered the men to make our position more defendable. In the morning, we would march back to the city.

There wasn't time to fortify the camp since we needed to do whatever we did by torchlight since it was nighttime. We had fires going throughout the night. That's what provided us with enough light to fight off the Jilldue, but setting up defenses was a different matter. You needed a good amount of light to see what you were doing. Torches are good to illuminate a path ahead of you, but the shadows they cast make it hard to know if the trench you dug was as deep as you wanted it or if the makeshift wall of logs tied together had any holes in it.

We needed something that would stop the Jilldue from launching another attack, and we needed it fast. As I was thinking what to do, the officer's words popped into my head: the Jilldue broke because I killed so many of them. They feared me. I drew my sword and approached the nearest Jilldue corpse. Holding down the head with my free hand, I began to chop the neck with my sword until I had beheaded the dead man.

Once the head was in my hand, I threw it down to the side, laid my sword down on the ground so as not to get blood all over the inside of my sheathe, and then picked up a firm stick that was beside me. I removed my knife and sharpened the stick's ends into fine points. When the blunt stick's ends became sharpened spearheads, I thrust one end into the ground, picked up the head, and slammed it on the other. A few soldiers gave me a horrified look, but most of them realized what I was doing and joined in. Soon, a wall of Jillduen heads was erected on the perimeter of our camp, providing us with security for the rest of the night.

As we marched back to the city, I knew we couldn't lure the Jilldue into a battle. They were the most slippery and illusive foes I had ever faced. As we descended the mountainside, I debated which other plans would work. When we arrived back at our headquarters, I knew Hiltole's strategy was the only one. We needed to take the Jilldue out of the war, but we couldn't do it by cutting their supplies or defeating their armies. What we needed to do was preoccupy them with something else.

I ordered the civilians in every town and city we held to evacuate within a month, informing them I was going to burn each city and town to the ground. A few packed up the day I gave the order, but most didn't. It wasn't until the second week when my men were openly carrying wood and pitch throughout the towns and cities, that more of the Jillduen civilians started to believe me, and more of them began packing up and abandoning their homes.

By the last week of the month, I had people surveying the cities and towns, looking for the best spots to start the conflagration. I felt relieved when someone told me that the last civilian holdouts were beginning to pack up their belongings. Back then, I didn't want to kill civilians. It was war, but that didn't mean you got to kill noncombatants. It would have been murder, something I was uncomfortable with in those days.

On the last day of the month, I gave orders to the incendiary brigade, and all five towns and two cities became alight. My small army waited at a junction on the roads connecting the two cities to meet the brigade members. They joined back up with us when the thick, black smoke reached the clouds. As I ordered the men to march, I knew the Jilldue were taken out of the war, and the campaign had been won.

Chapter Twenty-one

"I THOUGHT YOU WOULD HAVE TORCHED the cities and towns, regardless of the civilians," Jorn said after I ended my story.

"At the time, I didn't know how cruel the world was," I told him.

"Or you knew cruelty was a choice," my nephew rebutted.

"Perhaps," I admitted. "But enough pondering on the past. We should get to the palace and meet with your father. If we spend all our time discussing past wars, we won't have time to fight the current one."

I stood up from the table, and Jorn did the same. By the time we reached the war room, the sun was setting. I didn't realize how much time I spent telling Jorn about the war. Men ramble when sharing significant memories, especially when coated in pain and loss. I didn't prove to be the exception I usually was.

Maybe it's because I hadn't thought about the Jilldue and the Swadonilic Mountains for a while. Maybe it was because I wanted to think about something other than the hopeless war I was fighting. Maybe it was because I grew accustomed to having my nephew around and answering the boy's endless questions about the past. Looking back, I think it was all those reasons.

We found my brother in the war room, hunched over the table with the maps on it. Father would do the same while we were on the campaign, forever studying maps of geography and reading what felt like a never-ending supply of scouting reports. But there was always an air of control about him when he did. When you looked at him hunched over a table the aura of a great general surrounded him.

No such air adorned my brother. Rono was calm, an impressive feat considering the circumstances, but his eyes were not carefully studying the maps or dissecting the scouting reports as our father did. Rono's eyes frantically darted around the table's contents, desperately trying to find a way to preserve his kingdom and his city.

Despite this, I couldn't help but think this gave him a noble look since I knew he did not wish to preserve his place on the throne. If he did, he could have surrendered to Salroon under the condition he kept his throne. But my brother wanted to preserve Eshtar's sovereignty, knowing that his people would likely suffer under Diefetian rule. When we entered, I could hear him praying to Numveron and Pafix to end the war.

"Great King of Gods, with your guidance, I have brought peace and prosperity to this kingdom, undoing the damage of my father and using both to build a great temple in your honor. If I have done anything to please you, I ask you to bring a swift end to this war in Eshtar's favor. The Diefetians have attacked us, though we've done nothing to them.

"Master of War, terrifying Pafix, if Numveron, your king, declines my plead, and the righteous course is to be conquered, then I ask you to instill bravery in my soldiers' hearts. I ask that the martial honor of Eshtar will not be blemished," he finished.

Rono looked up. "I had hoped with Salroon fighting so many other wars, we wouldn't be in as tough of a situation as we currently are," he admitted.

"For all we know, the Diefetians are on the retreat everywhere else," Jorn pointed out.

"That wasn't your uncle's opinion before the war began, and he has been proven right for the most part," the king informed his son.

"How many have capitulated?" I asked.

"The Kyntrenbins, the Nutharicans and the Gofrundins have. The Renvolies hold on. There is a rumor they have rebuilt the ships they lost, and the Huderians are too prideful to surrender," Rono informed us.

"Has Salroon moved into Luiferia?" I asked.

"From what I've heard, the Diefetian war machine has stopped at the border, just as you predicted," he said.

"It's not as bad as I thought," I said. "Salroon could pull troops from the west to deal with us, but I don't think he will. He's got more than enough men to deal with us and capture the sword. And he risks a revolt in the west if he does redirect troops here."

"Looks like our situation hasn't changed much," noted Jorn.

"It has not. But if the Huderians surrender, we may see an influx of Diefetian troops. They're the last major land power Salroon has to deal with, and the fate of Renvoly will be decided on the seas," I said.

"Do we know if the Diefetians are on the march to besiege Kiholp?" Jorn asked.

"There have been no reports of a Diefetian army marching towards the capital," his father informed us.

"What is Salroon up to?" the prince wondered.

"Just because there have been no reports of an incoming army doesn't mean there isn't one on the way," I pointed out.

"Or it means Salroon is going to try and take the sword by having you killed, then try and take the capital," Rono said.

"I think that's more likely," Jorn gave his opinion.

"Why?" I asked, curious how my nephew was thinking about our current predicament.

"You don't just have *Hueik,* something Slaroon's been trying to get his hands on; you're the only hope for Eshtar. If anyone can win this war, it's you. If Salroon kills you, then he kills two birds with one stone," Jorn explained. "It's worth Salroon trying, and if you kill a handful of men but still die, then that's better than Salroon possibly losing hundreds assaulting the walls."

I smiled. "An excellent point."

"But, what if Salroon is doing something else?" the king asked.

"Like what?" I asked.

"Well, we're forgetting the gods told you Salroon was a servant of Allemar. What if the demon has instructed his vampire minion to do something else," my brother proposed.

"Brother, if we win the war and kill Salroon, then we won't have to worry about this talk of demons," I argued.

"Talk!" exclaimed the king. "You met with the gods and still think this is all talk. The Protectorate has confirmed that our enemy is a vampire and is in service to a demon. I thought you would believe what your eyes have seen and your ears have heard if nothing else."

"I've already admitted to the existence of the gods. But those worthless divinities you so fervently worship told me to kill Salroon and the vampires that follow him. Numveron himself even specified he didn't want me to fight the demon," I argued.

"For all we know, Allemar is making all of Salroon's decisions for him," countered Rono.

"Which doesn't matter. All that means is they have the same objectives," I said.

"What if they don't, and Allemar has Salroon doing something else, something we can't predict?" he asked.

"Why do you care? If Salroon wants to conquer Eshtar because his master told him to, then it doesn't change the fact we have to fight Salroon and the Diefetians," I argued.

"Our problems are bigger than defending the kingdom," Rono insisted.

"Bigger than the kingdom? Brother, have you become Emperor of the Continent while I wasn't looking?" I asked.

"Allemar is controlling Salroon, and Salroon is in the process of conquering the Continent. Whatever the demon is planning, the conquest of the Continent is only the beginning," he argued.

"Brother, you made me your military advisor to help you fight against the Diefetians, not to worry about the welfare of the whole Continent. You are King of Eshtar, and every other country on the Continent should not concern you unless they can threaten or aid your kingdom," I argued.

"One of us must care. It's not going to be you," he quipped.

"The world is a cruel place, brother. If you want to survive, you worry about yourself and your own," I told him.

"I remember our mother teaching us something different when we were younger," he commented.

"She also taught us the Protectorate was made up of caring, benevolent, and just gods. Her fate alone proves otherwise," I said.

"And your choices prove the world's cruelty stems from man's choices," Rono countered.

"That may be true, yet the gods did not step in and right all the wrongs I've made. They never tried to stop me. Aren't they supposed to be protectors? Shouldn't they have stopped me after I burned Ifeldum to the ground or made the ancient streets of Elmdi run with blood?" I asked.

"I don't think this is a helpful conversation," Jorn said before his father could respond to me. "What we should be arguing about is what we will do."

"He's right. We need to figure out what to do," agreed the king.

"There's not much we can do other than prepare for a siege," I said.

"What if Salroon sends someone to kill you and take the sword?" Rono asked.

"Then I kill them," I said.

"Perhaps you should go into hiding," the king proposed.

"That's funny, brother," I said. "And a foolish suggestion, considering you have no one else to fight this war for you."

"Then what's the plan?" Jorn asked.

"Find the Diefetian army," I said.

"Then do what?" Rono asked.

Suddenly, the door swung open, and a messenger entered. He promptly bowed to his king before handing him a rolled-up scroll. Once Rono opened it and gave it a quick skim, he thanked the messenger and dismissed him.

"What is it?" I asked.

"The Diefetians are besieging Tuldum and Gregoros again. Along with Swendufen in the south and Aponden in the east," Rono told us.

"Salroon's trying to cut us off, so we can't get help. If he takes all four, we won't have any means of resupplying our army. We'll have to rely on whatever stores we currently have since all of the roads that lead out of the country funnel into those four locations. We were worried about Salroon besieging the capital, but now he's trying to besiege the entire kingdom," I said.

"We don't have the resources to break all four sieges," Rono said. "If Salroon can't cut us off completely from trading with other kingdoms for supplies, he can greatly limit our options."

"It also means that if Uncle Bowv tries to escape with the sword, he controls all roads going out of the country," Jorn pointed out.

"That's never stopped me before," I said. "But you're right, and it's certainly part of Salroon's reasoning."

"I should have focused more on national defense instead of sacrificing it for trade," Rono grumbled.

"Don't be too hard on yourself. The kingdom was broken when you took the throne. You needed to build up the treasury, or else there would have been a revolution," I said.

"He's got a point, Father," Jorn agreed.

"I see your point, but what are we supposed to do? Gods know how many men Salroon has besieging each location. And who's to say that once we march to lift one siege, the Diefetians won't attack the capital? I might as well surrender," the king said, and a plan began to form in my mind.

"That may be a better idea than you think," I said.

"What in the gods' names are you talking about?" he asked.

"Surrender. Tell Salroon I thought the war was hopeless and took off with the sword. He'll hunt me down; he's got no choice, but it will be too late. I'll already have disappeared, allowing me to find Salroon and fight and kill him," I said.

"It's too risky," the king told me.

"It's either this or have your capital forcefully taken or starved into submission. It's your choice, brother," I said.

"How would you get to Salroon?" Jorn questioned before his father could respond to me.

"I have my ways," I assured him.

"Enough," Rono said. "I will not support you going to Salroon, even if it is to duel him again and risk him getting *Hueik*. Look at all the maps and the scouting reports, see if there is another way to win. And see if you can teach Jorn anything while you do so. I need to check on our spy problem. Keep what we have talked about between the three of us."

Rono left the room, and Jorn and I became the ones who were hunched over the table, studying maps and scrutinizing scouting reports. On the political map of Eshtar, I placed small, red wooden rings around the dots, representing that Tuldum, Gregoros, Swendufen, and Apenden were being besieged. Jorn nodded, saying that he understood what I was doing.

The scouting reports were in better order than I expected. The scouts had estimated about three thousand men at each location, meaning the Diefetians had a four-to-one advantage. There wasn't much I could typically do with three thousand men against twelve thousand, but fortunately for us, the enemy was not concentrated.

But there was the problem that Rono brought up. If we went to lift one siege, then that left Kiholp exposed. We didn't have enough men to defend the capital and break a siege simultaneously. Then, the problem was how long the defenders could hold out. They could hold out for a while if the Diefetians tried to starve, but it would be considerably shorter if the enemy assaulted the walls.

Tuldum was the most concerning. Although the garrison lacked men, the scouts reported that a ditch was built around the walls to deter escalations. Gregoros had been resupplied, while Swenduden and Apenden had the strongest walls out of the four.

But it doesn't matter how strong your walls are if you don't have enough men to man them. It was possible that both could fall with one determined assault by the enemy. I explained this all to Jorn and then asked what he thought.

"As far as I can tell, you're right, though I don't know much about strategy. But I think we have more to worry about than the sieges," he said.

"What else would we have to worry about?" I asked, wondering what Jorn had seen in the reports.

"Whoever Salroon put in charge of the sieges might be vampires. Every Diefetian official or commander we encounter turns out to be a vampire. Why wouldn't it be the same now?" the prince reasoned.

"A good observation," I said. If Jorn was correct, then Rono would no doubt want to deal with the vampire threat, which would make our situation more difficult than it should be. And we didn't know how many vampires there were.

Was there one vampire, or did a vampire lead each besieging force? We wouldn't know until they revealed themselves. I concluded there must have been four vampires, one for each siege. Salroon was attacking where he was attacking to control the roads out of Eshtar, so I wouldn't be able to make off with *Hueik*. Having a vampire at each siege would help ensure I would be stopped if I was trying to get out of the country.

My brother opposed killing Salroon outside of battle, but he would insist that the four vampires be dealt with. Rono wouldn't take an opportunity to achieve victory because it wasn't "honorable," yet he would risk defeat for honor's sake. There lay my problem. I would be sent to deal with the vampires, but I knew Rono wouldn't allow me to sneak into their camps in the dead of night and slit their throats.

I could have left then, frustrated by my brother's restrictions, and gone to kill Salroon, but I didn't want to. It had been years since I had been on campaign and longer still since I had a real challenge in war. Salroon, I would kill without hesitation, but he was a worthy opponent, and I respected him as a warrior and a general.

It was a long time since I had respected one of my enemies. At the end of my military career, just before I killed the Wretched King, I was unmatched in battle, and there wasn't a better general on the Continent, excluding the Wretched King. But by then, he had entrusted me with command of the entire Eshtaran army and was retired from military life.

When I abdicated and became the Terror of the Continent, no one could catch, kill, or outwit me. Time and time, when pursuers thought they had my clan trapped, I would always find a way out. Standing there hunched over the table, I realized I had been unknowingly craving a challenge. I smiled.

Then, I thought about how I was going to get out of the situation I was in. Or, more appropriately, how to get Eshtar out of its mess. It would be foolish to try to march to break the sieges. We didn't have the numbers to do that and defend the capital. And despite Rono's moral objections, I didn't have the time to go around killing the sieges' commanders. I would kill one or two, and then by that time, the others would have succeeded in their sieges. I needed a way to get the Diefetians to lift all four sieges without a fight.

For an eternity, I stared at the maps and reread the reports thousands of times, looking for a way to lift all four sieges in a single stroke. But lifting the sieges would not be enough. I needed a way to end the war. The only plan I could see was the one I proposed: have Rono surrender, tell the Diefetians I took off with the sword, and have them look for me while I found Salroon and killed him.

It was the only hope Rono had, and it got me what I wanted. As I thought about it more, I refined the plan, and it became even more viable. But some things needed to be done before I began. Information needed to be gathered from the heretic, I needed to convince a certain blacksmith to go against his king's wishes, I needed a plausible lie to tell my brother, and I needed to convince an old warrior to persuade my brother to sue for peace.

It wasn't hard to decide to go against my brother's wishes. He might have been king, but that meant nothing to me. The four sieges couldn't be broken by battle; we didn't have enough men, and I suspected the Diefetians had taken steps to reinforce their supply line to prevent another Tuldum. We needed to give the enemy an offer he couldn't refuse, and I wagered Salroon wanted the sword more than he wanted Eshtar.

He could easily do the latter, but the former was trickery. I could vanish; it could be years before anyone tracked me down. Salroon knew this, and his commanders knew it, too. If one of the commanders managed to retrieve the Sword of the Gods, their king would surely reward them for such a feat. If I was right, and there were four commanders, there would be a race for the sword.

It was our only option, but it was also a good plan. Though my brother was restricted by his morality, I was not. However, killing Salroon wouldn't be immoral because he was the king who invaded Eshtar without cause and sent Leernu to take *Hueik*, even if it meant killing Rono and me. And, of course, Salroon was a vampire, a demonic-spawned monster, making killing him beyond justifiable. But my brother was not willing to do what was necessary.

Looking back, I don't blame him. Rono knew diplomacy and politics, the latter a dirty game for sure, but both pale in comparison to the vile face of war. Salroon was the head of the enemy army, not some civilian. But I suggested we end the war and the threat to the kingdom by killing the enemy king. Killing the *vampiric* Diefetian king was one of the most moral plans I could propose. But I knew there was no way of convincing Rono; we inherited our father's stubbornness.

"I need to study the maps and the reports more," I told Jorn as I looked up from the table. "I'll be a while longer. Why don't you see if you can help your father with anything? I'm sure he's pretty stressed right now. If he says he doesn't need help, then get some rest. I feel we won't be getting much in the coming days."

Jorn nodded and left the room. I stuck around, still reviewing the maps and reports. I didn't lie since I still needed to look at both. I was trying to figure out the best place to lead the Diefetians on a chase. My concentration was interrupted when I heard Jorn's voice along with another one in the halls, then footsteps approaching the war room, and the door open.

As I looked up from the table, Hydela walked into the war room. She wore a plain dress, though she held herself in a regal manner. The look on her face left no doubt she despised me.

"Based on our last conversation, I thought you wouldn't want to speak to me," I said.

"And I thought you would abandon my husband at the first opportunity," she said.

"Looks like we were both wrong," I said, gazing back at the table.

"You're going to kill Salroon," she stated, and I knew she knew I was going to go against Rono's wishes.

"Considering he's been trying to kill me, I sure hope so," I said.

She sighed. "I've talked to Jorn and Rono. I know you're going to ignore my husband's wishes, track down Salroon, get him to fight you, then kill him," she told me.

"It is a possibility, albeit less probable, considering the queen believes it will happen," I said.

"I want you to do it," Hydela said.

"I must have misheard you," I told her as I looked up. "I thought you said you wanted me to pursue a plan, which your husband told me not to."

"Whether I like it or not, and as much as it pains me to admit it, you're the best hope for Eshtar since we have no other capable commanders," she said.

"My military reputation alone doesn't explain why you trust me. You think I don't care about my brother or the kingdom. So, why trust me?" I asked.

"I don't trust you to save the kingdom, Bowv," she said. "I trust you to do what you want: kill Salroon. His death will end this war."

"Belief out of necessity is the worst kind," I said.

"As it is the strongest," the queen assured me.

"Though I am not sure you can do the job considering the results of the duel," admitted Hydela.

"I know who I can talk to about winning," I said.

"Then talk to them, and don't lose this time," ordered the queen. "Salroon believes the sword you carry is the Sword of the Gods."

"You don't?" I asked.

"I don't think the Protectorate would judge you as worthy of wielding their weapon," she said.

"They didn't. The sword picked me," I informed her.

"Now that's just foolish," Hydela said.

"That's what I thought," I mumbled.

"You really do believe that's *Hueik*," stated the queen.

"Yes, I do, and I know the Protectorate is real, though they're useless," I answered truthfully.

"Bowv the Terror of the Continent admitting the gods exist. We must be living in the end times," Hydela commented, then shook her head and left the war room.

Chapter Twenty-Two

I WALKED INTO ILKON'S ROOM and was relieved to see the heretic turn his sea of scrolls into well-organized stacks, which crawled up the walls of his room rather than consuming the floor. Ilkon was there, reading a scroll on his desk. When he heard me approach, he looked up from his reading and greeted me.

"What do you need?" he asked.

"I need to know what Salroon did during our duel," I answered.

"I would think you would know better than I. You're the weapons master, not me," he said.

"Salroon muttered something under his breath just before he started attacking at a speed that should have been impossible. I need to know what he did," I clarified.

"Judging by your description, it can't be blood magic," Ilkon deduced.

"Blood magic?" I asked.

"The type of magic vampires can use after drinking blood," the heretic clarified. "Some people believe vampires need blood to sustain themselves, but that's a myth. They can eat food and drink water just like us. They need blood to activate their magic."

"None of the vampires I've fought did anything like that," I said.

"Probably because they drink blood in secret, they don't want to expose themselves. During the Vampiric Wars, it was far more common. And magic is nonexistent nowadays, partially thanks to the Protectorate Temple condemning it as demonic," the priest explained.

"There's no such thing as magic," I asserted.

"You thought the gods weren't real until you were granted an audience with them," Ilkon countered. "Chances are, when you encounter some magic, you'll change your mind."

"We'll see about that," I said. "But if it wasn't blood magic, what was it?"

"A prayer to Allemar," Ilkon informed me.

"A prayer?" I asked, skepticism in my voice.

"Allemar is the creator of vampires and is their god. Vampires can pray to him to gain short bursts of powers," the heretic explained.

"Then there's nothing I can do to prevent it," I concluded.

"Not that I am aware of, no," Ilkon said. "Barring, of course, an act of the Protectorate."

"Then there's nothing I can do to counter it," I repeated.

"Unless you get on better terms with them," he said.

I let out a laugh, which filled the room.

"Or not," Ilkon said.

"Well, thanks for the laugh," I said as I turned to walk out of the room. Ilkon may not have had a solution outside of religion, but the solution to my problem dawned on me while I walked over to the door.

"They may surprise you, Bowv," I heard Ilkon's voice behind me as I opened the door.

"A dull blade is more useful than the gods," I said as I left the room and went to find Glendeo.

The old man was in the lobby; for once, he wasn't sweeping. Instead, Glendeo sat at one of the tables with a rolled open scroll, a quill, and a small jar of ink. Several stacks of silver were off to the side, and I took out some pieces to add to it.

"You already paid for your room for several more nights," the old soldier told me. "What do you want?"

"A favor," I said.

"Ask someone else," he said.

"You don't know what I'm going to ask yet," I protested.

"Get someone else to do it. I owe you nothing," the old man said.

"The favor is specific to you," I told him.

"Still not interested. Letting you stay at my inn is a favor," Glendeo argued.

"Then I should take my silver back," I said.

"What do you want, Bowv?" he asked.

"I want you to convince my brother to sue for peace," I said.

"Why would I do that? And why would he listen to me?" asked the innkeeper.

"He'll listen because you're the most experienced veteran in the city and were one of Father's most trusted advisors," I explained.

"I wasn't his advisor," Glendeo argued.

"Not an official one, but you were. How often did you and Father walk around the palace talking about politics or the current war he was fighting? I remember those days, and so does Rono; that's why he'll listen to you," I said.

"And why would I convince the king to pursue peace?" he asked.

"Because you know we can't win this war," I answered.

"So, you'll have Rono surrender the kingdom, ending the war and freeing up resources and manpower for Salroon to chase you. Then you'll vanish and try to kill him," the old warrior deduced my plan. "Once Salroon is dead, Rono has grounds to object to whatever treaty he signed."

"Precisely," I confirmed.

"I don't know Bowv," he muttered.

"It's either this or see the kingdom strangled for weeks because Salroon wants to ensure the sword doesn't leave the country," I said.

"Since when do you care about the kingdom?" he asked.

"I don't. I care about killing Salroon, which is the best thing for me and the kingdom," I said.

"I would say yes, but I can't. Salroon bested you in the duel, and I don't like murder either," Glendeo said.

"No, I intend to fight him," I assured the old man. "But this time, I won't let him use the same advantage."

The old man went silent for a moment. "Fine, I'll do it."

"Good, and don't tell anyone I put you up to it," I ordered.

"Of course," he said as I got up from the table and began the walk to Billen's shop.

I reached Billen's shop about noontime. He was behind the counter for once and not outback at the forge. Bilen must have given the boy a break or was having him work the forge, which Billen would inspect later to see how well he could smith without Billen's supervision.

"What's the plan?" the blacksmith asked as I entered his shop.

"Straight to the point then," I said. "I'll tell you the plan, but first, you need to know my brother hasn't approved it."

"As if the king needed more reasons to hang you," Billen said. "Tell me anyway."

"The plan is: Rono surrenders, the war ends, and the Diefetians chase me to get the sword, though I manage to slip away and kill him," I gave the short version.

"How will you get to Salroon when he will send entire armies after you?" Billen asked.

"They'll be chasing me for a bit, but then I'll disappear without them realizing it, and they'll be chasing you," I explained.

"How do you suppose you do that?" he asked.

"I gather some men and have the Diefetians chase us down. We'll keep enough distance between us that they won't even notice that I've disappeared and you've taken command," I explained.

"I'll do it," he said.

"I thought you would need more convincing," I said.

"The war is pretty much lost," Billen said. "I don't think even you could figure out a way to win it through conventional means."

"Then it's settled. Don't tell anyone about this," I told him.

At that moment, the door opened, and Jorn walked in. The young prince gasped for air, and sweat poured down his face, making it obvious that he had run to the blacksmith's shop. "Father... needs... you," he gasped.

"Are we under attack?" I asked.

"No... the spy... has been... discovered," Jorn informed us between breaths.

"Spy?" Billen asked.

"There was one in the palace," I explained. "Rono and I believe the spy is why Ilonek was waiting on the road for us."

"You should leave," Billen said.

"Yes, I should," I agreed, then turned to Jorn. "Take your time getting back to the palace; your father and I can handle this."

I ran back to the palace and faired far better than Jorn. In addition to running around the back of the inn each morning, twice a month,

Glendeo would have me run around the city for hours. Combined with years of marching in the army and running as an outlaw, my stamina level was terrific. Not wanting to give the palace guards the wrong impression, I slowed down when I got to Glendeo's inn.

One of the guards outside the palace nodded to me as I entered and told me I could find Rono in the throne room. When I entered, I found my normally calm and collected younger brother pacing back and forth across the room. He was practically glowing with distress.

"I heard you caught the spy," I said as I approached.

"We have," he said.

"How?" I asked.

"When you told me Paderok was visiting a Diefetian trader in the mornings, I ordered him to follow. Nothing came up. Paderok wasn't seen visiting the trader on his morning walks, so I called my men off. My suspicions were removed until a squad of patrolling city guards noticed someone entering Ambassador Zimkoo's residence about two hours ago.

"After you killed Zimkoo and the emergence of our spy problem, I ordered the residence searched. Nothing was found, but I ordered the residence to be locked up and banned entry. When the city guards entered the house, they found Paderok uncovering a false wall and retrieving a scroll. The scroll had information Zimkoo was collecting about the military defenses of the city."

"Why did you send Jorn to find me if you caught Paderok red-handed?" I asked.

"Paderok claims he is innocent, and he was searching the premise on a hunch," informed the king.

"Of course, he does; he's a spy. Not everyone is as honest as I am when they confess to committing crimes, brother," I said

"I know he is, but I don't know if the Diefetian trader he supposedly has been visiting is involved in this," he said.

"And you're afraid the Diefetian will get away if you don't get Paderok to confirm he's been passing on information to the merchant, who then passed it on to the Diefetian army," I concluded.

"Yes," he affirmed.

"Let me down there, and I will get Paderok talking," I said.

"Torture is illegal, Bowv," my brother said.

"Since when?" I asked.

"Since I became king," he said.

"I'll scare him then; the man's terrified of me anyway. I won't have to lay a finger on him," I assured Rono.

"Yet somehow he will end up dead," my brother said.

"Then what do you want me to do?" I asked.

"I want you to track down this Diefetian merchant," he said.

"He'll run when he sees me since everyone in the city knows I'm working with you," I argued.

"He... has a point... Father," Jorn said as he walked into the room, looking more exhausted than when he walked into Billen's shop.

"I do," I agreed. "I told you to rest at Billen's."

"I took... a five-minute rest," he assured me between breaths.

"Then what would you advise?" Rono asked his son.

"Go down with Uncle Bowv to see Paderok and make sure he doesn't kill him," answered the prince.

Rono thought about it for a moment. "Alright, let's go, Bowv."

We descended the stone steps leading into the dungeon a few minutes later. Nothing adorned the walls, creating a barren feel I had grown accustomed to during my imprisonment. Paderok was in my old cell, sitting with his back against the wall across from the bed. He stood up as he heard us coming down the stairs. Rono and I walked over to the cell. Paderok did not speak.

"Do you have anything to say?" my brother asked.

"I do not," he said.

"You know why you are in here?" the king asked.

"I am," he said.

"And you still insist that you are innocent?" Rono asked.

"Yes, I do," Paderok answered.

"I have documents from Ambassador Zimkoo's residence detailing the city's defenses, documents you were found with while you were in the house, which I placed a ban on entering," my brother said.

Paderok fell silent. After Rono told him that, there was nothing he could do or say to get himself out of the cell.

"I also know that while on your morning walks, you pay a Diefetian merchant a visit," Rono said. "I suspect he is the one that passes your information to Diefet."

Paderok didn't admit his guilt, but his face was sullen, and his eyes had a slight downward gaze.

"It looks like I don't have to do anything," I told Rono, and my brother nodded.

Paderok's gaze shot up as fear coursed through his veins, pumped by a heart beating at a rate that could prove dangerous. I knew I couldn't lay a hand on him, but he didn't know that. If Paderok believed I could torture him and had the intention to, then he would be more forthcoming with information. I learned as a bandit, the threat of violence will get higher rates of compliance than actual violence.

"It appears so," my brother said.

"Just a couple of weeks back, I thought I was going to be the guy who would get executed," I said, placing a slight emphasis on "executed."

"A shocking turn of events indeed," my brother agreed with a grim look on his face.

"Why did you do it?" I asked.

Paderok didn't answer.

"What was it money, or did a Diefetian give you a mean look?" I asked.

The prisoner remained silent.

"Answer me!" I screamed, drew my sword, and approached the cell. Paderok jumped up like a sacred elk.

"Bowv!" Rono shouted. "Put the sword away."

I turned around to face the king. "He didn't answer me," I said as I sheathed *Hueik*.

"My father owed a debt to Merjohik," Paderok finally said.

"Who's that?" I interrogated.

"The Diefetian merchant I see every morning," said the courtier.

"Why did your father owe him a debt?" asked Rono.

"Merjohik saved his life a long time ago, but Father never had the chance to repay him," explained Paderok.

"The debt fell to you," concluded Rono.

Paderok nodded his head.

"You agreed to pass on information to him to pay it off," I reasoned.

"Correct," he said.

"How does Merjohik get information to Diefet?" asked the king.

"Through his caravan network, or at least that's what he tells me," informed Paderok.

"Who does he send the information to?" asked Rono.

"I don't know," admitted Paderok.

"Where is he?" the king asked.

"Probably gone by now since I've been arrested," Paderok guessed.

"Where would he go?" Rono pressed.

"Out of the country if he's smart," I answered for Paderok.

"We're done here," decided Rono. He turned away from the cell and proceeded to the stairs. I followed him.

"Let's go for a walk," he said when I reached the top.

He led me outside the palace and took a right turn. We walked along the side of the palace until we got to the courtyard. Much like the rest of the palace, it was made from stone. It had two deer at its entrance, each carved from a solid, large rock. As a child, I thought they looked so real they would startle and flee if I came too close.

The courtyard was a perfect square with four walls, one of which was a side of the palace. In the middle was a circle mosaic of four deer in the forest. Rose bushes and hedges sat along the perimeter, the only flora on an otherwise barren landscape. Four simple stone benches were along the mosaic, each corresponding to a cardinal direction.

There would have been less if Father had gotten his way. Everything that gave the place life, the rosebushes, the statues, and the mosaic, was my mother's doings. My father wanted the place as spartan as the rest of the palace, but my mother was adamant she wouldn't live in such a harsh place without a refuge. I don't know what she did. Father was the most stubborn man I have ever known, but somehow, she got him to add the statues, mosaic, and rosebushes.

Mother would tell Rono and me stories about the gods in the courtyard when we were younger. As she talked, we would forget our backs were sore from the lack of support and our butts were numb from sitting on stone. When Rono went to sit down, he chose the same bench. He leaned forward a little and put his hands on his face, covering his eyes. I didn't know if he was crying or processing the betrayal of Paderok. I gave him a few minutes before I spoke.

"What are we going to do about Merjohik?" I asked.

My brother removed his hands from his face, stood up, and approached me. "I don't know Bowv," he said, shrugging.

"He's probably already gone anyway," I told him.

"Then why ask?" he questioned.

"You looked miserable moping on that bench. Miserable kings are bad for morale," I said.

Rono shook his head. "Are you capable of empathy?" he asked.

"You didn't make me your advisor to be empathetic," I reminded him.

"No, I didn't," he said. "But did you ever have any?"

"What's with the questions? Less than a month ago, you would have said 'no,' so why are you asking?" I questioned.

"Did you love Mother?" he asked.

"What kind of question is that?" I asked, my voice elevated.

"A legitimate one, considering you killed our father," Rono whipped.

"You know I loved her," I snapped.

"How am I supposed to know that when after you killed Father, you became the most notorious criminal on the Continent?" he asked.

"Don't be ridiculous, brother," I said.

"Ridiculous? You've killed more people than the plaque," he yelled the last bit.

Rage began to stir inside me, but I kept it in check. "You know I cried for a week when she died. What are you trying to get at?" I asked.

He turned around, walked back over to the same bench, and sat down again. I walked over and sat down right beside him. Rono looked off towards the rosebush and spoke with a quiet voice.

"I realized today Paderok was the second man to occupy that cell whom I trusted and who betrayed me," he spoke, his voice almost a whisper.

"This is the second time a trusted court member has betrayed you. Must be tough," I told him.

He turned his gaze away from the rosebush and towards me. "I'm talking about you," he said.

Once he said it, I knew what he meant. Growing up, Rono placed immense trust in me. When I killed the Wretched King, I betrayed not just my father but also my brother.

"Why did you do it? And don't say 'necessity' like you told Jorn," he asked.

"I killed Father because he showed me power stems not from caravans or armies but from fear. I had to be the most feared man on the Continent, something I couldn't achieve while he was still alive," I explained.

"Power, that's why you did it? You never cared for power when we were young," he called my bluff. "I remember you as compassionate, selfless, and dutiful to our parents and the kingdom. What changed, brother?"

I fell silent and let a few moments pass before I spoke. "I have never known a woman more loving than our mother and a king more just than our father. But look at what happened. Mother died of the plague after helping to care for its victims, and Father, a righteous man, descended into wickedness. The most caring woman on the Continent died too soon, and the Wretched King reigned too long.

"Where were the great gods of the Protectorate, the ones Mother told us would intervene and set the world right when she took her last breaths? Where were they when Father started fighting wars for the fun of it and torturing prisoners for pleasure? Where were the gods when I witnessed atrocity after atrocity in war?" I asked.

"It wasn't about power," he concluded, his voice now a whisper.

Once again, he stared off, focusing his gaze on the rosebush. Silence fell around us with the speed of a sudden gust of wind. My brother's eyes remained distant and unconnected to this world. He sat there tossing around what I said in his head, trying to think of a response that would neutralize my nihilistic view.

It was the first time in my life he didn't have a counterargument. Looking at my brother sitting there speechless, I thought I had won. I didn't talk either, but I just sat there savoring the elusive victory I had sought for most of my life until I heard the sweat voice of a child, and like the waning tide, the celebration of my triumph was carried out to sea.

"Daddy," a little girl's voice broke the silence.

We both turned around to see a four-year-old girl with curly blond hair that ran down to her neck and wearing a blue dress that matched her yes, standing five steps from the bench. Neither of us had heard her approach.

"Kansaderi, aren't you supposed to be studying with the tutor?" her father asked.

"I finished early," my niece said.

"Kansaderi," pressed my brother.

"I did!" she whined and stomped her foot.

"Perhaps I should be asking what finishing early means?" her father thought aloud, then looked at her with a stare that would crack most grown men. It was the same uncompromising stare our father gave us when he knew we were hiding something. To Kansaderi's credit, she lasted much longer than Rono and I did when we were her age. Father typically had us spilling our guts within twenty seconds. My niece held on for at least thirty.

"Fine. I snuck out," she confessed. I heard dirt being scrapped in the hedges near us. Rono didn't indicate that he had heard anything.

"Why did you do that?" he asked.

"The tutor was going on and on about the war, how the kingdom's doomed, and wasn't teaching me anything. I thought I could be doing something else and snuck out," the little girl explained.

I laughed, and Rono turned to me. "Is something funny, brother?" he asked.

"Yes, she has so much common sense at her age. You're doing something right as a parent," I grinned.

"Don't encourage her, Bowv," he ordered.

"You're my uncle!" Kansaderi said with excitement and a small jump, then turned to her father and crossed her arms. "How come Jorn got to meet him, and I didn't?" she asked.

"Because I didn't want you to," Rono said.

"Why?" she persisted.

"Because I'm a dangerous man," I answered for him.

She turned away from Rono and towards me. "Father says we don't give up on family," she informed me.

"I think your father gave up on me a long time ago," I told her.

Again, she turned Rono, crossed her arms again, and gave her father a look similar to the one he had given her a few minutes earlier. She was silent, yet her look demanded an explanation from her father. He lacked one. I chuckled.

"I think she wants an answer, brother," I said.

"As do I," Jorn said as he walked towards us, and I heard dirt being moved again in the hedges, followed by a soft but assertive hush. No one else seemed to hear it. Rono and Kansaderi's attention was on Jorn

"This is a conversation for another time," Rono said.

"I want an answer," whined a persistent Kansaderi.

"And you will get one another time," her father said.

"Can I get one?" Jorn asked.

"No," the king said.

"Why?" an annoyed prince asked. "You sent me to war under his command and entrusted him to train me, then won't answer a simple question."

"It's because your father never gave up on your uncle," Hydela said as she joined our little group, walking in from the courtyard entrance. Hydela must have gone looking for Kansaderi and thought the girl went to the courtyard. Where else would a little girl wander off to in a stone palace?

I heard a twig snap in the hedges. Someone was hiding in the bushes, and I knew who they were.

"How could he give up on the older brother he admired as a child, who was so devoted to him and his parents? The brother who was there for him after their mother died. The brother who protected him from their father as he descended into wretchedness. The older brother he couldn't wait to see become king. Your father has never given up on your uncle. He doesn't want to admit it because the pain is too much to bear."

Rono looked towards his wife and smiled. "Well put, my love," he said.

"Uncle Bowv wasn't always a meanie?" Kansaderi asked.

"Not always," Rono informed her.

"Too bad the twins aren't here," Jorn said.

"They're hiding in the hedges," I said.

"I told you he heard us," an adolescent boy said from behind the rose bush.

"And I told *you* to be *quieter*," a girl's voice said.

"Dulnic, Fransya, come out," ordered their father.

With that, a cluster of branches close to the bottom of the hedges was pulled back, forming a small opening. First, Fransya crawled out, and soon, her brother followed. Both were covered in dirt. Fransya wore a forest green dress, while Dulnic wore a dark grey shirt and black pants. I was surprised when I saw that my niece and nephew were redheads. Dulnic's hair was more red-orange, off the ears, and away from his eyes, while Fransya's curly hair was auburn and only ran down to her neck. Both had green eyes.

"What gave us away? Was it when Dulnic moved around?" my niece asked.

"Or was it the twig Fransya snapped?" my nephew asked.

"Both, combined with your inability to sit still for a minute," I explained.

"You knew we were being watched and didn't say anything? And how in the gods' names did you hear the dirt being scraped?" Rono asked.

"They came minutes after Kansaderi. I could tell there were two of them since one hushed the other. You told me you had four kids. Kansaderi was already here, and Jorn should be resting from his run, so I figured the other two skipped their studies like Kansaderi. And I could hear them because when you are a wanted man, you pay attention to the noises around you," I told him.

"Speaking of studies, the three of you need to get back to them," their mother told them.

"But mom, we only just met Uncle Bowv," protested Fransya, who, by the tone of her voice, was trying to avoid going back to her studies.

"Yeah, I bet he has a bunch of cool stories to tell," Dulnic said enthusiastically.

"I have a lot of stories. None of your father would want me to tell," I said.

"Like how you killed our grandfather?" Fransya asked.

"The three of you go with your mother," Rono ordered.

"What about Jorn?" Dulnic asked.

"Yeah, what about Jorn?" Fransya asked.

"He stays here. We have matters to discuss," their father told them.

"Do I have to go back to the tutor?" Kansaderi asked.

"Yes, you do," Rono said. "Out of all of you, you only get tutored four hours a day because of your age, so it won't take too long to finish for the day."

"Aw," she said, and the four of them left the courtyard, leaving Rono, Jorn, and me alone.

"I don't know what to do," Rono said once they left. "Tell me you have a plan, brother."

"Since we don't have the number to break the siege, let me go after Merjohik. Paderok's right; he must have left the city by now. If I can catch him, he might have some information we can use," I said, seeing a golden opportunity to put my plan into motion with a slight adjustment. "He'll know if other spies are in the palace or lead us to a spymaster. We can't risk Salroon learning about whatever plan I'll come up with to break the sieges."

"We do need information, but we need to break the sieges too," the king said.

"Brother, right now, Salroon is trying to seal off Eshtar's borders, so I can't escape, not occupy its towns. I don't think the Diefetians will rush to take the cities; rather, I think they will wait to see if I come to break one of the sieges or get out of the country. Let me chase down Merjohik. It's a chance for me to gather more information to construct a proper defense. If I don't find Merjohik, I'll scout instead."

"What do you think son?" Rono asked Jorn.

"I think all we have left is desperate gambles," Jorn answered.

"Agreed," said his father. "What do you need?"

"A group of men, perhaps twenty, to track down Merjohik and Billen if he agrees to come along. He's a better tracker than I am," I admitted.

"You can have twenty of the men you took to Tuldum since they have the most combat experience," Rono told me. "But you need to bring Jorn."

"No," I said. "Having to train him will be a distraction, and I suspect he'll need to be ready for battle for this trip, which he is not. Have him train with Glendeo while I'm gone," I argued.

"Fine," my brother conceded. "Go get Billen and gather the men from the barracks. In the meantime, I'll interrogate Paderok some more and see if he has any information regarding where Merjohik could have gone."

"What do I do?" Jorn asked.

"Go see if you can convince Glendeo to give you some training," Rono told him. "Though after what your uncle has done with his training, he may refuse."

"Just have the old man look at what I've taught you. He'll at least do that. Now, I better get going," I said, walking out of the courtyard and returning to Billen's shop.

When I entered the shop, Billen's apprentice was behind the counter. When the boy saw me enter, he headed towards the back to get Billen. A few moments later, Billen walked down the hallway wearing an apron and sweat dripping from his brow.

"What is it now?" he demanded.

"Pack up your things. The plan is in motion," I said.

"Already? I knew you're efficient, Bowv, but a couple of hours is impressive even for you," he remarked. "I've already packed. Give me a few minutes to go to the forge and tell the boy what to do while I'm gone," Billen said, then walked back down the hallway.

Soon, we were entering the barracks. The color faded from the men's faces as we walked through the door. I heard a low groan from Halerod before he walked over to Jorn and me.

"Don't worry, lieutenant, it's a simple assignment," I reassured him.

"What is it?" he asked.

"The king has given me permission to take twenty men and track down a spy," I said, not wanting to demoralize them further.

"Simple enough," Halerod said.

"Since speed is of the essence, pick the fastest twenty men we took to Tuldum. They should be accustomed to difficult travel," I requested.

Within twenty minutes, Halerod had picked and assembled twenty men and were on their way with Billen to the western gate while I was returning to the palace to see if Rono had gotten the supplies ready or if he needed more time to prepare.

"You should be good to go," my brother said as I entered the war room. "Paderok said Merjohik probably headed west towards Diefet, so I sent the supplies to the western gate."

"Good, that's where the men are waiting," I said.

"I am praying Merjohik doesn't go another direction to throw you off," he said.

"I doubt it," I said. "He'll need to report Paderok has been compromised. Otherwise, Salroon will wonder why one of his sources in the palace has gone dark."

"True," he agreed.

"Unless you have something else to discuss, I better get moving," I said.

"Good hunting brother," he said.

I put my hand on his shoulder. "Hopefully, it will be, but if I'm not back in a week, start worrying. If I'm gone for two weeks and the kingdom hasn't fallen, think about surrender. I admire your will to keep fighting, brother, but sometimes it's better to admit you've been bested."

A grim expression came across the king's face. He clenched his teeth but soon nodded. I patted him on his shoulder, then left for the West Gate.

Chapter Twenty-Three

MY LITTLE GROUP WAS TWO DAYS FROM KIHOLP when I decided to put the next part of my plan into motion. BIllen was with me. The only problem was that I didn't know what to do about Halerod and the others. I could have lied to them and claimed getting chased by the Diefetians was the mission. But that would risk a mutiny when I disappeared, and I didn't want BIllen to have to deal with that since he would be the one in charge despite being a civilian. Instead, I told a different lie.

"Alright, as you have all probably figured out, there's more to this mission than tracking down a spy," I said while we were around the campfire, the warmth of the flame chasing away the cold air of the night's wind.

"Of course," sighed Halerod.

"We will be acting as a sabotage group, harassing the enemy, not just inside of the kingdom, but outside as well," I said, then glanced at Billen, who shrugged as if to say, "That's believable, why not?"

"However, the king has given me another assignment, which I must do alone. So, lieutenant, you're in charge when I leave in the morning. Billen is here to teach you the subtle art of sabotage and ensure you don't get caught by the enemy. Who, if you do your jobs right, will be hunting you down," I explained.

"And what's your assignment?" asked Halerod.

"Hunting down the spy is my responsibility," I lied. "I can get closer to him if I don't have twenty others with me." Halerod nodded.

The next morning, I went over the actual plan with Billen. I told him to stay out for about a week or two and maybe even do some sabotage or reconnaissance if the opportunity presented itself. Then, Billen and the men were to return to the capital to tell my brother I had disappeared. I stressed to Billen to suggest to my brother I might be resuming my criminal activities and to nudge his king toward making peace. Billen understood and wished me good luck.

It took me three weeks to reach the outskirts of the Aekwee Desert, having easily snuck out of Eshtar. All the Kingdom of Diefet lay within the Aekwee, and during my journey, it went unobstructed, which I hoped meant that Billen and the small group were keeping the Diefetians occupied. For most of recorded history, the Diefetians were isolationists.

The Diefetians took to trade to ensure they got whatever natural resources they couldn't get from the desert. The desert kingdom never had a large army because they never needed to. When an army marched into the long, barren expanse of the Aekwee, they never lasted long.

An invading army could find an oasis if its commanders knew where to look. But if the invaders reached a Diefetian town or city, which was purposely constructed far into the desert, they would run out of water when they arrived. Not wanting foreign traders to die as they wandered the desert, the Diefetians had trade outposts along the edges of the country, where foreigners would bring their goods to sell and Diefetian merchants would go to buy.

I had arrived at one of these outposts, knowing I would need to buy water to continue further and would have to sign on with a caravan heading to the capital to traverse the desert. The outposts were small villages with a few dozen buildings and enough soldiers to deter bandits. However, they were special in one way.

By Diefetian law, no citizens could live in the outposts, though they could stay there for a few days. This was to defend the kingdom. The Diefetians long realized the desert was their biggest strength in defending their kingdom. If they permitted the trade outposts to become full-fledged towns, they were making it easier for an invader to conquer them by not forcing them to march through the desert.

I arrived at the outpost closest to the Diefetian capital, Raeshek. The outpost's name was Ekwhil, and it didn't have much: a few inns for foreign and native merchants alike, a garrison for the small guard, which was about fifty men, and about a dozen shops that had sparsely furnished bedrooms on the second flood.

While living in the outposts was forbidden, sleeping overnight was allowed. Ideally, in the morning, someone coming in from the cities relieved whoever slept overnight, and the person relieved would take any profits back to the city. Constant traveling was necessary to ensure that the desert protected Diefet's wealth.

I came through there years ago, and not much had changed except for soldiers bolstering the outpost's guard regiment. In front of every third building, a soldier was stationed, and I counted at least two patrols: one for inside the boundaries of the outpost and another for surveying around it.

I found my way to the inn and signed on with a caravan heading towards Raeshek. Two and a half weeks later, I walked my camel through the Western Gate of Raeshek, beholding the marvelous sandstone buildings surrounding me. Because it can be expensive for the locals to import wood, there were no wooden signs outside shops. Instead, writing was etched into the sandstone, declaring the shop's name to whoever stood before it.

If words were chiseled out and a shop's name was carved above or below it, you knew it had changed owners. If the engraving of the shop's name didn't look worn, then chances are the shop was new. No chisel marks and a weather-worn name were the tell-tale sign of an old shop.

For the capital of a kingdom at war with most of the Continent, Raeshek didn't look the part. The city's streets were teeming with life wherever I walked. There were more soldiers than in peacetime, but that was to be expected, and I came knowing I would need to keep a low profile. At that time, Rono could have made peace with Salroon, and my brother wanted to capture me, too.

Getting to the palace was the easy part. Wearing merchant clothes in Raeshek is the best way to blend in. The soldiers didn't pay me any mind, but I knew I had to be careful when I approached the palace since some of the royal guards might have been the ones Salroon had taken to Kiholp with him.

When I approached the palace, I had no idea whether Salroon was there. My sources, whom I had contacted on my way to Diefet, had assured me Salroon was in Raeshek, but that information was weeks old by the time I had gotten to the capital. But the number of royal guards swarming around the palace confirmed that Salroon was there.

There are innumerable ways to get into a place where you are unwanted; chief amongst them is acting as if you belong. Even if no guards recognized me from Salroon's visit to Kiholp, I knew Salroon would have ensured each of his guards knew my description. Making my way in with a disguise was off the table. That left me with a break-in.

I spent the rest of the day examining the palace, studying every detail of its exterior. The Diefetian palace was unlike all the other buildings in Raeshek. It was a four-story building constructed of native sandstone accentuated with gleaming white marble, giving the palace a majestic glow in the light of the relentless desert sun. A ten-foot wall surrounded the palace, which was taller as far as palace walls go.

I knew from previous journeys that the king's chambers comprised the top floor's entire eastern wing. Salroon's predecessor, whom he usurped, didn't want to pay me tribute early in my bandit career. I snuck my clan into the city, assaulted the palace, and killed most of the king's guards until I got into his chambers. I told the old fool that he would have to pay double the tribute if he wanted to live.

Dangling out of a window, he agreed, but to teach him a lesson, I had my men burn down the royal treasury after we took the tribute. The king ordered riders to pursue us. When they caught up to my clan, we didn't leave anyone alive and left their bodies to boil on top of the infernal desert sands.

After about an hour of observation, I realized the route I used to enter the palace the last time was still there. On the western side of the palace, a section of the wall was falling apart, leaving holes that enabled someone to climb up it. From there, I doubt that the palace interior had changed much, if at all.

I would enter through a side door, ascend the steps only a short walk from it, and once I had climbed to the fourth floor, make my way down the hall to the king's chambers. I did all this without a hitch.

I had to hide from a few patrols of royal guards, but I reached the king's chambers in under half an hour. Though it was night when I made my attempt, lanterns gave me a small amount of light as I reached the door to the king's chambers.

As I entered the massive room, I saw a remarkable sight: the king of Diefet alone, without any of his guards, and his only protection was the sword attached to his hip. When he heard the door open and footsteps behind him, Salroon turned around and looked concerned, as if this was something he did not plan.

The look of worry only lasted for a moment and was soon cast aside with a chuckle, then a hardy laugh, which turned into a chain of laughter, causing the king to bend over as he laughed. I knew that was an opportunity to kill him.

All I had to do was draw *Hueik* and deliver a fatal blow. It would have been easy, but there was the problem. I wanted Salroon dead, but I didn't wish to murder. I wanted a fight. My reputation as a swordsman was at stake. After what felt like an eternity, the king composed himself.

"Here I thought I had you occupied halfway across the Continent, on the run while my soldiers hunt you down," Salroon said. "Yet you managed to sneak not only into the country but into my quarters without alerting any guards. This is remarkable even by your standards."

I drew *Hueik* and began to walk towards the king.

"After all you have seen, after all you have done, are you a believer now, Bowv, or do you still cling to your atheism like a sailor stranded at sea gripping onto a fragment of his wrecked ship?" he asked.

"It doesn't matter if I believe the gods are real," I said while walking towards him.

"I suppose it's because you're the Terror of the Continent," Salroon said as he backed away from me.

I shook my head. "You were never afraid of me. You and my brother were the only kings I couldn't scare."

"Then what are you?" he asked, drawing his sword.

"I am many things," I said, launching a feint that Salroon easily blocked. Our swords let out a ding as they met.

"A young man who witnessed the horrors of war," I said and attacked again; this time, Salroon chose to dodge, and I missed him by half of an inch.

"A son who witnessed his father become a monster," I said as I struck out at Salroon and heard the clash of blades as his sword intercepted mine.

"A prince who killed his king and abandoned the kingdom," I stated, beginning a series of attacks that tested Salroon's guard as I talked.

"A bandit who rose to terrorize a continent," I said, continuing my attack. As I spoke, rage built within me, giving me more strength and speed. Salroon's blocks were getting slower with each of my attacks. His eyes widened and glued to *Hueik*.

"A condemned man granted another chance," I continued as *Hueik* tore a gash into Salroon's free arm.

The vampire king let out a scream but still held his guard up. I didn't relent. My rage continued to build, fueling my attacks and allowing me to slip into a heightened state of consciousness. My reactions became superhuman.

"A veteran called to serve once again," I said as I faked high, reversed direction, and thrust my sword into Salroon's right thigh.

My attack grazed but did not pierce his thigh, having been knocked off course by the king's sword. The Diefetian let out an even greater scream that should have caused the guards to rush into the room. But the guards within earshot were dead. I didn't want anyone coming to the aid of their king too soon.

Salroon was hobbling backward, trying to create distance between us. It didn't work because he bumped into the wall farthest from the door. I followed him.

"But that all doesn't matter to you," I said. "What matters to you is that I wield *Hueik*. I am your end."

I had told Ilkon that I wouldn't give Salroon a chance to pull the same trick he used during our duel. I knew I had to prevent Salroon from praying to his god. And Salroon couldn't pray if he was busy blocking out what I was saying while defending himself.

Fury blinded me to exhaustion. I launched attack after attack, forcing the Diefetian king to concentrate on nothing save defending himself. To his credit, I could not break Salroon's defense.

"Why are you here, Bowv?" he asked, managing to speak after blocking yet another one of my attacks. "Even if you believe in the gods after what has happened, you're not your pious brother. Why do you want me dead?"

I didn't answer. Sweat ran down my brow as I struck at the king, swinging towards his left side. He parried. Instantly, I directed my sword to defend against his thrust to my chest, his first actual counter. The ring of clashing metal echoed throughout the room. My blade did not taste flesh, and my fury increased tenfold.

Like lighting, I stabbed at the king's chest, only for him to step back out of my reach. As he backed up, and my attack carried me forward, Salroon countered with an upward slash. As fast as a dropped anchor, I lowered *Hueik* and was rewarded by the force of colliding blades moving up my arm. Quickly, I disengaged and attempted another thrust.

Again, our blades met as Salroon parried. My sword was pushed to the side. The tip of Salroon's sword came shooting towards my face. I sidestepped to my right. We were now perpendicular to each other, with the Diefetian king's back facing me. I raised *Hueik* above my head and stepped forward, putting my full weight behind the descending chop.

But Salroon was too quick. My enemy pivoted and horizontally brought his sword up. *Hueik* crashed down onto it. I kicked out with my back leg. My foot slammed into the king's stomach, and he was pushed back. Salroon adeptly disengaged his sword and brought it back to guard, denying me an opening to take advantage of.

Then I did something that Glendeo would have screamed at me for doing: I charged. From the beginning of my training, Glendeo drilled into me that blindly charging an enemy was the most stupid thing a soldier could do. When Father took me on campaign, I witnessed plenty of single soldiers bravely charge forward, only to be impaled on spears. But this was different. I needed to keep the pressure on Salroon, and I had pushed him too far away from me to do that. I needed to get in close and fast, so I charged.

I wasn't surprised that when I got into striking distance, Salroon stabbed at my heart. Nor did the Diefetian king look surprised when *Hueik* met his blade for a parry. I slashed across with *Hueik*, but Salroon blocked my cut. He slashed out with his sword, and it was my turn to dodge backward. Not wanting to give Salroon a chance to take the offensive, as I fell back, I stabbed at the vampire's head, directing *Hueik* above his sideways moving sword that was now leveled with my upper stomach.

The Diefetian king snapped his head back, *Hueik's* tip missing his face by a hair's length. He retaliated with a thrust to my gut. If Salroon had been fighting anyone else, then it would have worked. The vampire's attack was faster than what most men could ever manage in their lives. But I had a sword in my hands since I was a child. I rotated my arm, swinging *Hueik* down and banging it into the vampire's sword. A loud metal ring filled the room.

I needed to finish the fight soon. The longer it went on, the more time I gave Salroon to pray to Allemar, and if he did that, then I knew I would be dead.

So, I attacked with speed. A feign up high. Blocked. One down low. Intercepted by the Diefetian's sword. Another feint high towards his head. The vampire raised his sword for a strong defense, but it was too early. I changed the destination of my strike. *Hueik* pierced my enemy's shoulder. Salroon cried out in pain. The Sword of the Gods began to glow.

Quickly, I pulled the blade out and launched a follow-up attack. Salroon blocked; it wasn't as strong as the others. Sensing weakness, I began a barrage of attacks. The clinging of swords rang out and echoed for an eternity.

Between my attacks, Salroon began muttering words in the same language he spoke during our first duel. A smile crept across the wounded king's face.

Refusing to be beaten again, I let out a guttural roar. This wasn't the enraged slaughter of the Jilldues after Queel's death; this was a duel to the death between two master swordsmen. My movements weren't blind and sweeping, battering lesser skill opponents, but precise, focused, and quick. My strikes soared toward my enemy like a hawk diving toward its prey.

The sound of metal slamming against metal became so frequent and loud that one would be forgiven if they thought armies were battling in the king's chambers. Salroon stopped his chanting, needing to concentrate on defending against my vicious assault. Every second, our swords clashed. Before one attack was finished, I began my next. Salroon scrambled to get his sword in a position to block. I increased my speed, attacking faster than any man should be able to do.

Beyond rage, a deep hunger for victory fueled me. The king's blocks came slow, and they weren't as sturdy. I pressed on harder. Then, silence suddenly swept away the clammer of battle. I had rammed *Hueik* into the vampire's gut. I whipped the sword out, and the king fell to his knees, then backward, hitting the floor. *Hueik* was now glowing with the luminance of two full moons.

"You're lucky," Salroon muttered as he lay on the floor, his eyes now glazed. "If I had finished that prayer, my god would have provided me with the power to kill you. But instead, you killed me."

"Death is what happens to those who rely on gods," I said.

The Diefetian chuckled, "I suppose that is a lesson you learned a long ago."

"It is," I confirmed.

"You have been a nuisance for a while now, but by killing me, you have become a full-fledged problem for my master," Salroon claimed.

"Your master?" I asked. "But you're the king."

Saloon let out another chuckle. "King of Diefet, yes. King of Vampires, no," Salroon informed me.

"Who's your master?" I asked.

"What's it to you, Bowv?" Salroon asked. "We both know you killed me out of wounded pride from our last duel and to preserve your reputation as a swordsman,"

"I want to know because you just said I've become a problem for him, which means he'll want to kill me," I explained.

"He wants the sword, as does my god. But the Vampire King won't want you dead for killing me. He'll hopefully be annoyed at my death, but he won't send anyone to kill you over it," Salroon said.

"Who is he?" I asked.

Salroon smiled and gave his last words, "The real question is, 'Who isn't he?'"

I stood there for a few minutes, thinking about what Salroon had said, then stopped. It didn't matter who his master was since he would still want the sword. Whoever this mysterious master was, he would send someone to try and take the sword from me. If I got lucky, it would be the master himself.

My train of thought was broken when I heard more royal guards rushing down the hallway. In moments, five royal guards entered the king's chamber, and within minutes, they were all dead.

More guards came, and more fell to my sword. *Hueik's* light began to dim, and when the last guards fell dead, the sword's glow faded completely. However, it was hard to realize since the blade was dripping with so much blood. The sight of a bloodied sword didn't stop the royal guards, nor did the bodies of their compatriots.

Under normal circumstances, I would be annoyed at their persistence. What reason did the guards have to continue their fight? I had killed their king, and they failed; it was as simple as that. For the first few guards, vengeance would have been their motivation for attacking me, but the others should have abandoned such notions when they saw their comrades' bodies.

Instead of being annoyed, I welcomed their persistence. I wanted every citizen in Diefet to know that there was no stopping me. Their king's royal guard couldn't protect him, and they couldn't manage to avenge him. The endless waves of royal guards relented when I got to the end of the hallway. I descended the stairs and got outside the palace without any sign of a guard.

When I exited the palace the same way I came in, there was a wall of royal guards, pikes lowered, blocking my path to both my left and my right. When they saw me, each phalanx began advancing towards me, hoping to either skewer me on their pikes or force me back into the palace, where I didn't doubt there would be more guards. I drew *Hueik* and thought about my options.

My thoughts were interrupted when the torches and candles in the palace and on the palatial walls extinguished, and the approaching guards stopped in their tracks. The night's air suddenly became several degrees colder. Out of nowhere, a man appeared before me. He was of average height, had a muscular build, and had the light brown skin of a Diefetian.

The stranger wore all black, but his clothes were not the roughly spun pants and shirt of a commoner but the finely tailored, silk clothes of a king.

You would think he was a king, except when you looked at his eyes. The stranger's eyes glowed red and possessed a hunger for domination.

"So, you managed to kill Salroon," the stranger said, his voice ringing with raw power.

"I assumed so since he hadn't finished his prayer, but I needed to see for myself. I knew you were capable, Bowv, but do you have any idea who you just killed? You killed one of the oldest vampires in the world. Salroon was dubbed a master swordsman before some of the first states were formed on the Continent. And you managed to kill him. Well done!"

"Allemar," I said.

"Yes, that's what you mortals have been calling me nowadays," the demon said.

"Why are you here?" I asked.

The demon laughed, "Not even intimidated, I see. I like that. I've come to congratulate you and provide you with a way out of your current predicament."

"Why?" I asked.

"Because I've been watching your progress, Bowv, and you are interesting. A young, noble prince, and a war hero at that, who kills his father and becomes the most feared bandit on the Continent. A devoted believer in the gods, he turned atheist, then when he meets the Protectorate, believes again, but replacing his disbelief with hatred in the process.

"Despite that, *Hueik*, the gods' weapon, chooses you as its wielder. Life would be so boring if you died here. And we both know the Protectorate isn't going to bail you out of this one, so I have to do it." With that said, the demon waved his hand, and the palace wall in front of me disappeared.

I looked at him with skepticism. "I don't buy it."

"I didn't lie," the demon defended himself. "I honestly find you amusing. But that's not to say I've given you all my reasons for wanting you to escape this predicament. Why don't I tell you another? There's no harm if I do. I don't want to see you impaled on Diefetian spears, Bowv, because I know what you are.

"No, I'm not going to say you're a killer; you've already accepted that truth. What you are, Bowv, and one of the reasons you fascinate me, is that you're a man broken by war, but not in the traditional sense. Nightmares, depression, or suicidal thoughts don't plague you. You're broken in another way. What war broke wasn't your mind, but your faith, your morality.

"War abolished your sense of right and wrong, placing it in its stead the apathy of nihilism and dissolved your faith, replacing it with a crusader's atheism. You became a villain to disprove the existence of the Protectorate. You're a curiosity, Bowv, an abnormality I can't see vanish just yet."

"I don't believe you," I said.

"Believe whatever you wish, but go on already. If I wanted you dead, I would have left you here to die. I don't have time to wait for you to decide because I have an important meeting. You'll have a few minutes to make up your mind before the guards unfreeze, and you have to find your way out of this situation. If you do decide the latter, make sure you don't die. I don't have much for entertainment these days." When he finished talking, he disappeared.

I knew I didn't have another way out, so I took Allemar's opportunity, ran past where the wall should have been, and put as much distance as possible between myself and the palace. From there, I stole a camel and headed towards the nearest trade outpost, beginning the long journey back to Kiholp and, without knowing it, ending a chapter of my life—one that started with me waiting for execution in a deary dungeon cell.

I Need You

This is my first book, and it's self-published. Due to budget constraints, I've done pretty much everything myself, including the cover art, although I used Grammarly for editing.

So, I need your help. Please tell people about this book, whether it be in person or online. And please leave a review. As an unknown author, reviews give me credibility and let people know if they will like the book or consider buying this book as a gift for someone.

I plan on writing at least a trilogy and have already started the first draft of my second book. However, how quickly I publish the second book greatly depends on how well this book works. I began The Terror and The Sword years ago, and I managed to finish it during a time in my life when I had a couple of hours a day to work on it. Those days are gone, so if The Terror and The Sword is successful, it will help me justify spending time writing the second book.

If you did like the book, there are a couple

# of ways to stay informed about what I am doing:

1. Follow me on BlueSky @trevorwarrenauthor.bsky.social. I will post updates there (like my progress on the second book) and answer questions about the book.
2. Subscribe to my email list at trevorwarrenhq.substack.com. You'll get updates via email, as well as my answers to questions that would be too long for Blue Sky.

Thank you for reading this book! I hope you enjoyed it, but if you didn't, I hope you find a good book to read.

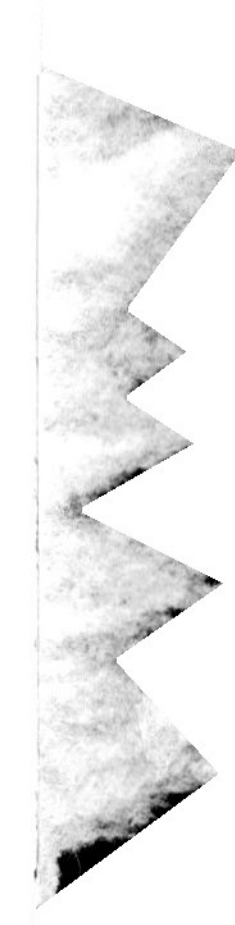